THE PARADOX FILES

Books 1-3

By

J.E. Taylor

The Paradox Files - Silencing the Siren

Book 1

A protector. A lost soul. A siren looking for salvation.

Kylee Paradox never expected to be a protector of humankind, but when hell's portals open and let loose the creatures of the underworld, she can't see any other way.

Armed with an ultimatum, Kylee has no choice but to embrace her new position as bounty hunter of the damned. Sending these monsters back to purgatory becomes her life's mission.

The only glitches in an otherwise noble pursuit are those who hold her fate in their hands. They forbid her from using her deadly siren song to lure the beasts back to the pit.

If she harms even a single innocent soul in her quest, Kylee herself will become one of the hunted.

Silencing the Siren
Chapter 1

THE SIGN OVER MY office door read *Kylee Paradox, Paranormal Investigator*, but I was really a bounty hunter of unnatural creatures. Honestly, I never expected to be a protector of humankind, but when hell's portals opened and let loose the creatures from the underworld, I didn't have a choice.

It was hunt, or be hunted. You can guess which choice I made.

Unfortunately, the perils of being a siren royally screwed up that plan. You see, if I employed my voice to snare these monsters— which, for the record, would be by far the easiest way to send them back to hell—it would drive any nearby humans beyond the edge of reason.

I was told there was no acceptable amount of collateral damage, especially if I was ever going to achieve my salvation. So, I had to curtail my greatest weapon and fall back on the warrior skills I had honed over the millennia.

I was kind of a badass.

This era was possibly the easiest to navigate compared to some of the umpteen centuries I'd walked the earth. It was so much easier to blend in and go unnoticed these days. But then again, everyone was preoccupied with their damn electronics. Unfortunately, I had fallen victim to the same technology pitfalls.

My computer buzzed, and I swiveled the chair around, dismissing the view of the Pacific for my oversized cherry desk. I glanced at the instructions that flashed on the screen, clenching my teeth in response.

I hated Fate. She was a bitch of epic proportion, and this latest order wasn't welcomed in the least. I hadn't been home in nearly a millennium for a reason. Now, she wanted me to go back and hunt one of my own. A siren had taken hold of the waters south of Crete and was making everyone within range of its voice go on murderous rampages. The latest nautical victim was big enough to make international news. A cruise ship had been exposed to the siren's song, and everyone on board was slaughtered.

I wondered if I knew the monster luring those poor souls to their death. As if Fate heard my musings, a name flashed on the screen. My stomach dropped as I stared at the display.

"You have got to be kidding me."

A swirl of smoke bloomed in the middle of the room. As it dissipated, the blonde bitch stood glaring at me from the center of the damned cloud. Standing in her signature ruby dress that flowed as if she also commanded the wind, Fate crossed her arms, looking down her aristocratic nose at me.

"I do not kid," she said. Her voice was about as icy as the Alaskan tundra.

"You really expect me to take down my brother?" I said, pointing at the screen.

A truly evil smile flashed, and I just wanted to smash that beautiful face in. She leaned on the desk, narrowing her eyes. "You will do as I order," she snarled.

"And if I refuse?" I crossed my arms. Two could play the snark game.

"I will personally escort you to your dungeon in hell." Her lips twitched from a thin line of anger to that of amusement. I never doubted this bitch enjoyed watching me squirm. "I know the devil has plans to punish you for your insubordination. After all, weren't you once his prize possession?"

Against my will, I shivered, and a rash of gooseflesh crossed every inch of exposed skin. The devil had kept me as his personal pet, his personal whore. When I didn't comply with his wishes, he kept me away from any form of water just for the giggles my suffering brought him. When I was nearly gone, he abused me and then threw me into a fish tank in his bedroom until I revived and bore aquatic demons for his amusement.

I couldn't imagine what the punishment for escaping his hellhole would be. I was sure it was far worse than my original stay in his dungeon. But was killing my own flesh and blood worth avoiding an eternity at the devil's hands?

"Would you kill your brother?" I asked, stalling, but the tilt of Fate's head as she studied me left me cold.

"What do you think?"

I thought she'd eat her own children, but I wasn't about to say that out loud. The choice tore at my insides, but I finally gave a nod. I had what was necessary to kill a siren. Neptune's trident was stored in one of my many hidden safes in my home on the San Diego shoreline. But the thought of sticking those spikes through my kin didn't sit well.

Maybe I could talk him out of continuing this insane plight. Convince him to hide, to lay low for a while, and maybe Fate would lose interest in bringing him in. I helped him escape when I had fled from hell and made him promise to keep under the radar.

He had kept that promise... until now.

Silencing the Siren
Chapter 2

I CROSSED THE THRESHOLD into my sanctuary. My shoreline home faced due west over the Pacific. This property had been mine for nearly a hundred years, and the house that stood now was more modern art déco than the turn of the century mansion that I'd once built. It had been destroyed by one of those cleansing fires that sometimes overtakes the California landscape.

The sunset tonight did not elevate my spirits. In fact, it did just the opposite. It made me yearn for the shores of Greece and the sight of broken wood planks drifting alongside blood, staining the pristine blue waters. I shut my eyes against the memories, as well as the molasses-colored Pacific.

Trudging up the stairs, I crossed the long hallway that opened to the living room below and stopped in front of the farthest bedroom door. I pressed my finger to the center of the doorknob and waited for the fingerprint to register. A panel slid open, and I stepped in front of it, allowing a scan of my eyes as well as the rest of my face.

The lock clicked, and I pushed the door open. The bedroom looked like any other middle-class bedroom. A four-poster bed rested against the far wall, along with a pair of nightstands. At the foot of the bed sat a large trunk extending the full width of the mattress. Along the wall to the right hung a picture window that had a built-in bench and shelving on either side, stocked with books and various knickknacks. The left wall behind the door had a long dresser that extended almost the full length of the room.

While everything looked like a normal bedroom, every piece hid some precious antique weapon, and only my prints, along with a surefire code, could open the treasure chests.

I stepped in front of the dresser and glanced at my reflection in the mirror. As forms go, the one I was cursed with turned heads no matter what I put over it. The less I covered, the more leers I got. My honey-colored hair fell in long loose curls, and I got questions about it at least once a week. I always got a cross expression when I said it was natural, like I'd somehow cheated the questioner out of some coveted hair secret. My eyes were the color of the Mediterranean Sea. I avoided mirrors just because one glance in my eyes triggered the sheer reminder of everything I left behind.

Fate transplanted me here in Southern California the moment I signed the paperwork. Of course, way back then, this was wild country. It wasn't known as the United States then. It was a tribal community of Aztecs and Indians, and I was a strange fit with my alabaster skin, blonde hair, and strange eyes. I think Fate did it on purpose. She wanted to see if I could withstand the scrutiny. I think she secretly hoped I'd fail and she could bring me back to the hell I escaped.

She certainly didn't expect them to worship me. I became known as Teo, goddess of sun and light, and that pissed Fate off. It was possibly the happiest time of my existence, and for a while, I forgot I was a fugitive from hell. It also gave me an appreciation of how special humans were. Their capacity to love and cherish exceeded my expectations, and it was then that I realized I wasn't put on this earth to destroy—I was destined to protect. It wasn't until a plague wiped out the natives that I truly understood just how fragile human life was.

I shook the thought out of my head and refocused, laying my hands on the fine cherry, pushing down on the wood grains. Warmth spread from my palms to my fingertips and back, then the lock clicked. I pulled my hands away and tipped the top of the cabinet to reveal an array of weapons. In the center sat the ornate trident, and I wrapped my hand around the cool metal. I lifted the heavy spear, careful not to let the tips touch me. While Poseidon's trident wouldn't kill me unless it pierced my heart, the tips of the fork would burn if they hit my skin while the weapon was in full form.

I closed the top of the bureau and laid the trident on the wood. Closing my eyes, I recited an old spell while splaying my fingers over the handle. *"Neptunus maris deus, fac mihi cessuros trident."*

Light bled through my eyelids, encompassing the space in front of me like a bright ball of fire. When it faded, I opened my eyes and picked up the small charm-sized trident, clasping it onto my charm bracelet with some of my other deadly weapons. Since the advent of air travel, I've had to hide my weapons in plain sight. I just hoped they would allow this on the plane. Since the terror attacks in 2001, air travel had been more difficult to navigate with any sort of weapon. I only had one close call with my bracelet, but I got out of it by gushing over the trinkets and the exotic places where I retrieved the charms. Luckily, I only had to throw away one of the charms, and luckily it was only a charm and not one of my true weapons.

Without lingering, I turned and walked out, re-engaging the security system as I shut the door behind me. I stalled in my bedroom doorway. Normally, I was packed and ready to go on a hunting trip before the sun dipped below the horizon, but this time was different. I really didn't want to go.

I hadn't seen my brother since the last time I was in the Mediterranean, and that was right around the fall of the Roman Empire. Our goodbye had been bittersweet, and now the memory of that final hug we shared tugged at my heartstrings.

"I can't do this," I whispered.

Pictures fluttered from nowhere, littering the floor of my bedroom with death and destruction. I scanned the massacre, and when my gaze fell on a dead child, I gritted my teeth and closed my eyes. Fate's message slammed home.

My brother was responsible for all this.

I stepped over the discarded photos and grabbed my suitcase from the closet. When I turned, all the photographs but the one that got me moving disappeared.

I stared at the terror frozen in the child's wide, dead eyes, the scream forever cast into her skin. I picked up the gruesome picture and sighed. My chest hurt with the weight of it. Children, while enamored with the siren song, were not affected the way adults were. This poor soul had not understood why she was being beaten to death; she only knew mind-numbing horror in those last moments, and that fear was showcased in her death.

This was what my brother did.

This was what I had to stop from happening again.

I put the photo into my suitcase for a reminder, because I knew I would need it when the time came to go into action. Otherwise, I might fall prey to the hurt in my heart or the screams in my head telling me this was as wrong as it got. My brain went into automatic, and I grabbed a handful of underwear, not bothering to count out the number. The same went for shorts and tank tops. I didn't even match up outfits like I usually did when I packed for a trip. There was no rhyme or reason in my packing. The only thing I made a mental note of were the two bathing suits I put in as almost an afterthought.

With a mishmash of clothes thrown into the suitcase, I zipped it up without a second look. I really didn't care if I had everything I needed. I slung the strap over my shoulder and grabbed my passport and travel purse on my way out of the bedroom.

After dropping the bag at the entrance to my kitchen, I put my pocketbook on the table and continued to the refrigerator. Nothing looked good. In fact, my appetite had all but fled since I received Fate's directive. But I also knew a twenty-plus hour plane ride would leave me famished if I didn't force food down my throat.

Instead of looking in the refrigerator again, I crossed to the pantry and pulled out a box of toasted oats cereal and a bowl. I settled at the counter with the milk and cereal within arm's reach and opened my laptop. Scanning the prices for last-minute flights, my best option was twenty-one hours for three grand. That wasn't bad considering the other flights on the list were pricier and added anywhere from four to eighteen hours to the trip. I wanted to get in and get out as quickly as possible, so I gave myself a week to do the job.

I did another search for marinas on Crete that rented yachts. Many of them were only day trip rentals which would not meet my needs. The long-term rentals required either a captain or a crew. A valid boater's license was not good enough. In fact, it wasn't even an option. I banged my hand on the counter. I closed my eyes and took a deep breath before I scanned the choices. I sent a note to the Heraklion Yacht Marina requesting a boat named *Michael*, which only required a skipper. I bit my nail waiting for the confirmation, and when it came through, I jotted down the name and the confirmation code before sending a note that I required the captain to have sound-canceling earphones for the trip. Once the email was sent, I closed my computer.

If I needed more time, I'd probably get slammed with another charge for both the flight and yacht, but my bank accounts could deal with almost anything. Most people only had a lifetime to save up for a rainy day. I had over forty lifetimes, so my reserves were well padded. Besides, if I finished early, I would take a hit, too, because there was no way in hell I'd be sticking around to the assault of memories that the Mediterranean Sea brought forth.

I poured another bowl of cereal, thinking that perhaps a full stomach would ease the pain in the pit of my abdomen. I was mistaken. It continued, and now that discomfort morphed into an acidic burn. I tossed the rest of the food out and opted for a walk. After navigating to the sliders, I stepped out into the cool evening and crossed the road to the beach.

The roar of the waves drowned out my thoughts as I settled on the sand, crossing my legs as I watched the dark water churn and roll. The tide crept towards me. Even if I dove in, the ornate tail I once had would not come back. That was forever gone the moment I signed up for this job. Sadness engulfed me as I sifted the white grains through my fingers.

The sand shifted next to me, and Alex, my neighbor, took a seat, handing me a glass of red wine with a crooked smile I adored.

"You look like your favorite pet died," he said with a gentle Texan accent and sipped his wine.

Alejandro Cervas was probably the only genuine friend I had in this current world. He had moved into the duplex next door a few years ago after an ugly divorce that left him with little more than the shirt on his back. He didn't see his kids often, but he raved about them any time he got the chance. Despite his near destitution, he seemed to have the secret of life nailed down. A good glass of wine, quiet conversation, and now and then a cigar were all he seemed to need.

I offered him a genuine smile and shrugged. "It's been that kind of day." I took a sip of the wine and swished it over my tongue, relishing the sweet dryness of it before swallowing.

"Anything you'd like to talk about?"

"No. Not really."

We stared quietly out at the ocean, sipping wine.

"Anything I can do?" he asked after a few minutes of silence.

There were dozens of things he could do to help me get my mind off the coming days, but every one of them would end up killing this quiet friendship we shared.

I shook my head. "I'm going on a business trip that will not be all that pleasant. If you could keep an eye on my place while I'm gone, that would be helpful."

His smile returned, and he gave me a nod. "My pleasure, senorita."

I leaned into his shoulder, gently bumping it with mine. He bumped me back. After he finished his wine, he stretched out on the sand, just staring up at the cosmos. When his gaze turned to mine, the trace of a smile disappeared.

"Do you think we will ever be more than this?" His deep voice sounded soft and unsure, but the fire in his eyes was as clear as the constellations in the sky above us.

"Do you value our friendship?" I asked, because I could only forecast heartbreak for both of us.

He would age.

I would not.

His body would fail.

Mine would not.

I had tried this before, and all I encountered was devastation. My heart was guarded from that kind of hurt because it would spawn my voice and send me on a direct path back to hell.

Not that I didn't screw around when the itch presented itself; I just didn't make it about feelings.

He stared up at the sky, still contemplating my question. His rugged, dark features always made me wonder what his ex-wife was thinking when she left him. He had the same complexion the Aztecs had and the physique that would make a goddess drool.

"Yes, I value our friendship, but why is it so bad to want more?" he asked.

I cringed at the question and how to explain it to him. "I enjoy living here and make it a rule not to get involved with the neighbors." I couldn't help my frown. My rule was solid, but it conflicted with my wants.

He sat up, and as I turned my attention back to the water, his finger hooked under my chin, pulling my gaze back to him. His deep brown eyes searched mine, and just the physical touch sent my heart thundering in my chest. Heat filled my cheeks.

"So... no attraction?" The hopefulness in the arch of his eyebrows belied the light tone in his voice, and I couldn't help but laugh. Hurt bloomed in his eyes, and the trace of his smile disappeared.

"It's not that," I quickly replied. "You are stunningly attractive, and sweet, and..." I sighed as his hand cupped my cheek. Despite being ancient, I always seemed to get flustered in these types of situations. Especially when I was attracted to a man who could greatly complicate my life.

"Alex..." I started, but his lips crushed my response. Whatever protest I had been planning to launch died in the tangling of our tongues.

The way he kissed was decadent. He pushed me back onto the sand, sending tendrils of heat through my form. His hand slid from my cheek, down the side of my neck. The slow progression of his touch locked my breath in my chest as his fingers gently caressed the side of my breast.

The logical part of my brain told me to stop him, but the tramp in me wanted his hand to keep going, to find the spot that drove me to release my voice, to capture his soul the only way a siren could. I moaned as his hand traveled lower.

Alex broke the kiss and stared down into my eyes as his hand found its mark, settling between my legs. He stilled and cocked his head.

"Do you want to continue this inside?" His gaze flicked to our houses and back, and his lips curved into that sexy smile I had seen a couple of times during the past few years. It was a smile that immediately made me damp.

I lay on the sand fighting just about every emotion until he applied pressure with his fingers, rubbing in a way that nearly unleashed the siren song from my throat.

"Alejandro." His full name rolled off my tongue in a soft whisper.

He returned his mouth to mine. His fingers worked the button on my jeans, and I gasped when he slipped his hand underneath the hem of my underwear. Still, I didn't stop him. Instead, my arms wrapped around his neck, deepening the kiss as his fingers slid inside my wet core.

He groaned in my mouth like a man who had been underwater too long and had found a pocket of air.

He pulled away from me. "Your place or mine?" he asked with a voice full of the same need throbbing in my veins. He climbed to his feet and helped me up off the sand, but before I could say which direction, he had me in his arms, and his lips crushed mine.

I didn't even remember the walk back or the sliders opening to my living room. It wasn't until he stripped my shirt that I noticed my surroundings. There was something desperate and possessive about his lips as they moved from mine down to the curve of my neck. My bra released, and I tossed it to the side before I tore his shirt off. His chiseled abs tightened under my fingertips. I clamped my mouth shut at the vibration in my throat.

The soft cushions of the couch met my back as he gently pushed me down. His mouth moved over every inch of my exposed skin while he worked on stripping my jeans and underwear. I reached down and grabbed his wrists.

He lifted his lips from my stomach, and his mouth formed a surprised o.

"I can't. As much as I want to, I can't right now." The wild child inside me screamed her discontent, but I had to be logical and rational, and honestly, I needed something to come back to.

"Kylee," he whispered, pleading with his gaze.

"We can revisit this when I get back." I grabbed my shirt.

He dropped his forehead onto my thigh.

"I'm not rejecting you."

He glanced up at me. "It sure feels like it."

"Look, this job..." I closed my eyes and took a deep breath. "What I'm going up against..." I opened my eyes. "If I'm not fully committed to it, I could die."

His eyebrows knit together.

"And if I know I'm coming home to this..." Heat filled my cheeks, and I glanced at the floor. "Well, let's just say it's a guarantee that I'll come home." I forced myself to meet his gaze.

His head cocked to the side, reminding me of an adorable puppy. "What exactly is your job?"

I sighed. "I run a paranormal investigation agency," I said, opting for the cover story rather than the truth.

He climbed to his feet and crossed his arms. "And you expect me to believe that?"

We had never once spoken about what I did. Our conversations were more existential and less vocational. The skepticism on his face irritated me. I slipped my arms in the shirt and stood, staring him down as I buttoned up. He raised an eyebrow as I plucked the mace off my charm bracelet.

"*Hoc maior gratia,*" I said, and the charm grew in my hand.

His eyes widened. I dropped the charm on my coffee table. The weight of the mace buckled the wood, and one of the spikes pierced it.

His ever-widening gaze bounced between mine and the ancient weapon. When he licked his lips and shifted his weight like he was going to flee, I crossed my arms. The motion seemed to snap him out of the shock.

"I'm going with you."

I uttered a laugh. "*Fac minorem,*" I said, and the mace shrunk back to the size of the charm. I plucked it off the table and put it back on my bracelet.

He stepped closer and reached out, running his index finger over the different charms attached to my bracelet. "I am going with you," he said again and met my gaze. "That way I can ensure you come back."

It was my turn to arch my eyebrows. "Excuse me?"

He closed the distance and pulled me into his arms. "I am not willing to lose whatever has started here. I'm going so I can keep you safe."

The absolute irony in his statement made me burst out laughing. He wasn't a god, or an immortal like me. He was a fragile human who had no business tagging along on a hunting trip like this.

"No. You are not coming with me. I'd be so worried about keeping you alive that I'd end up screwing up and killing both of us. I'm not putting that on my shoulders."

He pointed at the coffee table. "If you use that on whatever you're chasing, I'm coming."

"That won't kill what I'm going up against." I met his gaze. "That was just to show you I wasn't kidding about my job."

He held me close. "Are you a... witch?"

"No. I just happen to know a few spells that make it easier to transport what I need for the job."

"And how long have you been doing this?"

I stared at him, contemplating how to answer that. "All my life," I said, opting for more subterfuge.

He pressed his lips together. "And you've never gotten hurt?"

I rolled my eyes and tried to pull out of his grip. His arms tightened, holding me in place. He cocked his head, waiting for an answer. I was not going to give him a history of close calls, not with that overprotective glare now present in his eyes.

"Alejandro, let me go." I squirmed in his grasp.

"Look. I finally got the courage to make a move, and you seem to be on the same page, despite your earlier protest. And if there is a hair's breadth of a chance that you could get hurt..."

I stilled. "It's too dangerous for you to come."

"You realize saying that only makes me more set on protecting you."

"I don't need your protection. I need something special to come home to."

His grip loosened. "I need to make sure you're safe," he said softly.

The impasse seemed impossible to fix. I sighed. "I will be fine. Besides, you wouldn't be able to afford the trip."

His head cocked. "Where are you going?"

"Greece. Crete, to be exact."

He glanced at the suitcase, and his brow furrowed before he looked back at me. "Does it have anything to do with that cruise ship?"

The massacre on the ship made international news, and the fact that he jumped right to it made me stiffen in his arms. I opened my mouth to answer but thought better of it, clamping down on any response. Instead, I lifted a shoulder.

"Kylee, they don't know what killed those people. It could be some sort of virus for all we know."

"I know what killed them, and it wasn't a virus. That's why I have to go take care of it, so it doesn't happen again." I pulled out of his arms. "Now, if you don't mind, I need to get a decent night's sleep before I catch my flight."

He shoved his hands in his pockets and gave me a slight nod. He said nothing more, just turned and headed out of my house.

Silencing the Siren
Chapter 3

MORNING CAME FASTER THAN I wanted, given I had tossed and turned all night. By the time I arrived at the airport, the caffeine had finally kick-started my brain. I made it through the metal detectors without issue. As I sat waiting for the airport staff to start seating the plane, I clipped the bracelet around my wrist and leaned back, closing my eyes.

The last thing I wanted to do was alienate Alex. The bitter taste of regret filled my mouth, and I swallowed, reaching for the bottle of water I bought at the newsstand on the way through the terminal. I washed down the sourness and popped a piece of peppermint gum in my mouth, ignoring those around me.

I didn't have to wait long before the boarding call began. I got my carry-on bag, found my row near the back of the plane, stowed my bag in the overhead bin, and collapsed into the window seat. I glanced out the window and started mentally charting my approach to my brother. I was so absorbed in my thoughts that I didn't bother turning when someone settled into the seat next to me.

A waft of aftershave caught my attention, and I twisted to see who it belonged to. The physique of the man sitting next to me was as familiar as the aftershave. I met his dark gaze, and he offered me a nervous smile.

"What the actual fuck?" I asked before I could stop the words.

"I've always wanted to see Greece." Alex shrugged.

I closed my eyes and lay my head against the headrest. Whatever plans I had formulated all went out the window.

"Do you have any idea..." I opted to glance back out the window before I said anything that ears around me could pick up on and misconstrue. "I can't believe you did this," I muttered under my breath and sent a glare in his direction.

As the plane taxied down the runway, his hand covered mine on the armrest. I glanced at his death grip, then looked up at him. He uttered a nervous laugh. "I'm a little... anxious about flying," he admitted as the plane accelerated for takeoff.

I raised an eyebrow. "This is the safest part of this trip."

He gave my hand a squeeze but didn't say anything. Instead, he took a deep breath and closed his eyes as the plane left the safety of the ground. He paled a fraction and kept sucking air in through his nose and blowing it out between his lips until we leveled off.

His anxiety amused me and left me a bit humbled. I couldn't remember the last time anyone suffered through their own fear for my well-being. When his hand released mine, my stomach fell in disappointment. I glanced at him, sending him a slight smile before looking back out the window as we flew east over the vastly changing scenery of the United States.

"I have no idea what I'm going to do with you when we land," I said after passing over the Midwestern plains.

"I can think of a few things," he whispered. A dimple appeared in his reddening cheek, but he didn't look at me.

"Did you get a hotel room?" I asked. That dimple disappeared. He looked down at his hands and shook his head. "I was hoping you'd take pity on me." He gave me a hopeful sideways glance.

I sent a full glare at him. I didn't book a hotel room. I rented a boat for the week. There was no way I could have him with me. Not with what I was hunting. It was bad enough having a captain on board. One siren-psychotic man I could handle. Two would be difficult, if not impossible, especially when I had feelings for one of them.

"Alex..." The exasperation in my voice rang clear.

"I'm sorry, Kylee, but I couldn't let you do this alone," he said.

"I'm equipped for this. You aren't. Besides, I didn't book a hotel room. I rented a boat. And I cannot have you on board."

"I will be just fine. Besides, I do have a boating license," he said, sending me an endearing grin.

He did not understand, and I couldn't exactly enlighten him on a plane with strangers within ear shot. Instead, I glared.

"I'm not leaving your side." He stretched out in the seat.

Chivalry wasn't dead, but oh, how I wished it was. "I might just lock you in a trunk somewhere," I muttered under my breath.

He patted my knee and leaned over, planting a gentle kiss on my cheek. "I'm sorry if I have aggravated you," he whispered and then leaned back in his seat.

I sighed and glanced around. "While I adore your intent, I really can't have you on the boat with me. You are at more of a risk than I am." I met his gaze. "I know what did this. I also know what this thing can do to..." I bit my tongue before the word humans spilled out. "... to men."

A crease appeared between his eyebrows. "What is it?" he whispered.

"A siren." I figured if he knew what they did, he might back off.

The crease deepened, and his forehead wrinkled with confusion. Then his skin smoothed out, and humor filled his eyes. "A mermaid?"

I nodded and he actually laughed. He had obviously watched *The Little Mermaid* with his kids way too many times.

"You're kidding, right?" he said through his laughter.

I narrowed my eyes and pressed my lips together as the temptation to show him just how toxic a siren's song actually was to humans. But if I did that, I'm sure the plane would fall out of the sky and kill everyone on board, and I'd be the devil's plaything again.

"Sirens are deadly to humans. They poison mankind's minds, turning them into monsters. What happened on that boat was nothing more than a murderous rampage caused by the siren song." I chose my words carefully, hoping he would equate it to men, not all humans. I needed him to think I was safe on some level, and this ruse was the only way to do it.

His laughter faded as he studied me. "Will it affect you?"

I shook my head, opting for the silent response so he could draw his own conclusion.

"But it will affect me if I hear it?"

"Bingo." I pointed my finger at him. "Thus my insistence that you not come on the boat with me. It would be a shame if I had to kill you."

"How do you know all this?"

I glanced out the window, trying to form an answer that would hold water. "Because I have run across these things before. And I'm afraid the one causing this havoc was one I let go a long time ago. So, this is on me."

"You can't blame yourself," he said.

It was my turn to laugh. "Why don't you get some sleep? It's a long damn flight." I put the seat back and closed my eyes, avoiding any further conversation for the moment.

He squeezed my hand, and I squeezed back. Under all my angst, I was glad to have someone with me. Someone who could help pick up the pieces when all this was done.

Silencing the Siren
Chapter 4

I DOZED, BUT EVERY time I wandered into dreamland, I shot upright in the seat with my heart pounding without recollection of the dream that caused such visceral fear. Luckily, my restless sleep didn't interrupt Alex. He remained softly snoring in the seat next to me.

I stretched, giving up on the idea of sleep for the time being. My shifting stirred him, and he opened his dark eyes, sliding his gaze in my direction with a sheepish smile.

"Where are we?" he asked.

His voice turned deep and scratchy with sleep. It was the sexiest thing I had heard in a long time. I took a breath before glancing out the window. The vast blue of the ocean met my gaze.

"Over the Atlantic."

He glanced at his watch and then bit his lip with a raised eyebrow. "How much longer?"

I did the calculation in my head. "Around another fifteen hours."

"I didn't think this through," he mumbled and got up out of the seat, heading toward the restrooms in the back.

I watched him go and sighed. At least the transatlantic flights had bigger seats than domestic flights, so the comfort level was better. I climbed to my feet and followed his path. He stepped out of the restroom just as I stepped into the hall to wait. He held the door, and a small smile pulled at the edges of his lips. I paused and met his gaze, tilting my head at the sparkle in his eyes.

He leaned close. "I can think of one way to kill some time."

I understood that pseudo-smirk of his and gave him an eye roll before slipping in the bathroom and closing the door on his insinuation. I did my business, washed my hands and face, then rinsed the sleep taste from my mouth. When I glanced at my image in the mirror, his idea surfaced, and my cheeks reddened with heat.

I shook it off and headed back to my seat. Alex slid out and let me into the window seat. He pulled out his tablet and propped it on the tray. I glanced at the display and then at him. He was doing searches on sirens on Wikipedia, a site shrouded with a mixture of mythology and truth.

"What are you doing?"

"Research," he said. "Not the best way to spend my time, but I need to do something so I don't have an anxiety attack."

"Why are you anxious?"

He laughed and waved at the surrounding fuselage. "I'm forty-thousand feet in the air encased in a tin can. I don't fly for this very reason." He reached into his bag, pulled out a bottle of water, and gulped down half of it.

I didn't realize just how afraid of flying he was. I reached out and squeezed his hand before rifling around in my pocketbook for a deck of cards. "How about a little poker instead?"

He glanced at the cards in my hand and back at the screen, outlining the morbid dangers of my kind. He folded the cover over the text, stowing it in the pouch on the back of the seat in front of him.

"What are we playing?"

"Texas Hold'em," I said, drawing a smile in response.

"What are the stakes?"

I considered his question and shrugged.

"We have to be playing for something." The cock of his eyebrow turned my insides into warm honey.

"Okay, then you name the stakes."

He licked his lips and grinned. "We can't exactly play strip poker on a plane," he said with a light laugh. "So, how about... sexual favors?"

His hushed whisper sent a rash of gooseflesh across my exposed skin and a quiver of excitement down my spine. I had to draw a breath to not visibly shiver at the thought.

"What did you have in mind?" It was my turn to be coy.

His slow grin sent a rush of heat right to my center. "Are we upping the ante with each card turn, or did you want to set what the winning hands represent up front?"

I glanced at the card deck as my heart pumped liquid heat through my veins. The safer way was to set the limits up front, but then that wouldn't be as exciting as upping the ante for each hand. I took a deep breath and met his gaze.

"We can bet with each card turned. The ante starts with a kiss on the cheek, and we go from there. However, the, um, mile high club is only available if you have a royal straight flush. If you call it, you have to show your hand. No bluffing." I figured the odds of that were slim, but if I didn't put the rule on the table, it was one I was sure he'd bluff about just to get me bent over in the bathroom.

His cheeks turned rosy pink, and he smirked. "Sounds fair. Wagers to be paid up after each hand?" he asked with a hopeful lilt.

"Depends." I glanced around the plane.

Alex scanned the sleeping passengers and shrugged. I guess the thought of someone waking up to find us engaged in sexual favors didn't deter him. As a matter-of-fact, his smile widened. I shuffled the cards and dealt the first two to each of us, then put the deck aside. I glanced at my first card and stifled a smile, forcing my face to betray nothing. The ace mocked me, and I bet on it alone without viewing the second card. I waited for him to weigh in.

"I'll start with a kiss on the lips," he said.

"Check." I cut the deck before I flipped the first three community cards.

The flop contained an ace, a jack, and a three, none of which were in the same suit. Now, I had to think of what exactly I wanted from him. My odds of winning with a pair of aces looked really good.

He bit his lip and looked from his cards to the ones on the tray. "I'll raise to a French kiss."

I wanted to see the turn card before I started upping the stakes. "Check." I grinned and let him cut the deck this time. I flipped the turn. Another jack. That made things interesting. I met his gaze, waiting.

His lips twitched. "Hand job through the jeans."

"Check," I said.

I turned the river. A three, which didn't help me at all.

"Oral in the restroom," he whispered with a grin.

"I'll see your bet and raise it to oral right here in the seat." My heart sped up just thinking about how taboo that was, but the thought of him kneeling on the floor lapping me underneath one of the airline blankets made me ache between my thighs.

He blinked at me and then glanced around the cabin at the sleeping passengers before looking at his cards. "Check," he said, his voice cracking. He turned his cards over. He had a full house with jacks and threes. His grin widened as my heart dropped.

I turned my hand over, showing the ace, and then moved it to reveal the other card. A five of diamonds.

He swiped up the cards and lifted the table, shifting in the seat with the biggest grin I had ever seen.

I pressed my lips together against my smile. Hell, it wasn't as if I had never dreamed of seducing Alex this way. I just never thought I'd actually be doing it on a plane full of passengers. I threw the blanket over his lap and glanced around to make sure the stewardesses weren't starting their rounds. The passengers in the aisle across from us were sound asleep. I unbuckled my seatbelt and dropped to my knees on the floor. He lifted the seat divider and put one of his legs up on the seat and leaned back, pulling the covers up to his chest as I crawled under the blanket.

His pants were quickly unbuttoned, and the zipper undone, leaving me with a view of dark, tented boxers. I pulled his already hard member free from his pants and cursed the fact I didn't look at my second card. But I couldn't begrudge him that much. I probably would have made the same bet on an ace high pair.

I drew his tip into my mouth, and his sharp intake of breath made me smile, as did the stall of shuffling cards. I thought about tucking him back in and taking my seat because, technically, I had met the bet. He didn't up the ante to swallowing, but I knew that wouldn't be fair. He won the hand and deserved a proper blow job.

The airline tray came down, giving me very little room to work with. His hand threaded into my hair, pushing me to swallow more of him than I was prepared for. I nearly gagged on the pressure in the back of my throat. His grip on my hair tightened, moving me in fast, deep strokes until his hips thrust, forcing his entire length into my mouth, along with a flood of hot semen. I swallowed and received almost a purr in response.

His body shook once, and then his grip on my hair loosened. When I pulled away, he tucked himself back into his pants and shifted again, moving so I could slide back into my seat. The blanket remained draped over him, but his face carried blotchy red patches. He met my gaze as I buckled in.

I wiped my mouth and reached for the gum in my bag, offering him a piece before I unwrapped one and popped it between my teeth. The mint explosion was welcome, overriding the salty aftertaste.

"Damn," he whispered and started shuffling the cards again. "I might need a nap." He leaned over and caught a kiss before he focused on the cards.

He dealt the first two cards, and this time, I looked at both. A pair of queens, but I didn't want to start out too cocky. It wasn't like either of us had issues losing. Most times, whatever the favor, we would both win. I just wanted the reciprocal action.

"Check," I said.

He stared at his cards. "Hand job."

"Check," I said, stifling a smile.

He rolled the three cards. Two hearts and a diamond, all low. My pair of queens seemed to be the best hand, but I wasn't sure I wanted to bet more than a hand job yet. There were two more cards to be flipped, and the sparkle in his eyes had me worried.

"Check."

"Check." He rolled the turn card.

Another heart. This time a six to go with the three and four, making the option for a flush a possibility as I glanced at my queen of hearts.

"Hand job under the clothing," I said.

"Oral, here in the seat," he said, staring at his cards.

"Check."

He flipped the river. This time it was the eight of hearts. A flush beat two pair.

I smiled. "Mouth and hands," I said, raising my eyebrow.

He blew a stream of air out of his lips. "Mile. High."

"You don't have a royal straight flush."

He turned his cards, revealing a straight flush, eight high. While it wasn't a royal straight flush, it was close enough, and I couldn't really deny him, not with that hungry look in his eyes.

"That's not what we agreed to," I said as he stowed the cards in my pocketbook and folded up his tray.

He took my hand, led me to the restrooms, and pulled me inside before the nearest stewardess turned around. Before I could protest, his mouth covered mine, and his hands wandered over my ass. He broke the kiss and dropped, pulling my pants and underwear to the ground.

"Turn around," he whispered.

I obeyed, staring at my reflection in the mirror and then his dark eyes behind me. He reached his hand around to my stomach and slid lower, finding my clit with his fingers. The slow circling of his fingertips drove me half mad. With his other hand, he closed the toilet lid.

I stepped out of one of my pant legs and widened my stance as much as possible in the small space. It had been centuries since I felt this kind of heat, this kind of connection with anyone. When his finger penetrated deep inside me, I clamped my mouth shut on a moan.

He wasn't gentle like he had been last night on the beach. His gaze locked on mine and was half mad with desire. He swept my hair to the side and planted a kiss on my neck, right on the spot that made me shiver with anticipation.

The moment he entered me, I thought I would lose it. The siren song made it as far as the back of my throat before I caught myself. I wanted this man. I wanted his soul, his devotion, his love. As we rocked together in the tiny space with his fingers and his manhood creating a magic in me I had never experienced, I realized just how deep my feelings for him ran.

"Kylee," he whispered and squeezed me tight, burying his face into my shoulder as he shivered with the force of his release. He pulled me with him as he sat down on the seat, huffing against my back. "What am I going to do with you?" His fingers hadn't stopped, and I arched as my body finally responded to his caress the way he wanted me to.

I clamped my hand over my mouth as the waves crashed over me. His soft chuckle in my ear brought me back to the present, to the fact we were in a bathroom on a plane over the Atlantic.

His hand stilled, and his forehead landed on the spot between my shoulder blades. "Now, I seriously need a nap."

I leaned down without uncoupling and pulled my pants to my knees. I wasn't ready for this warmth inside me to end, so I leaned back into him and sighed. "Me too. But I don't want to fall asleep in here."

He snorted a laugh and stood, forcing the uncoupling. "Sorry," he said when I whined. "I'll let you clean up." He scooted around me and gave me a kiss before slipping out of the bathroom. I closed the door and engaged the lock to do my business.

By the time I got back to the seat, he was already asleep. I climbed over him to get to the window seat and curled up alongside him, using his soft shoulder as a pillow. My eyelids drooped, and his soft snore followed me into sleep.

Silencing the Siren
Chapter 5

THE JERK OF TOUCHDOWN shocked both of us awake. I wiped my eyes and glanced out at the Heathrow terminals. We didn't have to switch planes, but for several of the passengers, this was their final destination. I stretched in the seat and looked at Alex.

"Morning." He rubbed the slight stubble now present on his cheeks. "Did we...?"

I allowed a smile to surface. His sheepish question amused me. I nodded.

He exhaled and grinned. "I was afraid it was another vivid dream."

"You have vivid dreams about me?"

Alex chuckled. "Since the day I met you."

"Really?"

"Yes. But you and I both know I haven't been ready for anything other than friendship. At least not until recently. And then I was afraid of screwing up our friendship, so I didn't make a move..." He shrugged and studied his hands.

I knew he had dated in the last few months, but he never seemed to be interested in the women he found through an internet dating service. Some of his date stories were hysterical, but he never clicked with any of them. Each time he'd share a disaster date, I had to admit the outcome didn't disappoint me the way hearing he had a date had.

"What changed?"

"Something about how vulnerable you looked last night hit a nerve, and it made me realize how much I cared about you."

"So my vulnerability prompted you to make a pass at me?"

His lips twitched into a smirk and he shrugged. "I've seen you worked up before, and I figured if I was wrong, you might not be inclined to beat the crap out of me for taking a chance. If I was right, I figured maybe I could wipe that lost look out of your eyes."

I stared at him, contemplating whether I was irritated at his timing or humbled by his sweetness. I chose the latter and leaned in, pressing my lips to his prickly cheek. "That's sweet."

He blushed. "I'm glad I took the chance, but I really need to warn you. I'm not sweet. Sometimes I can be a little possessive and overbearing without meaning to be. At least that's what my ex told me. So, I'm asking you to tell me if I start behaving like a lunatic. I don't want to ruin whatever we started."

I let out a chuckle. "You mean like jumping on this flight thinking you'd be all hero-like and save me from whatever big bad I'm going up against?"

His face reddened even more, and he shifted in the seat. "Well... yeah. Kind of like that."

I patted his thigh. "I forgive you, but only if you listen to me when we get to Crete and stay on the island."

He bristled and glared. "And if I don't?" He crossed his arms.

"Then you will probably die."

His eyes widened.

"And I would hate for that to happen," I added, to soften his shock.

"Is there anything I can do to come with you and be protected?"

I glanced out the window at the airline hub. My gaze landed on the airman directing the planes with his orange cones and his noise-canceling earphones. I turned to Alex, my eyebrows raised.

"If you get something like that, it might work, but to be sure, I would want the combination of some noise-canceling ear protection, along with music playing or something, so there is no chance that if the siren sings, you'd be lulled to your death."

He followed my gaze and nodded. "I'd be willing to do that so I'm close enough to help if you need me. But if I can't hear anything, how am I supposed to know you need my help?"

"We'll figure something out." I wouldn't ever call him to action against my brother. Alex would be torn in two within seconds. The wisdom of having him onboard the boat was also in question. If the captain went homicidal, then I was putting Alex at risk. But then again, if I was fighting my brother, the captain could be used against me.

This whole situation was a losing battle. I closed my eyes as the new passengers heading for Greece started boarding the aircraft. We only had another four hours on this plane and then a short layover in Athens before the hour-long puddle jump. I honestly couldn't wait to get out of the stale air and get to the shoreline. I needed sea air. I could feel the dryness of being bottled in an aircraft for sixteen hours. It wasn't pleasant when I was away from the ocean for any period.

Alex's hand threaded into mine. Whatever color had been in his cheeks previously had gone. He looked almost ashen green. The unmistakable jerk of the plane pulling away from the gateway registered.

"I think my motion-sickness medicine ran out a long time ago."

I shuffled through my pocketbook, pulled out some gum, and handed him a couple of sticks of peppermint. He grabbed them from me and stuffed them in his mouth so quickly I had a moment to wonder if he even unwrapped them. His jaw worked, tightening and loosening as he chewed. A little of the green left his complexion, and he offered me an uneasy smile as the plane taxied to the runway.

"Just a few more hours," I whispered. He squeezed my hand. "Think you could, uh..." He raised an eyebrow, and his gaze moved from mine to his lap and back.

I laughed and shook my head. The noise of the airplane didn't drown out the conversations happening around us.

"It might take my mind off the, uh, unease pummeling every muscle in my body." Alex still sported a hopeful look.

"Not happening, Casanova."

"I know. I'm just trying to get my mind off..." His free hand fluttered in front of him as he waved at the interior of our plane.

"You want me to talk dirty to you?" I asked softly.

He let out a laugh. "That certainly wouldn't hurt."

I leaned close to his ear and whispered, "Mud."

The guffaw that escaped him was louder than either of us expected, which led to both of us cracking up. We laughed hard enough that he didn't really notice the takeoff.

When he started winding down, I added, "Grime."

That wound him up some more, but the grip on my hand belied the laughter coming from his lips. I turned his head towards me and planted a kiss. He drew a breath in and held it.

When I pulled away, his gaze locked on mine. "Maybe we should just kiss for the rest of the flight," he said. The clouds now blocked all views of the landscape. The plane climbed above the cloud layer and then leveled out.

"When did you figure out you were attracted to me?" he asked.

I met his chocolate gaze and sighed, thinking back to the day he moved in. I watched his bronze-skinned back as he carried his things from the moving van into his condo. He glistened in the midday sun, and the edge of his gray sweatpants darkened from the trails of sweat flowing down his skin. His bare muscles stood out from the exertion. I'd considered asking if he needed help, but I was enjoying the view too much.

"The day you moved in."

"So, we both have wasted four and a half years?"

"No. We became good friends." I glanced out the window at the cloud bank below us. "Besides, if we had jumped in right away, it never would have lasted more than a few weeks. I would have been the rebound. I'm not interested in being anyone's rebound. Been there, done that. It never ends well."

His hand relaxed around mine, and he leaned back in the seat. "Good point. But still, the idea that I missed the intensity we shared earlier for the last four years..." He shook his head and sighed. "Seems damn foolish."

"Well, maybe we will have a chance to make up for lost time." I didn't know if we would or not, but just saying the words seemed like the right thing to do. I certainly hoped to explore this further, despite my initial reaction on the beach. Yes, I wouldn't age, but Alex had quite a few years before he hit the standard of old. Perhaps if we made it out of this alive, I would tell him exactly what I was and give him the option.

If he knew the truth, would he still be all in like he seemed to be at the moment?

"What's going through your mind?"

I shrugged. "I'm wondering if you'll stick around once you get to know the real me." I closed my eyes and sighed at the fact the automatic editor of my words seemed to have been left back in San Diego. If I hadn't been a little sleep deprived, I would have never said that aloud.

"Kylee, there isn't anything you could do to drive me away."

I leveled a smile of sorts. "You may rethink that statement after all this is done."

Silencing the Siren
Chapter 6

ATHENS. I STOOD OUTSIDE the airport, taking a few deep breaths before I had to go back inside. The sweet tang of the ocean entwined with the air, soothing the dryness in my skin even though I couldn't see the water beyond the mountain range. The feeling of home wrapped its arms around me. I sighed at the melancholy that came with this homecoming.

Alex looked like he had been stuck in a plane for close to a day. His usual neat hair had become the bedhead look that most men spent hours cultivating. His long black eyelashes barely covered the dark circles under his closed eyes, and the bristle on his cheeks gave him a rugged look that I liked better than the smooth, clean-shaven cheeks I was used to. He took a deep breath of fresh air.

Being outside did us both good. The sea air bred life into me, and I was thankful to be so near my only true means of survival. When he finally opened his eyes, he smiled.

"I don't think I want to get back on a plane for a while," he said.

"We still have another flight left to go to get to Crete, but the bonus is we have enough time to grab a decent meal, and the flight is only an hour."

"Can we just stay put for a day or two? Go sightseeing instead?" he asked.

The way his brown eyes begged reminded me of the cutest puppy in the world. I almost said yes, but I knew a day or even an hour detour from this hunt meant someone else might die.

"I can't, but you're more than welcome to stay behind and see what Athens has to offer."

His gaze hardened, and his lips pressed into a thin line. He shook his head. "As much as you'd like that, I'd never forgive myself if something happened and I wasn't there to back you up."

"We aren't the dynamic duo," I said, rolling my eyes. I reached for the door.

His hand landed on my arm. "I didn't mean to piss you off."

I stopped. "You didn't. I'm just tired and a little hungry."

He nodded. "Me too. Let's go find some food before you jam me on a plane again." He opened the door and let me lead the way through the gates.

I decided on La Pasteria because I wanted a proper meal as opposed to getting my food at a counter like a fast-food stop. Although, I could probably stand through the entire meal after close to eighteen hours on a plane.

They sat us at a small table near the concourse, and I was content to people watch. When I glanced at Alex, he was staring at me. I shifted and tried to hide my unease behind a smile.

"How can you possibly look as beautiful as you do after being on a plane for so long?" He blinked and blushed after the words tumbled out.

His kind ramblings made my smile a little less forced, and I reached across the table, caressing his cheek. "I kind of like the stubble," I said, ignoring his question. I may look good, but the anxiety wracking my body left me with more knots than a bored sailor.

The waitress came over and took our orders. I got a simple linguini in clam sauce and a glass of white wine. Alex ordered chicken parmesan and a beer. When our drinks came, he raised the bottle.

"To exploring whatever this is," he said.

I tapped my glass against his and took a sip, thankful he hadn't toasted to the success of my mission. I wasn't sure I could drink to that right now. Eventually, I would have to tell him what I was and who I was going up against, but for now, I'd just enjoy my meal and his company.

Halfway through our food, he paused and studied me. "Do you regret what happened between us?"

"No. Not at all. Why?"

"You are unusually quiet."

I took a deep breath and gazed out on the concourse and the flow of passengers scurrying from one point to another. "I have reason to be." I turned back to him. "But this is not the time or the place."

"Are you okay?" he asked after a few moments.

Was I okay? That was a good question. Before we landed, I would have said yes, I was great. But now that I was here, too many memories seemed to resurface. I looked down at my half-eaten meal and pushed the plate away.

With a slow shake of my head, I softly said, "No."

He reached over the table and took my hand in his. Just his mere touch seemed to soothe the growing beast inside me. Gratitude welled up as tears that I quickly blinked away. But I wasn't quick enough.

"I'll be right back." He stood, disappearing around the corner. When he came back, he collected our carry-on bags and took my hand. "We're good to go." He led me out of the restaurant.

I let him take me to our gate, where he found a quiet, unoccupied corner.

"What is going on?" he said, his voice low and concerned.

"Alex—"

He put his hand up, stopping me. "I've known you long enough, Kylee, so please don't pass this off as jet lag or some equally insulting excuse."

I stared into his worried eyes. "I'm not sure how to say this."

He waited quietly while I considered my words. "What if you were sent on a mission to kill one of your siblings?"

He uttered a sharp bark of a laugh before the humor faded from his face. "You're serious." My slow nod answered his question, and he leaned back in the chair and glanced out the window. "I don't think I could do it."

"What if they were responsible for at least five thousand deaths, and if you didn't stop them, there could be countless more?"

His gaze snapped back to mine, and he huffed, crossing his arms. "I thought you said it was a siren." An undertone of sarcasm laced his voice.

The sting of tears burned my eyes. "It is." My words caught in my throat, and I wasn't sure he heard me because his expression didn't change. I cursed under my breath at the sudden swell of emotion. I shook my head to get a hold of the rising panic filling my soul.

I didn't understand why it was so damn important for this man to understand. After all, he was just a mere mortal. The plane ride had done something to my ability to keep distant. My mind drifted to the way he had claimed me in the bathroom.

"My brother killed those people, and I need to stop him before he does it again."

Alex leaned forward. "Why didn't you just tell me that? Why did you have to make up something about a damn mystical creature?"

Anger flared under my skin. "I did not make it up, Alex. My brother is a fucking siren, and I told him to lay low, but the idiot didn't listen to me, and now I have to take him out or I'll end up..." My brain caught my mouth before I told him I'd end up in hell. That was too much for him to absorb right now. His incredulous glare told me I had let too much slip. "I have to stop him before he pulls this shit again, and unfortunately, that means I have to kill him."

Alex slowly sat back in the chair with an unreadable expression.

"Really?" he finally asked and raised both eyebrows.

It wasn't that cute, endearing expression I was used to on the San Diego beach. This was a challenge with some dangerous undertones.

I had half a mind to show him just what kind of damage a siren could do. "Yes," I growled through clenched teeth. Self-preservation kept me from letting loose.

His skeptical gaze dropped to the bracelet around my wrist with all my little trinkets, and the snark in his expression softened. He sucked the side of his lip between his teeth, and when his gaze came back to mine, it wasn't as angry, but it still held a million and one questions.

Unfortunately, the concourse had started to fill up, and I couldn't get into this without strangers overhearing. It was never good to talk about killing someone at an airport. Alex's gaze wandered as people took the seats around us.

"We will talk about this when we land."

There was no leeway in his statement, and the warrior in me bristled. I never took kindly to being told what to do, but I let it go. He had a right to know, especially since he walked into a relationship with me without a clue.

Silencing the Siren
Chapter 7

THE CALL FOR A flight interrupted our silent stew. I looked at my ticket and stood. Alex didn't follow.

"I don't think we are sitting together on this flight." He showed me his ticket, and he was right. My seat was in the sixth row of the plane, and his was in the twentieth row. A part of me was relieved, enough so that I ignored the uneasy smile on his face and turned, boarding with the premiere passengers instead of waiting for him. I was situated in my seat when he walked by. Our eyes met, and he offered me a terrified smile, trying to feign bravery.

"You'll be fine," I said, and he nodded, but I doubted my words did anything to settle him. Guilt bit at me, and I glanced back to see him slide into a window seat.

"Would you like to sit with your friend?" the woman sitting in the aisle seat asked.

"Thanks for asking, but he's a big boy. He'll be fine," I said.

"Yes, but will you be, dear?" she asked.

I met her gaze with a smirk. "I'll be fine," I assured her, amused by the grandmother's comment. I needed the break. I needed the quiet without that questioning look. I also needed Alex to noodle on his own thoughts for a while. Maybe once we landed, he wouldn't corner me and force my hand.

Even if he wanted to talk once we landed, we'd have precious few moments before I went out on the boat I chartered. I would not allow the man on board if he didn't have those sound-canceling earphones, so that was a detour we would have to take, although I had no idea where to procure such things nowadays. I had requested that in my charter notes, and I hoped like hell the captain heeded my request. Otherwise, I would have a rabid man on board, and my brother would be the least of my worries.

As soon as we were in the air, I headed back to use the restroom. Alex's gaze was locked out the window and his hands clamped on the armrests. I paused at the seat.

"How are you doing?" I asked.

His head snapped in my direction. His eyes were like saucers of raw fear, and the smile looked as forced as his voice sounded when he said, "Just fine."

I traded a glance with his seatmate and continued on to the lavatory. Something about leaving him to deal with his fear of flying didn't settle well. When I stepped out of the bathroom, he was there, waiting for the facilities.

He stopped me from passing and pulled me close. "If your brother is one of those things, what the hell does that make you?" He didn't wait for a response. Instead, he slid into the bathroom and closed the door.

Retching noises came from inside and I paused, focusing on him instead of the sting of his question framed in accusation.

"Are you okay?" I asked through the door.

"Airsick." Then he retched again.

I put my hand on the door, sighed, and headed back to my seat. There wasn't a thing I could do for him right now, and it looked like there would be no peace when we landed.

"How's your friend?"

I glanced at my elderly seatmate. "Airsick. He doesn't do well on planes." I leaned closer. "And he followed me here, so..." I shrugged and gave her a smile.

She gasped. "He's a stalker?"

"No, not at all. It's really more complicated than that." I glanced out the window. "I guess he just didn't want to hit the pause button on what we started before I left."

Her hand fluttered to her lips. "That is so sweet!"

I couldn't help the smile that surfaced. "Yes. Incredibly sweet, but not incredibly practical."

She patted my knee. "Sometimes those are the best people to have around."

I looked over my shoulder to see if he was back in his seat. It was still empty. I chewed my bottom lip as worry prickled my skin. I unclipped my seatbelt and stood just as he came out of the restroom. He smiled sheepishly. After making sure he made it to his seat, I slowly sat down again. The ding of the seatbelt sign came on, followed by the announcement to right our seats and prepare for final approach. I collected my things, stowed them under the seat in front of me, and followed the stewardess's directions.

The minute the wheels touched down, seatbelts across the plane were undone, and the passengers started gathering their things. For a moment, I entertained fleeing the plane and letting Alex fend for himself, but he would likely be foolish enough to follow me.

I stayed in the seat until most of the passengers departed and then stood to retrieve my bag just in time for Alex to stop and let me lead the way.

"I honestly thought you were going to bolt," he said as we walked through the concourse.

"The thought crossed my mind."

We stepped outside, and I raised my hand to flag down a cab.

"I'm not sure what to do with the conversation we had at the airport."

I glanced back at him. "Look, I didn't ask you to come with. In fact, I expressly said no for this very reason. If I'm worried about you, I'm more apt to make a mistake, so unless you want me dead, I suggest you table this conversation for later."

A cab pulled up then, and I threw my bags into the trunk and slid inside, waiting for Alex to do the same.

As soon as the door closed behind him, I said, "Heraklion Yacht Marina, please." I turned to Alex. "If I said I was, does that change the way you feel?"

He blinked and leaned farther into the seat. My heart sank at the torn expression on his face. He stared at his hands for a moment and then gazed back at me with the slightest shake of his head.

"So you've done some of the same things as your brother?" he asked, his voice soft enough for me to pick up over the rumble of the cab's engine.

"A long, long time ago, yes."

He paled. "How long ago?"

I chuckled and looked out the window at the passing scenery. "How far back does Crete civilization go?" I asked the cab driver.

He rambled about archeological discoveries dating as far back as seven thousand BC, but that the first evidence of pottery was dated between three thousand BC and twenty-five hundred BC.

I watched Alex's profile as the cab driver explained the Minoan civilization and the timeline of the rise of modern civilization. His gaze turned to mine, silently asking the million dollar question. Had I seen the dawn of true civilization?

In fact, I had, but the devil caught me before I could see the accurate measure of progress of the Bronze Age. By the time I escaped the devil's prison, the crude wood boats that easily smashed on the rocks had turned to more structurally sound wooden vessels. A part of me wanted to use my voice to tempt the sailors, to claim their souls and witness the destruction. I could only envision how those vessels sounded as they crashed upon the jagged rocks.

Fate had intervened before I had another taste of death.

Alex's pallor improved. When we stopped at the marina entrance, I peeled off the fare as Alex collected the bags.

"You look damn good for your age," he muttered under his breath.

I stopped and faced him. "Alejandro Cervas, you were the one that insisted on making a pass and jumped on a transatlantic flight in some sort of misguided chivalry."

He shifted and nodded.

"So, does this change what we started?"

He laughed and shoved his hands in his pockets. "I don't know. I'm tired as hell and need some solid sleep. Who knows, maybe this is just a bizarre dream, and I'll wake up with you in my arms in your house."

"Before you get some sleep, we need to find you some of those noise-canceling earphones."

He stepped closer with a crooked smile. "So, if I asked you to sing for me?"

"I would say no."

His smile disappeared. "Why not?"

"It would kill you."

“Oh.”

Nothing like a death threat to ruin the mood. I turned and glanced at the boats. The only one I recognized was the *Christy*. But that wasn't the one I had tentatively rented. I didn't wait for any more of this crazy conversation. Instead, I headed toward the office to secure my ride.

Silencing the Siren
Chapter 8

"WHAT DO YOU MEAN the boat I chartered was rented to someone else?" Frustration welled into my voice.

The bell over the door rang. I didn't bother turning around since I already knew it was Alex just by the trace of his aftershave.

"Is there a problem here, honey?" he asked.

I spun towards him. "The boat I thought I had chartered was already rented out, and all that is left is that one, which comes with a three-man crew," I spouted as hot lava formed in my stomach, spreading in the form of a panic attack.

If I took that boat, it would mean four men to contend with, not two. I was badass, but I wasn't sure if I could handle four siren-crazed men, especially if they were all as big as Alex.

"We don't need a crew," Alex said, looking past me at the rental agent. "We don't even need a captain, but I understand that's required." He crossed the office and put his arm around me.

"It's either that or we can offer you a day cruiser," the heavyset rental agent said.

I traded a glance with Alex. I couldn't afford to just take the day cruiser. I needed to go out farther than what a day trip rental would allow.

"Fine," I sighed. "But the crew is required to wear soundproof ear protectors for the trip, like I had specified in my original request."

"About that, ma'am, they asked if that was truly necessary."

Alex's arm tightened around me like a vise. Perhaps he saw the flash of anger in my eyes. I certainly felt it, along with the resulting pounding in my head.

"I'm afraid we must insist," he said.

The rental agent gave a single nod. "That will be seventeen thousand euros."

"Excuse me? That's double what I had reserved."

"I am sorry, but we explained it is truly first come, first served."

They had explained, but I thought I had been clear that I would compensate them for holding the boat I wanted. Apparently, this schmuck didn't get the message. I had no choice. Sure, I could've gone to another port and hope for a rental that would meet my needs, but I was tired and needed a nap before I headed to the last spot I saw my brother before Fate pulled me from the sea.

I pulled out my wallet and nearly threw the credit card at the rental agent. He rang us up and went through the regulations before waving us towards the boat.

I climbed aboard, and Faraji, the host, took our luggage and gave us a tour of the boat. He introduced us to Taavi, the cook, along with Captain Hagan. All three were sizeable men.

Captain Hagan cleared his throat. "I do not understand the request for noise-canceling headphones."

"Do you have them?" I asked.

He glanced at Alex and then back at me, nodding. "Yes. I have a pair for you as well, but I wasn't aware that another passenger was going to be with us."

I smiled and hooked my thumb towards Alex.. "He can have the extra pair. As soon as we clear the port, I would appreciate you all putting the headphones on."

"Yes, ma'am."

"I think I am going to take a little nap," I said with a yawn. "Please wake me up when we get to the south shore." I reached into my pocket and pulled out the coordinates. "This is our first destination." I handed it to the captain before I headed down to the cabin.

Alex followed and collapsed face first on the bed. When he lifted his head, meeting my gaze, I laughed.

"What are you doing?"

He opened his mouth and closed it before any words came out. Then he rolled off the bed onto his feet. "I'm sorry. I just assumed." He turned towards the stairwell and the second bedroom.

"Alex?" I said as he took the first step. He turned towards me. "If you want to stay, that's okay with me."

The change in his expression was immediate, and it warmed my soul. His smile brightened the room. He closed the door at the base of the stairs before crossing back to the bed. This time, he didn't just drop onto the bed; instead, he stripped to his boxers and climbed under the sheets, hugging the pillow.

I thought the man was asleep before I slid under the covers next to him. I glanced at his thick black hair and ran my fingers through it. He turned his sleepy gaze to me at the touch.

"You okay?" he whispered.

I stared up at the ceiling and then out the window at the blue sky, shaking my head. "I'm not sure how I'm going to get this done."

He propped himself up on his elbows, but didn't speak. He studied my face with an expression I couldn't read.

"How old are you?" he asked.

My eyebrows rose. "That's not a question you ask a woman."

A smirk appeared. "I know you don't go mermaid in the water, so what do you really look like?"

I sighed and rolled away from him. I didn't want to have this kind of conversation. Besides, I barely remembered what I looked like, but I remembered my brother. Mermaids and mermen were not Ariel or even that chick from *Splash*. We were scary creatures with voices like a host of angels.

"Kylee?"

I turned, meeting his brown-eyed stare. "Fate turned me into what you see, and I've been like this for multiple millenniums. I don't change. I don't age. This is it."

He ran his finger over my cheek and then over my lips. "It could be worse. You could look like that rental guy."

I burst out laughing. I couldn't help it. He joined me with a low chuckle.

"Come here." He rolled on his side, pulling my back to his chest, spooning me in his arms. "Get some sleep, and then we'll figure out what to do with the three stooges upstairs."

Silencing the Siren
Chapter 9

THE SOFT KNOCK ON the door woke me. Awareness of Alex's light snore filtered into my consciousness, along with the continuous knock. I opened my eyes to the dark room, and every synapse in my body roared to life.

It shouldn't have been dark.

I pulled the door open with no memory of crossing the distance and stared into Captain Hagan's eyes. "What the hell?" I snapped and waved towards the dark room behind me.

"Neither of you woke, so we continued our heading and have set anchor for the night."

"You aren't wearing the ear protection." My body reacted before I could stop it. I pulled Captain Hagan into the dark room and flipped him to the ground, kicking the door closed and drenching us in darkness.

The light by the bed came on, and Alex sat up, his eyes as wide as the Captain's on the floor at my feet.

"Kylee," Alex barked.

"He kept going, and none of you have the ear protectors on." I stared Alex down until movement out of the corner of my eye drew my attention back to Captain Hagan. He was attempting to get up. I jabbed the heel of my palm into his temple, knocking him out.

"Are you insane?" Alex jumped out of bed.

I glared at him. "I have no idea how far out we are, or even if these men heard the siren call. I can't take the risk." I flipped open my suitcase and grabbed a skein of rope. "Are you going to help me?"

"Help you do what?" he asked and ran his hand through his hair, making him look much more harried than I felt.

"Tie the captain up so he can't hurt himself or anyone else."

Alex didn't understand the danger; that was clear from the horrified expression on his face. When he didn't move to help, I unraveled the rope and rolled the captain onto his belly, pulling his wrists behind him.

"Is this really necessary?" he asked.

But I didn't stop until the captain's wrists were bound tight and the end of the rope was anchored around the bed footing. "Do I need to tie you up?" I asked and stood.

He laughed a high-pitched laugh and shook his head. "Besides, I'd really like to see you try." He crossed his arms, cocking his head and giving me a crooked smile.

I stepped close, narrowing my eyes. He reached out, but I knocked his hand away. His eyes widened, and the smug smile faded.

"Kylee, I was just kidding." His voice was soft, his gaze sincere.

This was the Alex I knew, and I relaxed, pushing the warrior inside down, along with some of my guard.

I nodded and took a step back, distancing myself. "I need to get the headphones for you and the captain." I turned and headed upstairs.

Neither the cook nor the host was in the main cabin. I crossed to the sliders leading out to the deck. The two men were sharing a smoke, and neither were wearing the protective earphones.

The fact that they were laughing and talking and not displaying any hostility gave me an indication that perhaps I overreacted. I opened the slider and peeked out. "Excuse me, but can you tell me where I can find those earphones?"

The two stopped and glanced at me. Both tossed their cigarette butts in the water, and that's when I heard the soft crooning in the distance. That low melody that humans didn't recognize at first. I knew I was in trouble. I turned, trying to retreat as fast as I could, but Taavi, the cook, was faster.

He grabbed my arm and spun me towards him. I used the inertia of my spin to deliver a blow to his chest with the heel of my hand. His "oof" greeted my maneuver, and he went sailing back into Faraji. Both of them tumbled out onto the deck.

Out of the corner of my eye, I saw the earphones on the corner of the console and grabbed two pairs. I knew I should stay and take care of these two, but if I didn't get these on Alex and the captain, I'd be battling four men instead of just two.

I turned and ran smack into Alex's chest. He stared beyond me at the ocean night. I cursed under my breath.

His gaze lowered to mine. "Shit," he muttered and clamped his eyes and mouth shut. His entire body went rigid. His face scrunched in pain, and he forced his wrists in front of him, surrendering himself to me.

For the first time in my life, I witnessed what someone resisting the siren's call looked like, and it took me by surprise. I stared at him, dumbfounded, until the pitch of the song changed, growing louder and more insistent as Jeremiah got closer to the boat.

I knew my window of opportunity was mere seconds. I whispered a spell, and the small cuffs on my bracelet grew to normal size. With a twist of my wrist, I had the handcuffs open and was able to get one cuff tightened around Alex's wrist before weight slammed into me.

I flew past Alex onto the floor, yelping at the sudden pain in my hip. I may be quasi-immortal, but that didn't mean I didn't bleed or bruise. This one was going to take a bit of healing. If I didn't get this under control within the next few minutes, I might be put in a very compromising position.

I hopped to my feet before Faraji reached me and executed a foot sweep, knocking him down. Alex still stood in place, but his eyes were open and locked on the handcuff dangling from his wrist. Taavi wasn't far behind Faraji, and I took him down with a spin kick, knocking him out cold.

Alex's attention moved from the metal to me. His gaze turned into a glare. He lifted his cuffed hand and pointed to it. The move held more of an accusation than words would have.

I cursed under my breath because I might have to hurt him. Before I could take a step in his direction, arms wrapped around me like a vise, trapping my arms to my side. I threw my head back, but all I connected with was a chest. I kicked my legs back, struggling in his grip.

"Alex, help me," I said.

His face scrunched in pain. "Let her go." He took a step forward. His face smoothed out.

"Fuck you," Faraji growled close to my ear.

"She's mine," Alex said through clenched teeth, closing the distance. His fists clenched.

I shivered at the murderous glare. I wasn't sure whether the fire in his eyes was fueled by the siren song or just someone manhandling me.

My heel hit Faraji's shin just right, and he roared. His grip slipped, and I was able to scissor my arms wide and break his hold. My feet hit the ground, and I reached to my right, catching his shoulder and arm in my grip, and rolled him right over my hip. He landed between me and Alex. I took a step backwards, looking for some distance.

That was a dangerous move. I stumbled on Taavi and landed on my ass a few feet behind him.

Alex closed the distance and stopped, staring down at me, his expression transitioning between concern and anger. I rolled back and climbed to my feet, looking between him and Faraji, who now stood right behind Alex.

Taavi moaned from the floor. My skin flushed hot with panic. I met Alex's gaze, and the man I had fallen for was not there anymore. A feral monster had replaced him with one thing in its sights.

Me.

"I don't want to hurt you." I put my hands out, assessing the chances of getting Alex and Faraji neutralized before Taavi gained consciousness.

Alex's slow smile sent a shiver through me.

"Oh, but I want to hurt you." He stepped over Taavi. The darkness in his eyes reminded me of the devil.

I froze, but the jangle of his handcuffs pulled me out of my momentary paralysis. He pounced, and I moved, grabbing his reaching arm, and using his motion against him to slam him into the wall behind me.

I turned and ducked under Faraji's hook, coming up with my shot to the side of his face and knocking him off balance. That gave me enough time to thrust my knuckles into his temple. Faraji crumpled to the ground just as Alex tackled me.

We rolled across the floor, and he ended on top. He grabbed my arms and slammed me against the wood grain beneath me. His grip was tight enough to bite into my skin. A low growl came from deep in his throat.

"Damn it, Alex, you don't want to do this," I hissed up at him.

"Every time you tell me I don't want something, I see red," he snarled, but he didn't make any move beyond that first slam.

The groans from the other side of the room permeated my brain. I took a quick look at the two men slowly coming to.

"Baby, if you don't want to see me ravaged by those men, let me go. Let me take care of this." I used the softest, most seductive voice I could without engaging my song, praying it would reach my Alex.

He blinked and glanced toward Faraji and Taavi. His eyes flashed just as his face turned almost a purple red. He snarled and let go of me. I let him get to his feet before I swept him to the ground. I needed him safe, not in the middle of this battle.

"I'm sorry, baby," I whispered and slammed his temple.

At the very least, he would be disoriented long enough for me to get him somewhere where he couldn't hurt himself. I dragged him out on the deck, threaded his free arm around the outside railing, and snapped the cuffs closed.

I leaned over and placed a kiss on his forehead, then went inside to find those headsets before the others woke up. I grabbed a pair and went back outside to fit them over

Alex's ears, praying that it might stop the degeneration of his mind.

I stepped inside, and the main floor was empty. Neither Faraji nor Taavi were anywhere in sight. My skin went cold. The siren song was loud enough to be close, and I couldn't hear any shuffling in the room over my brother's damn voice.

"Jeremiah, shut the fuck up!" I screamed.

The song stalled, and a nervous heat filled my bones. My brother was close enough to hear me scream. I slunk farther into the room, holding my breath as I inched past the helm, which was one of the few places someone could hide. By the time I got through the room, I knew they were no longer here, which meant they either disappeared to our quarters or the crew's quarters.

I turned back towards where I cuffed Alex and froze.

"Looking for these things?"

His voice hadn't changed in all these years. I stared into the neon-blue eyes of my brother. He held fistfuls of hair from each limp body in his grasp. Faraji and Taavi stared aimlessly toward the stars as their wet clothing dripped on the deck. Their blank expressions faced me, while their bodies faced the water. Jeremiah had snapped their necks, twisting them one hundred and eighty degrees. The faint stench of urine mingled with the sea air.

My heart slammed in my chest. Alex was still out there. I had to control my breathing, otherwise I would end up hyperventilating. Jeremiah might not know about him or the captain yet. Especially if they both were still unconscious, but the moment he sensed them, they were as good as dead.

My brother tossed each body to the side. They slapped the deck like wet fish, bringing a heinous smile to Jeremiah's face. His form held gray-green scaled legs that would return to a single powerful tail once he was submerged in the water. He stepped inside the cabin with a glare that clearly conveyed I was next.

"Jeremiah, please don't."

He stopped, staring at me through narrowed eyes. "How do you know my name?" His wet voice filled the room.

I forgot what we sounded like in our native form. The song differed from the voice. I had seen humans piss their pants at the sound of us talking. It had a terrifying, gravelly quality, as if we had a pint of sand in our cheeks while trying to talk around a gallon of water. It sounded like a walking corpse.

"I was the one who got you out of hell." I stood tall. I looked nothing like I had the last time I saw him. I had hidden him away before Fate got her grubby little hands on me.

A guttural growl gurgled in his throat. "She is dead."

"No, Jeremiah, I'm alive. It's me, Kylee." I opened my arms wide. "This is what Fate did to me."

He charged. "I killed her!" he shouted and swiped his clawed hand at me.

I jumped back, but not far enough. His nails dug bloody welts across my abdomen, shredding my shirt.

"I killed her a thousand times," he roared and swiped again.

This time I threw myself backwards over the edge of the couch, rolling over the cushion until I landed on my feet on the other side. Adrenaline burned through my veins as I set myself for the next attack.

"Stop this shit right now!" I commanded.

A muffled yell from downstairs pulled his attention from me. My heart dropped. The captain was an innocent, just like the crew members that my brother killed, and he didn't have a headset on.

I scrambled, trying to put myself between this evil version of my brother and the stairwell. Jeremiah's backhand hit, knocking me clear across the room. I slammed into the wall with such force, I swore my skull cracked.

Dazed, I tried to force my eyes to focus. The siren song mingled with the high-pitched whine in my head. My brother disappeared down the stairs. I used the wall to climb to my feet. Shaking my head just made the world tip worse.

A blurry duo stepped into the room. I covered my ears at the sharp knifing sounds, but even with them covered, I heard his command.

"Kill her." Jeremiah took a seat in one of the captain's chairs to watch the massacre.

The captain crossed the distance with his wrists free of the bonds I had left him in, but the rope stretched between his tightly clasped fists, taut with the pressure. His angry gaze dropped from my face to my shredded shirt and my bare legs. When his eyes traveled back up my body, he snapped the rope.

I tried to move, to turn and run away, but the rope caught me under the chin, yanking me back. The captain tightened it like a noose, cutting off my ability to breathe. I grabbed at it as he yanked harder, pressing his body against my back, pinning me to the wall.

The suggestive movement of his hips pulled a chuckle from my brother. I clawed at the rope, trying to get a little slack to draw a breath. The rope loosened for a second, long enough for my underwear to be ripped off. The captain's hands pressed against the wall on either side of my head, pulling the rope in opposite directions, closing down my trachea.

If I didn't act now, I would not survive. The captain rubbed himself against my backside, and just as he pulled away, readying himself to take me, I stomped my heel on the top of his foot with everything I had left.

It was enough to stun him, but his grip on the rope didn't let up. I tried to twist, but he body slammed me against the wall. My head hit the wood, and I saw stars. He tried to force my legs wide. I kicked my heel upwards. His thighs tightened on my ankle before I reached my goal. My strength was waning, and my lungs burned.

One of his hands dropped away from the wall, and the rope around my throat loosened. I jabbed my elbow back, connecting with a set of ribs. I followed with my other elbow. The captain grabbed my ankle and twisted, knocking me to the ground. I stared up at him holding my foot. His pants were crumpled around his ankles. I realized he no longer held thc rope.

I kicked with my free leg, hitting home. His grip on my ankle released, and I rolled away, peeling the rope from my neck. I stood, using the upward movement to jab my palm into his nose. He went flying backwards onto the floor, his body jerking uncontrollably until he stilled. A small stream of yellow, pungent urine escaped.

I closed my eyes for a second. After the reality that I killed the captain settled, I turned a glare at my brother. "You bastard." My raw throat only produced a hiss.

He stood and crossed the room, cornering me. I had no more strength to fight him and no voice to defend myself. His sharp claws penetrated my shoulder, and I let out a squeak of protest.

If I died now, Alex would surely die. Just the flash of his face in my mind set my blood on fire. I yanked away from my brother just as the horn of another fishing vessel reached my ears.

Jeremiah's blades retracted. "I'll be back. Be a good girl and just sit down until I get back. You, I want to kill slowly. I want to sap your strength right from your bones." He smiled and disappeared out the front. A splash followed, along with the lull of his voice.

Silencing the Siren
Chapter 10

WITH EVERY MUSCLE IN my body hurting, I crawled towards the deck, dragging the dead captain with me. Each movement came with the assault of one of my brother's memories. Somehow, when his nails penetrated my skin, I received some sort of nightmarish transmission. The devil sent our spawn one by one to drag Jeremiah back to hell, but my brother killed every one of my daughters.

The last one Lucifer sent was a dead ringer for me, right down to the sea-colored eyes. I recognized that child. She had been my first, but she was faithful to the devil, shunning me. She went after Jeremiah with a vengeance, but was not strong enough to resist his song, even with the devil's blood running through her. The little witch made my brother believe she was me. No wonder he wasn't buying my story.

I stopped at the control panel and pulled myself up, flipping the switch to lift the anchor. Then I continued towards the deck and the dead crew members. I used the remainder of my energy to push all three of them off the edge into the Mediterranean Sea.

I stumbled to Alex and checked his pulse as the drift of the sea took us south. He was still breathing. I said a small prayer to keep it that way. My head dropped into his lap as exhaustion, pain, and my brother's memories swirled in my head.

If Alex woke and killed me, so be it. At least I would be with him until the end. My eyes closed, and blackness sucked me under.

THE CLANG OF METAL against metal pulled me from slumber, and my eyes opened to the morning sky. Alex banged his wrists against the bar, his teeth bared in aggravation. I rolled away out of range and dragged myself up on the railing. My movement caught his attention, and his glare landed on me.

He blinked as his gaze traveled from my head to my toes, and then his eyes closed. A crease appeared between them for a moment.

"Did I..." His eyes opened, and his gaze met mine.

I shook my head. "No."

"I can't hear." Panic filled his voice.

I stepped close enough to pull the headphone away from his ear. "I covered your ears. I think we are far enough away to be out of range, but I'm going to leave them where I can cover your ear quickly if I need to, just in case." I recovered his ear and headed inside. I needed something to wash the sour taste from my mouth and I couldn't leave him standing out on the deck all day. I grabbed a chair for him to sit in and a bottle of water for both of us.

"Where is the captain?" he asked as he took a seat in the chair I offered.

Instead of answering, I offered him a sip of water, holding the bottle for him while he quenched his thirst. I moved the headphone away from his ear and took a seat a few feet away.

"Unfortunately, no one else survived, and I think the only reason I'm still breathing is another ship came into the area." I rubbed my sore face and stood to retreat inside. I needed some form of clothing instead of just a torn shirt. I slid on my bathing suit and cover-up because anything else would irritate the cuts across my stomach, and the light fabric would be perfect in the hot Mediterranean sunshine.

I rifled through Alex's bag and found what I deemed would be a comfortable pair of shorts. I would also have to figure out something in the way of a commode for him because he would not be un-cuffed until I figured out how to reverse the effects.

I knew of only one way to do that, but even after the heinous way Jeremiah treated me, I wasn't mentally or physically ready to run Neptune's trident through him. I needed a good meal and a little more rest before I took my brother on.

I stepped outside with Alex's shorts in my hand. "I figured you might like a pair of shorts instead of just your underwear."

He nodded. "I could use a shower."

"Not going to happen, hon." I placed the shorts on the arm of the chair and pulled the underwear he put on before our flight off him. I smiled up at him as I took the shorts in hand. "I could leave you commando, if you'd like."

He rolled his eyes. "I'd prefer not to get a sunburn on my dick. But before you put my shorts on..." He turned and leaned into the railings, relieving himself in the ocean. "Now you can help put those on," he added when he finished.

I pulled his shorts up to his thighs, and as I stood to finish dressing him, I realized my mistake. I had stood between his arms. He slammed me into the railing and smiled down at me.

The intensity in his eyes both thrilled me and sent a shiver of fear to my core. His mouth dipped as if he was going to kiss me, but the gentle graze of his lips slid under my jaw instead. His tongue skimmed my neck, and his teeth clamped down on my earlobe.

The sudden pain of teeth cutting into my flesh pulled a gasp from me.

"Let me out of these cuffs," he whispered through clenched teeth.

"I can't," I said, trying not to whine from the pain gripping my ear.

"I'll tear your throat out with my teeth if you don't."

His grip on my ear increased. I cried out. He pressed harder against me, trapping my hands between us. I let go of the edges of his shorts and grabbed his cock, applying enough pressure to convey that I meant business. The pressure on my ear let up, but he didn't let go.

"Alejandro, you are hurting me." I squeezed harder.

"That's the point, Kylee." His strained voice whispered in my ear.

I dug my nails in. Alex recoiled with a gasp, giving me a window. I slid out from under his arms and out of reach of his only true defense. He glared at me from over his shoulder, my blood dripping from his lips. I circled behind him and hiked up his shorts before collapsing in the chair a few feet away from him.

"You still want to kill me?" I asked.

He smiled with blood-smeared teeth. The crazy was back. I closed my eyes, burying my face in my hands. The only way to free him of this curse was to kill Jeremiah. I got up to go inside the cabin.

"You can't leave me here," he said.

I stopped with my back to him, debating what to say. I turned, crossed to him, and put the headphones back on. I didn't want him getting to where self-harm came into his mind. At least he was still in murder mode, which gave me a bit of hope. Once the disease advanced to the suicidal stage, there was no going back, even if the host who caused it was eliminated.

I left him cursing up a storm and went to find food. Maybe a decent meal would give both of us a small reprieve. I shuffled around the kitchen, finding eggs and bacon, and I whipped them up along with a few slices of toast. I brewed coffee, too.

With a fully loaded tray, I headed out to the deck, setting the food down on the table in the center. Instead of attending to Alex, I ate my fill and leaned back in the seat, sipping my coffee and assessing his mood. His gaze was glued to the plate piled with eggs and bacon.

"Are you going to behave?" I asked.

When he didn't respond, I nearly laughed at my stupidity. The man couldn't hear me, so I finally picked up the plate and a fork and stood. His gaze followed the plate until I stopped a foot away from him, and then he finally met my gaze and licked his lips.

I took a piece of bacon and fed it to him, leaving a large, last piece because I didn't want my fingers near his teeth. At least he still had some reasoning skills. For that, I was thankful. He ate every bite I gave him, and when the plate was empty, I set it on the table and grabbed the coffee I made for him.

I held the cup while he took a sip and closed his eyes. "You certainly know how to treat your prisoners," he said, opening his eyes again. The glare was there, but it was clouded by gratefulness.

I moved the earphone and said, "Yeah, well, I still care about you." I replaced it and brought the plates back to the kitchen to clean up the dishes.

The mundane activity seemed to clear my mind. I debated on staying inside or going out on the deck and subjecting myself to his heckling and glares. I needed rest, and I needed to figure out a plan, but I also didn't want to leave him alone. I grabbed a couple of waters and went back out into the sunshine.

I put one of the bottles in his hand and sat down with mine. He stared at the plastic and then at me. "What the hell am I supposed to do with this?"

"Figure it out," I said, mouthing the words as articulately as I could. It was his problem right now. I wasn't in a helping mood beyond feeding him. I turned and took the seat that looked out over the sea. No landmasses were visible from any direction. I sipped my water, letting the scenery calm me.

"You really were one of those things?"

I turned, meeting his stare. He had been out cold when my brother was on the boat. Or so I thought.

He chuckled a little. "I played dead. Especially after he snapped Taavi's neck."

I looked away. I didn't want to discuss this with his warped mind. Alex was a smart man, and he knew me well enough to play psychological games with me.

"Well, were you?"

I nodded without making eye contact.

"Will you turn into one of them again?"

Disgust laced his voice, and I cringed. I shook my head. The form I had now was forevermore, at least until I was delivered to the gates of hell. Then who knows what the devil would do?

"Are you going to look at me?" His voice echoed over the water.

I stood and marched over to where he stood, moving the earphone. "You were not even supposed to be on this trip!" I got right in his face, letting the anger of the situation surface. "You decided you just had to save my ass. Well, you did a bang-up job of that!"

He recoiled and blinked in a way that led me to believe I reached the true man and not this thing driven to violence by my brother.

"I nearly was gang raped because I was so concerned about you." My skin heated with the fury filling me. I pointed to the rope burns around my neck. "The captain thought it would be fun to choke me to death while he banged me." The emotions coiling inside wound up to where I was now yelling. "And my brother doesn't believe I am who I am because the devil kept sending my offspring to kill him. He never saw me in this form, and in his mind, he already killed me!"

The color leaked from his face.

"So any chance I had of talking him out of continuing this insane path he has taken is gone. I have to kill him in order to save your ass." I poked him in the chest and took a few steps back before I did anything more. "The only reason I'm not unlocking you and letting you finish me is what would come next."

He cocked his head, and his forehead creased.

"I'll spend the rest of eternity at the hands of Lucifer. I crossed him once by freeing my brother and escaping from hell. He's had millenniums to stew over that, and the time I spent at his mercy before will look like a fun trip to Disney Land in comparison." I took a deep breath. "If I fail, I end up at Lucifer's mercy. If I use my voice and an innocent dies, I end up in hell. If I free you, you will kill me, and at this point, I'm not sure I would stop you. If that happens, I end up being filleted for the rest of eternity."

Alex slowly sat down.

"May God have mercy on me, because when I take my brother's life, I know where he is going. I'm sentencing him to an eternity of anguish."

My vision blurred, and I swiped at my hot face, wiping tears I didn't realize I was shedding.

"Damn it, why did you have to get on that plane?" I collapsed in the chair, facing him.

Silence fell between us.

"You... you had children?"

I met his gaze. "Lucifer's favorite pastime was taking advantage of me and dropping me back in his fish tank until I birthed his hideous spawn. I had zero choice in the matter, so no. I did not have children. I had abominations."

Silencing the Siren
Chapter 11

THE CALM OF THE sea lulled me. I stood on the bow at the farthest point from where Alex was chained. The soft crooning of Bruno Mars filled my head, but it still didn't take away the burn of Alex's silent disappointment. I couldn't deal with the disgust written on his pursed lips, as if I had given him a sour lemon instead of the facts. His judgment, along with Jeremiah's memories, raked at my nerves.

It was one thing to deny I ever had offspring when I had very few memories of them, but seeing each of their deaths through Jeremiah's eyes left me unable to cope. Each spawn that he killed took a piece of his sanity, turning him into the lunatic I saw last night.

I wondered if the same would be said of me after I slayed him.

The railing under my hands vibrated as if Alex was intentionally banging it. I tore my earphones off my head and turned towards the back of the boat.

"Kylee!" Alex's hoarse voice called.

I made my way aft, stepping onto the deck. His gaze was glued to something starboard, and I squinted into the sunlight, shielding my eyes with my hand. Light reflected off the hull of another boat coming in our direction. It was far enough away for the sound not to reach us yet, but I had a sinking feeling they weren't just heading on a lucky trajectory.

I tapped Alex on the shoulder and he jumped. His head swiveled toward me, and the tension filling his form eased a fraction. I stepped inside and took the helm, firing up the engines. I wasn't sure where to run, but I knew there was no other option.

It was probably a pirate craft, the Hellenic Coast Guard, or the boat that had saved my ass last night. Either way, an encounter would be no good. I couldn't explain Alex to a right-minded person, and I certainly couldn't let him loose, even if I was ordered to. If it was a pirate vessel, I wasn't sure what would happen.

I glanced starboard, and the single boat in the distance was now three. My heart dropped. There were no flashing lights, so my logical mind ruled out the Coast Guard. While it still could be Jeremiah's victims, I highly doubted they would be sane enough to launch a multiple craft attack.

Which left the only logical explanation. Pirates. After all, this was a hell of a boat, and it had just been drifting on the wind until a few minutes ago.

"Shit," I muttered and set course for the Egyptian coast.

With the autopilot set, I had to get Alex off the deck. Otherwise, he'd be killed instantly by whoever stepped on board. I muttered an incantation, and a key charm grew to a normal size. I unclasped it from my bracelet. With a few strides, I crossed to Alex, moving his earphone.

"If they board, we're both dead." I unhooked one cuff and stepped back.

He glanced at me and turned, heading inside. I followed a safe distance behind, and when he disappeared into the head, I went back to the helm. He came out a few minutes later and stopped a few paces away from me.

"Why don't you take a seat," I said, concentrating on pushing the engine as fast as the thing would allow. "And put those things back on," I added, nodding towards the earphones hanging around his neck.

He stepped behind me and grabbed my arms, slamming me forward over the console. His hands were already moving, pushing my swimsuit down enough for his fingers to access the warm recesses between my legs. My shoulder hit the engine kill switch. I tried to push him away. I could not have this distraction.

"Alex, we need to get the hell away from here," I said, but the urgency in my voice was lost in his purr as his fingers slid inside me.

His hand in the center of my back kept me facedown on the hard surface as his stroke became more of an assault.

"I need this," he whispered. His hips thrust forward, filling me with his length.

I cried out, but it was more from the surprise of his entry than pain or fear. His fingers manipulated my sensitive nub in slow circles. Whatever arguments I had were lost in the sensation of him rocking in and out of me in such slow strokes that I thought I would go insane.

The hand planted in the middle of my back slid to the base of my neck and snaked to the front of my throat. His grip tightened as his stroke increased. He pulled me to his chest, squeezing my windpipe hard enough to restrict my breathing, but not enough to close it down.

The sensation of him fucking me, along with the pressure on my neck, turned on an all-consuming fire that wiped my memory of danger. All I had was this moment, this pleasure laced with pain.

His hand moved from my throat, and he pulled my legs wide, lifting me until I kneeled on the edge of the helm. I pressed my hands against the edge of the backsplash, pushing into each of his thrusts. When he pulled away, I moaned, feeling empty without him, but then his cock breached my ass.

My moan shut off when his hand clamped around my throat again. His other hand resumed playing with my clit, creating a delicious heat through my body.

"Cum for me, baby," he whispered in my ear while his fingers still caressed me. His length slammed into me, pulling out a wheezing gasp. "I want you to drench the helm," he added, speeding up his movement.

He knew how to manipulate a woman's body with his hand. I had a moment to wonder what his mouth would be like before his teeth bit down on my shoulder, creating a new pain that blended with the bliss. I panted beneath his hold as he growled my name low in his throat.

My body tightened in anticipation of the buildup pooling in the center of my being. His grip tightened in response, cutting off my airway. My body didn't have the presence of mind to panic. Not at first, not when all my pleasure centers were pulsing with the need to release.

I bucked with the power of my orgasm, unable to draw air into my lungs, my body clenched with the strength of it. He pushed deep into me, crying out my name as he released with such force it caused another orgasm. This time, I did exactly as he had asked—I came so hard I sprayed the console.

His grip on my throat didn't release. In fact, he squeezed tighter as his body shuddered with aftershocks. I grabbed the cuff still clasped to his wrist and tried pulling. His lips found the nape of my neck, and he nibbled on the skin.

I yanked harder.

"Just go with it, Kylee," he whispered in that cold, empty voice.

The languid aftereffects of a soul-searing orgasm disappeared, replaced by the burn in my oxygen-starved lungs. He had me in a position that I could do little more than flail my arms. I tried pulling my legs together, but between the pressure on my throat and his hand still continuing to play me like a human guitar, I couldn't find the strength to move my body in a way to break his grip.

White spots filled my vision. I scratched at the hand around my throat. I bucked and one of my legs came out from under me. I used it to push off the console, sending the two of us onto the floor. The impact made his grip slip, and I twisted, rolling away from him as fast as I could. I coughed, gasping for air as the spots covering my vision faded. I pulled my bikini bottoms back in place and climbed to my feet.

He lay on his back, staring at the ceiling, his chest rising and falling with his exertion. A tear spilled from the edge of his eye as he slowly turned his gaze to mine.

"I don't want to kill you. I really don't. But I have to." He sat up.

My chest hurt from more than oxygen starvation. Murder reflected in his eyes. I executed a roundhouse kick, connecting with his head, praying it wouldn't kill him.

He went down hard. I paused a minute before I crossed to check if he was still alive. My fingers searched for a pulse, and when I found one, I let out a shaky breath. My throat closed on the sob building there. Somewhere, some angel was looking after this man.

I was sure I'd have a lot of explaining to do when he finally snapped out of the siren's spell, but for now, the bruise on his temple had already grown into a knot that would likely hurt for weeks, much like my nearly crushed windpipe.

The roar of the engines gave me a start. I glanced out the window, judging distances. I had a choice. Safeguard Alex or try to outrun the fleet of three boats closing in. I glanced down at my unconscious ward and made my decision.

I dragged Alex into the bathroom, looking around to make sure nothing he could hurt himself with was within reach. I sat him on the commode and cuffed him to the plumbing. He would be uncomfortable, but he would also be alive.

Once the headphones were secure, I wrapped gauze that I found in the first aid kit under the sink around his head, including his eyes to make sure the headset stayed in place no matter what. He would be disoriented as hell, but I didn't care. At least he would be safe and had an added bonus of being perched on the loo.

I exited and closed the bathroom door just as the boats flanked the yacht. I ran my hand through my hair and glanced at the soiled helm. There was nothing I could do about cleaning it at the moment.

The unmistakable smell of sex filled my nostrils, and I prayed those who were boarding wouldn't catch it on the air, especially if they were siren influenced. There were too many of them for me to fight back. My heart banged in my chest. I had a split second to figure out a plan.

I collapsed on the floor within sight of the door, saying a brief prayer that this was the right course of action. If I was wrong, there could be dire consequences, and I would have to tap into my siren voice to save Alex's ass.

Silencing the Siren
Chapter 12

FOOTSTEPS OF AT LEAST three people shuffled onto the deck. I made the muscles in my body relax. I hoped I would look like an unconscious woman to whoever boarded our vessel.

It took me a few moments to nail down the language they spoke. Arabic. My mastery of languages helped, but for some reason, the dialect they were using was foreign to me. I only could pick out one of every few words. Something poked me, and I allowed a small moan to come from my lips. I fluttered my eyelids open but let them close again after getting my first view of seven men with machine guns.

A slap stung my cheek, and I resisted the punch that almost got away from me. Instead, I blinked my eyes open and slowly glanced around, letting my eyes widen. I tried to scooch away from the men like any sane woman would do if they were woken to a room full of men with guns.

One of them grabbed my hair, showing it to the others, telling them I would bring a lot of money on the black market. The other argued I was damaged goods. The one with my hair crouched next to me.

"Where are the men who did this to you?" he asked in perfect French.

I just stared at him. He tried again in Italian and then finally tried English.

I let my chin quiver and shrugged. "I hurt him and he stumbled that way." I pointed towards the deck. The only other area accessible from off the deck was the crew quarters.

The fool looked up and pointed the group towards the deck, leaving only the two of us in the cabin. His grip on my hair loosened, but it didn't release.

"How did you hurt him?" he asked, using a calm voice, but he was clearly assessing me.

"I kneed him in the balls," I said. "And the last thing I remember is him stumbling out there, and then I blacked out."

The gun was slung over his shoulder behind him, and the others were out of eyesight. I shot the heel of my palm up, catching him under the chin with all the aggravation mixing in my blood.

The audible snap of the jackass's neck sounded through the room.

I dragged him behind the helm and yanked the gun off his shoulder. After checking both the clip and the safety, I set the gun to controlled live fire. Positioning myself behind the kitchen counter where I could see both the deck and the front of the boat in the mirror above me, I leaned back and went over my options. I was too far away from the bathroom where Alex was bound to protect him from any stray bullets.

I was tempted to use my voice, but the ramifications if any of them got loose would be catastrophic, so I hunkered down and waited. If they all didn't come up at the same time, or if they came from opposite directions, I'd have to do something drastic. But until this played out, I wasn't going to get my panties in a bunch.

A radio squawked, and I jumped, but luckily my trigger finger didn't squeeze. I glanced around at the man I just killed and cursed under my breath. Shuffling noises below stopped, and then the fast patter of feet in both directions reached my ears.

Damn it all to hell. The element of surprise was gone, and now they would run in here with guns raised, if not already blazing. I took a deep breath and closed my eyes. The wisdom of this wasn't even on the map, but I couldn't let them shoot up the place.

I opened my mouth, willing the siren inside me to come forth. The first note was soft, almost soothing. The pounding feet slowed to a stop for a few beats before resuming at a slow pace. They arrived from both directions at the same time, their guns pointing at the ground now that I had them in my spell.

I altered a couple of notes and then stopped, waiting and watching the men in the mirror. The expressions changed on almost all the pirates, confusion turning to rage and guns raised, pointing at one another. I ducked farther down and covered my head the moment the bullets started flying. My ears rang with the discharge of so many weapons in the enclosed space. When the last body fell and silence blanketed the room, I stood from my hiding place.

Just to be sure, I squeezed the trigger, burying a bullet in each head before I ran to the deck where the boats were moored. I sprayed almost the full clip into two of the three hulls. I swung to the third one and faced the only person manning the boats. He pulled a sword and went to hop onto my deck.

The last of my bullets nearly cut the man in half. He fell back into the only viable boat. The others were already taking on water. I untied the sinking vessels and went inside to gather the dead. It took me a while to get them all in the boat where my sword-wielding foe had made a valiant, but vain attempt.

Untying the last skiff, I pushed it away from the yacht, emptied the rest of the bullets into the boat, and dropped each spent weapon in the sea, waiting until the boats had nearly submerged before I headed back inside. I stopped dead in the doorway, my eyes nearly bulging out of my head at the sight of a live pirate.

His gun was trained on the middle of my abdomen, and he smiled. None of the bullets had hit him. I never saw where he had hidden. In my haste to get these shits off my boat, I hadn't done a head count.

"Hands up," he said, but his voice wasn't clear. It was nasally and slurred like that of a person who had no mastery over his tongue.

The truth hit like a boxer's jab. This pirate was deaf.

I obeyed, putting my hands in the air. The fact that he was deaf saved his life, but now I was at his mercy. By the glare he leveled at me, I didn't think he was capable of compassion.

He pointed the gun to the spot in front of him. I slowly crossed, wondering if there was a chance to get out of this. I stalled a few feet away. His face scrunched in fury, and he tapped the floor right in front of him.

I took another step. My mouth went dry.

"Right here!" he bellowed and pulled the trigger, sending a round into the floor.

I stepped to the spot he shot. His backhand spun me onto my knees.

"What happened?" he barked and grabbed my cheeks, forcing me to look at him.

"I... I shot them." I knew lying wasn't an option.

"No. Before. Downstairs, we ran and stopped. Then they all went crazy killing each other!"

I shrugged, my mind spinning to come up with a creative answer that would freak him out enough for me to get the gun out of his hands. "I don't know. I heard someone singing and then all hell broke loose. That's exactly what happened before the captain of this boat tried to kill me." I pointed to the bruises on my neck, praying this asshat knew enough about sea lore to make him nervous.

The anger thinning his lips turned into wide-eyed fear. His gaze darted around the boat. I went to stand, and the barrel swung back in my direction. His eyes narrowed as he studied me.

"Take off shirt," he commanded.

With shaking hands, I peeled off my cover-up, revealing my skimpy bathing suit, along with the scrapes and cuts of the last few days, some of which still oozed.

He grabbed a handful of my hair and pointed the barrel against my cheek. "I sell you."

I laughed, but he jammed the gun between my teeth. I gagged on the oily barrel, trying to recoil. I had no power over this crazy, deaf fuck.

"You my slave," he snarled. "You obey or die."

As if to make his point, he jammed the barrel of his gun farther down my throat. He pushed me back and pointed to the helm, handing me a slip of paper with coordinates.

I started the engine and plugged the coordinates into the computer, glancing at the location. He had me going to a port in Libya. I couldn't bring Alex back to land. Not with the sickness in him. I changed the direction, taking us opposite what I had plugged in, into the heart of the Mediterranean.

My only hope was to find my brother.

Deaf boy jabbed the gun into my lower back, hard. I turned, and he pointed to the ground in front of him. This time, an evil smile spread over his lips.

"Kneel and suck me, slave."

Jesus, I just stepped into the wrong pile of shit. I sank to the floor, and the barrel kissed my temple. A muffled cry came from the bathroom, but the deaf man with the gun didn't register Alex's angry rant the way I did. It was as if the action of this bastard brought my boyfriend out of the blackness I knocked him into.

I blinked at the mental reference. Boyfriend. What an odd thought to have right before I choked down another man's cock. The pirate tapped my temple. I glared up at him with my lips pressed together.

Instead of issuing another threat, the deaf asshole grabbed my elbow and jammed the gun into the center of my hand. The roar of the discharge filled the space. Pain locked down my ability to breathe. Then my exhale came in the form of a scream. I pulled my shattered hand to my chest as tears blinded me. Alex's rant changed from threats to my life to threats to whoever was harming his woman.

"Suck," the deaf fuck commanded, tapping my temple again.

My mouth was still open with pants of pain. He didn't care that I might bleed to death while giving him a blow job. All he cared about was his slave obeying. I had been in that position once before. I froze at the demon smile on this bastard. It reminded me too much of Lucifer.

My chest seized, and air wheezed in and out of my lungs. He reached for my arm again. This time, he might blow my hand clean off. I raised my good hand to the front of his cargo shorts and fumbled with the belt. I had sucked enough cock in my lifetime, but this was different. I had never been forced to give head. If I didn't find my brother, this would be my future until whatever benefactor bought me tired of my wiles and killed me. This was my penance for using my voice against humans and failing to bring my brother down the first time.

I unzipped the man's pants to the sound of Alex kicking the doors, stomping on the floor and screaming as if it had been his hand that had been shot to hell.

Deaf fuck pushed me away, cocking his head. He caught the vibrations of Alex's freak out. Hell, even I felt them through the floor, since any bounce of the hull shot waves of agony from my hand through the rest of my body.

I reached for the trident on my bracelet as deaf boy moved the gun toward the bathroom. The incantation fell from my lips. "*Deaus Neptunus in mari nascuntur tridentem istum mihi.*" Before the bastard knew what happened, the weapon grew and impaled him, slicing right through his body with a searing sizzle. The gun went off. He emptied the clip as he fell, shattering the sliders and drawing a bullet line through the ceiling. The gun lasted longer than he did.

I recounted the shrinking spell, "*Neptunus maris deus, fac mihi cessuros trident.*" The trident retracted back into the charm size in the palm of my hand. I clasped the bloody charm back onto my bracelet and headed to find the first aid kit. My hand needed attention before I could address another dead body.

Silencing the Siren
Chapter 13

I SEARCHED EVERY ROOM on the boat except the bathroom where Alex was chained looking for another damn first aid kit and came up empty. I stopped in front of the bathroom and took a deep breath. When I threw the door open, his flailing and carrying on abruptly ceased. His entire body stiffened when my fingers grazed the front of his face. I pulled down the strip covering his eyes, leaving a bloody streak on the gauze.

"What the hell happened out there?" he asked.

It took me a minute to realize the red on the side of his head wasn't from my hand. I nearly ripped the gauze off his head in one sweeping motion. He winced as I pulled the headphones off. I stared at the welt cutting through his ear and followed the trajectory to the wall behind his head. A hole the size of a bullet met my gaze.

I sat down hard on the floor. A stray bullet from the shootout had torn through the gauze and must have knocked the headphones off enough for him to hear part of what happened. My good hand covered my mouth as I met his glare.

"What happened?" he snarled.

I found my wits and stood, putting some distance between us while I addressed my mangled hand with water from the sink.

"I used my voice and made them shoot each other. Unfortunately, there was a deaf one with them who lived." I clenched my teeth against the burn of clean water and glanced at Alex. "Your kicking and carrying on saved me."

He gave a huff and nodded towards my hand. "It certainly doesn't look like I saved you."

I bit my lip and slowly wrapped my hand in gauze. What I really needed was the ocean water and its healing properties. Instead, I poured some hydrogen peroxide on a towel and dabbed the cut along Alex's head and part of his cheekbone.

He winced away from my touch.

"Sit still."

"What are you doing?"

"I'm cleaning your gunshot wound." I stopped and glanced at him. "We both got lucky today. You've just got a flesh wound."

If the bullet had been even a half an inch to the left, he would have died. My hands shook as I cleaned the wound. The blood had already clotted, but he would have a visible scar on his cheek for a while.

I stepped back and leaned against the door. "I tried to secure the headphones with the gauze. That's why you couldn't see, and as much as I know you don't want me to do that again, I have to."

He went to argue, but I splayed my fingers at him, stopping whatever rant he was about to launch.

"I can't deal with you right now. I need to take care of the hole in my hand first." I turned and went to the helm to shut the engine off. I needed the ocean. I needed the warm waters of the Mediterranean. I needed the magic of home.

I dropped anchor and went to the bow of the boat. The deck was a god-awful mess. I knew I'd have to climb up that way, but for now, I needed a clean view of the sea, not one marred with death.

I dove off the bow, bracing myself for the pain of the water hitting my hand. It did not disappoint, and I gasped, nearly sucking in a lungful of water. I surfaced, coughing and sputtering. Forcing the water I inhaled out of my throat kept my mind off the debilitating agony gripping my hand. I slowly moved towards the stern, taking small strokes to stay afloat.

By the time I reached the back of the boat, the pain eased to a dull throb. I reached for the rail and held on for a moment, bringing my injured hand into view. The bones had already been reconstructed, and the skin was just beginning to thatch back together. I squashed the urge to itch it and dunked it back under the surface.

This was one of the curses of my existence. The ocean had always healed what ailed me. Cuts, bruises, and breaks all disappeared after a dip in the sea. It revitalized me, but there were limitations. I was sure death was one of them, but I was never dumb enough to play out that curiosity.

I glanced down at the only other limitation that I was aware of. The only wounds that hadn't healed were those delivered by another siren. Cuts still traversed my stomach, and the wound in my shoulder still oozed. My stomach held red welts, but that shoulder wound needed addressing.

I climbed out of the water, taking as much care as possible to avoid the blood streaks on the deck, but it was nearly impossible. When I stepped back into the bathroom, Alex's eyes widened.

I glanced in the mirror at my unmarred neck. The bruises on my face were gone as well, and my hand, while itching to high heaven, didn't show any signs of a bullet shattering it.

"You never wondered why I used to go swimming at odd hours of the night?" I picked up the bottle of hydrogen peroxide and dumped a healthy amount into the wound on my shoulder. It bubbled and continued to ooze as I searched the cabinets for something more convenient than a strip of gauze and bigger than a Band-Aid.

"Why didn't that heal?" he asked, nodding towards my shoulder.

"Because it's from another siren." I didn't go farther into the lore with him. Instead, I found a larger bandage and pressed it over the wound.

"So... if you died, all I would have to do is dump your body in the ocean and you'd come back to life?"

I rolled my eyes at him and turned to leave.

"I'm asking a serious question."

"The dead don't rise." I stared at him for a moment, and that hopeful glint in his eyes faded. "I need to find another pair of earphones for you."

"Why?"

I stopped in the doorway and hung my head before I glanced back at him. "My voice is the only thing that will get me close enough to my brother to use this." I flicked the trident charm on my bracelet.

"I'm already doomed," he said. "I'd really like to hear your voice in my head."

"Killing my brother will break the spell on you."

His eyebrow rose.

"And anyone else still afflicted with the siren sickness."

I left him to noodle on that while I started the tedious work of cleaning the cabin, including getting rid of the last body. There was only so much I could do, even with the strong cleaners I found in the staff quarters. I had no idea how long I scrubbed, but I couldn't get it all clean. There was too much blood on the fabric. Luckily, I was able to get the floors clean, and at least

Alex had been quiet while I cleaned the cabin and deck. I had left the bathroom door open so he wouldn't feel so isolated.

When I finished, I grabbed the headphones along with earbuds that had been downstairs in the captain's quarters. He had an iPod in the charging station, and I plucked it from the base before heading back to Alex. He glared at me when I stepped into the room. "There's no chance you'll let me out of here, is there?"

"Afraid not."

He lashed out with his foot, and I caught it with my free hand before it connected.

"Do I need to tie your legs up too?"

The angry grimace transitioned into a playful smile. "Is that what you'd like to do?"

"Not particularly," I answered and slid to the side of the toilet where his legs couldn't reach. "I would really like *my* Alex back, because I think I might have fallen in love with him during the flight over here."

He blinked up at me and didn't fight as I fit the ear buds in and then placed the headphones over his ears. I chanced a quick peck on his lips before setting the iPod to shuffle and hitting play. I stepped away.

"I think I've been in love with you for a couple of years now," he whispered.

I paused in the doorway and met his gaze. For a moment, a shadow passed over his eyes like I wasn't supposed to hear what he'd just said. I gave him a nod and made my way to the newly cleaned helm. I lifted anchor and turned over the engine, letting it idle while I checked the historical coordinates.

The nice thing about this vessel was it had a log of wherever the boat engaged the anchor. I set course for the first anchor of our journey.

Silencing the Siren
Chapter 14

THERE REALLY IS NO easy way to prepare yourself for killing someone. Let alone someone you love. No matter how many times I rolled it over in my head, I still came back to the option of talking sense into him. Logically, it sounded like a valid plan, but I knew better. Even if I looked like I had the day we escaped from hell, I'd still have a hard time convincing him of who I was.

"Damn it," I muttered, shaking the thought out of my head.

If one lived, the other died. My gaze traveled to the bathroom as the twilight created long shadows across the cabin. Alex had broken out in song a few times when something familiar came across the tunes I had on continuous shuffle. He was as tone-deaf as they came, and it was so endearing that tears sprang to my eyes.

The navigator beeped, and I glanced at the coordinates. This was where we were anchored the last time my brother struck. I shut the boat down, dropping the anchor.

Waiting was never my strong suit. Alex's intermittent singing pulled my attention away from detecting the siren song enough times for me to become truly annoyed.

I stood, and that was when I felt the tilt of the boat. The stern dipped, and I moved so I could see the deck.

Jeremiah climbed the step, his legs still forming, so his steps weren't steady yet. I glanced towards the bathroom. Alex had gone unusually quiet. Maybe he felt the disturbance, too.

My brother let out a soft scale of notes, as if he were testing the ship. I unclipped the trident and held it in my fist. The tongs singed my skin, but I ignored the discomfort, holding tighter instead.

When he stepped through what used to be the doorway, his eyes narrowed in my direction.

"You really shouldn't have used your voice again, Jeremiah," I said, my voice full of sadness.

He paused. I couldn't bring myself to utter the incantation that would bring the trident to full form. The resistance to killing my little brother kicked in. This was the boy I used to rock to sleep in my arms after our mother abandoned us. This was the kid I used to play hide-and-seek with in the coral reefs. This was my brother.

He hissed at me in such a way that I took a step back. "Why aren't you affected by my song?" he growled.

"Because I once swam in this sea and sang alongside you, luring humans to their death. Then the angels came and sentenced us to an eternity in hell."

He bellowed with rage and charged. I stood my ground, pivoting at the last moment. He sailed past me and slid to a stop, spinning back in my direction to launch at me. This time, I wasn't fast enough. His backhand caught my cheek, sending me falling to the side. I used the inertia to roll back on my feet.

Anger welled up inside me, exploding to the surface as a roar. "Why? Why did you break our pact?"

"The only pact I ever made was with my sister, and she is dead!" He moved towards me.

I tried to dodge to the side, but he still caught me, slicing across the same shoulder he injured before. I screamed and spun out of a direct hit. The look in his eyes was far beyond reason. He was going to tear me apart piece by piece if he had his way. Even knowing this didn't bring forth my self-preservation. I couldn't kill him to save my soul.

He closed the distance and shoved with his palms. I flew into the wall next to the bathroom entrance. The impact dazed me, but not enough for me to lose my grip on the trident. I glanced to my right and met Alex's wide-eyed stare.

The next moment, Jeremiah had his hand wrapped around my neck. He lifted me off my feet, slamming me back into the wall.

"No!" Alex yelled.

Jeremiah's attention jerked to the bathroom and the clear view of Alex tied to the toilet. "What have we here?"

His grip constricted my voice so I couldn't say the incantation to make the trident big. I couldn't defend myself, either. Struggling in his grip, I kicked out, but my human form was no match for Jeremiah. He was going to kill me in front of Alex.

"*Hoc maior gratia!*" Alex cried from the bathroom, using the same words I used to make the mace grow in my living room.

My right wrist grew heavy, and I realized just what Alex had done. I twisted my hand and gripped the handle of the mace, bringing the spiked ball straight up between my brother's legs.

His breath came out in an 'oof,' and then his grip on my throat disappeared as both his hands grabbed his private parts. I swung the mace like a bat while I had a moment of reprieve. It connected with his temple, knocking him to the ground. My bracelet snapped when I dropped the mace. I gave Alex a quick nod of thanks before moving out of Jeremiah's reach.

His glare lifted to me as blood dripped from the side of his face. The damage the supernatural tools I wielded were always significant no matter the creature. It was as if the weapons were charmed in some fashion, and it was no different against Jeremiah. I could hurt him with any number of weapons, but only one would kill him.

He let out a growl as he climbed to his feet. Instead of coming after me like I assumed, he turned towards Alex like a predator cornering his prey.

Hot venom filled my veins, and my protective instincts flared. My voice rose from the depths of my soul, singing a lullaby that I used to sing to Jeremiah when he was little.

His head whipped in my direction, and jaw dropped. He stopped dead in his tracks, turning towards me. I continued singing, and every fiber of my being screamed at the injustice of this moment. My skin burned with it, along with an ache in my chest that would overwhelm me if I let it.

He stepped towards me like he was in a dream, lulled by my song. My voice hitched. He swam in my vision and I blinked. Hot paths traced my cheeks. They did not stop, even as the song smoothed out in my throat.

Between verses, I whispered Neptune's incantation. *"Deaus Neptunus in mari nascuntur tridentem istum mihi."* And the trident grew to full height.

Jeremiah's gaze moved from me to the weapon I now held, and his eyes widened. I let the last verse roll from my lips, pulling his attention back to my tear-stained face.

"I'm sorry," I whispered and jabbed the business end of the trident towards his chest.

He parried, but not fast enough to miss the sting of the trident tearing through his arm. He bellowed his anger and grabbed for the staff. I twisted away, cutting his chest with the sharp point on the end opposite the trident fork.

His claws scraped my back, tearing the flesh as I spun. I stumbled back and caught myself before I fell. I aimed the forks at my bother as we circled.

"Kylee!" Alex's voice barreled from the bathroom.

I didn't pay any mind to Alex. I couldn't. Not right now. I was too engaged in this battle to let my attention wane. If Jeremiah got hold of the trident, I was dead.

"You share the same name as my dead sister." His gaze sharpened now that he was no longer under my siren spell. He jerked towards me.

I flinched, jabbing the weapon. He sidestepped and grabbed one of the trident forks, yanking me off balance with a bellow as the gold burned his skin. The trident slipped from my grasp, and I hit the floor flat out. The trident clattered a few feet away. I scrambled to my feet, diving for it.

The kick in my side sent me flying into the cabinets on the far side of the room. The shock of it left me disoriented until I drew a breath. Air seemed to revive the wild beast, twisting my bones inside me. I moaned at the pain searing my left side. I tried to get to my hands and knees, but I couldn't quite manage it.

My eyes focused on seeing Jeremiah step into the bathroom, out of sight.

"No," I whispered, but even speaking was painful.

Metal scraped against metal and Alex howled. I forced myself to my hands and knees just as Alex came flying out of the bathroom. He landed on his ass on the floor without headphones, and the cuffs were no longer on his wrists. The impact knocked an ear bud out of his ear.

He scrambled to his feet as Jeremiah stepped in the doorway and pointed towards the discarded trident.

"Kill her," Jeremiah ordered and sang the haunting tune of our ancestors. The one that incited murder in our victims.

Alex's body tensed, every muscle vibrating with the curse. He stepped towards the trident as if he wore lead shoes. His singular focus was on the weapon, and there was nothing I could do to stop him. If I engaged my voice, Alex would be doomed.

"You bastard," I whispered, glaring at Jeremiah as I pulled myself to my feet.

He stopped singing, turning his attention to me. "Come on, big sis. Let's hear that voice of yours. Let's see what you can do?"

Alex picked up the trident and stared at the tongs and the diamond embedded just above the staff. He twirled it and inspected the sharp point before turning his gaze to mine.

The darkness that lived in his eyes pulled a shiver from me. My Alex was no longer; he was my brother's puppet now. His movements were smoother as he turned and pointed the deadly dagger at me.

I couldn't bring myself to stop him, no matter how much my brother cajoled. Alex stopped in front of me, holding the trident out in front of him as if he was handling a bo staff in a martial arts class.

Jeremiah stepped behind him and tilted Alex's hand so the point was in line with my heart. He stepped back and smiled over Alex's head.

"Kill her," he said again, this time in a melodic whisper. One Alex couldn't ignore.

I met Alex's fogged gaze. "I love you, Alex."

The mist cleared for a fraction of a second. Just enough for my Alex to make an appearance. He jammed the trident backwards, spinning and lunging at the same time. The forks bit through Jeremiah's stomach. He let go of the staff as Jeremiah screamed in agony.

My brother's face transformed into a mask of fury, and he lurched forward, impaling Alex through the right side of his chest. Alex's cry mixed with my brother's growling roar as he continued towards me.

I grabbed the tip and muttered the incantation before Jeremiah could impale me. "*Neptunus maris deus, fac mihi cessuros trident.*"

Alex bellowed his pain and collapsed as the trident staff shrunk.

The minute he hit the floor, I said the magic words again. "*Deus Neptunus in mari nascuntur tridentem istum mihi.*"

The trident shot forth like a lightning bolt, but this time, the aim was true. The middle fork pierced right through my brother's heart. My chest ached and my throat tightened against the sudden swell of tears blinding me.

Jeremiah's eyes widened, and he looked down at the tongs embedded in his chest before his gaze returned to mine. "Kylee?" he whispered and then slowly sank to his knees. He transformed into his native merman form.

"I'm sorry, Jeremiah," I whispered and pushed harder until the bottom of the trident forks burned into his chest.

His tail banged the floor a couple times, and I waited until his last breath wheezed out of his lungs before I commanded the weapon to shrink back to trinket size. His body crusted over like an ancient sea coral that had been exposed for too long, freezing him forever in death.

My gaze moved to the trinket in my palm just before my knees gave way. I dropped to the floor and crawled to Alex. His breath was labored. I rolled him on his back, his pained gaze meeting mine.

"Kylee," he whispered and coughed blood.

I reached for my charm bracelet and found my wrist empty. I frantically scanned the boat cabin. I scrambled to my feet and stumbled across the room to where the bracelet lay still attached to the mace. My shrinking incantation sounded slurred, like I had a little too much wine, but I guessed that was from the bang on my head. I connected the trident charm and filtered through the rest of them until I came upon a delicate decanter. I twisted it off and crawled back to Alex, sputtering the right spell to make the ambrosia vial expand.

Thankfully, Alex was still breathing and conscious. I poured three drops in his mouth and peeled his shirt up to reveal the hole where the spike had gone through. I poured five drops of the ambrosia on his skin surrounding the injury.

"I'm sorry, sweetie. This is going to hurt." I rolled him over. He just groaned. This time, I poured what equaled a quarter cup of liquid right into the puncture and then turned him on his side.

He gasped as I held him in place. I capped the decanter, whispered the spell to shrink it back to charm size, and clasped it on my bracelet.

"I know it hurts," I said, as his jaw tightened. "But it will heal you."

"What is it?" he asked through labored breaths.

"Nectar of the Gods."

His eyebrows rose. "Immortality?"

I guessed he knew Greek mythology. Chuckling, I shook my head. "While it has healing qualities for humans like the ocean does for me, it does not make you immortal." I stoked his cheek gently. "Although one could argue that it can help you cheat death a time or two."

He laughed, but his laugh turned into a convulsing cough that sprayed blood everywhere. A wad of blood came up. Then he settled down with a groan, leaning into me. His breathing was less labored now, less like a wet rag than before. I lifted the shirt in the back and smiled at the entry wound. Instead of being an inch in diameter, it had shrunk to the size of a bullet in the short time we sat here. In no time, his skin would be smooth and unmarred.

I closed my eyes, and the world swam.

"KYLEE?"

A wet hand caressed my cheek. Weightlessness gripped me, yet my entire body felt heavy. It was an odd sensation.

"Kylee, please wake up."

The words whispered at a distance, but they pulled at me, drawing me closer.

"Please, please, wake up."

Lips drifted across mine. The softness was welcomed and sweet, and his breath tickled my face. Splashing taps on my cheek made me turn away.

"Kylee?"

My name hung on the air, and I blinked my eyes open. Alex's concerned gaze met mine. I lifted my head and winced. My muscles didn't like me very much, and I couldn't quite figure out where I was.

"Where are we?"

"We are in the emergency float on the deck. I filled it with sea water, so it's kind of like a kiddy pool." He wiped my cheek with water and helped me sit up. "It's not exactly clean, but I think it did the trick."

"What happened?"

"You passed out."

I had to suppress a 'duh.' The last thing I remembered was his wound healing, and then everything went black. I waited for more of an explanation.

"I think you might have crushed your entire ribcage and possibly shattered your shoulder. The back of your head was bleeding. I'm sure you have a hell of a concussion, and I think you may even have cracked your cranium. I have no idea how you did what you did at the end." He stopped and wiped his face. "Luckily, I remembered what the ocean did for you before. So..." He waved at the pool and gave me a shrug. "I didn't know if it would work, and I didn't have any magic elixir like you did."

My back stung to high heaven, but at least breathing didn't hurt like it had before. The water healed some of my ailments, but not the cuts from my brother's claws. I did a slow assessment of all my limbs, torso, and head. I seemed to be in one piece, even though my head still felt fuzzy.

"Kylee?" he asked after a few minutes of silence.

I turned to look at him.

"I remember... everything." His gaze dropped away from mine and he stood, retreating into the cabin now that he knew I was okay.

I climbed to my feet and stepped out of the makeshift tub. Glancing at the red-tinged water produced an unpleasant shiver. I had to have been bleeding pretty badly to turn an entire lifeboat full of sea water red. Either that or someone put food coloring in it as a poor joke.

Each step pulled at the cuts on my back. I winced as I walked carefully into the cabin. Alex was sitting on the couch, dripping bloody water all over the place. I almost said something, but a quick glance around quieted me. All the furniture in the room was splattered with blood, and the floor had a thick puddle where Alex had fallen. The crusted shape of my brother still sat in the same place as well.

The entire scene looked like it was cut right out of a B-horror flick.

"Are you okay?" I asked as I approached him.

Alex shook his head. "I tried to kill you more than once and I..." He waved towards the helm. A blush bloomed in his cheeks, spreading to his entire face. "I don't really know what that was." He avoided my gaze.

"You are a very strong man."

He covered his face with his hands.

"Look at me, Alex," I whispered as I took the seat opposite him. It was a struggle, but he finally met my gaze. "You resisted my brother's siren call more than once. That is something I have never seen before."

"I tried to kill you."

"Yeah, well, that roundhouse kick I did could have killed you, too. And my brilliant idea of making those pirates shoot each other nearly got you shot. A half inch the other way, and you would have died."

"I deserved it." His lips pressed together, and his brow creased in that familiar look of self-loathing.

I used to see that expression on his face any time he got into an argument with his ex-wife. "Don't do that."

"Do what?" His sharp gaze jumped to mine.

"Blame yourself."

He bit his lip and stared at me. "Kylee, I was still in there."

"I know. I'm still breathing."

His eyebrow went up.

"You have no idea how much willpower it takes to refuse to follow a siren's orders. My brother gave you a direct order to kill me. You didn't. Instead, you attacked him. That doesn't happen. Ever. I have seen husbands kill their wives and mothers slaughter their children without a blink. I've seen brothers and sisters turn on each other." I stopped and closed my eyes. "You are the only man that ever resisted. Why?"

He laughed. "Are you seriously asking that?"

I nodded.

He leaned forward. "I jumped on a plane and traveled halfway around the world to make sure you were safe. However misguided that was, that is not done simply out of friendship." He looked down at his hands clasped between his knees. "Did you mean what you said to me?" His gaze pierced through me with a mixture of hope and dread. "Or was that just said to reach whatever was left of me?"

I swallowed, and it was my turn to look away. A part of me didn't want to admit to the adoration I felt for him. It was much easier to admit my feelings when I thought we were both doomed.

"Kylee?" he asked, drawing my gaze back to his.

"Yes." My answer was quiet and small. "I meant it."

He leaned back on the couch, relief smoothing the lines in his face. "I thought you might have been feeding me some bullshit just to survive." He glanced at his soiled shirt and my bloodstained bathing suit. "I need to get some clean clothes on." He stood and held out his hand. "Come on."

I took his hand and let him lead me downstairs to the bedroom we hadn't been in together since the first day of this catastrophic cruise. He led me into the shower and turned the water on, pulling me inside with him.

Neither of us had cleaned up since we left California, and the hot water stream felt like heaven until I turned my back into it. I winced as my cuts took a direct hit.

Alex quickly washed himself with the body wash and shampoo and then did the same to me, taking care to avoid getting soap directly in my cuts. The water ran red for longer than I cared to see, but it soon turned pink and then clear. He shampooed my hair twice, and it felt like I had entered nirvana. His fingers were gentle and soft as they kneaded my scalp.

After I was all clean, he turned me towards him and wrapped his arms around me, bringing me to his chest.

"Thank you for saving me," he whispered in my ear. "I know what you had to sacrifice in order to do that."

I hugged him back, the numbness of my actions thawing, and with it came the tears. Tears mourning my brother's death, mourning all the death and destruction he created. Alex held tight while I cried. When all my tears dried up, I pulled out of his grasp.

He shut the water off and wrapped a towel around his waist. He grabbed the second towel and dried me off before he turned me around to inspect my back.

"I think you might need stitches for a couple of these." His finger traced my skin between cuts, then he opened the medicine cabinet.

"The first aid kit is in the bathroom upstairs," I said as he shuffled through the cabinets in the bathroom.

"Just wait here. I'll be right back." He stepped out of the room.

I sat on the toilet seat waiting for him, letting the numbness take hold of both my mind and my body. When he came back, he wore shorts and a T-shirt. He pulled me into the bedroom where he had the entire first aid kit laid out on the bed. He pulled the vanity stool over and sat me down on it before working on my back.

He dabbed something cool and soothing on the burning cuts and I sighed.

"So what do we do now?" he asked as he continued to work on patching me up the best he could.

I remained quiet, mulling it over. I wasn't sure if he was asking about us or our current situation, so I went with the safer bet. "I have no idea how we're going to get this boat back to port and explain the loss of the crew and the condition of the cabin upstairs."

He huffed a laugh. "I wasn't asking about the fucked up predicament we are in."

"Oh."

He turned the stool, so I faced him and continued patching the front of my shoulder. Once he had the bandage in place, he met my gaze.

"How does this work?" He pointed between the two of us.

"You know what I am and what I've done. But you don't know everything." I stood and rifled through my suitcase, pulling on a pair of shorts and a comfortable loose tank top before I turned to him. "If there is ever going to be anything more between us, you need to know what my deal is."

He closed up the first aid kit and patted the corner of the bed next to where he sat. His expression was neutral. Unreadable.

"I have a paranormal investigation agency, but that's not what I'm doing here. This trip was something I was ordered to do."

"By who?" he asked cautiously.

"Fate. I work for her as a kind of bounty hunter."

"Fate?" He laughed at me like I was shoveling shit in his direction.

The air shifted, and I cringed. I had hoped I wouldn't have to deal with Fate until I got home. Alex shot to his feet and stepped back into the side table. His eyes widened at the vision of the queen bitch herself. I stood, putting myself between her and Alex. The tight set of her lips and the blaze in her eyes left me shaking.

Her signature red dress billowed as she pointed her finger at me. "You violated the rules," she growled.

"I did what you said. I killed my own flesh and blood." My teeth clicked closed so tight that my jaw hurt.

"You employed your siren," she spat back.

I nodded. "Twice. But no innocents died as a result."

Her hands balled into fists. "I should drag your ass back to Lucifer right now," she said with all the fire and fury written on her face.

Alex's hands curled around my shoulders. "I don't think so." He held on to me like I could be yanked from his life at the whim of the woman standing before him, which was an accurate assessment.

Her fiery gaze moved from mine to his. "She also violated her contract by telling you about our deal." She crossed her arms. "So what punishment do *you* deem fitting for breaking the rules?"

Alex stared Fate down, blissfully unafraid of the woman. "She killed her own brother. What more do you want from her?"

"Do whatever you want to me, but leave him alone," I said as a hot flash of panic filled my form. My heart jumped into my throat, pounding hard enough to make breathing as difficult as it had been after my brother crushed my ribs.

Fate was a fickle bitch, and she could yank him out of my life just as easily as she could yank me back to hell. And she enjoyed tormenting me. I wouldn't put anything past her right now, especially with the lack of fear coming from Alex.

She stepped closer, glaring down at me.

"If you so much as harm a hair on his head, I'll open so many goddamned portals that this earth will be overrun by monsters, and you will not have your little bounty hunter to clean up the mess." The ultimatum slipped out of my mouth in a feral growl. After all the shit she had put me through, if she yanked Alex from this world to spite me, I would do damage on a cataclysmic scale.

Fate blinked at the venom in my voice, and perhaps she heard the truth in my words because she took a step back, distancing herself. Her eyes narrowed as she studied me. She pulled a book out of her skirt ruffles and ran her perfectly manicured nail down each page before she flipped to the other side, continuing page after page while we waited for her sentence. She slammed the book closed and glared at me, sliding the book back into her pockets.

"You are a lucky girl. The people who died on your watch were already on death's list, and he isn't." Her gaze moved beyond me to Alex and back. "But I cannot let your transgression go unpunished." An evil smile spread across her lips.

I went to speak, but she reached out with her hand and yanked at the air, pulling her fist tight. My body jerked, and I inhaled at the sudden release from my throat. For a moment, I thought she'd cut it wide open, but then Fate held her hand over a vial. Light filled the glass, and she corked it.

"That should teach you," Fate purred before she blinked out, leaving a swirl of smoke in her place.

My legs turned to jelly, and I took an unsteady step before sitting on the side of the bed.

"She's quite the bitch." Alex crouched down in front of me. "Why don't you tell her to go pound sand?"

I met his gaze and opened my mouth. No sound came out. My hand went to my throat. The skin was intact, but I could no longer speak. Fate had left me a mute. She stole my damn voice.

"Kylee?"

I pointed to my throat.

His eyes grew. "What did she do?"

I tapped my throat and waved bye-bye.

"She took your voice?"

I nodded and closed my eyes, hanging my head. I took a breath and gathered my wits. Lots of people existed with less.

Do you know sign language? I signed slowly, hoping I had the gestures correct.

He just stared at my hands. I could have been signing ancient Greek to him for all he knew. I'd have to teach him how to read what I was saying, but in the meantime, we had more pressing issues to attend to. Like how to explain the condition of the boat and not end up rotting somewhere in jail in Greece for the rest of our lives.

Silencing the Siren
Chapter 15

WE STOOD LOOKING AT the dingy in the cargo hold. It was one of those nice proactive lifeboats. The inflatable one Alex had used as my healing tub wasn't the only one on board. I was glad the captain had given us a full tour of the boat before we set sail, because otherwise I would have never dreamed up this plan.

"Are you sure?" Alex asked.

I nodded and typed a message to him on his tablet. *It's the only plausible way for us to get out of this.*

We had hashed out every other scenario, from cruising into harbor with the boat as is, to calling for help, and everything in between. Our only hope of being let on the plane home was to get into the lifeboat and head back with the story that we escaped when pirates took over the yacht. It weaved the truth together and would explain quite a lot if any of the bodies or boats were found. Every other scenario landed us in a jail cell.

"It's risky. They might find this boat before we get to shore," Alex said, rubbing his chin. "But maybe if they do, it will lend credence to our story."

I think the bizarre massacre on the cruise ship might help our situation too. Let's see what we can gather. We are close to two hundred miles southeast of Crete, so in all likelihood, we are looking at five days in that thing before we hit land. I finished typing, handed him the tablet, and turned my back on our escape route, heading back into the belly of the boat.

"We can't fare too well," he said. "Escaping in a well-equipped dingy is kind of suspect."

I paused at the door and nodded. I hoped there wasn't anything he was attached to in his suitcase. I just needed to make sure we had enough food and water to survive an extended time in that little boat.

I did a walk-through on the main floor and grabbed an armful of waters, as well as a couple handfuls of snacks, before heading to the bedroom. I emptied my backpack and dropped my broken charm bracelet in the inside pocket before placing the water and snacks in the bag.

From my suitcase, I grabbed a change of clothing and did the same for Alex.

I started to leave and then turned back, grabbing our wallets, phones, and passports and shoved them in the same pocket as my bracelet. I hesitated at the doorway, thinking about my patch job. I grabbed the first aid kit, and with the bag, headed back to the cargo hold and Alex waiting with the boat now in the water.

"This thing has a sail," he said with a smile and glanced at the two things I held. "What did you end up grabbing?"

I opened the backpack to show him our stash.

"Clothes?"

I nodded and put the tablet in the bag as well. I hoped the battery lasted more than a few hours. It was the only efficient way to communicate with Alex.

"I wouldn't have thought of that." He reached his hand out to take the bag.

I handed it over, along with the first aid kit, and then let him help me in the boat. He climbed in and pushed off, glancing at the luxury yacht with a sigh.

"It's such a shame," he mumbled and took a seat next to me on the bench, handing me one of the oars.

We rowed in tandem, watching as the boat drew farther and farther away. Neither of us spoke or typed. We just watched as the sun breached the horizon, coloring the sky. Our slow row was hypnotizing. We kept it until the sun rose higher in the sky.

"I need some water," Alex said.

His voice reflected the scratchy dryness that my mouth held. We both pulled our oars in, and I unzipped the backpack, pulling out two water bottles and handing him one. I reached in again and pulled out a couple of protein bars, which we both tore into just as heartily as the water.

"When did we last eat?" he asked after he inhaled the food and drained half the bottle of water.

Yesterday morning, before the pirates boarded. I typed on his tablet and handed it to him. I returned my attention to my water, taking small sips to savor the liquid.

"Shit. No wonder I'm a little dizzy," Alex said as he hoisted the dingy sail.

He adjusted the angle so our heading continued to the northwest. Then he settled in the seat next to me, drinking the remainder of his water in the same conserving sips I was taking.

The wind picked up, moving us along at a decent clip. He didn't feel the need to fill the silence with talk. He just sat holding my hand as we moved back towards civilization. Thankfully, we were in the Mediterranean, which was fairly calm in relation to the open Pacific. Not that there weren't strong currents or bad weather; it was just less prevalent than in the open ocean where one can go thousands of miles without sight of land. The widest point between land masses was less than a thousand miles. Where we were, unless we started drifting due west, we only had four hundred miles between Greece and Egypt, and we had been dead center when we left the yacht behind.

"I'm in need of a nap," Alex said, meeting my gaze. "Can you man the helm while I catch a little shut-eye, and then I'll cover you?" Dark circles under his eyes punctuated his exhaustion.

I nodded and traded places, taking the rudder from him to make sure we kept on our track. I wasn't tired in the least. Something about sailing quietly on the water had invigorated me. Besides, the cuts on my abdomen, back, and shoulder would probably make sleep impossible.

He leaned over and placed a kiss on my cheek. "Wake me if something happens." He crawled under the canopy at the front of the dingy. He was snoring within minutes.

I let him sleep until the sun dropped on the horizon. Along with the twilight came exhaustion, and my head bobbed. I jerked in place, forcing myself to stay awake long enough to hand over the post.

I kicked Alex's foot, and he shot up, nearly banging his head on the canvas canopy.

"What?" Panic laced his question as his gaze darted left and right. When it landed on me, he stared as if he wasn't sure where he was. He rubbed his face and glanced at the darkening sky. "You let me sleep all day?"

I nodded and yawned.

He climbed out of the hull and took over steering while I crawled to where he had been and attempted to find a comfortable position. The minute I closed my eyes, my eyelids acted like a deranged movie plex where the last few days kept flashing over and over until I thought I'd scream.

I finally silenced the angst and drifted into a restless slumber. In my dream, the trident pierced Alex's heart, and my brother drove a stake through mine. We died on that pole together until Fate came and dragged me by the hair, kicking and screaming all the way into Lucifer's lair.

My penance in hell wasn't being Lucifer's whore. No. It was much worse. My voice was taken from me, and I couldn't utter a sound. And then they put me in a room where I had to watch as Alex was slowly torn to pieces in front of me.

"Kylee!"

Alex's voice broke through the nightmare as his hands shook me awake. I opened my eyes and flew into his arms, nearly knocking both of us over the edge of the dingy.

"Hey," he whispered in my ear as I clung to him like a frightened kid. "It's okay. It's all over."

I would have thought I'd be the one consoling him after our encounter. Especially since he'd had no beliefs in the supernatural less than a week ago. He seemed to have rolled with this much smoother than anyone in my past.

I pulled away and brought my hand to his cheek. The smoothness that had been there this morning after our shower was now marred with prickly stubble.

It was just a nightmare. I typed out on his tablet.

"I was surprised I wasn't plagued with them all day," he said. "Did you want me to drop anchor and hold you so you can get some sleep?"

I leaned back, studying him before typing. *I'm not a damsel in distress.*

His lips pressed together in a smirk, and he looked out at the water. "I never insinuated that you were," he said, while trying not to smile at me. "I just thought..." He met my gaze. "I don't know what I was thinking," he admitted with a laugh. "I keep forgetting you've been around longer than I have. I was just trying to offer you some comfort."

That's very sweet, but I'm not sure you holding me would help with the nightmares.

He glanced at my words. "Okay, do you want to tell me about it at all?"

I shook my head and cuddled next to him on the bench. I picked up the bottle of water at his feet and took a sip before returning it to its spot. We had been on the sea for less than twenty-four hours and had cracked open the third bottle.

We might need to slow down on the water. I typed and looked up at the sail as it barely flopped in place. *We have at least two more full days.*

"Which means you need to get some actual sleep. We have to alternate in order to cross the distance as quickly as possible." He folded the sail. It wasn't doing much with relatively little wind. He tossed the anchor overboard. "I don't expect us to get very far without wind, and I don't have the energy to row alone, so we are going to get more sleep and conscrve some energy in case we have to do some rowing in the morning. Okay?"

I couldn't argue with his logic, so I let him pull me down onto the hard hull. His shoulder made for a soft pillow, and the heat from his body kept me warm. I closed my eyes and thought, *Just for a few minutes*.

Silencing the Siren
Chapter 16

HOLY BRIGHTNESS. I TURNED my head away from the light and into a hard knob. I blinked my eyes open and stared at an elbow. It took me a moment to place where I was, and I nearly chuckled. The only thing that stopped the laugh from escaping was the origin of the light. It wasn't the sun. It was a spotlight.

I shook Alex awake. His groggy gaze met mine, then squinted into the light. He shot to a sitting position, scraping his head on the canopy in his haste to get up. The person holding the light lowered it a fraction. Beyond the bright spot sat another small craft.

"Είσαι καλά?" a voice called from beyond the light.

Alex traded a glance with me. While I understood the question asked in Greek, he obviously didn't, and without a voice, I couldn't answer.

"Are you okay?" the voice asked in English this time.

"Who are you?" Alex asked in a wary voice.

"Coast Guard," the man said.

The tenseness in Alex's form released, and he slumped. "Thank God," he said. "We're banged up, and she needs stitches. I did the best I could to fix her up before we escaped, but I'm not a doctor."

The skiff closed the distance, and someone tied a rope to the pad eye of our lifeboat before they pulled alongside us.

Alex helped me to my feet, and just before he handed me over to the Coast Guard, I pointed towards the backpack, meeting his gaze.

"Don't worry. I won't forget what little we have left." He gave me a tired smile.

I crossed over into the skiff with the help of three military-built men in uniforms.

"What's your name?" the one holding my arm asked.

I glanced at him and tapped my throat with a shake of my head.

"She hasn't spoken since we were attacked on the yacht we rented," Alex said as he stepped into the skiff with the backpack hanging over his shoulder.

A flashlight shined at my throat, and the owner of the light actually winced. I hadn't had cause to really study myself in a mirror since my brother died, but I ventured from the man's face that I had some nasty bruises from when Jeremiah tried to strangle me to death. A crushed larynx would be a hell of a reasonable fabrication, and I was glad Alex's explanation spawned the thought. It certainly would explain my loss of voice.

"We'll get you to a doctor in no time," the man said after he shut off the light. He sat me on a bench and wrapped a warm blanket around my shoulders.

Alex took a seat next to me with a blanket wrapped around him, too. He put the backpack between his feet and threaded his hand in mine. The simple gesture warmed me more than the blanket.

They brought us to a bigger cruiser, helped us aboard, and brought us into a sheltered area while they headed toward Greece's mainland.

A formal looking gentleman in a neatly pressed uniform came in and took a seat across from us. He pulled out a pen, scribbled on the clipboard he held, and then finally looked up at us.

"I am Commander Angelis with the Hellenic Coast Guard."

His heavy Greek accent was hard to miss, and the fact he remained all business sent off alarms in my head. I gave him a nod and traded a glance with Alex.

"I'm Alejandro Cervas, and this is Kylee Paradox." Alex put his hand out, and the commander stared at it for a moment before he shook it. The pause was enough to set the mood. This would not be a pleasant conversation.

"Were you aware that Captain Hagan and his crew were murdered?"

I stared at him and slowly nodded. Alex hadn't been conscious when the captain died. I made a motion for something to write on, and the commander handed me a pen and paper.

We were attacked by something; I wrote. If they found the boat, the crusted statue of my brother would go a long way to substantiate the partial truth I was spinning. *Alex played dead, and before the something killed me, another boat came into the vicinity, and the thing took off. But before it left, it promised it would be back for me.*

I glanced at Alex, and he gave me a nod before I handed the commander the paper.

Commander Angelis raised an eyebrow as he read my note. "You expect me to believe this?"

I stood and let the blanket drop from my shoulders so I could lift my shirt, showing him the deep gashes Jeremiah's nails left. And then I turned so he could see the same on my back. I pulled the shirt down and took a seat.

Alex draped the blanket around me again. "It did that to her," he said, meeting the commander's sharp gaze. "Whatever the hell *it* was."

The commander leaned forward and handed the paper back to me. "What did you do next?"

Alex started to answer, and the commander glared at him. "I want to hear this from her."

I glanced at Alex, then held the pen to the paper once again. *We ran. That thing took the bodies with him into the sea and took off. I wasn't waiting around for him to come back and finish us. We lifted anchor and headed away as fast as the yacht would take us. Unfortunately, we didn't get very far before pirates attacked the ship.*

I handed the sheet to him and waved my fingers for more. He handed me another piece. Before I continued, my hand fluttered to my throat, and I blinked back the mist that covered my eyes.

The pirates... Well, they wanted to sell me to the highest bidder back home, but wanted to make sure I'd be worth the money. They nearly killed me before the men turned on each other. It gave us the opportunity to escape. We'd been drifting in that lifeboat for a few days.

I handed the last sheet to the commander and avoided eye contact. This was the dicey part. If they didn't believe us, we were going to be screwed for a very long time.

He read the note, closed his eyes, and wiped his face before clearing his throat.

"And where were you during all this?" he asked Alex, his voice as accusatory as it had been before.

"I was in and out of consciousness for part of it and then just blazing mad. But Kylee kept me out of harm's way and got me down to where the lifeboat was. Her voice was gone by that point, but she was able to get me to understand we needed to escape. We left just as gunfire broke out in the main cabin."

He studied us, his gaze traveling from Alex to me and back like he was measuring the level of bullshit we were feeding him. There was something under the accusation in his eyes. Something haunting. I had an epiphany and pointed at the papers. He handed me one.

I wrote, *How many men on this ship died?*

When I handed him the slip of paper, he recoiled, his eyes widening before shooting to mine. His composure melted, and he crumpled the paper and looked away.

This man was looking for answers. Answers as to why his ship became a war zone. A mythological creature wasn't good enough. Especially since he himself had been affected by my brother's siren song. There were too many haunting glances at me not to be right about this.

I tapped the floor with my foot, bringing his attention back to me.

"Six," he answered and paled. "One by my own hand, and I need to know why."

An ensign came in, interrupting the conversation. He handed the commander a photograph. Commander Angelis stared at the picture for a good minute before his gaze rose. Whatever color had remained on his face faded, leaving him almost green. He blinked, glanced up at the ensign, and handed me the photo.

"Was this on the yacht when you boarded?" he asked with a tremble in his voice.

I looked at the black-and-white photo of Jeremiah frozen in death. A shiver rippled through me, and I dropped the photo as if it were burning my fingers. My hand went to my throat. I shook my head, trying to swallow the bile that had risen in my esophagus. The revulsion and horror filling my form hit like a fastball to the abdomen.

Alex put his arm around me. "That was the thing that nearly killed us," he said, staring at the photo face up on the floor.

I glanced at his pale profile. His aversion to the photo was as real as mine. I could feel it in his grip on my shoulder and see it in the tension of his jaw. When he raised his gaze to the commander, the man across from us flinched.

Commander Angelis ran his hand over his face. "That is a statue," he said, denying what he must know as the truth.

In these parts, there was plenty of speculation regarding mermaids and sirens. Especially after what happened to that cruise ship.

"It wasn't when we saw it, and it had legs, not the damn tail you see in that picture. The face is the same, and so are the clawed hands," Alex snapped. "If you have any doubts, measure the statue's damn hand and compare it to the bruise on her neck." He hooked his thumb in my direction. "Or measure the spread of the thing's claws and compare them to the cuts on her stomach and back if you still have doubts."

The commander's gaze moved to my throat. "If you wouldn't mind putting your hand over the shape of the bruise," he said to Alex.

"Excuse me?"

"Do it," he snarled.

I lifted my chin and turned toward Alex. His hand was much smaller than my brother's, so I had no issue with the request. At least it might ease the obvious angst the commander had in relation to us.

Alex did as he asked. The commander mumbled under his breath.

"Thank you." He picked up the paper from the floor and waved the ensign guarding the door over.

I caught the whisper to have someone measure the hand on the statue and for the ensign to measure the mark on my throat. He gave a nod and stepped out. When he returned, he had a piece of string that he used to span the bruise. With the length measured, he left us alone with the commander.

"I don't believe in mythology..." Commander Angelis stood, glancing out over the ocean. "But I heard the most haunting songs before all hell broke out on this ship. It was like what you described happened to those pirates. And if I allow myself to believe for a second that a merman did this to all of us, I will be put in a padded room for a very long time." He turned to us. "Why did we stop? Why didn't we slaughter ourselves until everyone was dead like on that cruise ship?"

I pointed at the picture and made the writing motion. He handed me another piece of paper.

If that truly is the being that attacked us, perhaps his death released us all from the siren's control.

He stared at my note and then met my gaze. "You heard the song?"

Both of us nodded.

His expression hardened. "You killed the crew members of that boat?"

We both shook our heads.

"The crew attacked Kylee." Alex looked at the ground and closed his eyes. "I did, too. She defended herself pretty well, considering four men were on the attack, but neither of us killed the crew. She did her best to keep us from harming her or each other. I guess that thing wasn't satisfied with how things were playing out and decided to take things into its own hands."

The commander glanced at me, his eyes narrowing. "You were not affected?"

I shook my head and grabbed another piece of paper. *No, not in the same way the men were. I tied the captain and Alex up to keep them safe. That creature snapped the necks of the other two and then let the captain loose with instructions to kill me. Alex was already unconscious. When I nearly knocked the Captain out, that thing got angry, broke the captain's neck, and came after me. Just before he did the same to me, another ship came into the vicinity.*

I stopped writing and looked up at the commander. My heart sunk. It was his ship that made it so my life was spared. I handed him the paper as tears welled up in my eyes. Six crew members paid the price instead of me.

He read my words and then met my gaze. I pointed a shaky finger at him and twirled it around to indicate the ship. The truth of it all slammed home, and I buried my face in my hands. If I had only killed Jeremiah that first time, the commander's ship wouldn't have been influenced by the siren.

Commander Angelis kneeled down in front of me and pulled my hands from my face. I met his gaze through prisms of tears. The hardness in his features softened.

"I think that may have been us, and to know our arrival saved two people from death is more than I could have hoped for."

I glanced at Alex, and he squeezed me to his side.

"Thank you," Alex said. He relayed the depth of my gratitude with those two words.

The commander gave a nod, climbed to his feet, and left us alone.

"I'm sorry, Kylee," Alex said softly, and pressed his lips to the side of my head.

I wasn't sure why he was apologizing, but I accepted his warm condolences.

THE COMMANDER AND CREW let us be for the remainder of the trip. Neither Alex nor I got any rest, and we didn't talk. I just leaned into him, thankful for his warmth and quiet strength. Numbness settled into my bones, taking any discomfort from my injuries.

We arrived in Athens just as the sun kissed the surface of the sea.

"Miss?" an ensign said, sticking his head in the room we sat in.

I met his gaze and raised an eyebrow.

"We have medics waiting on shore to take a look at you."

I glanced at Alex. I just wanted to go home.

"You need to get your back looked at before we get on a plane," he said, as if he read my mind.

I sighed and nodded. I climbed to my feet and took an unsteady step. Alex grabbed my elbow, steadying me before he grabbed our backpack. The minute we climbed onto the dock, a medic swept in and escorted both of us into the nearest building on the base.

I was given a johnny to put on. They tried to remove Alex from the room, but I kept his hand in mine and shook my head.

"I'm staying," he said.

"We need to check you out too," the medic said.

I pointed to the floor in the room, still clasping his hand.

"She wants me to stay. I don't have an issue if you check me out in front of her. And if I'm reading her correctly, she feels the same."

I nodded, thankful for his accurate interpretation of my actions.

"Fine." The medic handed Alex a johnny as well. "Get changed and the doctor will be in momentarily."

Alex helped me out of my shirt and into the garment, then he traded his shirt for the johnny and took a seat next to me on the bench. He didn't bother asking if I was okay. I thought by then he knew better, so instead, he took my hand in his and gave it a squeeze.

I returned the motion as the doctor walked into the room. She was a beautiful, dark-haired Greek woman, and she gave me a soft smile.

"Hello, I'm Doctor Romanov. I understand you haven't spoken since the attack," she said, looking at some notes scribbled on the clipboard she held. It was strange not seeing a doctor with a tablet like in the states, but perhaps they weren't as advanced as that here on the coast guard base.

I nodded and lifted my chin to show my neck.

Dr. Romanov put the clipboard down and crossed to me. Concern displayed in tiny wrinkles around her mouth. She pressed lightly on either side of my Adam's apple. I winced. She made me stick my tongue out while she flashed a light down my throat, but I knew there was no actual sign of damage. Fate had just stolen my ability to speak, and no medical doctor could restore it.

"Did you cough up blood?" she asked.

I shook my head and glanced at Alex.

"No, she didn't," he said. "I think her back and shoulder need more attention at the moment than her throat," he added as the doctor kept tinkering with my neck. "I did my best to patch her up, but I still think stitches are necessary."

The doctor glanced at him before returning her gaze to me. "Does it hurt to swallow?"

I shook my head, then shrugged and pointed to the sides of my neck. I signed the muscles were sore, but not my throat directly.

"Your muscles are sore?"

I nodded. *You know sign language?*

She stared at my hands and gave me a nod. "Yes. As far as the muscles in your neck, they will be sore for a while. You sustained some really nasty bruises." Her glance jumped to Alex in a manner I didn't like.

He saved me, I signed. *So don't give him that look. He's got a head injury, if you hadn't noticed.*

Dr. Romanov took a long breath. "Okay. Let's look at your back." She walked to the other side of the table. She pulled off the patchwork that Alex had done. "Your boyfriend is right. You are going to need quite a few stitches."

I traded a glance with Alex, and he shrugged.

"I told you it wasn't pretty." He squeezed my hand.

"I wouldn't talk, mister. That bruise on your forehead is pretty nasty." The doctor stepped around to the front of me.

"I'm fine," Alex said. "I just need about thirty hours of sleep after I eat a four-course meal."

His comment brought a smile to my lips. It had the same effect on the doctor as she shined her light in each of his eyes.

She returned to me and slid the johnny off my shoulder to inspect that wound. When she finished, she met my gaze. "You are one lucky lady. It looks like this missed the tendons and just hit bone. If this had been a half inch in either direction, you wouldn't have been able to use this arm. At least not enough to keep fighting whatever attacked you two."

I shrugged and glanced at Alex. *I'm not sure I could have kept fighting if it wasn't for him,* I signed.

The doctor nodded. "I'll be back with the nurse, and we will get you sewed up."

Thank you.

Dr. Romanov and the nurse who had got us settled in the exam room worked together to stitch up my shoulder and the gouges in my back. They then sent us on our way with enough bandages to get us home to the states. I stopped at the marina store and bought both Alex and me some flip-flops for our feet before we got into the cab that the base had called for us.

I leaned back in the seat and winced. Any pressure on my back pulled at the stitches. I leaned forward enough so my back didn't press on the vinyl. Alex slid inside next to me with the backpack.

"Where to?" he asked softly.

Airport, I mouthed and made the hand signal for an airplane taking off.

"The airport, please," Alex said to the driver without hesitation.

While he didn't know formal sign language, he was reading me pretty damn well, and I was thankful for that.

The cab driver dropped us off and waved away payment, telling us the coast guard had covered the cost before he drove away. Alex and I turned and took in the airport, and I wondered if there was even a flight today.

When the airline clerk told us there wasn't anything until tomorrow morning, I almost burst into tears. I nodded and wrote a note to please book us on the earliest flight possible, then I handed over my credit card to cover the charges for both of us.

"I assume there's a hotel in connection with the airport?" Alex asked after our tickets were all squared away.

"Yes." She pointed to our right. "If you go through the doors at the end of this hall, you will come to a passageway that connects with the hotel."

"Thank you." He took the tickets and my hand and led me away from the airport terminal.

I felt like a walking zombie, numb except for the discomfort of my back. I let Alex take charge. He booked us a room and got me settled under the covers before he slid into the bed next to me. I remembered nothing beyond his soft peck on my lips and then the shifting of the covers before darkness yanked me under.

Silencing the Siren
Chapter 17

RINGING YANKED ME OUT of a sound sleep, and I rolled, wincing at the pain in my back. I glanced around the room and at the empty spot beside me, disoriented. My attention finally turned back to the nightstand next to me and the buzzing phone. I picked up the receiver and got an automated wake-up message.

Alex stepped out of the bathroom with a towel wrapped around his waist and rubbed his wet hair with a second towel. "Hey, sleepyhead." He flashed a smile. "Was that our wake-up call?"

I nodded and tried to stretch, but the movement pulled a silent gasp from my lips.

"You might want to clean up and change before we go sit on a plane for another eighteen hours." He sighed and stepped back in the bathroom. "Thank you for having the forethought to grab a change of clothes," he called from behind the door.

They had said for me to wait at least twenty-four hours before I took a shower, but I needed to feel clean after everything we had been through. As soon as Alex vacated the bathroom, I slid inside and turned on the shower.

"They said to wait a full day," Alex said from the doorway.

I turned and sent him a glare, daring him to stop me. He raised his hands and stepped out of sight. I left the bandages on until I finished cleaning my body and hair. The adhesive peeled off easily, and once I had all the bandages I could reach removed, I wrapped my hair in a towel and loosely draped the other around my body.

I stepped into the room, and Alex looked up. I pointed at him and then turned so he could remove the last soaking bandage I couldn't reach. He pulled the fabric away from my skin, took the towel I held, and blotted the skin in between each cut.

The man had such a delicate touch that I closed my eyes.

"Do you need me to put the spare bandages on?" he asked softly in my ear.

His proximity stirred a need deep within me. It was the first emotion I'd had since we stepped off the coast guard boat. I nodded, not because I couldn't patch myself up, but because I just wanted him near me. I needed to feel something more than this vast emptiness that had overtaken me.

Once my wounds were covered, he handed me my clean clothing. I took them with me back to the bathroom, dressing and finishing the motions of cleaning up. Thankfully, the hotel supplied us with toothbrushes, toothpaste, and deodorant, so at least I felt human when I stepped out of the bathroom.

Neither of us bothered to pick up our dirty clothing. I think we both just wanted to get home and leave all reminders of what had passed behind. I handed him his wallet and his passport from the backpack before pointing at the door.

"You're in a rush." He pocketed his documents before hooking his thumb at the cart of food behind him. "Didn't you want something to eat?"

I shook my head. I wasn't hungry. I hadn't been since the numbness took hold.

"You need to eat something." He picked up the apple and tossed it to me as he folded a pancake and shoved it into his mouth. He wiped his hands on a napkin while chewing and swallowing the pastry. "Ready?"

I nodded and took a bite of the apple. The juicy sweetness soothed my throat. I knew at some point I'd be thankful he insisted I eat something, but as we left the room, I tossed the half-eaten fruit in the garbage and closed the door. My mood soured with each uncomfortable step.

As soon as we settled our bill, I headed straight to the airport terminal. I wanted away from this side of the world and the memories that would haunt me for the next thousand millenniums thanks to that demanding bitch. And now I couldn't even have a decent conversation because of her slanted view of justice.

Thousands of years had passed since I found joy in destroying a human life, and I had lost all taste for it. In a way, I was glad Fate stole my voice, but it really wasn't necessary. I would never again engage the siren. Not at the expense of a life. Using it to lull my brother had been enough to kill that urge on the spot.

Alex tried to engage me in conversation, but I tuned him out, preferring to wallow in what might have been as opposed to the cold reality that I killed Jeremiah. Once we were seated on the plane, I closed my eyes.

"Kylee?" he whispered. He took my hand in his and gave it a squeeze. "You did the right thing."

I took his iPad and typed, *I know. But it still doesn't fix the hole his death left in my heart.*

Alex leaned over and planted a soft kiss on my cheek. "If there is anything I can do to ease your pain, please let me know."

I stared out the window and then grabbed his iPad back. *We need to learn sign language because this typing shit is for the birds.*

"Well, we have close to nineteen hours trapped in this fuselage, and I know neither of us is in the mood for a repeat of the prior trip, so..." He handed me the iPad. "Have at it."

Silencing the Siren
Chapter 18

WE WALKED INTO MY home, and Alex dropped the backpack on the kitchen island. I fished through it and pulled my bracelet out.

"What are you doing?" Alex asked.

I yanked the trident off the chain and held it up, meeting his gaze. *I need you to say the spell that returns this to normal size.* I signed slowly. He had picked up a lot in the nineteen hours we were stuck on the flight, but I still had to go slow enough for him to process it.

His mouth moved as he translated what my hands were saying. "You need me to say a spell?"

I nodded and scribbled it down. I hesitated before I handed him the note. I could see him testing out the spell and one or both of us being speared by the trident as a result. *But wait until we get upstairs and I tell you to say the spell, okay?*

He nodded. "I'll wait until you give me the go ahead," he said, and I handed him the paper.

Alex studied the words as he followed me up to my weapons arsenal. Thankfully, I didn't use a voice-controlled code for access. Otherwise, I'd be screwed. As it was, I would need Alex to recount whatever spell was necessary to use my tools, or I'd be shit out of luck the next time I had to go take down a monster.

I pressed the code into the door and positioned myself in front of the scanner. Alex let out a low whistle.

"Impressive," he said after the lock disengaged.

I crossed to the long dresser and laid my hands on the specific spots needed to open the secret cabinet and waited, relishing the heat that flowed into my hands from the scanners. The audible click announced the completion of the process, and I opened the dresser lid. I dropped the trinket in the center of the velvet holder and glanced over my shoulder. Alex stared into the cabinet in appreciation at the array of knives, daggers, and other deadly weapons.

"Damn, girl." He met my gaze. The utter appreciation reflected in his eyes made me shift. I didn't deserve idolization.

I rolled my eyes and tapped the paper in his hand.

"Oh, yeah." He cleared his throat and repeated the words on the paper. His pronunciation was off, so nothing happened.

I bit my lip. *Do you remember how I said it on the boat?*

He stared at my hands, and the color in his cheeks faded a notch. He closed his eyes. His lips moved, but no sound came out at first. Then his eyes flew open, and he spoke the exact words I used after he had collapsed. "*Deus Neptunus in mari nascuntur tridentem istum mihi.*"

Light flashed over the trident, and we both squinted as it grew to its full glory. Seeing the dried blood covering the forks, and the handle sucked the air from my lungs. I plucked the note from Alex's hand and dropped it into the case before I slammed the top closed.

I grabbed his hand and literally dragged him from the room, slamming the door behind us. I leaned against it, still trying to draw a full breath, but my lungs didn't seem to be on the same page.

"Kylee?"

I turned and signed, *Thank you.*

His goofy, uncomfortable smile appeared. "Any time," he said. "I guess."

We stood staring at each other, and his smile faded. My heart dropped at the seriousness of his expression. It was as if he were seeing me for the first time. I thought it was doubt I glimpsed, but then he moved, pinning me to the door.

His lips captured mine, and he kissed like a drowning man clawing his way to the surface. It was frantic and full of everything he had held back since my brother died. His hands gripped my arms, harder than I thought he intended. When he finally broke the kiss, the intensity in his gaze reminded me of what he looked like on the boat just before he ravaged me.

I shivered and kept his stare.

"I want to do this right this time," he said, his voice husky with the need so obvious in the hardness now pressed against me.

I didn't have a witty response, especially since my hands were down at my sides. I wanted to say something like there was no helm for me to spray, or if he wanted me to bend over. I wanted to say anything to keep this intensity from burning out.

Instead, I broke his grip on my arms and yanked him back to my lips. I needed this as much as he did, and the pain of my injuries only heightened my desire to wipe out all conscious thought.

He whisked me off my feet, and I pointed towards my bedroom. He didn't need to be told twice. In my room, our clothing came off in such a flurry, I thought we might have charged the air. The electrical current between the two of us reached the insanity level bordering on combustion.

He pushed me back onto the bed and kneeled on the floor, pulling me until my knees rested on his shoulders. Just the mere thought of his tongue inside me created a warmth through my entire form.

The frantic pace at which our clothing came off halted. He grinned as his tongue traced the inside of my thigh from my knee to my hip joint. He did the same with my other leg before kissing my stomach. Each time he avoided my pussy, my breath hitched.

He navigated my abdomen up to my breasts, using his hands and mouth to tease me. He knew what I wanted, but he was hell bent on taking his time. I had no voice to protest. I was at his mercy, and what a sweet mercy it was.

He kissed me, rolling his tongue with mine in such a sweet ride that I sighed into it. Then he traveled back to where he started. With a sparkle in his deep brown eyes, he lowered his head and sucked my sensitive nub. His tongue started a dance that left me panting.

His fingers breached my core, sliding in and out with such a patient slowness that if I'd had a voice, I would have screamed. When he finally pulled away, the emptiness caught my breath.

"Roll onto your knees," he said in a commanding tone, one I couldn't deny.

The minute my ass was in the air, he grabbed hold of my hips and slid inside me. His stroke was slow, so slow I thought I was going to lose my mind. The lack of being able to purr my satisfaction frustrated me, heightening every sensation.

His hand traveled from my waist to my clit, and his damn fingers started that slow roll, bringing me to the next level. I had a feeling I knew what was coming. When he slipped out and into my ass, I hissed air between my teeth.

He slowly pushed his entire length inside and then pulled me to his chest. His fingers kept playing with my clit, and his other hand rolled the hard nubs of my breasts between his thumb and forefinger, creating a delicious heat that nearly undid me.

"Cum for me, Kylee," he whispered in my ear. His hips started their circular roll, creating such heat inside my core that if I'd had my siren voice, it would have been released without my permission.

This was too good to be true. Too pure to last, but I reached back and grabbed his hips, forcing him to move faster and harder. His fingers responded in kind, playing with me like I was a prize concert fiddle.

When his hand moved from my breast to my throat, I tightened, but somehow it also heightened every sensation. He squeezed, narrowing my air channel, but not hard enough to close it.

This was decadent and exciting, and my body responded in a rush of wet heat.

"That's it," he groaned in my ear. "Oh, fuck, Kylee. Cum for me!"

His orgasm hit like a wave smashing into my G-spot, and I arched into another epic release. I came for him just like I had on the boat, but I had no sound in my open-mouthed scream of ecstasy.

He released my throat and pulled out of me, spinning me onto my back and burying his face in my wetness before I could draw a full breath.

He lapped and toyed with me until I writhed with my hands holding fistfuls of his hair.

He made his way up my body to claim my mouth with his. In one motion, his cock filled me, pulling another wave of heat from me. In all my years of existence, no one made love to me the way he did. He was demanding and hard, and he knew exactly what buttons to press to push me over the edge.

I grabbed onto him and rode the magic until we were both too exhausted to move. He finally rolled off of me, and we both stared at the ceiling, our breaths heavy with exertion.

We slowly turned our heads to look at each other. I smiled first, and he followed with that grin that made my insides melt.

Why the hell did your wife leave you again? I signed.

"Honestly, Kylee, I don't want to ruin this moment by talking about my ex. Okay?" His fingers threaded through mine, and he brought my hand to his lips. "Besides, I have experienced nothing like this before."

I scrunched my eyebrows together and pulled my hand from his to sign, *What do you mean?*

"You. This intensity. It's like it's going to swallow us up and spit out burned ash. I honestly didn't think this kind of connection actually existed."

I didn't think it existed either.

"So, in all the years you've been here..." He held my gaze.

I have never experienced this. It is beyond reason.

He arched his eyebrow and rolled onto his side, propping his head on his hand. His fingers traced my cheekbone and his lips pressed against mine. When he pulled away, he whispered, "Marry me."

My mouth popped open, and I blinked at him as I shook my head. *I did that once. No thanks.*

"So have I, but I've never been surer of something in my life."

I pressed my lips together. *I don't need a certificate to tell me how I feel. And I certainly don't need a priest to dictate to me the rules of engagement.*

His eyes followed my hands, and he sighed, meeting my gaze. "Just think about it. I can't go back to being just friends."

I can't go back to that either, but marriage isn't the only option here. I knew this might be hard for his Roman Catholic mind to wrap around, but I just didn't believe in the human concept of marriage. My heart would always be his, but his eternity and mine were very different.

His eyebrow cocked, and a smile played on his lips. "Are you suggesting we live in sin?"

The way he whispered it and made his eyes grow wide drew a silent laugh from my chest. He broke out in a full grin when I shrugged.

He pulled me into his arms. "I don't know about you, but I'm ready for that thirty hours of sleep now."

I pressed a soft kiss to his lips and snuggled, shifting so he spooned me.

His soft breath tickled my ear. "I love you, Kylee," he whispered.

I wished like hell I could say those words back to him. All I could do was sign them, but it seemed woefully inadequate.

AS TIRED AS MY body was, my mind wouldn't let me rest. I stared out the window, wondering how someone could love something as dark and ancient as I was. Dusk turned to night, but sleep didn't come. I lay in Alex's arms while his snore filled the room.

I gave up on trying, since my mind was constantly circling around the entire trip. The things I did wrong. The lives that were lost because I didn't act sooner. They all haunted me as much as my own actions. The coldheartedness of killing my kin just wouldn't let go of my soul. I slipped out of Alex's arms, dressed in a pair of shorts and a T-shirt, and headed out to the shoreline of the mighty Pacific.

I dipped my toes in the water and took a seat on the damp sand. The sea called to me, wailing its sorrow for another mythos laid to rest. Warm tears burned my eyes and my throat as I searched for an excuse not to drown in the pain encompassing my heart.

I thought Alex would be enough to push away the hurt, but he had only kept it at bay for a little while. Now it came with a vengeance.

I killed my own brother.

I murdered the boy I rocked to sleep when we were young.

I watched the light fade from his eyes and his form turn to crusted coral.

It was as if Neptune had my heart in his tightly closed fists. My chest hurt from the weight of what I had done. My head dropped onto my arms as the tears came. I made no noise, but the sobs constricted my chest further, pummeling every muscle in my back with their force.

I didn't know how long I sat on the cold sand with my tears mingling with the sea. I couldn't draw a full breath, and if I had a voice, I thought I would be screaming at the top of my lungs until I blew my voice box. The injustice of what I had done viciously raped my mind, pushing me closer to an edge I did not want to tumble over.

A hand landed on my shoulder, and my heart seized in my chest, locking my breath in my throat as I jerked away from the touch. Alex's eyes met mine, and one glance at my face etched immediate concern in his face.

He dropped into the sand next to me and pulled me onto his lap.

I didn't know how to rein in this hurt. I didn't know how to survive this devastation. It was beyond anything I'd ever had to withstand. Right now, the idea of Lucifer's floggings seemed tame in comparison.

For the first time in my life, I needed help picking up the pieces.

"Shhh," he cooed in my ear. "Everything will be okay. I'm not going anywhere, I promise."

His words calmed the stormy seas within me, and the tears dried up as he continued to coo and stroke my hair, gently rocking me in his arms.

His calm confidence that things would work out wormed its way next to the ruins of my soul. A strange sensation weaseled its way into my body, creating a pins and needles effect in my limbs, as if I were finally waking from an extended and very lonely nightmare.

It took me a moment to put a name to it, and when I did, I nearly jerked in Alex's grasp. The sensation seeping into me was my heart finally finding a true home.

I had no idea what I did to deserve Alex, but right now, I thanked the gods for delivering him to me. Being in his arms felt like heaven, and for the first time since I received Fate's directive all those years ago, I dared to believe I just might have found my salvation. And it was in Alex's arms.

The End

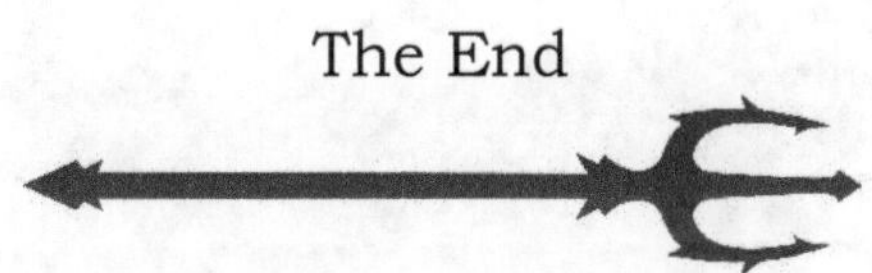

Continue The Paradox Files with book two, WAKING THE SIREN.

The Paradox Files -
Waking the Siren

Book 2

Kylee has another mission and a new ally, but will it be enough to battle the desert heat?

Virtue and devotion.

Who would have thought those two qualities could get you killed? When a bicorn terrorizes Las Vegas, that's exactly what this murdering beast targets.

Kylee Paradox is given the mission to bring this monstrosity to justice, but the desert does not bode well for a siren. In fact, it could be just as deadly as the monster she is hunting.

Waking the Siren
Chapter 1

I T HAD BEEN NEARLY a decade since I slayed my brother, and I was still mute from Fate's punishment. The witch had stolen my siren out of spite, and as I stared over the aquatic scenery from my office window, I wondered if I'd ever get my voice back.

My computer buzzed, interrupting my wandering thoughts. I swiveled the chair around, dismissing the view of the Pacific for my oversized cherry desk. I glanced at the instructions that flashed on the screen, clenching my teeth in response. The next menace on my list was a bicorn. I hadn't run into one of those bastards since the fall of Rome.

It seemed one had come out from hiding and started a killing spree. Culling the virtuous and devoted men of... I stared at the city and let out a silent laugh. What the hell?

Las Vegas?

That was not expected. My fingers poised over the keyboard to question my handler's judgment. The last place I wanted to go was the desert. Besides, everyone knew there was no virtue left in Las Vegas.

I slammed my nails against the proper keys and sent the city with a question mark.

The space between my desk and the door shimmered, and the newly crowned Fate stood before me. This girl was stuck somewhere between teen and adulthood, and she seemed much softer than the bitch who had been on the job since I escaped the binds of hell. But as anyone who encountered me knows, looks can be deceiving. Word on the street was this little young thing was the one who killed the wicked witch.

I still had yet to pass judgment on whether she would follow in her predecessor's footsteps or not. As if she understood my hesitation, she slid a printed instruction paper onto my desk, tapping it for emphasis before she settled in the overstuffed chair.

"Yes. Las Vegas. And this bicorn thing is killing people that aren't on my list. I'm sure you remember the imbalance that occurred the last time someone started reaping those that weren't on the list," she said in her soft, young adult voice that made me want to strangle her for stupidly passing up human existence for this godforsaken joke that was immortality.

I huffed at her. I remembered the catastrophe as well as she did. It caused another breach in Purgatory, which has kept me busier than I cared to admit. At least Fate and Death had a handle on the beast from the inner realm—Leviathan. I'd hate to be the one who had to corral that monster.

I remember, but, really, isn't there anyone else? I signed.

She raised an eyebrow. "Do you see a line of bounty hunters behind me?" She hooked her thumb at the space over her shoulder.

This wisp of Fate was definitely not a pushover.

But it's the desert, I signed. Being that far away from the ocean was bound to create some issues for me. I never strayed that far for very long, and the desert was one place I avoided at all costs.

Fate glanced out the window and sighed. "Lake Mead is nearby, and if you're in a pinch, you can always take a dip in the fountain at the Bellagio."

I stared at her and cocked my head, narrowing my eyes. *It's not the ocean.* My hands moved faster with my agitation.

She sighed. "I know. But you're the only one I have at my disposal."

You've got Leviathan, I signed.

She laughed a full laugh that was both endearing and grating. "Can you see Levi in Las Vegas?"

Okay. She had a point. Leviathan in his true form would likely destroy the city like something out of a bad *Godzilla* film. I slowly shook my head before turning my chair around so I faced the sea.

"Ms. Paradox, I know this is hard," she started.

I glared over my shoulder at her and then twisted my chair so she could see my hands. *It's Kylee, and you have no idea what the desert does to me, do you?* I looked back at the ocean while silence filled the room.

Fate stepped into my line of sight and leaned on the windowsill. She shook her head, and her chocolate eyes softened. She really hadn't been in the position long enough to see what the effects of being land-bound did to me.

Three days. That is all I ever have away from the sea. Seventy-two hours, and then this form breaks down. I waved at the Barbie-doll figure I was cursed with. *It starts with dry skin, which isn't that uncommon away from the water, but the dry skin leads to my hair becoming like corn husks left in the sun too long.*

"Can't you bring moisturizer?" she asked, but it wasn't in the least bit sarcastic. She was honestly thinking human moisturizer would work.

Fate, you really are clueless, aren't you? I signed, wishing for my voice so she could get the nuance of sarcasm.

"First of all, please, call me Julia." She shifted. "Every time I hear the name Fate, I think of that bitch that had this job before me." She shivered and glanced out the window. "And as for being clueless, yeah. I am. In case you hadn't noticed, I'm kind of new here, and the only thing I have about you is the contract you signed." Her gaze swiveled to mine. "But I do know the contract is binding, and I can't change that, even if I wanted to. You will be released when the last creature is returned to where it belongs. So, why don't you enlighten me?" She crossed her arms and raised an eyebrow.

Well, Julia. I paused and met her stark stare. *If I don't get back to the sea by the time five days have passed, I look like a dried up corpse.*

"What happens after five days?" she asked, cocking her head like a puppy.

I don't know. I have never gone beyond five days away from the sea. Five days is brutal enough, and I've never wanted to push that boundary. At that point, it takes me something like three months to recover. But that is under normal conditions, like the Swiss Alps or the Russian tundra or even the Midwest. The desert is an entirely different beast. If I don't find this thing in the first couple of days, the chances of me having the strength to kill it... I clenched my hands and shook my head.

Fate glanced at me and blew a stream of air through her lips. She turned, facing the ocean. Her bottom lip sucked between her teeth as she pondered my words.

There wasn't anything more I could add to the conversation, so I waited for her to speak.

With a nod, she turned towards me. "I need you, Kylee. And not just for this job. You're the only one I have that's bound to bring these things in. So, I guess I have to make sure I get you some solid intel, so you can get in and out before any actual damage happens. We will try to shoot for wrapping this up within three days, okay?"

I blinked and leaned back in the chair. The idea that she was going to help in any way was a new one. The old Fate got off on seeing her patsies suffer just enough to understand who had the upper hand. This girl didn't seem to be the overbearing type at all. Firm, but not nasty.

I nodded. Feeling bold, I asked, *Do you think I can get my voice back before you send me on this job?*

Julia glanced out the window with a sigh before she looked down at the floor.

I waved my hand in her field of view. *Well?*

"I'm not sure how," she finally said after staring at my hands. She met my gaze. "I'm not sure if it's as simple as giving you the vial or not. But we can try when I bring you the instructions, okay?"

Okay. I bit my lip and asked my next question. *Can you tell me how close this will bring me to my salvation?*

Fate pulled out her cell phone and pressed a few buttons before she swiped her finger across the screen multiple times. With a sigh, she said, "There are still a few hundred creatures topside, and unless they go rogue..."

I moved my gaze out to the ocean. A few hundred wasn't insurmountable. It actually was more palatable than not knowing had been, but her last statement really burned. I counted to five to keep my temper in check.

What do you mean 'unless they go rogue?'

"I wasn't planning on hunting them down," she said in a small voice.

So, I'm just stuck here? I balled my hands into fists.

She opened her mouth to reply, and creases appeared in her forehead. Her mouth closed, and she sucked her bottom lip into her mouth, offering me what looked like a consolatory shrug. "If they aren't hurting anyone, I'm not bound to bring them in," she finally said.

And my contract isn't finished until they all are brought in.

She nodded slowly. "Assuming there isn't another breach," she said, scrunching her nose in disgust. "Why would you ever sign such a shitty contract?" she added and pointed at her phone.

I was well aware of the many nuances of that fucking contract. However, this last bit of news grated on my nerves like a desert sandstorm.

I met her gaze. *Because the alternative was worse.*

Fate glanced outside again. "I still would have bartered," she mumbled and slid the phone into her pocket.

I was young and foolish and didn't think I had a choice. In the meantime, can you please figure out how to restore my voice?

The girl nodded. "Let me go get you the intelligence you'll need for this trip. In the meantime, pack and be ready for my instructions." She blinked out, leaving a soft breeze in her wake.

I had a feeling that this new Fate would be more of an ally than her predecessor. I always

thought the old one wanted me to fail. That bitch
had wanted me back in the confines of hell.

Waking the Siren
Chapter 2

I STEPPED INTO MY home on Ocean Front Walk and smiled at the orange sky beyond the wall of glass facing the beach. The entire back of my house faced west, so I was blessed with amazing sunsets. Every sunset in progress left me breathless and longing for the days where all I did was swim in the tropics. Of course, those were also the days I lured sailors to their death.

My house was bigger than Alex and I really needed, four bedrooms in a sprawling white setting, but those extra bedrooms came in handy for hiding all my antiquities. I had enough of an arsenal hidden away to be considered a military fort, but these were not the normal military grade weapons. They were the only artillery that could take down supernatural monsters. From simple gemstones that could neutralize garden variety ghosts, all the way to daggers made of stone or wood used to kill beasts from hell.

A bicorn could only be killed with a dagger made of pink ivory wood. I prayed I still had the ones I used all those centuries ago, otherwise I would have to figure out a way to get the wood and make another knife, and there really was no time for that. I turned away from the sun melting into the watery horizon and climbed up the stairs, opting for sweats before I pilfered my artifacts.

After I changed, I descended to the living room and opened the sliders to let the cool sea air filter through my house, recognizing my motions for what they were—procrastination. Rummaging through my weapon store was bound to bring up some unwanted memories, and I was doing everything in my power to avoid going into the third bedroom.

You're being ridiculous, I thought and glanced at the stairwell. My stomach growled, reminding me I needed to eat. I stood at the foot of the stairs, pushing both my dread and my hunger pains away, and trudged up the steps, wishing Alex were home instead of off visiting his kids.

The door to the third bedroom beckoned me, growing in my mind's eye like a funhouse mirror, distorting my vision. I closed my eyes, trying to remember the last time I stepped foot in that room. I shivered. It was the night we got home from killing Jeremiah. Just the thought of his name brought a stabbing pain to my midsection, and I nearly doubled over from the agony.

The hardest job I was ever assigned was taking down my brother. He had gone rogue and was killing sailors off the coast of Greece. Jeremiah wouldn't listen to reason, and my only option was to use my siren. I was always stronger than Jeremiah, and my voice lulled him long enough to pierce his heart with Neptune's trident.

No one should have to kill their kin. The urge to use my siren song died along with my brother, as did some of my inherent caution.

Fate scolded me for breaking the rules, and she reminded me of the price for innocence lost. She reminded me of what was waiting for me in hell. I have not been the same since. Her punishment left me mute, unable to speak, unable to laugh. Unable to ever use my siren again.

Alex noticed my lack of vigilance, too. The last few jobs we were hired for turned out to be more closely aligned with a suicide mission, as opposed to just a run-of-the-mill haunting. We had both been banged up more than either of us cared to admit, but unfortunately, it came with the job. Going up against the supernatural was always a crapshoot, especially without a voice to utter any sort of spell to keep the entity in line. Fortunately, my will to survive had always been strong. I really didn't know how to give up.

Besides, if something happened to me, I wasn't sure what Alex would do. He kept promising me he would break into hell to bust me out, but he was just a frail human who had no idea just how impossible that would be, especially since I was certain he was bound for the pearly gates.

Since my brother died, I had been closer to the breaking point than I had ever been in all the years walking this earth. The rebellion was right there, just under the surface, looking for a reason to break the rules. And my hatred of Fate didn't help quell the need to cry mutiny.

Alex seemed to be the only one who could tame that wild side and keep me grounded. If he had been killed in Greece, or if that witch had seen fit to yank him from my life, I would have already gone off the reservation.

I mulled over the difference between the old Fate and Julia. If the queen bitch had issued the order to go after the bicorn, I would have got my voice back and let loose my siren from the top of the Bellagio just to spite her. The results would have been epic, and just entertaining the idea was almost akin to issuing a dare.

Now that I met Julia in person, I wasn't sure I could betray her in such a spectacular fashion. Especially if that little thing really killed the old Fate. If the rumors were true, then my chances against her would be slim, especially since she was Death's girlfriend.

Enough stalling! I scolded myself and reached for the access panel, stepping in front of the scanners. Once I typed in the access code, a screen opened, and light scanned my face. An unmistakable click followed, and I reached for the doorknob.

Hesitation drew my breath in a sharp inhale as I turned the knob. The room remained the same as the last time Alex and I had stepped inside. My gaze pulled to the long dresser where Neptune's trident was stored, but thankfully I would not have to see the weapon I had used to kill my brother all those years ago.

The dresser was not where my pink ivory wood blades were. Instead of turning toward the bureau, I crossed to the trunk at the foot of the four-poster bed.

Kneeling before the finely crafted trunk, I found the buttons and pressed them in the precise order to unlock the hidden compartment. The click alerted me that my memory was as good as it was the day I set each of the locks. I pushed open the top, and instead of neatly folded linens, the display case of ancient and ornate daggers hidden underneath the blankets was now in full view. I slid the glass aside and picked out the two wooden knives.

"You have a case?"

My heart squeezed. I jumped at the baritone voice behind me. On instinct, I leaped to my feet and spun, nearly launching one of the daggers.

Alex put his hands out. "Whoa there," he said, his eyes wide.

I lowered my arms, but considering my hands were otherwise occupied holding the weapons, I couldn't answer him. I turned back to the trunk and pulled out the sheaths, then slid each blade into its holder before I closed the display case and the trunk, reengaging the locks.

Alex waited patiently for me to lock up my arsenal and followed me into the bedroom. I threw a suitcase on the bed and dropped the knives into it, and then I turned to him. Before I started explaining this new job, I stepped closer and palmed his cheek. Gray circles remained under his eyes, making them darker than normal.

You look tired, I signed.

He offered a half smile and a shrug. "Any time I deal with Mallory, it's exhausting." He caught a gentle kiss.

The way he said his ex-wife's name always came out like he just swallowed bitter medicine. To say he disliked the woman was an understatement, and I couldn't blame him. She had thrown a proverbial shit fit when she found out he had moved on.

The minute Mallory found out Alex was living with me, she tried to get the courts in Los Angeles to take away his visiting rights. I had gone with him to court, and when they realized I was a mute, he gained some sympathy from the judge, and Mallory lost her case. But that didn't mean she would make things easy. She had full custody and his visiting rights were limited to one weekend a month and one week a year, but she made it so the week was when the kids were in school. That meant Alex had to go stay in a hotel to see them. Mallory wouldn't allow them to come to San Diego under any circumstances, and she wouldn't let him see the children if I was around.

For someone who threw the man away like an old pile of trash, she certainly wasn't taking his attachment to me as if she was over him. If I could get away with it, I would gladly go slit her throat. Unfortunately, she was an innocent, and I would be trading my life with Alex for eternity in hell.

The man in front of me would never forgive me for that. As much as he wished her ill will, he also knew she took good care of his children. His tolerance of her was admirable, and another reason I adored him.

"So, a job?" he nodded towards the suitcase.

I nodded and spelled out *Las Vegas* with one hand.

Alex's sexy lips twisted into a smile. It was as if those two words revived him. "So my efforts to get you to a Vegas wedding chapel finally wore you down?"

I rolled my eyes. Alex had made proposing to me an annual event until a couple years ago. At that point, he stepped up his efforts and started asking me almost every month. It was as endearing as it was frustrating. We had been over this so many times, but the light dancing in his tired eyes pulled a sigh from me. I cocked my head and raised my eyebrows in my 'Really?' expression.

"Come on!" He purposely gave me those sweet, wide eyes that I had a very difficult time saying no to. "It'll be fun," he added when I pulled out of his grip.

I shook my head. *This is a job,* I signed. *One that you probably should hang back for.*

"Like you really have a choice," he said.

I crossed my arms. This was the same argument we have had for the last ten years. He knows I'm immortal and can kick ass in any sort of combat situation, but he still insists on putting himself in harm's way just to ease his mind. He thinks he keeps me safe, and in a few of the cases that worked out. But with a bicorn who targets those with high moral virtues? No. Not happening.

Alex, this is as dangerous for you as going after my brother was.

His face fell, as did his arms, and he stared at me. Rightfully so. I hadn't mentioned my brother since the night we got home from that trip and he consoled me on the beach. Neither one of us had mentioned Greece in years, so my bringing it up held weight.

"What are you going after?"

A bicorn, I signed.

He blinked, and his gaze jumped from my hands to my face. "An acorn?" he asked with a crease between his eyes.

All the seriousness of the conversation went out the window. I cracked up. I was laughing at him and he knew it. His face turned red, and an embarrassed smile surfaced, breathing some levity into the evening.

B-I-C-O-R-N, I signed slowly and waited for him to say each letter before continuing to the next.

"What the hell is a bicorn?"

I went to the tablet on my nightstand and typed in the term, scrolling through the search results until I found the most appropriate lore. He scrolled through the text and closed down the screen.

"So, it devours faithful and devoted husbands?"

I nodded.

"We aren't married. Yet." He crossed his arms.

I raised an eyebrow. *It targets faithful and devoted lovers, and unless you've been messing around behind my back, that describes you.*

"And this thing looks like a horse?"

I shook my head. Images from Rome snapped off in my mind. The true form of a bicorn was a hideous display—a faceless two-legged animal with a hole full of razor-sharp teeth in place of a mouth, claws that could shred humans in one swipe, and no eyes to speak of. But they gravitated towards beauty, taking on stunning forms to seduce their victims.

They can take any form they want, I signed.

He stared at my hands, and then his gaze rose to meet mine. Instead of asking more questions, he stepped in and delivered a kiss that stalled my mind.

"I'm going," he whispered as his lips moved to my neck. This was his tactic when he didn't want an argument, and for the most part, it worked. He sidetracked me with his lips and his hands, both caressing and possessive.

This time, however, I pushed away long enough to sign, *No, you're not.*

He acknowledged my hand signals by lifting a single shoulder before moving me to the bed, and from that point on, my hands were otherwise occupied.

Waking the Siren
Chapter 3

ALEX ROLLED AND PROPPED his head on his hand. He traced lazy circles on my bare stomach. His gaze followed his movement as if he were in some sort of hypnotic trance.

I snapped my fingers to draw his attention. His fawn-brown eyes met mine. A soft smile formed on his lips, and he leaned over, giving me a small peck.

"I love you," he whispered.

I love you, I signed back. God, how I wished I could say those words out loud. Somehow using my hands to say it was not enough.

"Marry me," he said.

The hopeful lilt I was used to wasn't present in his words. It was more of a statement as opposed to a question. I didn't answer him. Instead, I stared at him and sighed. He closed his eyes, rolling away to sit on the edge of the bed and pull on his jeans. He stood, keeping his back to me as he ran his hands through his hair. Every muscle flexed.

"We've been together for ten years. I just don't get why you are so opposed to pledging your heart to me."

He didn't turn around. I knew just by his clipped tone and stress visible on his back that he was pissed. He headed towards the bedroom door. I scrambled out of bed, cutting him off.

Please don't be mad, I signed.

But Alex didn't bother looking at my hands; he just stared me down. He inhaled enough so his chest puffed out, then he shook his head. "I can't deal with this right now." He skirted around me. A few moments later, the slider downstairs opened and shut.

My heart thundered in my chest. In all this time, I had never seen him go silent in his aggravation with me. He had yelled, stomped, cursed up a storm, and even thrown things a couple times, but this quiet anger turned my blood into ice. I pulled clothing on as quickly as possible and sprinted to catch up to him.

He had planted himself at the edge of the surf, letting his feet get wet with each wave. I stepped in front of him, blocking his view of the endless Pacific. He didn't meet my gaze, but the muscle in his jaw tightened.

"Leave me alone right now, Kylee. Otherwise, I might say or do something I'll regret."

The softness of his voice terrified me. I crouched in front of him. *Marriage is a commitment of forever,* I signed. *Your forever and mine are vastly different.*

His eyes narrowed and his jaw clenched. "You keep saying that." His growl matched his glare. "And it pisses me off. I've given you everything, even giving up time with my kids for you, and you can't get past making a commitment?" He made finger quotes as he spat out the word *commitment.* "What makes you think you'll live longer than me, anyway?" He stood and turned north, trudging up the beach, sending small sprays of sand with each step.

I stared after him. *Because that's how it always works out.*

Instead of chasing after him, I left him alone, but it wasn't out of consideration for his wishes. It was out of the raw fear of losing the man. I wasn't sure what would happen when he returned, but I knew if I didn't let him work this out in his head, this would be the end of us.

Didn't he understand that he already had my heart?

I took a seat on the sand and folded my arms on my knees. Water caressed my feet with each wave. The solace I usually found near the ocean was absent. My chest hurt from the weight of his words, and I leaned my forehead on my arms, wondering if I was the one being ridiculous.

"I'll sign a prenup."

I glanced up at him. *What the fuck?*

"You heard me." He crossed his arms.

I climbed to my feet as the burn of his words raked my skin. *You think my hesitation is because of money?*

He shrugged and looked out over the water. "It's the only reason I can see why you won't say yes to me. You're worried I'll bleed you dry."

The fury that filled me was unwarranted, but he knew damned well the money meant zero to me. I wished I could voice the litany of sarcastic responses crossing my mind. Instead, I just lifted my middle finger and spun to head back inside.

His hand clamped down on my upper arm. I reacted and had him on the sand under me with my fist, ready to dole out some justice. I caught myself, uncurling my fist before it did the damage that vicious part of me wanted to do. He didn't even flinch.

"Go ahead," he growled.

No. I went to stand and distance myself, but he again grabbed hold of me.

"You don't give a shit about me," he said through clenched teeth.

All the fire inside fizzled out. *Yes, I do. I just...*

His grip on my arms loosened, and I sat back on the sand.

I glanced out at the dark waters. *Every time I've made a commitment...* I shook my head and folded my hands in my lap. Whether I wanted to admit it to myself or not, I had already committed to him more than I had to anyone else in my lifetime. I knew the real reason I avoided making it legal. The minute I allowed that to happen, this relative bliss would be yanked away from me.

He sat up and hooked his finger under my chin, forcing me to look at him.

"Finish the sentence," he said, but there was no anger there. "Please."

I lose. My vision blurred, and a hot path cut down my cheek. *And I can't lose you.*

His eyes closed, and his chin dropped to his chest. His hand threaded into my hair, and he pulled me into his arms. I buried my face in his shoulder, hating how vulnerable and exposed I felt.

"You won't ever lose me," he whispered in my ear and planted a kiss on my cheek.

His words should have calmed the fear in my soul, but they only made it burn brighter. I would lose him. It might not be for another sixty years, but he would slip away just like all the other humans who had ever become close enough to find the chinks in my armor.

I pulled away. *You can't come on this one with me.* I wiped the tears from my cheeks.

Alex closed his eyes for a moment. When they opened again, a flash of anger hardened his gaze. "Was this all an elaborate ploy?"

I shook my head, stopping him. *I'm afraid.*

A crease appeared between his eyes, and his head cocked.

This wasn't a normal statement coming from me. I had never once admitted to being scared in the entire time I had known him.

"This thing in Las…"

One shake of my head halted the beginning of his assumption. It wasn't the bicorn that scared the shit out of me.

He pointed to his chest, and his eyebrows arched. I slowly nodded.

He broke out in a smile. "I scare you?"

I oscillated my hand back and forth like a see-saw and shrugged. While most of the time I wished for my voice, right now I wasn't sure I could articulate the fear so he would understand. I tried anyway.

What we have together is perfect, but the minute I step into a chapel and profess my love for you in front of God... I curled my hands closed.

"What do you think will happen?"

I didn't want to spell it out. I didn't want to curse what we had.

The air shimmered next to us, and I was relieved that I didn't have to answer him. Instead, we both stared at the vision of the young Fate standing within arm's reach.

I climbed to my feet, and Alex warily followed my lead.

"Who are you?" Alex asked.

"Julia." She extended her hand.

Alex looked at me and I signed *Fate.* His eyebrows rose, and he glanced at Julia again.

"You can't be much older than my daughter." He shook her hand.

"And?" Julia gave him a ghost of a smile, as if waiting for him to say more.

Alex just stared at her.

She turned her attention to me. "I identified a pattern for you. It seems the bicorn is attacking newlyweds, but we haven't been able to figure out if it's because of booking the honeymoon suite at the various hotels, or if it's connected with a chapel."

Julia wasn't telling me anything I didn't already know from my research earlier today.

"The hotels don't have record of any new employees that have started in the last couple of months, but there are a few chapels that have had new employees start in that same time frame." She handed me a piece of paper with the names and addresses of the Las Vegas wedding chapels with new employees. "I have nothing more right now, but if anything comes up, I'll get you the information as soon as I can."

What about my voice?

Julia reached into her pocket and pulled out a vial. She held it out to me. "As I said before, I'm not sure how to reinstate it."

I snatched the glass filled with light out of her hand just in case she was inclined to pull it away. Without so much as a thank you, I pried the cork out and brought the rim of the opening to my lips. I inhaled the contents. Bitter and burning air flowed down my throat. For a moment, I thought she had slipped me a hot chili pepper instead of the essence of my voice.

Instead of pulling the glass away, I forced myself to inhale deeper until the vial was empty. Whatever magic had been sealed in that bottle for ten years passed into my cells, creating heat that nearly drowned me.

Fear as cold as the arctic layered over the heat, and I closed my eyes, pushing it away as I attempted to clear my throat. I opened my eyes and met Alex's wide gaze.

Alex. My lips formed the word, but no sound came out. Nothing but air over my teeth. Whatever had been in that vial couldn't have been my voice.

I snapped my gaze to Fate.

This isn't mine, I signed.

"It was clearly marked as yours." She shifted her weight. "Fate had a lot of little... trinkets, but that vial was in your folder along with your contract."

I stared at her, unsure of how to contain the heat burning in my veins. The sharp bite of fingernails in my palms harnessed the building anger. I slowly unclenched my fists.

"I wasn't sure if there was something else that was needed to restore your voice. There weren't any instructions in the file." She kicked the sand in front of her as she looked out at the water. "I'm sorry," she added.

"What's in this for you?" Alex asked, crossing his arms. His suspicion of the girl came across in his tone and his glare.

Julia turned her gaze to him. "Excuse me?"

"Why are you helping?" he asked, waving at me.

"Because the desert could kill her." She pointed to me. "And she's the only bounty hunter I have at my disposal."

Alex's gaze whipped to mine. "What is she talking about?"

Great. This was just what I needed. I sent a glare at Julia and then signed, *Being away from the ocean for more than a few days isn't good for me. If I'm away too long, well, let's just say it could take months for me to recover.*

"Jesus, Kylee, why the hell didn't you tell me about this?" He ran his hand through his hair and turned away.

"I'm sorry about your voice. If I find out anything more, I'll let you know," Julia said before blinking out.

Instead of addressing Alex, I glanced at the paper and the names of three different chapels in Las Vegas. He scanned the beach before stepping in front of me and plucked the paper out of my hands.

"You are going to explain." It wasn't a request. The hardness in his features had returned.

My skin flushed hot at the order, and I clenched both my hands and my jaw. After counting to five to keep my temper in check, I relaxed. *I can't be away from the ocean for an extended period.*

"Define extended," he snapped.

I've never been away for more than five days, and as I said, it took months to recover from that. Julia was trying to help by getting me some solid intelligence on where this thing might be so I can get in and get out like that. I snapped my fingers. *So there is less of a danger.*

"And when exactly were you going to tell me this?"

I bit my lip and shrugged.

The paper crumpled in his hand. "This isn't going to work." He headed towards the house.

My heart leaped into my throat at his snarled statement. It took me a minute to recover, but then I followed him. He paused before closing the slider, allowing me to step inside before he shut the door.

He tossed the paper onto the counter and grabbed a beer from the refrigerator before meeting my gaze with a blatant glare.

I lifted my hands to speak.

"Don't." He splayed his fingers at me. "Just don't."

I curled my hands to squash the need to apologize, and he drained the entire beer in one long pull. He let out a burp and slammed the bottle down on the counter. Instead of commenting, I headed upstairs to finish packing.

I closed the suitcase and latched it before hauling it off the bed. When I turned, Alex was leaning against the doorjamb with his arms crossed, watching me.

"I'm trying to figure out what I'm going to do with you." He sighed.

I froze in place and stared at him. The fear that raked my skin on the beach was back, and it kept my hand securely around the handle, unable to engage in conversation.

"How many husbands have you lost?" he asked.

I blinked and held up three fingers.

"Right after the weddings?"

I glanced at the floor and shook my head. I raised two fingers and met his gaze. The first died of old age. But the other two times I allowed access to my heart and agreed to be bound in marriage, my husband died almost immediately after the declaration. One within the first week and my second marriage ended violently within hours of our nuptials. All three died in my arms. I couldn't go through that with Alex, not with how incredibly intense our connection was.

"Do you think maybe Fate had something to do with that instead of God?"

I opened my mouth, but nothing came out, so I dropped the suitcase. *I don't know.*

"Doesn't that seem a much more logical explanation than you feeling like you're cursed?" He approached me and stopped within reach. "After all, you have told me dozens of times you thought she got off on your misery. That she wanted you to fail."

Damn his logic. That fear still tugged at my heart, but Alex had a point. I shrugged.

"It makes perfect sense to me."

No matter how logical it seemed, it still didn't calm my nerves. It didn't quell my intuition, which was having a fit among fits. I trusted that little voice in my head more than Alex's shot in the dark. He stepped closer, clouding my thought process.

You are not coming to Las Vegas with me, I signed.

His jaw tightened. "Then you aren't getting the list."

He had never been this difficult before. I put my hand out expectantly.

He tapped his temple. "It's in here. I memorized the names of the chapels before I ate the damn paper."

I took a step back as my eyebrows rose. The shock of his words caught up to my brain, and my jaw clamped closed. *Damn you!*

His lips formed a smile, but it was not friendly.

I pulled my phone from my pocket, but he plucked it from my hands and chucked it across the room, where it smashed against the wall.

"I am going with you, Kylee."

His growl, along with his actions, was sufficient enough to freeze me in place. His glare bordered on dangerous.

I glanced at my shattered phone. I had one other way of contacting Fate, and I picked up my suitcase, bound for my laptop downstairs.

"It's gone," Alex said, as I crossed the threshold into the hallway.

I stopped and turned. *What is?*

"Your computer. You have no way of getting the information you need without me."

I glanced over the railing at the empty kitchen counter and spun in his direction. I wasn't sure whether to call his bluff. Hotels had business centers, but I knew it would take too much time to hack into my private and very secure server to get to my communication tools. Fate was not on speed dial, and without my hardware, I was cooked.

The thing that burned even more was Alex knew exactly what he was doing.

What. The. Fuck?

"I meant it when I said I was going, but you keep insisting on brushing me off like I can't take care of myself, or you, for that matter. I have learned enough over the last ten years for you to consider me your equal. I'm your damn partner in all this, but every time you get a call for business, you try to bench me. It isn't happening. It's almost as aggravating as your inability to commit to me."

The suitcase dropped with a thud. *Inability to commit?* I waved at the house surrounding us. *I don't call this a damn inability to commit. Just because I don't need a legal document the way you do doesn't mean I am not committed to you. What the hell is wrong with you tonight?* My hands moved in a flurry equal to that of the inferno raging inside me.

He closed the distance and towered over me. "What is wrong with ME? What the fuck is wrong with you?"

Both our chests rose and fell, and the air between us sizzled with hostility.

Pack your fucking bags, I signed, and he blinked. I took a minute to savor the widening of his eyes before I added; *I guess we are going to Las Vegas.*

Waking the Siren
Chapter 4

ALEX DROVE IN SILENCE with his foot heavy on the gas. When I reached for the radio, he sent a glare in my direction, stopping me from trying to lessen the tension with a little music.

"I'm sorry I broke your phone," he said after an hour on the road.

I kept my hands folded in my lap and gave him a nod. The uncomfortable quiet settled over us again. I started picking at a hangnail to distract myself.

"What if you brought ocean water with you?" he asked, breaking the stillness.

I rolled my hand, prompting him for more because I was unsure of where he was going with his question.

"It's kind of late now, but what if the next time you have to go inland, you bring a couple gallons of seawater with you? Would that help you survive longer away from the ocean?"

What? To drink?

He glanced at my hands and shook his head. "No, to soak in. To heal if need be."

I had never really considered that, but I guess it would be similar to when he filled the life raft with sea water to heal me after my brother died. I shrugged when he looked at me.

"It might be something to try in case we decide to go see the largest ball of twine." His dimple appeared for an instant before it disappeared.

I stared at his profile. I was still pissed off at the crap he pulled on me, but I couldn't help the silly grin that surfaced. Twine. Who thought these things up? I turned towards the window so he wouldn't see my smile.

"So, you think you'll want to go see that someday?"

I glanced back at him. *No.*

His lips toyed with a grin, and he looked back at the road. "No, you don't think it would work, or no to the world's largest ball of twine?"

No to the ball of twine.

"Still mad, huh?"

I nodded my hand in the "yes" motion. I half expected him to tell me he was, too. But to his credit, he kept his mouth shut. Silence engulfed us once again, and I glanced out my window at the clear night sky.

"I don't blame you," he finally said. "I was a bit of an ass."

You think?

He glanced at my hands and snorted. "Yeah. Not my finest moment. First the shit with Mallory, and then all this with you. I just can't seem to win with any of the women in my life right now."

What happened with Mallory? I signed. I knew he looked tired when he got home, but we started talking about the job, and I never asked how his kids were.

"She wants more money. She's using our situation against me." He glanced at me and then back at the road. "She doesn't want the kids exposed to us, especially since we are living in sin. She doesn't want them to think what we are doing is okay, and they are at the age that us living together could affect their morals." Venom filled his voice, and his grip on the steering wheel tightened. "She fed me some bullshit about how her lawyer thinks they have a case."

A slow burn started in the pit of my stomach and I glared at him. *You proposed to me to appease your ex-wife?*

"No, I proposed because I'm in love with you. I'm tired of games and half truths, Ky. I need more, and I don't give a damn that you're immortal and I'm not. I want to marry you because without you, I'm not whole." His grip on the wheel loosened, and he sighed.

"And for the record, I got mad because Mallory got into my head." His bottom lip slid between his teeth. "I don't know what the hell she was thinking, but she made a pass at me."

I remained silent, but my heart picked up and my skin flushed hot. I didn't know whether to be angry or scared, so I let both emotions duke it out.

He glanced at me. "I told her to back the hell off because it would never happen. Not even if she was the last woman on earth."

I exhaled a breath, and the heat faded.

"She then launched into a rant of epic proportions. She sure knows the buttons to push and the things to say that trigger hefty doses of doubt in my mind."

What did she say?

"She said you obviously didn't love me. Not if you weren't willing to marry me."

You told her I didn't want to marry you? I signed.

Alex stared at my hands and then focused on the road. "Yes. When she started hammering me about us living together, I made the mistake of saying that it wasn't my choice that we weren't married right now. And Mallory took that as an open invitation to throw herself at me."

I looked out the window, but his hand slid onto my thigh and gave it a squeeze.

"I got mad because I thought maybe she had a valid point."

I couldn't deal with Mallory and her games. Nor could I make any comment about the murderous thoughts that paraded through my head. Instead, I focused on the more immediate destructive actions of his.

While that explains your explosion on the beach, that does not explain eating the list and destroying my phone and computer.

He chuckled. "Your computer is fine. I just hid it in the oven, which we both know would be the last place on Earth you would look for the damn thing. I said I was sorry about the phone, though." He glanced at me. "You not telling me that being away from the ocean is dangerous didn't help. In fact, it just compounded my doubts along with everything else."

Alex offered me a shrug and shifted his hand onto the console between us. I slid my fingers through his as a peace offering. He closed his hand around mine and squeezed.

"I'm sorry," he whispered.

I squeezed back and focused on the dark outside the window, allowing all the horrifying things I wanted to do to that woman dance through my mind.

"Are you okay?" he asked after a few more minutes of silence.

I met his gaze, nodded, and pulled my hand from his. *Just trying to figure out which weapon in my arsenal would be appropriate to use on Mallory.*

He laughed. "I can only imagine." When his laugh wound down, he said, "You know you can't go after her, right?"

You would get custody of your girls, I signed.

He shook his head. "As much as it would be a relief for us, it would crush my girls, and I could never do that to them."

I know, I signed, but he couldn't stop the decadent fantasy playing in my head.

"You're still imagining stripping her skin off, aren't you?" he said.

I tried to hide the smile that surfaced and looked out the window. His chuckle confirmed he got the message, and I snuck a sideways glance at his handsome profile. He was more beautiful than Achilles had been, and I couldn't blame Mallory for regretting her choices. Alex had become more handsome in the last ten years than that first day I met him.

"I need to grab a coffee before we leave civilization." He pulled off the highway into a gas station. He got out of the car, and I admired his backside as he headed inside the convenience store. He came back with two coffees and handed me one as he took the driver's seat.

"So what hotel are we going to?" he asked and started the car.

Bellagio.

"Nice." He put the car in gear and pulled back onto the highway.

Are we okay? I asked.

He stared out the windshield. "I think so," he finally answered. "I mean, I'm still a little irritated with you, but that's my problem, not yours." He took a sip of his coffee and put it back in the cup holder next to mine. "I'm not going to lie. There is a part of me that wants to cut and run, but my heart won't allow me to walk away."

His words didn't settle my unease; in fact, they compounded it. I was glad when he flipped on the radio and started singing along to the music. His complete lack of tone made me smile. He rested his arm on the console with his fingers inches from his coffee.

I slipped my hand over his, and he gave me a crooked grin. The rest of the drive was filled with soft music and his off-key crooning. It was times like these that I wanted to join in, but even if I had my voice, that would never happen. Not while Alex was by my side. I couldn't condemn him to madness.

Waking the Siren
Chapter 5

THE WAY THE LIGHTS brightened as we drove closer, intrigued me. I had never been to Las Vegas, and all I knew about this city was what I saw on television and in the movies. The growing glow in the distance captured all of my attention.

"You look like a kid who has just come down the stairs at Christmas," Alex said, breaking the quiet between us.

I grinned and nodded. *I have never been to Las Vegas.*

"You've never been here before?"

No. I try to avoid deserts, remember? I signed.

"Well, then, we need to do this so you get the full effect of the strip." He moved into the right travel lane just as we passed exit thirty-two. He took the next exit, turning right, and then almost immediately took a left onto South Las Vegas Boulevard.

As we passed a golf course, the famous WELCOME TO FABULOUS LAS VEGAS sign stood out against the overload of neon in the distance.

The amount of people out made me both grin at the spectacle and grimace at the task of finding the bicorn in this activity. However, I was thankful this wasn't New York City, where crowds were still milling about long into the wee hours of the morning. By the time we passed the MGM Grand, I cursed silently at both the sensory overload of lights and the increase in the nighttime population. In this part of the strip, it was more like the Big Apple than I cared to see.

Alex shifted in the seat and glanced at the clock. "Did you eat anything earlier?"

I shook my head.

"I didn't either."

I raised my eyebrow.

"The paper didn't count," he muttered and sent a sideways glare. "Want to grab a bite after we check in?"

A smirk played on my lips.

"Food. A bite of food," he said after a quick glance in my direction.

I'm here on a job, not a vacation, I signed.

"We have all day tomorrow to find your bicorn. I'd just like a relaxing meal before we get down to business. Besides, I'm fucking starving."

We could do room service?

"I'd rather go out right now."

I almost detected an eye roll in his tone, but he kept his gaze on the road. His rebuff of spending the night in the hotel with me hurt, and I touched his sleeve. *Did you want me to get separate rooms?*

His gaze lingered. "What do you think?"

An icy shiver found my spine, and I wasn't sure whether he was being coy or an asshole. *I don't know. That's why I'm asking.*

"No, Kylee, I don't want separate rooms. I just need a good meal before we do anything else."

I gave him a nod as he pulled into the Bellagio and parked in the arrival lane. We grabbed our bags from the trunk, and Alex handed the keys to a valet. He took the ticket the kid handed him and started towards the check-in counter. I grabbed his arm and pointed towards the Chairman's Lounge.

The arch of his eyebrows made me smile.

Only the best.

"I guess so." He held the door for me.

We stepped up to the counter, and I started signing. The desk attendant stared blankly at my hands before looking at Alex.

"Kylee Paradox. Penthouse Lakeview," Alex translated.

I rummaged in my purse for my license and the credit card that I had made the reservations under. I handed both my pieces of plastic to the concierge. He typed on the computer before glancing up and handing my cards back.

"Your room is all set, Miss Paradox. Will Mr...." The attendant looked at Alex.

"Mr. Cervas," Alex said.

"Will Mr. Cervas be staying with you?"

I nodded and smiled. I signed three words, and Alex stared at my hands before his gaze rose to mine, registering surprise before he recovered.

"I'm her fiancé," he said, and his voice cracked as the word rolled off his tongue. He coughed and cleared his throat. "Can you tell us where the nearest steak house that's still open might be?"

The concierge glanced at the clock. "STK next door at the Cosmopolitan is still open and serving for another hour. Would you like me to reserve you a table?"

Alex blinked and glanced at me. I gave him a nod.

"That would be perfect."

"I will have a car out front for you in..."

"Fifteen?" Alex said.

"In fifteen minutes." The concierge handed me the room keys and showed us a map of the hotel and where the rooms were, as well as the hotel amenities and casinos. He snapped his fingers, and a bellhop appeared and took our bags.

Alex and I followed the bellhop up to the penthouse suite. Our bags were brought into the bedroom as we took in the strip from the living area. I handed the bellhop a twenty and signed, *Thank you.* He gave me a slight bow before he left us to our own devices.

The minute the door closed, Alex said, "Bathroom."

I pointed towards the bedroom, following him, and veered into the bathroom marked HERS. Alex gave a laugh as he stepped into the HIS restroom and closed the door. I relieved myself and splashed water on my face before making my way back to the living room.

Alex stood in front of the window, his hands buried in his pockets. I knew a comment was due based on what I had him tell the desk attendant, but he just turned and gave me a nod.

"Ready?"

I nodded and patted my stomach, which was already making itself known with a low grumbling growl. The minute we stepped outside, a chauffeur opened the town car door for us.

Thank you, I signed.

You are very welcome, Miss Paradox, the chauffeur signed back.

I grinned and glanced at Alex. His lips curved in that bemused smile I was used to as he slid into the seat next to me.

"We both appreciate that you are proficient in sign language, but Kylee isn't deaf. Her hearing is as sharp as a bat's."

"Yes, sir." The chauffeur gave a slight bow and closed the door. When he slid into the driver's seat, he looked back at us. "I understand you are going to STK's next door?"

"Yes, thank you," Alex said.

The drive was no more than a blink, and we were under STK's canopy. The chauffeur rushed to open our door for us. Alex slid out and both he and the driver extended hands to help me from of the car. A girl could get used to this kind of treatment.

I took Alex's hand and gave the driver a conciliatory smile.

"Shall I pick you up in an hour?" he asked and closed the car door.

I think we can walk, but thank you, I signed.

Alex said, "It's a nice night. I think we'll walk if you don't mind." He pulled his wallet out and handed the driver a ten-dollar bill.

"Have a nice evening," the chauffeur said.

We waved and headed inside.

Alex stepped up to the hostess box. "Hello, the concierge over at the Bellagio called in a reservation for us?"

She looked at the paper in front of her. "Miss Paradox and Mr. Cervas?"

"Yes, ma'am." Alex leveled his winning grin at her.

The hostess grabbed two menus and led us into the heart of the restaurant. Considering it was after ten, the place was busier than I anticipated, but the hostess weaved through the tables until she sat us down at a table with a view of the Bellagio fountain. After the hostess poured water and left us alone, Alex glanced at me.

"Fiancé?"

I shrugged. I had initially booked the room on the premise of it being for a wedding night extravagance and that my husband-to-be was meeting me here sometime either tomorrow or the next day. I hadn't expected Alex to be with me. Hell, when I booked, I didn't even know if Alex would be back before I had to go.

It was either that or say you were my father. Which would have been a stretch, don't you think?

He let out a laugh. "Well, I guess thank you for that. But I'm still confused."

I looked at the recent news stories of missing persons here, and most of the recent ones were newlyweds, so that aligns with the list that... I paused because I was hesitant to use the word Fate. *The list you ate. So, when I made the reservations, I made them under the guise that I was getting married in Las Vegas this week.*

Alex bit his lower lip and glanced out at the fountain before sliding his gaze back to me. "What if I hadn't come? What would you have done?"

Nothing. I was planning on being done with this job long before the fictional wedding date and just bailing at that point.

Alex nodded and picked up the menu. "What do you want?"

I glanced through the offerings. Steak with lobster topping and béarnaise sauce sounded divine. I folded my menu and waited until Alex looked up.

"Let me guess. Some sort of steak and lobster combo?"

Six ounce with béarnaise and the hearts of romaine salad to start.

"Do you want any sides?"

I shook my head, and he folded his menu as well. As if that signaled our waitress, she stepped to the table.

"Hello and welcome to STK Las Vegas. My name is Pepper, and I'll be your waitress tonight. Can I get you drinks to start?"

"Actually, we know what we'd like," Alex said. "She will start with your hearts of romaine salad and then have the six-ounce medallion steak, medium, topped with lobster and a side of béarnaise sauce. I will have the same, except make mine a ten ounce." He handed Pepper the menus.

"Anything to drink?"

Alex raised an eyebrow in my direction, and I shrugged and waved for him to make the choice for me.

"A bottle of the house cabernet would be fantastic," he said.

Pepper thanked us and stepped away.

No scotch?

"Cabernet goes better with steak."

The sommelier approached the table with the bottle of wine and poured a splash into Alex's glass. Alex swirled the wine before taking a sip. He closed his eyes, and when they opened, he gave a nod. The sommelier filled our glasses and set the bottle on the table before he took his leave.

Alex lifted his glass. "To us."

I lifted mine and clinked it against his. We both took a sip and then the fountain show began, capturing our attention. The waitress delivered our salads as soon as the show finished.

"So, what does tomorrow look like?" Alex asked as we dug in.

I took a few more bites before I put my fork down to answer his question. *You tell me. You have the places on that paper up here.* I tapped my temple and resumed finishing my salad.

He huffed and shifted in his seat. "This might make tomorrow a little easier." He placed a square velvet box on the table between us.

My fork stopped halfway to my mouth at the sight of the ring box. My gaze jumped to his. His hands folded on the table in front of his empty salad plate, and his eyes held a dare I didn't want to entertain. I slowly resumed eating until the last of the greens were gone.

A busboy came by and cleared both plates.

Against my better judgment, I reached for the box. Alex's hand landed on mine, stopping me.

"You have to say yes before you get to see what is inside."

I pulled my hand away and leaned back in the chair.

"We are going to be visiting wedding chapels tomorrow. Wouldn't it be more believable if you were wearing a ring?" Alex whispered. A smile appeared on his face and he leaned back, his gaze focused on something over my shoulder.

The waitress stepped into view with our plates. "Can I get you anything else?" she asked as her gaze bounced from Alex to me.

I shook my head, still staring at Alex.

"Thank you, this looks fantastic," Alex said. As soon as the waitress was out of hearing range, his smile faded. "I've done the romantic proposals, the begging proposals, along with everything in between. This..." He waved at the box. "This is my ultimatum proposal. Marry me. Tomorrow."

Or what?

"You already know the answer to that." He dug into his meal.

I thought your heart wouldn't let you?

He glanced at my hands and then met my gaze. "I love you, Kylee, and I'd gladly lay my life down for you. But I won't wait by the sidelines anymore. I can't. So if your choice is to say no, then all those fears you confessed on the beach will come true. You will lose me. But it will not be because of some angry god, or some misguided sense that the universe is out to get you. It will be because you chose that path." He pointed his fork at me like a freaky exclamation point and then went back to eating his dinner.

My heart clamored in my chest and sweat broke out on my palms. It was my stomach growl that allowed me to focus on something other than the swirl of emotions accosting me. I allowed my hunger to take precedence and focused on the food in front of me. The box mocked me throughout the meal, making it impossible to enjoy the fine cut of beef. Still, I cleaned the plate.

Alex stared out at the scenery, sipping his wine and waiting. Now that there was no more food on my plate to distract me, I had to face his ultimatum. I had to make a decision. What irked me was he was right. He had bent over backwards and asked me in every conceivable way to marry him. Some of which would have been deemed the perfect proposal in a majority of women's minds, but I was too concerned with Fate striking him down to say yes.

With the change in guard, did I really have a valid fear anymore?

I reached for the box because life without him wasn't a life at all.

Alex's gaze snapped to mine. That distant, hard look he wore from the moment we left San Diego disappeared. His breathing picked up. His lids rapidly blinked, as if he was trying to grasp the meaning of my actions. Tears filled his wide eyes, but they didn't spill over, giving them a bright sheen. Then every muscle in his face relaxed into a smile that could light up the night.

I stopped with the box in front of me, measuring what I wanted to say, but before I could start signing, the waitress popped up at the table.

"Can I interest you in dessert or coffee?" Pepper asked.

"We are all set, thank you," Alex said, but he never lost eye contact with me.

"I'll take this whenever you are ready." She put the leather bill holder on the corner of the table.

As soon as she stepped away, Alex whispered, "I thought..."

I love you enough. I signed in a flurry before I flipped the box open. My hand fluttered to my mouth, covering my dropped jaw. The box had not only a stunning engagement ring, but equally dazzling wedding bands.

It wasn't my matching sapphire studded platinum rings that formed the lump in the back of my throat. It was his wedding band. His steel band had an ocean wave pattern that matched the sapphires in my ring. And the thing that tightened the muscles in my neck and pulled tears to my eyes was the beautifully etched tail coming out of the wave.

"I gather I did okay?"

If I had my voice, the laugh that would have escaped would have been high-pitched and nearly hysterical. Okay. He did more than okay, and when he reached over and plucked the engagement ring from the velvet, I dropped my hand from my mouth and offered the shaking appendage to him.

The ring fit perfectly. I stared at it and then down at the wedding bands. *When?*

He laughed softly. "The week we got back from Greece. And I just finished paying for them last month."

He closed the box and slid it back inside his pocket. Beams of happiness nearly shot out of every single cell. His smile captured his joy.

"Think we can pay for dinner now and get back to that penthouse?"

The light sparkling in his eyes set my insides on fire. *Oh, hell yeah.*

Waking the Siren
Chapter 6

W E BARELY HAD THE hotel room door closed before he slammed me into the wall, pressing his entire form against me as his lips claimed mine. Before I knew it, he had me on the couch, stripped free of clothing. The man was in ravage mode, and I was so hot I thought I'd flash over.

Our tongues twirled in a sensual dance, and when he pulled away, I wanted to whine. But it was impossible to voice my discontent. The minute his teeth nibbled my ear, my disappointment vanished. His hands slid down my sides, creating a delicious tingle through my skin.

Alex ran his tongue down the line of my neck, and my skin broke out in gooseflesh. I arched into his mouth as he suckled my breast. I ran my fingers through his hair while he went from one nipple to the other, sucking until both were hard and I was wiggling under him.

He knew what I wanted. He played with me, moving lower at a pace that would have made a glacier look like a speedster. I think he licked every inch of my belly in his slow progression south. When he avoided my core and attended to the inside of my thighs instead, I thought I would scream.

God, if only I had a voice.

My eyes rolled back in my head the moment his tongue hit the mark. I arched and silently moaned. Vibrations formed in the back of my throat, and I snapped my mouth closed. The only time I ever felt that sensation was when I used my siren. The shock cooled me to the point I lost track of what Alex was doing.

That was soon rectified as his tongue circled my clit in that way that drove me wild. Whatever thoughts I had fled, and my body drank in every masterful move of his, responding with a rush of wetness every time he hit that magical spot.

When he abandoned the space between my legs, I tightened my grip on his hair. His dark eyes met mine as he worked his way up my body. He paused at my breasts again before his lips found mine. His member filled me with one thrust, knocking the air from my chest.

After the first few thrusts, Alex tempered his pace and took a deep breath. He met my gaze as our hips moved in a slow concert. His grin appeared, and his eyes sparkled with the intensity of the moment.

I mouthed the words; *I love you.*

"I love you, too," he said, his voice a husky growl as he tried to hold on to this a little longer.

His hips sped up, grinding into me in a way that let a tidal wave loose within me. My head tilted back in ecstasy. Alex's eyes clamped shut, and the muscles in his neck and arms tightened. His groan accompanied his release. His eyes opened, meeting my gaze. His jaw tightened with the aftershock that went through both of us, and then he relaxed, nearly collapsing on me.

"I need sleep," he whispered in my ear and kissed my cheek.

I raised an eyebrow. He was usually good for at least two rounds.

He chuckled. "I'm exhausted, babe. I've had one of the worst days of my life and I never thought it would end this way."

I cocked my head. He was familiar enough to know my questioning look.

"I honestly thought with everything that happened with us today you would have told me to shove the ring up my ass." He climbed to his feet and offered me his hand. With little more than a quick look at the clothing carnage spread across the room, he led me into the bedroom.

I glanced at my hand, at the ring he gave me, and the reality tingled through my form. I was getting married tomorrow. Holy shit.

His grip loosened, and he grabbed his toothbrush from his bag and stepped towards his bathroom.

The turndown service had placed fancy chocolates on our pillows. I snatched mine, popping it into my mouth before I headed off to clean my teeth.

With my mouth tingling with the minty taste of toothpaste, I stepped back into the bedroom. Alex was already burrowed under the covers, and he rolled towards me with an exhausted smile.

Are you serious about tomorrow?

His smile faded. "Yes. And unless we find this bicorn, we'll be getting married three times, so you might want to wear something other than those killer heels you packed."

I slid under the covers while his words sank in. I glanced at him and then shifted onto my back. *I need a dress.*

"I need a tux, so that will be the first order of business in the morning." He propped up on his elbow and delivered a quick peck. "Tomorrow night, you can return the favor." He nodded towards the living area of the suite.

Before I could respond, he turned so his back faced me. He was snoring before I figured out how to turn out the lights. I stared at the ceiling, watching the patterns made by the neon of the city below. Thoughts twirled in my head, alternating between getting a wedding dress and taking down the bicorn.

My eyelids grew heavy, and before I knew it, the two themes converged into one giant,

strange dream sequence that left me tossing and
turning all night.

Waking the Siren
Chapter 7

SUNSHINE PAINTED THE ROOM. I rolled over to see an empty bed. The clothing I had worn last night was draped over the chaise lounge by the window and Alex was nowhere in sight. I sat up just as he stepped into the room with a breakfast tray.

"I figured a hearty breakfast would get us through today." He set the tray on my lap before hopping over to the other side of the bed and slipping under the covers next to me.

The tray held two plates piled with pancakes, strawberries, and bacon. It was an odd combination and my absolute favorites. He poured syrup over my stack and then did the same with his, and we dug in.

The light fluffy pancake drenched in syrup nearly melted in my mouth. It was like a little slice of heaven before a long and possibly grueling day. I leaned over and gave Alex a peck of a kiss and signed *thank you* before I focused all my attention on clearing my plate.

"I looked up places that rent tuxedos, and there are a few in the area that also rent wedding dresses," Alex said as he wiped his mouth.

I glanced at him for a moment. The thought of renting a dress didn't sit well with me, and I scrunched my nose at him.

"You don't want to rent a dress?"

I shook my head and took my last bite of the delicious breakfast.

"You think you'll find something just like that?" he asked and snapped his fingers, the lilt in his voice echoing the doubt etched in his rugged features.

I gave a wave at my form and raised an eyebrow. He didn't understand women's clothing or the one blessing with this body in this century. I was model-perfect, and most off-the-rack dresses fit like they were made just for me. I had no doubt I would find something suitable. I just had to make sure my blades would fit under the skirt because I was not going into the belly of the beast without protection.

He chuckled. "Go clean up." He nodded towards the bathrooms as he took the empty tray from my lap and put it on his nightstand.

What about you?

"I took a shower after I ordered breakfast." He leaned back on the pillows and grinned, lacing his fingers behind his head. "I'm all clean if you feel the need to delay for some reason."

I gave him a coy smile, and while the offer was tempting, the clock was ticking. Getting sidetracked by morning sex would only lead to another nap, and then half the day would be gone. We had some serious ground to cover before I withered away to a dry husk. If that happened, I wouldn't have a prayer in hell at taking down the bicorn.

Rain check, I signed and grabbed my bag.

"I'm holding you to it!" His words followed me into the bathroom.

The warm water revived me, and by the time I stepped out of the bathroom, I was all primed for a day of success with one knife strapped to my leg and the other to my arm before sliding into my shirt.

I stepped out of the bathroom and smiled at Alex. He had dressed and tried to neaten up the bed while I bathed. His gaze washed over me, and an eyebrow rose.

What? You don't like black? I signed.

"Not on my wedding day," he said. "And certainly not yoga pants and flip-flops. Although, that top is sexy," he added and shoved his wallet into his pocket.

I wasn't exactly planning on getting married. I only brought clothing suited for agility and comfort in this heat. Besides, you're not any fancier. I waved at his casual polo shirt, shorts, and sneakers.

He huffed at me. "Your knife isn't exactly hidden in that, either." He crossed to me and flicked the end of the sheath that poked out of my sleeve.

Knives, I corrected. The sheath on the inside of my thigh was well hidden, even under yoga pants. *Well, depending on what dress I get, you might have to wear this instead of me.* I pointed to the exposed end on my arm.

The creases in his forehead smoothed out, and he took my hand in his. "You have room in your purse for this?" He held out the box with the wedding bands in it.

My chest tightened, but I nodded and opened my pocketbook for him. He dropped the box inside and led me out the door of the hotel room. As much as I loved the man, my internal warning bell sounded as we crossed to the elevator. One glance at the smile playing on his lips, and I shoved the anxiety aside.

A limousine waited for us at the curb, and the driver opened the door as we stepped outside into the sweltering heat. I almost wilted from the dry air, but the inside of the cab was nice and cool.

Alex slid inside and rattled off an address to the driver. I gave him a sideways glance after the door closed and the limo rolled down the driveway.

"You didn't want to rent a dress, so I'm taking you to the best bridal boutique in Las Vegas." He grinned. "I'll drop you off and go get my tuxedo. Do you think you'll be able to find a dress in an hour?"

An hour is plenty of time, I signed. At least I hoped an hour would be enough. This time, I wanted perfection. I didn't want to settle for the first thing that fit.

"You can tell me if that's not enough time," he added.

I think an hour is good as long as they can fit me in. If I have to wait, it might be a little longer.

"I had the concierge make an appointment, so you won't have to wait."

I leaned over and kissed his cheek. *Thank you.*

We pulled up in front of Couture Bride and Alex helped me out, leaving me with a peck on the lips.

"I'll see you in a little while." He shooed me towards the door.

I watched him go and then entered the shop. The girl at the table looked up and smiled.

"Do you have an appointment?" she asked, and I nodded. "Name?"

Kylee, I signed.

She just stared at my hands in that panicked expression of those who don't have a clue. Instead of taking on the bitchy attitude that crept up my spine, I made the motion of a pen. She handed me a pen and paper with that pleasant smile plastered back on her lips. When I handed her the paper, she checked her list and stood.

"Right this way, Miss Paradox. We are expecting you." She led me to a large dressing room with an array of dresses hanging from the racks. "Your fiancé was kind enough to give us your size when he called this morning, so we

237

pulled all the dresses that would allow you to walk out today with the dress of your dreams." She gave me a nod. "Ellie will be right with you. In the meantime, be our guest." She waved to a small table with coffee and finger foods.

Instead of indulging in the sweets, I started looking at the dresses hanging from the racks, quickly ruling out a great deal of them. I found a half dozen that piqued my interest and put them on the empty rack in the corner. When I finished my first inspection of the selections, I unclipped my knife from my arm and dropped the sheath into my purse. I didn't want to catch it on any of the dresses as I held them up one by one in front of the mirror.

I stood in front of the mirror with one of the WToo designer dresses held up to me, and while it was beautiful, I couldn't imagine trying to fight off an enemy in a strapless dress. Begrudgingly, I put the Soliel back on the rack along with one other strapless gown I had chosen from the mix.

Leaving me with four options. Before I could narrow it down any further, a small woman who looked no more than eighteen stepped into the room.

I'm sorry, she signed. *I got tied up with another client.*

That's okay. It gave me a chance to narrow down the choices to these. I waved at the four dresses hanging next to me. All of them had some form of silk and lace with a fitted bodice and an A line skirt that would allow me to be agile as well as hide my dagger without detection. Function was just as important as beauty for me today.

She gave me a smile and signed again.

I put my hand up, stopping her. *I can hear, so if you'd like to speak, that is perfectly fine with me.*

She blushed and glanced at the ground. *I'm deaf,* she finally signed.

I had only encountered a couple of deaf people since I lost my voice, and I never knew how to apologize for my assumption. Here, I would be in the room with this woman for a while. It wasn't like I could make awkward excuses and leave, so I gave her a nod and a smile.

I'm sorry.

It seemed inadequate, especially when she waved her hand at me like swatting away a puff of smoke.

Which one do you want to try on first?

I chose a silky Tolli dress. She asked if I wanted help. I shook my head, and she waved to the dressing room. I stepped inside and she handed me the dress. The moment the curtain closed, I stripped down to my lace underwear and unclipped the knife from my thigh, hiding it in my clothing before I stepped into the dress and pulled the straps over my shoulder, leaving the back open.

I walked out of the dressing room area and pointed to my back. Ellie approached and zipped me up. The dress fit loose and it just didn't have that wow factor. My gaze moved from my image in the mirror to Ellie's. She had that same so-so look that I did until she met my gaze, and then her beaming smile sparked.

It's beautiful, she signed.

Yes. But it isn't the dress.

She gave me a slow, knowing nod and waved towards the select few I chose. I pointed to my back, and she unzipped the silk. I didn't bother with the dressing room. Instead, I dropped the dress, stepped out of it, and handed Ellie the garment to hang back up.

This time I chose the Watters dress. This one had illusion tulle and detailed lace, neither of which felt scratchy against my skin like some of the other dresses. This one was soft and sexy, as well as functional.

The moment I pulled the tulle over my shoulders and the sweetheart neckline molded to my breast, I knew this was the dress. The skirt swayed as I moved in front of the mirror. Ellie stepped behind me without prompting and zipped the back in place. She even went as far as buttoning the top buttons. The dress fit as if it were custom made for my form. I stared at the beauty of it.

Do you have shoes in size eight? I asked as I pulled my gaze away from my reflection.

Ellie nodded. Her gaze scanned me and her eyes reflected awe in the same way mine did. And then she hurried from the room.

I stared at the dress. The detail in the lace was subtle and did not overwhelm the dress like some of the other gowns. It accented the sweetheart neckline. I ran my hands over the fabric, smoothing it out before I combed my fingers through my hair, styling it to fall over one shoulder. The illusion was complete. I grinned like a little girl who had just been given a lollipop bigger than her own head.

The door opened, and Ellie came inside with three shoeboxes and something sparkly in her hand. She crossed and handed me a bedazzled headband. I handed it back with a shake of my head. As perfect as the headband would have been, I didn't want to have anything in my hair that might be used as a weapon.

Ellie set the headband aside and offered me the shoebox instead. I grinned at the name on the box. Paradox. Paradox London Pink Scrumptious, to be specific. The open-toe lace shoes were ideal for the dress I stood in. The fact this sales girl seemed in tune with the perfect accents impressed me. I plucked a shoe from the box and pulled the skirt of the dress high enough so my foot peeked out from under the fabric. Ellie took the shoe from me and crouched down to help me put it on.

Once both shoes were on my feet and the skirt settled back in place, Ellie stepped back and gave me a nod, along with a wide smile.

I love it, I signed, still staring at my reflection. Alex would love it, too.

Did you want to try on the other two dresses before you decide?

I shook my head. I didn't need to go any further. This was the dress I was meant to marry Alex in, and every cell in my body rejoiced with the decision. *No, this is the one. This is just perfect, especially with the shoes.*

Are you planning on wearing the dress out of the shop? She asked.

I bit my lip. As much as I wanted to surprise Alex, I also didn't want to put us in the position of being separated at the chapels today. If I didn't leave with the dress on, I would have to change somewhere, and that made both of us vulnerable.

I nodded. *But I'd like to have you bring my fiancé in here for a more private reveal if you don't mind.*

I don't mind at all. If you'd let me take the dress, I'll go have it pressed while you settle the bill and then we will get you set for your big day.

Taking the dress off actually stung. I didn't want to part with it, but Ellie's kind smile and helpful directions were enough to settle my nerves. I threw on the bathrobe she offered me and grabbed my purse, heading for the front counter to pay for the dress.

Ellie appeared at the counter and handed the cashier the billing slip and another piece of paper. The cashier glanced at the note and smiled up at me as Ellie disappeared.

"Ellie is getting your dress pressed and ready for you, so once we are done here, you may return to the dressing room where she helped you, okay?" she said as her fingers glided along the computer keys. "That will be $3,273 dollars." Her gaze left the screen in front of her and met mine. "How would you like to pay for that?"

I fished in my purse, pulling out my wallet, and handed the cashier my credit card. The entire transaction took less than five minutes, and I was back in the dressing room before Ellie returned. In the time I had gone to pay for the dress, the racks of gowns had been discretely removed, leaving only the mirrors, different seating options, and the reality that the room was much larger than it originally looked.

My clothing still lay heaped on the chair in the dressing area. I exhaled. I had thought no one would come into the room, but at least they didn't touch my clothing. If they had, they were in for a hell of a surprise. I glanced at the bathrobe wrapped around me. The cloth fell to just shy of my knees, which was more than enough fabric to hide my dagger. I quickly strapped the sheath around my thigh and sighed. If Ellie wanted me to put the dress on over my head, I'd have to figure out a creative way to lose the bathrobe without revealing the weapon.

I shoved my clothing into my purse and zipped it up before heading to the coffee and pastries table that had sat untouched since I arrived. I picked up a toothpick and speared a cheese cube. The cheddar square tasted fresh, and I followed it with a small cracker before grabbing a water. I took a seat in one of the overstuffed chairs and waited for Ellie to return.

Waking the Siren
Chapter 8

I GLANCED AT THE clock. Time had ceased to move since Ellie came back and assisted with getting my wedding dress on. I paced across the floor with the train trailing after me. It had been a little over an hour since Alex dropped me off, and each passing minute amplified the dread in my soul.

Ellie came into the room. *He's here,* she signed and hurried over to me, leading me to the elevated platform in front of the mirrors. She placed me and puffed out the train so it trailed down the step. *Facing the mirror is more dramatic, and you in that dress deserve a dramatic reveal.*

Thank you, I signed and folded my hands in front of me. Taking a deep breath, I gave a nod, and she went to the door and opened it.

Alex stepped inside, looking as handsome as I had ever seen him in a designer-fitted tuxedo. His dark hair was perfectly styled the way I adored, cropped close on the sides, and tall and thick on top. His shoes shined just as much as his eyes.

"Wow."

It was as if his voice triggered my ability to move. I turned and smiled.

"You look like an angel." He held out his hand, and I took it, falling into the hug he offered. "My beautiful angel," he whispered in my ear.

I love you; I signed when he stepped away.

"Come on. Let's go get married." He pulled me towards the door.

I grabbed my pocketbook on the way and gave Ellie a wave as we left the bridal salon.

Alex helped me into the back of the limousine and slid into the seat next to me. He rattled off another address and then glanced at me with that hungry smile.

I waggled my finger at him. *Save those thoughts for tonight.*

Even though I shut off the idea for the moment, I could feel the heat pool in my core at the promise in his gaze. I reached into my purse and pulled out the second dagger.

Alex glanced at it and pulled the blade from the sheath. He opened his jacket and dropped the blade in the inside breast pocket. I raised my eyebrow at him.

"Large pocket protector for a large pocket," he whispered and put my palm on his chest over where he stashed the knife.

My gaze dropped to my hand, and I pushed harder. I couldn't feel the knife.

"I told them it was a tradition for my family and that I needed a jacket that could have an antique letter opener stowed in the pocket in a way that the guests would never know." He gave me a shrug and patted his chest. "They came through."

They certainly did. The fact Alex was protected made those internal alarms inside me quell to a quiet blare instead of the relentless roar they had been all morning.

The limousine pulled into the county clerk's office. I cocked my head.

"Marriage license." He opened the door. He turned and put his hand out to help me from the seat.

I grabbed my wallet out of my purse and then took his hand. Alex had done the paperwork online this morning before I woke and it was all ready for us to pick up. We showed our drivers' licenses and signed our names where the clerk told us. Then we were off with the document that gave us permission to tie the knot.

When the limousine pulled into the Bellagio again, my hands formed the question, *Why?*

"Copies," he whispered and hopped out the door. A few minutes later, he emerged and slid into the back. "Little Church of the West, please," Alex said to the driver.

"Yes, sir," the driver replied.

We pulled up to this lovely old chapel surrounded by greenery, as if it were something from a mountain town in Montana instead of in the middle of the desert. The quaintness of it tickled me, reminding me of some of the ancient places of worship I had seen long ago in southern California.

Alex and I exchanged a glance, and he put out his hand. I went to place my hand in his, and a smirk crossed his lips.

"The rings," he said.

My mouth formed a surprised *O* before I turned and rifled through my purse, pulling the small box out. I handed it to him, and it disappeared into one of his pockets.

"Now you can give me your hand," he said.

Heat filled my cheeks as I climbed out of the limousine after him. The driver tipped his hat.

"I will wait for you in the back parking lot." He nodded towards the hint of asphalt that could be seen beyond the grass.

"Thank you," Alex said, as I signed the same.

He pulled the original wedding certificate out of the inside pocket of his coat and took my hand. I stared at the building, wondering if we were walking towards a new life or our demise.

"Are you okay?"

My gaze moved to his, and I forced a smile.

His eyebrows rose. "That's kind of a scary smile."

I rolled my eyes and pulled my hand from his. *I'm nervous.* It was hard to admit just how unsettled I was, and I couldn't say for sure if it was the act of marrying him or the fact we could be walking into a trap.

"Nervous?"

I nodded and patted his breast pocket. The one holding the blade.

His features smoothed out, and his soft laugh filled the awkward silence. "You're worried about the job, not about marrying me?"

I nodded and the tenseness in his muscles eased, although mine were still as taut as a tightly wound string. His hand landed on my lower back and guided me towards the building in a patient but firm manner.

"Relax and enjoy the moment. We'll deal with the monster later," he whispered and opened the door for me.

I stepped inside, and my radar went up. Each face I looked at could be the bicorn. I tried to recall how I flushed the last one out. It hadn't been easy, but I had the luxury of time since I was so near the shore. However, one thing I remembered was the thing had taken on the most stunning female form, almost as beautiful as the goddess Venus herself. As I glanced around the lobby, none of the faces I saw fell into the stunning category. Cute and pretty, yes, but drop-dead beauty wasn't among them.

Would the thing be that cunning?

My brain grappled with that and I finally ruled it out as the receptionist turned her attention to us. Run of the mill cute or pretty wouldn't make a virtuous man crumble.

"Hello," Alex stated. "I called this morning."

The receptionist, whose nametag announced her as Karen, glanced at the list in her hand. "Mr. Cervas?"

"That's correct," he answered and handed Karen the original marriage certificate we filled out at the town hall.

"Right this way, sir. We are almost set for you two." She smiled at me and added, "You are stunning in that dress."

Thank you, I signed with a smile.

Karen led us to the entrance of the small chapel and had us wait to make sure things were ready.

You called?

"Yes. Most places you can't just walk in and get hitched anymore. So we have reservations, like at a fine restaurant." He made finger quotes around the word reservations and winked at me.

So who is the newest... I stopped as the doors swung open.

Karen smiled and stepped out of the way as the music started. I immediately recognized "Just the Way You Are" by Bruno Mars, which was the song Alex always sang to me whenever I was down. I loved his off-key version. This specific detail made me smile.

He tugged me forward. I fell into step with him as we crossed the distance between the doors and the altar, where a pastor waited for us.

Karen handed the pastor the paper and stepped to the side next to a photographer, who snapped a picture of us. He lowered the camera as the pastor cleared his throat.

"Dearly beloved, we are here in the sight of God to join Alejandro and Kylee in holy matrimony. Marriage is an honorable estate, not to be entered into lightly but thoughtfully and reverently." He looked at the paper in his hand and then back at Alex. "Alejandro, will you have this woman to be your lawful wedded wife? Will you love her and comfort her, honor and keep her in sickness and in health, and forsake all others as long as you both shall live?"

"I do."

The pastor turned to me. "Kylee, will you have this man to be your lawful wedded husband? Will you love him and comfort him, honor and keep him in sickness and in health? And forsake all others as long as you both shall live?"

I do, I signed.

He glanced at Karen. She gave him a nod.

"Do you have the rings?"

Alex pulled the box out of his pocket and handed it to the pastor. The pastor opened the box and handed Alex my ring.

"Please repeat after me," he said.

Alex slid the ring on my finger and recited our vows. "I, Alejandro, take you, Kylee, to be my wife. I promise to be true to you, in good times and in bad, in sickness and in health, and I will love and honor you as long as we both shall live. Please accept this ring as a token of my love and fidelity."

I took the ring and slid it on Alex's finger and followed the pastor's directions in sign language. *I, Kylee, take you, Alejandro, to be my husband. I promise to be true to you, in good times and in bad, in sickness and in health, and I will love and honor you as long as we both shall live. Please accept this ring as a token of my love and fidelity.*

After he received another nod from Karen, he continued, "Those whom God hath joined together, let no man put asunder. We who have come together today have heard the willingness of Alejandro and Kylee to be joined in marriage. You have come of your own free will and, in our presence, have declared your love and commitment to each other. You have given and received a ring as a symbol of your promises. Therefore, by the power vested in me by the laws of the state of Nevada, I take great pride and pleasure as I declare you husband and wife. You may kiss your bride."

Alex leaned in and pressed his lips to mine as the music started again. The magical moment was interrupted by the flash of a camera. Alex pulled away from me and grinned. Another flash captured the moment, and we turned towards the photographer for another handful of pictures as the pastor and Karen signed our certificate. The photographer stopped long enough to sign as our second witness before we were escorted out of the chapel.

Karen led us to the reception desk and handed Alex a card with website directions to access digital copies of the photographs. She made each of us sign the certificate again, and then she stamped it with a seal.

"Would you like us to file this for you?"

Alex glanced at me and then nodded. "Yes, please."

"Your photographs will be ready for viewing in just a moment. You are welcome to have a glass of champagne while you wait." She waved towards a seating nook with a fresh bottle of champagne and two glasses. A monitor sat just beyond the bubbly.

"Thank you, Karen." Alex led me away. "You were going to ask who was the latest hire?" he whispered in my ear.

I nodded.

"Karen is their newest employee. She's been here for about a month," he said as he poured two glasses and handed me one. "To us," he added and tapped his glass against mine.

I raised my glass and then took a sip. My gaze moved beyond Alex. Karen was busy with paperwork and never glanced our way. Instead, she focused on the next bride and groom who had been waiting for us to finish.

"Do you think it's her?"

I shook my head. Alex studied me and I shrugged. *Think stunning, not mousy cute.*

A smirk formed on his lips. "Kind of like you?"

Heat filled my cheeks, but before I could answer, the photographer stepped into our nook.

"Hello, Mr. and Mrs. Cervas." He extended his hand to us. "I'm Mark. Your photographs are available for viewing." He reached over the table and turned the monitor on. "Your wedding package includes a wedding album with a dozen photos. As we go through them, please let me know which ones to mark. Additional pages cost one hundred dollars each, so keep that in mind."

He smiled and started clicking through the pictures.

I didn't realize how many he had taken in the short time we were in the chapel and by the time we were done, we had it narrowed down to twenty photos. My favorite was Alex's grin after he kissed me. The man's eyes sparkled even on film. We forked over the money for the album and arranged for it to be delivered to the hotel later in the day.

Alex wrapped his arm around my waist and led me out of the chapel to our waiting limousine. When he slid into the seat next to me, he took my face in his hands and planted a lingering kiss.

"Back to the hotel?" the driver asked when Alex pulled away.

"No." He glanced at his watch. "We need to get to the Wee White Wedding Chapel, please."

The driver's brow creased.

"We didn't like what they offered here. We're looking for something a little more... unique," Alex said. "Besides, we have a reservation at two. If we don't like that one, then we have one later this evening as well."

"Yes, sir." The driver pulled out of the parking lot.

A few minutes later, we pulled into the Wee White Wedding Chapel. Alex held his hand out as the driver came around to open the door.

"The ring," he whispered as he slid his off and dropped it into his pocket.

I took it off at his direction with a little more than a pang in my heart, but we couldn't exactly walk in wearing the rings and pull off the getting married thing. Not if we truly wanted to catch the bicorn.

My ring disappeared into the same pocket as his, and he pulled out one copy of the marriage certificate and took my hand. The moment we stepped inside, I knew the bicorn wouldn't be party to the chaos inside. There were several chapels and another dozen brides and grooms standing around, waiting. The staff rushed from one to the next, and it did not give anyone the time to make an impression. Besides, there was not one stunning woman in the lot.

Still, we waited in line until we stood before the desk.

"Name?" the middle-aged woman at the counter said around a mouthful of chewing gum. She was possibly the most repelling creature I had seen in a while.

"Oh, hell no." Alex turned me around, marching towards the door.

I glanced around one last time before we stepped into the sunshine and oppressive midday heat.

What?

"The receptionist was the newest employee," he said as we marched to the limousine.

I actually snorted, surprising both of us, but the silent laugh pushed more air through the back of my nose than I expected. *Yeah, if the bicorn was hiding in that form, it would be starving by now.*

Alex burst out laughing. "No shit." He opened the door for me and climbed inside after I was situated.

"That leaves us with the Vegas Wedding Experience, but we have the rest of the day to relax. They could only fit us in tonight just before they close."

I waved at the dress.

"We could go back to the hotel, where we can both get comfortable," he said with a grin.

"Back to the hotel?" the driver asked.

"Yes, please," Alex answered. "We will need a ride tonight to the Vegas Wedding Experience, though."

"That's a nice venue. They offer a limo service as well. Would you like the concierge to arrange it for you?" the driver asked and focused on the road.

Alex glanced at me and I shrugged. "Sure," he said. "That would be great."

Do you think the spa could fit me in for a mani-pedi and possibly hair and makeup? I signed and pointed to the driver.

"My w..." Alex faltered and corrected himself. "My fiancé wants to know if the spa at the hotel has a slot for her to get a manicure and pedicure along with her hair before we go to the chapel tonight."

"Let me check." The driver called into the hotel. "Does a four o'clock appointment work for you, Miss Paradox?"

Four is perfect.

"She said that is perfect."

I leaned back in the seat and closed my eyes for the remainder of the ride.

Waking the Siren
Chapter 9

THE MOMENT WE STEPPED into the hotel room, Alex reached for me. I batted his hand away. *We are not going to ruin this dress. Not if we are going to get hitched again tonight.*

"You are my wife right now." He wrapped his arm around my waist and pulled me against him. "And I want to make that official," he purred in my ear.

I rolled out of his arms and turned, pulling my hair to the side so he could unzip the dress. I glanced over my shoulder at him and raised an eyebrow.

Alex slowly unzipped the back of my dress like he was unwrapping a china doll. I appreciated his delicate touch just as much as his care in folding the dress over the chaise lounge. His tux was folded with care as well, and then he faced me. His boxers were already tented with his desire.

His gaze flowed down my body, stopping at the sheath on my leg before continuing on.

I reached to unclasp it.

"No, leave it on." He moved in front of me. "It's fucking hot."

Kinky, I signed.

He grinned and pushed me back on the bed, relieving me of my lace panties before he filled me with one hard thrust.

"I have been waiting to do this since I laid eyes on you in that dress." He closed his eyes and slowed down his pace with a sigh.

I moved with him at that insanely slow pace that drove me wild, especially with the way his pelvis ground against mine. Making love to Alex was always a spiritual adventure—from the decadent and kinky to the sweet like right now, he knew how to make me lose my mind.

He leaned forward, claiming my mouth in a heated kiss. His hips matched the pace of his tongue, lingering at first but then increasing into a wild frenzy that ended with a groan as my nails raked his back with my release.

The kiss broke, and he stared down at me with a sleepy smile. "I love you, my dear wife."

I smiled and gave him a peck. My stomach growled, and I looked at the clock on the nightstand. I didn't have enough time for room service before my salon appointment.

Alex glanced at the space between us. "And here I thought *my* stomach was loud." He rolled away, stretching out next to me.

I took him in, and my smile widened. This exquisite man lying next to me was my husband. The reality hit like a tidal wave, and my vision blurred. I blinked back the heat pooling in my eyes and sat up before Alex caught the tears. I crossed to my suitcase, looking for anything that would be appropriate for a pedicure and still hide the knife from view. Nothing fit the bill, but then I remembered the yoga pants stuffed in my pocketbook.

"What are you doing?"

I waved at my naked body and wiggled my fingers, hoping he would get what I was saying.

"You still have a little time," he said with a grin.

Instead of turning, I headed to the bathroom and relieved myself. I also took a minute to splash cold water on my face to wash away the tear stains. With my emotions in check, I walked back into the bedroom.

Where's my pocketbook?

"In the other room. Why?"

Yoga pants for the pedicure, I signed and crossed into the other room. My purse was on the coffee table. I grabbed both the pants and shirt and headed back to the bedroom.

Alex was still sprawled out on the bed with his hands behind his head. He watched as I picked up our discarded underwear and dropped it on our formal wear.

"Going commando?" he asked.

I shrugged and pulled the pants on over my bare ass.

He propped himself on his elbow. "I think we should do that tonight."

I laughed at him. *Seriously?*

"Yes." He grinned.

I sucked my lip between my teeth as I considered it. *Okay.* I slid my top over my head and gave him a smile. After grabbing my flip-flops and purse, I blew him a kiss and headed out of the hotel room.

Waking the Siren
Chapter 10

THE SPA EMPLOYEES AT the Bellagio certainly knew their way around pampering a woman. From the relaxing foot soak to the deep tissue massage on my calves, I thought I had entered nirvana, but then came the hot towel wraps and green tea lotion for an invigorating end to the pedicure foreplay.

The chair I sat in had those slow massage knobs that climbed up my back to my shoulders in hypnotizing circles before returning to my lower back. The endless loop left me feeling more like silly putty than a bride. I chose a blood-red nail polish for both my toenails and fingernails. I figured I was already married, and tonight's follies were more for show, anyway.

As soon as the nail pampering was over, I was escorted into the hair salon where the hairdresser put my hair in a braided cascading up-do that put the bridal magazine pictures to shame. I stood in front of the mirror looking at the thick but loosely braided cords at the sides of my head that lead to the web of beautiful curls tickling the nape of my neck. It was gorgeous.

I was pleased, and my monetary tips showed it. When I walked into the hotel room, Alex looked up from the couch, and his eyes widened, almost like they did when he saw me in the dress for the first time. He put down the book he was looking at and stood. He looked fine standing there in just the tuxedo shirt and pants. The jacket lay neatly across the couch next to him.

I blew him a kiss and headed towards the bedroom to get dressed. I didn't have much time left before we had to be on our way. Instead of pulling the shirt off over my head, I stretched it over my shoulders and down my body, stripping the yoga pants with it. The shoes came first, and I buckled the lace sandals before I stood and picked up the dress. The hard part came when I tried to zip it up. I only had the reach to get it to the middle of my back. I needed Alex and crossed to the living room.

He turned towards me when I tapped the wall. I pointed over my shoulder before signing, *Can you zip me up?*

His lips formed the perfect smile. "I didn't think it was possible, but you look even more beautiful than you did this morning." His pants tented, and he shifted as he crossed to me. A blush crept into his cheeks.

I raised an eyebrow at him before he stepped behind me. I swear the man could be as bad as a teenage boy standing in a stiff wind.

"Commando has its drawbacks," he muttered and tugged gently at my zipper until it reached the top of the dress. "The photo album from this morning came." He pointed towards the table. "Want to see?"

Do we have time?

"Just enough for you to at least take a quick look." He handed the album to me before he slid his coat on.

I flipped open to the first page, and my chest squeezed enough for my breath to draw in. Alex's grin captured my heart, and having this memorialized struck a chord deep inside me, bringing those alarms to the surface and ruining the relaxation the last two hours had created in my muscles. Doubt crept in, and a part of me wanted to grab him and hop in the car to head home, where I knew he would be safe.

I looked up at him, and that spectacular smile graced his lips, melting my resolve even further. I knew if I continued to flip through the photos and let these emotions take control; I was going to back out of this job.

And I didn't have the autonomy to do that. I closed the book and placed it on the table, trying to shake the dread clawing at my insides.

I'll look at them later. Let's go before I change my mind.

His smile faded, and he stepped close. "It's a little too late for that."

I rolled my eyes and palmed his cheek, slowly running my thumb across his lips. The desperate need to run from this desert oasis filled every cell. I leaned in, catching a quick kiss before I heeded my own internal alarms.

Let's go catch this bitch so we can go home, I signed as I stepped away.

His cheeks flared. "I thought you meant you changed your mind about marrying me." He let out a small chuckle. "I really need to stop assuming you mean me when you say shit like that."

Yes. You do. I gave him a smile and took his hand.

Alex checked the pocket of his coat for the hotel key before we stepped out of the room, and I gave his breast pocket a pat as well.

"It's there. That's the first thing I made sure of when I put the jacket on," he said as the elevator opened. "And the rings are safely tucked away, too. I think I want the photo package from tonight, as well," he added.

I shrugged. I didn't care. The photo album sitting in the hotel room was enough for me, but if he wanted pictures of me with my hair all decked out, I didn't have a problem with that. As a matter of fact, it was downright sweet.

Okay. I smiled as we stepped into the lobby.

Heads turned as we crossed to the entry. A town car with the wedding venue logo plastered on the side was already waiting for us outside.

"Mr. Cervas?" the driver asked as we approached. There was something vacant in his gaze, but it could be just the end of a long day.

"Yes," Alex confirmed.

The chauffeur for Vegas Wedding Experience opened the door to the back of the town car for us. Alex helped me inside before taking the seat next to me.

I really didn't want to be in the car going towards danger, but then again, if this didn't pan out, we would only have one more day before my body broke down. The caviar hair treatment I received at the spa actually rejuvenated my hair, but that had nothing to do with the fish eggs and everything to do with the fact they stored the delicacy in sea water.

The slow pattern of Alex's thumb on the side of my hand pulled my attention back to the moment. He watched the passing scenery with an expression I couldn't read. I squeezed his hand, and he glanced my way with a smile that held tension at the corners of his lips.

I wasn't the only one on edge. I squeezed his hand harder.

"I'm good," he whispered. "Just nervous that this place isn't going to be everything we want," he added and brought my hand to his lips. His gaze traveled to the driver and back to me.

So I wasn't the only one who caught the weird vibe of nothingness from our driver. He looked pleasant enough, but there was no personality there. Unlike the chauffeurs at the hotel, who all seemed to be talkative and jovial.

I pulled my hand out of his and signed, *Did you remember the wedding license?*

Alex snorted a laugh. "Yes. I have the license and the rings. I have everything we need, so just relax, hon."

"She doesn't speak?" The driver's gaze locked with mine through the rearview mirror for a moment before traveling to Alex's.

"No. She can't speak," he said in a clipped tone that was neither friendly nor welcoming to encourage any more conversation.

"You must really love her to marry a deaf-mute," he muttered from the front seat.

"She isn't deaf," Alex clarified with a hard edge in his voice.

The driver's eyes never changed as he glanced at the two of us. No remorse or surprise at Alex's comment. Even his mumbled apology lacked emotion and sincerity.

My spine tingled with warnings. I wished Alex had had the hotel service take us to this wedding venue instead of using their service. We were heading into the devil's lair without an escape plan.

Waking the Siren
Chapter 11

WALKING INTO THE VEGAS Wedding Experience lobby wasn't anything I was prepared for. Unlike the bustle of the last place we stepped inside, this one was almost too formal for my tastes. Add to that the fact that everyone working in the place could have landed a modeling job on the spot.

I traded a glance with Alex. He wore the same expression I envisioned on my face. Both of us were overwhelmed.

A petite woman with glasses and an appointment book approached us with a smile.

"Mr. Cervas, I presume?" she asked and extended her hand.

Alex shook it and gave a nod.

"I am Beverly. We spoke on the phone this morning. We have you all set for the sunset ceremony. If you will follow me." She led us to the right. We crossed through an empty ballroom and out onto a terrace over a secluded lake. "Martin is all set over at the gazebo and ready to officiate the ceremony. So is Shea, our photographer, who will discuss photo packages with you after the wedding. And Justin is all set to take you back to your hotel after you wrap up with Shea. Now, you also mentioned you would need witnesses?"

"Yes, and at least one of them needs to read sign language," Alex said.

"Yes, that is outlined in the notes here, and I am well versed in multiple languages, including sign language." Beverly smiled up at us and put her hand out. "The license?"

Alex pulled the last copy out of his pocket and handed it over.

I was too preoccupied with the scenery to pay close attention to what the two of them were discussing. The gazebo faced west, and the sun had dipped enough to be visible between two mountain peaks in the distance, reflecting a bright orange path on the water leading to the wedding altar. The sky had turned deep blue with the clouds colored in pinks and purples stretching towards us. It was magnificent.

And distracting. The beauty of this place was hypnotizing.

While Beverly was pretty, the photographer standing with the preacher landed in that stunning realm that worried me.

How long has the photographer worked here? I signed.

"She's only been here a little under a month, but I can assure you her resume and portfolio are impeccable."

I nodded and offered what I hoped was a sincere smile. Beverly led us to the gazebo, and as soon as we stepped onto the path leading up to the outdoor altar, soft music piped through the speakers. The sun dipped lower on the horizon. Everything about this magical situation was wrong. The place was too perfect, too staged, and it was the ideal hiding spot for a bicorn. I glanced at Alex.

He sensed me gazing up at him and glanced my way. "I love you," he whispered as we walked into the monster's lair.

The ceremony was almost word for word as our actual wedding ceremony this morning, but much more surreal with the sun setting behind the officiant. I let my guard down, and when Alex kissed me, I let the kiss linger, melting into him and forgetting for a moment that we stood in the presence of danger.

When the kiss broke, we stared at each other and smiled. The click of the camera pulled us out of the moment. A moment I did not want to end because as soon as we stepped away from this altar, we were back in hunting mode.

Alex seemed to sense my hesitation and wrapped his arms around me in a hug. He twirled me around in a circle and set me on my feet again with a laugh. The sparkle that appeared in his eyes gave me an indication of what type of thoughts were parading through his head, but with another snap of the shutter, his demeanor subdued.

"Are we all set?" he asked, glancing at Beverly and the clergyman.

"We just need your signatures," Beverly said.

We crossed to the podium at the side where our certificate lay. Beverly and Justin, our driver from earlier, had already signed as witnesses, and we signed our names as well.

"I'll make sure this gets filed with the county clerk in the morning," Beverly said as she took the form. "I'll leave you in the trusted care of Shea, who will walk you through the photo packages and see to it you get the perfect representation of your special day."

She shook both our hands. "Congratulations," she added before she strolled towards the main ballroom.

We turned towards Shea.

"Mr. and Mrs. Cervas, congratulations. It has been a pleasure photographing your special occasion this evening. If you will come this way, I can upload the pictures for your viewing and go through the various packages we offer."

Even her syrupy voice grated on my nerves. I shook her hand first, and her face tensed a fraction when her fingers wrapped around mine. It was so quick that I almost didn't catch it. With Alex, she held his hand a few moments longer than necessary, and a spark twinkled in her eye.

Distracted by the nearness of our most likely candidate for the bicorn, I had to still my need to rip the knife from my sheath and bury it in the monster's evil heart. There were still people around, still receptions occurring in the other area of the building. I couldn't do this in public, not if I hoped to get out of here without being arrested.

I traded a glance with Alex, and he gave me a wink.

"We'll take all of them, please," he said as we shuffled through the photos. They were just as gorgeous as the ones in the album back at the hotel, but these had the mountain sunset as a backdrop. "Digital copies," he clarified. "With the release to print at our leisure."

Shea beamed and took Alex's credit card, disappearing into the office.

Justin gave us a nod and headed out of the lobby.

Shea came back with our card and the receipt, along with a card that had instructions on how to download the files.

"I will upload these to the website on the card tonight. I just want to warn you, you will need to download them within thirty days or there is an added charge for reloading them to the website," Shea cautioned and stapled the receipt to the instructions.

"Thank you." Alex folded the receipt, slipping it into his coat pocket before he replaced his credit card in his wallet.

She shook our hands. "I believe the town car should be waiting up front for you. It has been a pleasure," she said and then disappeared, leaving us alone in the lobby.

Alex went to say something, but I shook my head. I took his hand, and we headed out to the car.

Justin stood holding the door of a different, bigger car. This time, he wore a smile that seemed much warmer than earlier. The cab had a single leather bench seat across the back and a stocked bar on the side behind the driver's seat. A privacy shield separated the driving cab from the back as well. It was almost akin to a mini limo. In the middle of the bar sat an uncorked bottle of champagne with two champagne flutes.

"Would you like me to do the honors, sir?" Justin asked after we settled in the car.

Alex glanced at the bottle and then at Justin. "I think I've got it."

"Very well, sir." He closed the door.

The minute the car engine started, the door locks engaged. Alex was too busy prying the cork from the bottle to notice. With the cork safely out, he poured us each a glass.

"To us," he said. "May we have a long and happy life together."

We tapped the glasses and took a sip. I didn't detect any odd taste in the bubbly. Apparently, neither did Alex because he downed the glass and set it aside.

He went to take my still half-full flute, but I pulled it away, finishing it before relinquishing the glass to him. Without a hint of caution, he tossed the cup onto the counter and took my face in his hands.

"I love you, Kylee Cervas." Then he crushed my lips in a kiss that promised all sorts of naughty things when we got back to the hotel.

If I wasn't so pre-occupied about catching the bicorn, I would have melted under it.

A wave of dizziness hit me, and I pulled away from him. He blinked at me, and his forehead wrinkled quizzically.

"Ky..." he started, but never finished. His eyes rolled up into his head, and he slumped in the seat next to me.

The soft hiss coming from the air conditioning ducts caught my attention just before the blackness took hold of me.

LITTLE BY LITTLE, LIGHT bled into my consciousness. Whispers came and went, but I couldn't make out the words. The fog clouding my brain cleared, but my body was still too heavy to listen to my commands to move. My last memory in the limousine snapped my eyes open and catapulted me to my feet.

The only fixture my gaze locked on in this bland room was the large window a few feet in front of me. Alex was on the other side of the glass, tied to a chair, still wearing his tuxedo. His head lolled to the side, and his mouth hung open in a stupor, but he didn't look like he had been harmed.

My heart slammed against the walls of my chest. I went to step towards him. A yank on my arms brought reality to the forefront. Both wrists were bound in rope and anchored to metal hooks on the floor. I couldn't reach the window, even if I strained forward. I tried kicking out in front of me, but it was just too far. The burn of frustration flushed my skin, and I silently cursed.

I glanced around at my surroundings, looking for anything that might aid in my escape, but there was nothing within my reach. Even the table at the back of the room wasn't accessible. The tools on the table froze me in place. It looked like Lucifer's torture chamber had been moved topside. Ropes, whips, knives, and even some horrific toys meant to tear someone apart from the inside out lay organized on the table.

Silence overrode my senses. The door opened. Four men, including our driver Justin, stepped into the room. Their empty smiles mimicked each other, and I shivered, trying to dredge up the facts of exactly what the bicorn did to their female victims. If the table behind me was any indication, I was in for some serious pain.

Men were left as vacant, shriveled shells, the life sucked out of them and their soul. Their soul fed the damn beast, dying just as surely as the bodies the monster left behind.

I wished to hell we had driven ourselves to the venue.

Shock as strong as an electrical current flowed through my form as a woman crossed into the room behind the four men. I blinked and my eyebrows rose. She was not who I expected.

Beverly, the petite wedding planner from the Vegas Wedding Experience, chuckled at me as she crossed the space, holding the sheath that had been strapped to my thigh. She stopped less than a foot away, pointing the leather at me. "I never expected to find this on you," she said, her voice harsher than the one she used at the venue. "Where did you get it?"

I shrugged. With my hands bound, my ability to communicate was stunted. I had to keep up the pretense as long as possible to give Alex a fighting chance. If he woke as groggily as I had, this bitch could easily throw him off his game.

She hissed at me.

I mouthed, *Something old.*

Her eyes narrowed at me. "Did you just say 'something old?'"

I nodded. *Family heirloom.*

"Really?" Sarcasm laced her voice, and she turned to the closest minion. "Handkerchief," she ordered and put out her hand. He obliged, and she wrapped the cloth around the hilt of the weapon, pulling it from the sheath. The leather fell to the floor. Her free hand cupped my cheek. "You really expect me to believe that crap?"

Before my eyes, Beverly changed to my mirror image. Horror filled every cell, and with it came a blinding pain searing my side. I couldn't even cry out as the knife pierced through my insides. Both devastation and fury filled me. She was close enough to me to take the only opportunity I had at my disposal. I head butted the bitch.

The impact left me woozy, but it was worth it. My mirror image stumbled back, yanking the blade from my side. Her dainty nose was twisted at a broken angle, and blood dripped down the front of the image of my dress.

I smiled at my handiwork.

She wiped her face. "Bitch!" she snarled and pointed the blade at my face as she stepped in again. Grabbing a handful of my hair, she forced my head back and pressed the point to my throat. The raw fury reflected on her face coursed through my body like acid, burning away all logical thought.

"I was going to let my boys kill you while I claimed your husband's life, but I think it will be more painful for you to watch me drain him of all his humanity instead. I'm sure you'll see the sweet irony in all this when he is the one who strangles you to death."

Fuck you.

Her lips pressed together, and a snarl came from her throat. She stepped away and glanced at her minions. "Have at her boys. Make her suffer, but she needs to be alive and aware when he comes in here. He gets to do the honors, understand?"

They nodded and all their eyes turned to me, narrowing with evil undertones. The first punch hit where the bitch had stabbed me. Acute pain spiraled through me, and my knees gave out. I dropped to the floor, trying to shield myself from the next blow, but one man grabbed a handful of my hair and yanked me to my feet. My scalp screamed.

Alex's mumbling through the intercom paused the punch fest. I pulled in a breath of air, staring at his groggy form. His eyes blinked, and he glanced around the room, calling my name. Beverly, wearing the facade of me, gave me the most horrific grin.

"I want her to witness this." She waved towards the window. "And no toys. Not yet. I also don't want to hear a peep from this room, got it?"

I struggled to break the binding holding me in place and opened my mouth in a silent scream. The lack of ability to voice my distress bloomed a rage inside me that compounded when the bicorn stumbled out of the room.

Alex stopped yelling and just stared at her, blinking at the image of me with a bloody knife in my hand. He closed his eyes, and his sigh of relief came through the speakers.

I was so focused on him, I never saw the punch coming. One of the bicorn's minions sucker punched me in the side she had stabbed me again. Sharp pain shot from the wound, dropping me to my knees in a silent scream. Air locked in my chest as another grabbed a handful of my hair, lifting me back to my feet.

The agony was so acute that I missed what Alex had said to the thing on the other side of the mirror. The bicorn nodded and crossed the distance, dropping to its knees before Alex. It used the knife to cut the binds holding his ankles and one of his wrists before putting the weapon on the ground.

I squirmed, trying to get away from the next hit, but the struggle was useless. I needed to find a different strategy. I focused on the pain, using it to find the strength I needed. Using the leverage of the ropes, I executed a sidekick, connecting with Justin's groin as he stepped in to deliver another blow.

He went down hard, with an *oof*. The glare he sent gave me an indication that I was going to pay dearly for that, but before I could turn my attention back to the window, another punch yanked the air from my chest.

"What are you doing?" Alex raised his eyebrows and glanced at the mirror in front of him and then around the empty room. "Kylee," he said again, this time in more of a whispering growl I knew intimately.

The bicorn's hands slid up his chest as the filthy thing pressed its lips to his, stopping whatever argument he might have been launching. It was so very much like something I would do that I tilted my head back in a wail that should have broken the glass in the mirror. But only air rushed out of my mouth.

Justin slammed his fist into my cheek. I went down. My cheek flared as if someone had hit it with a blowtorch. Stars filled my vision. Again, one of the thugs grabbed my hair, pulling me to my feet. The scream in my scalp had gone numb. He pulled me far enough forward that I was bent over and my arms stretched at my side, straining both shoulders. The shit held my head back far enough, so the only thing filling my vision was the bicorn unbuttoning Alex's shirt. When it started kissing its way down his chest, I thought my brain would explode.

"Are you going to untie me so we can get the hell out of here?" Alex asked, but I knew that voice. That tone of we-shouldn't-be-doing-this-but-please-don't-stop filled my ears.

Another punch hit my side, lifting me off the ground. But it was nothing compared to the mental agony of seeing Alex succumb to the wicked monster. Tears welled in my eyes, blurring my vision, and my throat tightened.

The bicorn shook her head. A smile crawled across Alex's lips.

"Kinky," he whispered over the sound of his zipper being lowered. "Ah, fuck, Ky," he nearly groaned, and his head went back against the seat. His free hand slid into the nest of braids on the bicorn's head as he guided the pace of its strokes.

I hadn't realized Justin had lifted my dress until hands gripped my waist, pressing into the cut with the same force as his entry. My gaze was glued to the scene on the other side of the window. The soul-sucking bitch was deep throating him. Giving him the blow job I had called a rain check on at the hotel.

The asshole holding a handful of my hair leaned forward. "You are going to swallow me like that before this is over," he whispered in my ear before his teeth clamped down on the sensitive tissue. He laughed and tugged on my ear until warm liquid ran down my neck. He stood and delivered a blow to my side.

Justin pounded me with brute force, mimicking the fists hitting my torso. Each thrusting blow nearly tore my shoulders from their sockets.

Alex groaned, even as my violations continued. Alex's essence slowly seeped from his body with every vile stroke of the bicorn's mouth. His cheeks hollowed as his eyes rolled back with rapture.

Agony overwhelmed me all the way down to the cellular level. The cry forming in my soul vibrated in the back of my throat, and I forced out my dormant siren. The haunting melody escaped, filling the room. Hope and horror glimmered inside me.

The ecstasy etched in Alex's face disappeared. Wisps of his soul snapped back in place. His gaze shot to the glass, and swear it locked on mine, and I kept singing, damning him just as much as the soulless minions abusing me.

The only one in the vicinity with a soul heard my song, and it was going to be the death of me.

His gaze dropped to the thing sucking his dick. Shock skittered over his features. He moved faster than I imagined he could and had the knife from the floor embedded in the thing's throat before it could stop him.

He kicked it away from him and reached into his pocket. Relief swept over his face as he pulled the other dagger from his breast pocket. Once he cut through the binds, still holding his hand to the chair, he stood and zipped himself back up. Disgust weaved into his features, peeling his lips away from his teeth in a snarl as he glanced at the mirror.

My heart soared even with the pain wracking my entire form. I had no control over the bicorn's minions. They were too far gone to be influenced by my siren. My voice failed as another fist connected with my rib cage, piercing my lung with fragments of broken bone. I coughed blood. Fists continued to pound my body, bruising and breaking without hesitation. My shoulders screamed at the torque of an angle they had me in, and if Justin kept up the pounding pace he was at, both shoulders were going to dislocate.

The bang of the door being kicked off its hinges didn't stop the assault on me, although the one holding my hair let go and moved in front of me.

"It's your turn to swallow cock," he said, reaching for his zipper.

I caught the rage flash over Alex's face before the minion blocked my view of my doomed husband.

Before this soulless asshat could unzip his pants, fresh blood poured from him, drenching me. He fell to the floor in front of me, his throat sliced wide, almost to his spine. Alex's roar filled the space, even as Justin continued his assault, tightening his grip on my side to the point his fingers dug into my cut.

With a growl, Alex slammed the knife in the man's face to my right. The wet sound of him ripping the blade out of flesh followed. Before the man fell, Alex brought the blade across the distance to my left. Another rain of blood splashed over me. The maniacal fury in Alex's face caught my breath in my chest. He disappeared beyond my field of vision.

The hands gripping me ripped away from my skin, as did the brutal force pounding my insides to a pulp. A high-pitched scream filled the room, and it was shut off an instant later.

The rope around my right wrist snapped, and I fell, turning my head so I wouldn't break my nose on the floor. My cheek hit hard enough to create white stars in my vision. Then whatever binds holding my left wrist in place released. I lay still for a minute, trying to assess the overwhelming damage to my body.

"Kylee." Alex's soft voice pierced my mind.

I glanced up, wincing at the motion. Just moving my head hurt. I struggled to lift onto my elbows.

Alex crouched in front of me, his white shirt bloody from his carnage. I looked around me at the four dead men. My gaze landed on a dismembered penis, and I now understood what that high-pitched scream was for. A satisfied flush rushed through me at the twisted justice. The knife dripped thick red gore onto the floor near me. I slowly pushed myself into a kneeling position.

Alex handed me the knife, took off his tuxedo jacket, and put it over my shoulders as my teeth clicked against the shock, trying to overcome my body. His hand reached out and cupped my cheek.

"Your voice is beautiful," he whispered.

Tears flooded my vision and spilled over, creating hot paths down my cheeks. I had damned the man I loved. Silent sobs ripped through my battered body. He helped me to my feet before covering my mouth with his, trying to silence the violent shakes filling my form. His soul seared to mine, and despite the pain his grip on me caused, I melted into the kiss.

Both his hands gripped my cheeks tentatively, as if he thought I would crumble under his touch. The knife weighed down my right arm, and I didn't have the energy to lift it to return the sweet gesture.

His sudden inhale yanked the air out of my lungs in a painful pull. The kiss broke, and his wide gaze met mine before dropping to the hand still holding the knife.

A crease appeared between his eyes. "Ky..."

He sank to his knees and fell forward onto my legs. The dagger he had stuck in the bicorn's throat was now embedded in his back. Beyond him stood Beverly with a vicious smile. Alex had speared her throat, but he hadn't pierced her heart, which was the only way to kill a bicorn.

"Bitch, that soul was mine," Beverly hissed.

Rage encompassed me. With the flick of my wrist, the knife in my hand sailed true, carrying with it the power of my fury. I leaned forward, screaming my siren. The two-way mirror and all the glass in the vicinity shattered at the pitch of my voice.

The bicorn's smile faded. Her gaze fell to the ivory wood blade sunk to the hilt in her chest. She fell over backwards like a tree dropping. When her body hit the floor, the facade of Beverly disappeared, leaving the hideous, faceless creature in its place.

I fell to my knees next to Alex. His eyes focused for a fraction of a second, and then went dull. His spirit slammed into my body with the force of a hurricane, fusing to my cells, becoming a part of me, unlike those ancient doomed souls of my past who satiated my hunger and just disappeared like they never existed.

Alex was the only siren victim that melded with me like a new strand of DNA. I could feel him in my soul, which meant when I finally faced the music, Alex would be there with me, sharing in my torture. Sobs clenched my chest.

My siren self flared, letting loose a wail of sorrow that lingered in the air.

Waking the Siren
Chapter 12

I DIDN'T KNOW HOW long I lay with my head on Alex's shoulder. His shirt was paper thin and see through from my tears. My throat hurt from the siren screams, and every muscle felt as if I had gone through a meat grinder. I wrapped my hand around the hilt of the knife in his back and pulled. The strain ground the broken bones in my chest, and a whine escaped from the back of my throat.

I climbed unsteadily to my feet and tucked the knife back into the breast pocket of the tuxedo jacket I still wore. My bare feet crunched over the shattered glass as I crossed to the door, ignoring the symphony of pain each step produced.

I needed the ocean. Otherwise, I would die in this desert hellhole and drag Alex to hell with me. The memory of his warm embrace filled me, and my breath hitched. My vision blurred under a steady stream of tears as I stumbled outside.

A small parking lot circled around the vacant building, and only two cars sat in the lot. Even the windows of the automobiles were shattered. I approached the shiny black town car we had gotten into at the wedding venue last night, and my reflection came into focus. I let out a silent huff. I looked like a cross between the bride of Frankenstein and Carrie with the rat's nest that was my hair and the blood streaking my dress.

I tried the door handle, expecting resistance, but there wasn't any. I tumbled onto the glass-covered seat. The keys dangled from the ignition. I closed my eyes and turned the switch. The engine roared to life. The GPS system blinked on, and I typed in the Bellagio.

The directions said I was twenty minutes away from my destination. I leaned on the steering wheel, fighting another bout of tears. With the last of my energy, I put the car in gear and headed for the hotel with both my mind and body on autopilot.

I pulled into the valet service at the hotel's private entrance for gold customers, thankful we had booked a suite. Walking through the hotel lobby in the condition I was in would have scared the crap out of everyone. At least here, the number of people turning white and gasping was limited.

The hotel manager intercepted me halfway to the elevator.

"Miss Paradox?" he asked.

I tried to step around him, but the movement caused me to cringe in pain. I raised my left hand, showing him the rings.

"Mrs. Cervas," he corrected. "Are you hurt?"

I met his gaze, leveling my most serious stare, mentally telling him to get the fuck out of my way.

"Where is Mr. Cervas?" he asked, his voice dropping to almost a whisper.

My chin trembled, and this time I walked around him. I got to the elevator with no one else stopping me. In the room, I reached for the zipper and nearly fell to my knees at the motion. After a few tries, I pulled the knife out of the coat pocket and sliced through both sleeves, stepping out of the bloodied mess that had once been my stunning wedding gown. I crossed to the shower, still holding on to the ivory wood knife.

You need to get out of here. Alex's whisper filled my ears, but I ignored it.

I needed to feel clean, but even the spray of the shower hurt my bruised skin. Red flowed from my hair and my skin, but I forced myself to stand in place until all that flowed was a thin pink line from the stab wound in my stomach.

Drying off was another hellish nightmare, as was putting clothing on, but I did every necessary motion until I was dressed and my hair was combed free of knots. I glanced at the nightstand next to Alex's side of the bed. My car keys sat there, along with the valet ticket and a notepad with a scribbled note I hadn't seen before. I limped to the side of the bed and picked up the paper.

Just going to set up a few things and grab us some breakfast. I'll be back soon. Love you. A.

Tears burned my eyes. I folded the piece of paper and put it into my bag. I grabbed the car keys, rolled my suitcase into the living room, and sat on the couch, just staring at the photo album. With effort, I picked up the book and placed it into the suitcase.

Halfway to the door, I stopped and backtracked to the tuxedo coat crumpled on the floor next to the ruined gown. I squatted and rifled through the pockets, finding the photo instructions from the ceremony last night. Something about leaving that behind seemed as wrong as leaving Alex at that abandoned property.

I struggled to my feet and dropped the card in my purse. Numb to my injuries, I crossed back to the elevator and stared at the stains on the tile floor as it descended. I stepped out in the lobby to a flurry of activity, including a swarm of police. The manager pointed at me, and a couple of police officers crossed, blocking my path.

"Mrs. Cervas, we would like to take you to the local hospital," the female officer said. Her badge announced her as Detective Mills.

I stared at her and let go of the suitcase handle. *I just want to go home.* I signed and bit my lip, pushing down the rush of feelings clawing their way to the surface.

"We need to check you out." She reached for me. "You are still bleeding." Her voice was soft, and concern laced her eyes. Her hand landed on my shoulder, and I winced. "Please, ma'am. You are in shock. Let us help you."

I couldn't move my feet forward. Instead, I blinked at her and cocked my head, swallowing hard. I had to get to the ocean. My injuries were substantial enough that if I was brought to the emergency room here in Las Vegas, I would never leave.

I need my home. Please, just let me go. Tremors started in my chin, and my vision blurred. *Please. I can't stay here. I just... I can't.*

She followed my hands and glanced at her partner before meeting my gaze. "Can we just ask you a few questions before you go?"

I turned my glance toward the hotel manager and lifted the valet ticket. He nodded. I turned back to the police officers. Most of my brain was still in a fog, but something about Detective Mills's gaze made me sense sympathy.

Questions?

They traded a look. "Do you have any recollection of anything that happened to you this morning?"

I reached out for the handle of my suitcase to steady myself. A high-pitched whine filled my ears, and I gave her a slow nod.

"Then you know you are injured," she said.

How do you know?

"There were recordings," she said. "Recordings of everything," she added softly.

That seemed like a thing that bicorn bitch would do to tide her over between attacks. I glanced at the floor, my mind filling with a measure of trepidation. I used my siren, but I had no idea if it translated over to digital recordings. Good God, what had I done? I blinked and forced myself to meet Detective Mills's gaze.

"What do you remember?" Detective Mills asked.

I kept hold of the suitcase. *Everything,* I signed slowly and then moved away from them.

"What was that thing?" Detective Mills's partner blurted out.

I stopped. Because of my injuries, twisting around to face them wasn't an option, so I held up my hand and spelled out, *Monster.*

Silence resounded behind me. I limped towards the exit where my car sat behind the broken one I had left at the curb earlier.

"Mrs. Cervas, you need to be looked at. Please, at least let me take you down to the emergency room," Detective Mills said as she ran up beside me.

No. I can't stay here. I signed after the valet took my bag from me and stowed it in the trunk. *If you saw the videos, you know why.*

The detective tilted her head in sympathy.

He was my everything. Now, I need to go tell his children that he's dead. I can't do that from a hospital bed here.

The debate in the woman's eyes raged, and then she reached into her shirt pocket and handed me her card. "I really should take you to the hospital here," she muttered under her breath. "At least let me know you arrived home safe, okay?"

I glanced at the card. It had both an email and a phone number. I gave her a nod. She helped me into the car and shut the door. I pulled away, each turn of the wheel wrapping my midsection in a high state of anguish. The pressure I had to exert with my foot was a new hell that kept me alert.

By the time I pulled into my garage, I was ready to just plow through the back wall, keep driving down the beach, and let the water claim me. But Alex's narrative in my head kept me breathing, kept me as close to sane as possible. I turned off the car and closed the garage door.

It took me a few minutes to get the car door open. I swung my legs out and struggled to my feet. The moment I stepped away from the security of the vehicle, my knees buckled, and I collapsed onto the cold concrete.

Get your ass up, girl.

The strength of Alex's voice in my head jumpstarted my muscles. I pushed myself to my hands and knees. While I would have preferred to just stay on the concrete until my heart gave out from shock, I did not want to sentence Alex to an eternity of Lucifer's revenge.

I crawled to the door and pulled myself up. The pain almost loosened my siren, but I clamped my mouth closed and forced myself to walk towards my lifeblood. The ocean beckoned.

I had been in dire circumstances before, but I wasn't sure if I had ever been this close to death. The hundred yards of sand stretched before me seemed insurmountable, especially under the midday sun, leaving the sand scalding on my already scraped and cut bare feet.

Come on, honey, just a few more steps.

His soft whisper gently pushed me forward. I stumbled into the surf, dropping to my knees as a wave flowed over me. The water charge infused me, squeezing my form, turning every broken bone, every torn piece of flesh, and every bruise into liquid agony.

My blood sizzled in my veins, and if I had a voice, it would have been screaming as I writhed in the surf under the pure torment.

Healing had never been pleasant, but this... this was a whole different class of torture.

White spots dotted my vision. I attempted to crawl to the safety of the sand, but the water pulled at me, trying to claim my soul in the same manner I had claimed Alex's. Relentlessly rolling me under its will.

Darkness threatened, and I fought it as vehemently as I had fought all manners of creatures over the years.

Unfortunately, this was not a battle I was destined to win.

Waking the Siren
Chapter 13

SAND SCRAPED MY CHEEK. I lifted my head, blinking my eyes open. I didn't recognize the surrounding landscape. Instead of taking a closer inspection, I rolled onto my back, assessing my current condition. The clear night sky met my gaze. I blinked a few times, trying to bat the crust off my eyelashes.

I had stumbled to the water during the midafternoon. My brain couldn't grasp the idea that I had been tossed around in the surf for hours like an untethered skiff drifting at sea. It was a miracle this human form didn't drown.

I scanned the night sky and found the Big Dipper. It was low enough in the sky to be an hour or two after dusk. My house was close to a mile from this spot. I tentatively climbed to my feet.

Halfway home, the events of the day barreled back into my numb form and I stumbled, landing on my knees. A tidal wave would have been a kinder punishment. The sorrow scratched every surface of my skin while wrapping its elastic arms around my chest, squeezing until I couldn't draw a breath.

Tears burned my eyes, my throat, and cut warm paths down my sand-brushed cheeks. I had lost in the past, but not like this. Not to the point I had difficulty envisioning any kind of tomorrow.

If Alex wasn't riding shotgun with my soul, I probably would have gone suicidal.

Bullshit.

"Shut up." Only a whispered hiss of air came out between my lips. The water hadn't repaired my voice box, at least not to the degree I needed to be coherent.

No. I won't shut up. Not when you need a reality check. I will always be here, Ky. Always. His voice echoed in my head.

I wanted you by my side, not trapped in my head. Damn you. I told you not to come, I told him.

If I hadn't come, someone else would have died.

I opened my mouth to argue and snapped it shut. He was right. With the lack of time to really study the venues or the employees, I wouldn't have been able to narrow it down so quickly, and another couple would have paid the price.

I turned you into a murderer. My hands slowly formed the core of my sin, following the flow of my thoughts.

You did not. Seeing what those animals were doing to you... That did. His tone turned feral, and the exhale of a deep breath followed. His voice was calmer when he continued. *I would have gone psycho even without the influence of your voice.*

I stood and continued back to the house. The door to the garage was partially opened, and I couldn't remember if I closed it or not. I turned on the light, scanning the space. My gaze locked on the path of blood from the car to where I stood.

I shut the door, crossed to where the keys lay, swiped them off the floor, and popped the trunk. Pulling the suitcase out was much easier than carrying it down from the hotel room. I brought it inside.

The light on our answering machine blinked, but I ignored it. Instead, I pulled out the photo album and took a seat on the couch. My wet clothes squished against the leather, but I didn't care.

With my heart pounding in my throat, I opened to that first picture. The one where Alex wore the grin I loved. I ran my fingers over his face and bit my lower lip to stop the trembling. My ring shined in the overhead light. I closed the book. I couldn't go any further.

I had no idea how I would ever function normally with the pressure of his loss constricting my chest.

One breath at a time, babe. Just one breath at a time.

The End

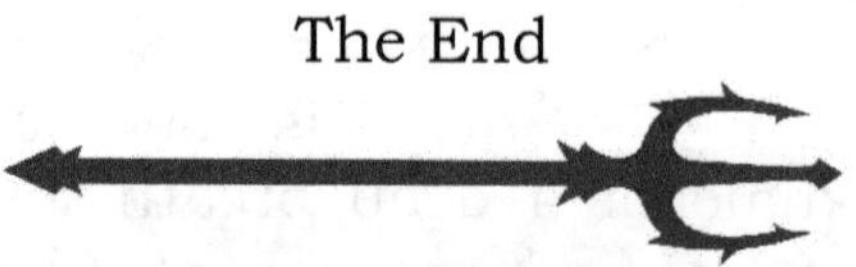

Continue The Paradox Files with book three,
HUNTING THE SIREN.

The Paradox Files - Hunting the Siren

Book 3

In the aftermath of the massacre in Las Vegas, Kylee Paradox has no choice but to run.

Her siren caused innocent lives to be lost, and now Fate is bound to carry out Kylee's punishment for breaking her contract.

If Fate catches her before she can find a loophole, Kylee will be on a one-way train to a tortured eternity in the fiery pits of hell.

Hunting the Siren
Chapter 1

MY MIND KEPT RETURNING to the moment I lost Alex.

I couldn't turn off the litany of mistakes I made that led to such a catastrophe. The entire horrifying ordeal looped endlessly in my head as the television droned in the background. Each time my mind's eye relived him slipping from my grasp, a piece of my heart died.

The wedding album sat untouched on the coffee table. I couldn't get past the first page without my chest constricting tight enough for my breathing to stop. I was sure the rest of the pictures would produce the same acute pain.

The answering machine kept clicking on as the detective in Las Vegas implored me to pick up. I couldn't help the aggravation that flushed over my skin at her stupidity. I had no god damned voice. How the hell was I supposed to answer the phone?

The next time the machine picked up the call and her voice came over the speaker, I actually lifted the receiver, but instead of putting the phone to my ear, I tapped it on the counter. Silence filled the line, and I went to disconnect.

"I'm an idiot," the detective mumbled. "Mrs. Cervas, I apologize for my repeated calls. Tap if you can hear me."

I thought about just hanging up. Instead, I tapped the phone.

"First, are you okay? Tap once for yes, twice for no."

My body had been healed by the ocean, so now it was all a mental game. I knew I wasn't right in the head, but she wasn't asking about my state of mind. I tapped once.

"Thank God," she whispered. She was silent for a moment. "Do you have the ability to video chat?"

I tapped the phone once.

"Do you still have my card?"

I thought about the soggy papers I pulled out of my pocket and tapped the phone twice. She rattled off her video chat number, and I quickly scribbled it down and then put the useless phone back on the charger.

I scanned the apartment for my computer.

Oven. Alex's soft voice filled my brain. Having the narrative of my dead husband in my head for all eternity was going to suck. Each time I heard the musical timbre of his voice, my chest tightened, and my lungs forgot to work.

It took me a moment to recover, and then I turned towards the mostly unused kitchen appliance. If he hadn't told me where he had hidden it on our way to Las Vegas, it would have taken me months to find the damn thing, considering my laziness in the culinary department. I still couldn't believe he sabotaged my electronics and destroyed Fate's instructions in order to make it impossible for me to insist he not come along. If only he had just listened to me in the first place.

I sighed and lugged the laptop back to the couch, propping it up on the wedding album. With a few keystrokes, I had my video call program up and I typed the detective's number. The computer buzzed twice before the frame filled with Detective Mills's face.

"Mrs. Cervas, thank you for calling me back. I apologize for my lack of etiquette before, but we hadn't heard from you, and honestly, I was a little worried."

I am okay; I signed. *I'm sorry I didn't call as soon as I arrived, but I wasn't in any condition to carry on a conversation.* I still wasn't, but at least I didn't look like death anymore. Her concern touched me.

"We have some questions that you might be able to help with."

Her gaze turned away from the camera longer than what I considered normal and her lips scrunched in a way that made me think she was chomping on the inside of her mouth as she formulated her questions. When the detective's gaze came back to the screen, she sighed and shuffled through some papers in her hands.

"You referred to that thing as a monster," she started and left that statement hanging.

I nodded and rolled my hand for her to continue.

"Our forensic experts are stumped. We have no idea what the hell it is."

Do you know what we do? I signed.

"No," Detective Mills said.

We own a paranormal investigation agency.

Her eyebrows went up. "Do you know what that thing was?"

A bicorn. An ancient being that eats the souls of the virtuous. At least that's what the lore says, I signed. I had nothing to lose by giving her this information. I had already lost everything that mattered to me.

"Bicorn?" She glanced at the papers in her hands again. "How do you know?"

You've had missing persons' reports recently, right?

Her eyes narrowed. "Yes," she said, drawing out the s.

We watch for things like that. Plus, it gave us the excuse to finally get married. If we had been wrong, we would have had an exceptional honeymoon. A lump formed in my throat, and I closed my eyes, willing the tears not to spill over. The heat descending on my cheeks told me I failed at that, too.

"You purposely came after that thing?"

I nodded, and another stream of heat flowed from my shut lids.

"Even in your condition?"

I opened my eyes. *What condition?*

She glanced at the paper in her hand. She licked her lips and opened her mouth to speak. It took her a minute before she formed any words, and when she finally looked up at me, she said, "The forensic tests on your blood..." She let out a shrill laugh. "You're pregnant."

My eyes widened, and my jaw fell. The words hit like a brutes punch. My hand dropped to my stomach.

"You didn't know," Detective Mills whispered.

I shook my head, confirming her statement. Stunned didn't describe the numbness that grasped me. Millenniums had passed, and I certainly hadn't been a saint over the years, so this news rattled me. I thought Fate had made me unable to conceive.

Alex's quiet chuckle filled my mind, and I shivered. Our child would never know his father's off-key voice. Our child would never know the strength of his arms or the compassion in his heart. Sadness enveloped me, and with it, another deluge of tears.

"Mrs. Cervas?" Detective Mills said softly. When I looked up, she continued. "You might want to get that checked out just to make sure everything is okay."

I nodded slowly, but I wasn't sure I could bring myself to make a doctor's appointment. I didn't want another tragedy on top of losing Alex. The fear I felt daily when he was by my side was unbearable, but whatever had taken hold of my body the moment the news of my pregnancy tumbled from the detective's lips had me paralyzed in place.

She blew a stream of air out and glanced at another sheet of paper.

I harnessed the untamed stallions that were trampling my heart and pulled myself together.

"Are you okay with continuing?"

Yes. I nodded.

"We wanted to ask if you were sure there was no one else in the building when you left. Perhaps someone hiding?"

I shook my head, and my throat constricted. My heart started that wild gallop again. *I didn't see anyone when I left. Why?*

"We think there might have been someone else there at the time."

I cocked my head as my internal alarms ramped up.

"We think they took one of the cars from the parking lot and drove to the town of West Canyon, which is only a quarter mile down the road." She turned one paper in her hand toward me.

A picture of a red Volvo with the windows blown out filled the computer screen. "Do you remember this car?"

That car had not been in the parking lot with the town car. My heart plummeted and a high-pitched buzz filled my ears. When Detective Mills pulled the photo away, I shook my head.

No. Why?

"The couple driving this car slaughtered an entire neighborhood before an off-duty police officer shot them down."

The buzz in my ears grew, and my vision tunneled.

"Mrs. Cervas? Are you okay?" Detective Mills asked.

I reached out and closed the computer without signing anything. The hot flush of panic jumpstarted my muscles. I moved faster than I had since I stepped back in my home. I vaulted up the stairs and threw a suitcase on the bed.

What are you doing? Alex asked.

I didn't bother answering him. I needed to get out of here as fast as humanly possible. I stopped at my bedside table and grabbed a permanent marker from the drawer. With a shaking hand, I drew a failsafe sigil on my wrist. It looked like a weird weather vane with squiggly lines and dots between the four points. I had painted these on all the doors in this house when we got back from Greece. From that day forward, Fate had never set foot in my home.

I would need to do the car as well, because as fast as I could pack up, I was out of here.

What. Are. You. Doing? Alex blared in my head.

Running.

Silence blanketed me. I still felt Alex's restless soul, so I knew he was in there. I didn't have time for a conversation with him. I needed to get my shit and boogie, because as soon as Fate figured out what happened in Las Vegas, I would be on her hit list.

Once my suitcase was filled to the brim, I took the largest duffel bags I had and hit my weapon rooms. Knives, daggers, machetes, hatchets, arrows, spears, katanas, sabers, spadroons, and all manner of sharp weapons dropped into the biggest bag. All my spices and crystals went into the next one.

In the third bedroom, I stopped in front of the long cabinet that contained Neptune's trident. The trident was the only weapon that could kill me, and I thought twice about freeing it from the boxed trap. I would be safe as long as it was locked away.

I stepped away from the bureau with my cache in hand and headed back to my bedroom. I placed everything on the floor and scanned the room. My gaze landed on Alex's clothes basket. Before awareness settled in, I had crossed and dropped to my knees next to his discarded clothing. I pulled out his old chambray work shirt and brought it to my nose. The subtle smell of his deodorant clung to the shirt, along with a mix of sweat and aftershave.

Kylee. His sigh filled my world.

I slipped the shirt on over mine and started down with the first group of bags. When the trunk was full with the packed luggage, I pulled the permanent ink pen from my pocket and drew the same sigil on the inside of the trunk before I closed it. I stood with the keys in my hand.

I didn't have a destination or even a plan in mind. Wherever I ended up had to be near the ocean. There was no other way I would survive. The tropics were the logical choice, but I wasn't getting past the border patrol with the trunk full of weapons. The Gulf of Mexico would be the next logical place, but I knew it would only be a matter of time before someone found me.

The Pacific Northwest was too close.

I needed to figure out a place they would never look for me. And I had to get there without traveling a shore route. My gaze drew to the back door and the sea beyond as I entertained a comment Alex had made on our way to the desert.

Use the fish cooler, Alex replied.

I nodded and jammed the cooler in the back seat. With two gallon jugs, I jogged to the shore, filled them, and trotted back to fill the cooler. I made four trips and then one more to fill up the jugs. With ten gallons of water, I was ready. I paused at the driver's door and glanced at the house.

I pocketed my keys and went back inside for two things. My hidden stash of cash and the wedding album. With the attaché case full of cash stowed under the driver's seat and the wedding album in my old backpack, along with my purse on the passenger seat, I pulled out of my garage.

I took one last look at the house I shared with Alex and pulled away, heading east with only a random thought.

Maybe I would stop to see the world's largest ball of twine.

Hunting the Siren
Chapter 2

MY EYELIDS DROOPED AS the sign announcing Phoenix passed. I needed to find a hotel to crash, but I wanted to at least be on Interstate 17, heading towards Flagstaff first. Luckily, within a couple of miles after merging onto 17, signs for a Red Roof Inn exit saved me from dozing at the wheel.

I didn't even remember my head hitting the pillow.

The light blazing in through the open curtains yanked me from a pleasant dream. Alex's embrace faded, and reality crashed into me. I rolled onto my back and stared at the ceiling. Emptiness filled me to where I entertained just lying in the bed until my cells broke down.

Thirst drove me to my feet. I shuffled into the little hotel bathroom and unwrapped one of the plastic cups. After three cups of cold water, I met my gaze in the mirror. My eyes widened at the state of my hair. I had only been away from the ocean for less than twenty-four hours, but my hair looked like I had been desert-bound for three days. A dry husk.

I turned and glanced at the clock. It was barely seven in the morning. Panic filled me. My decomposition was happening at a speed that would lead me to death a hell of a lot faster than an intervention from Fate. I grabbed the hotel key and went out to the car, grabbing one of the gallon containers. Once inside the room again, I plugged up the tub drain and poured the gallon into the shallow bath.

The seawater clung to my skin, soaking in like I was a sponge. The progression of hydration scaled up my abdomen to my scalp. Everything tingled as the pirated ocean water performed its healing magic. When all that was left in the tub were droplets of water, I stood and glanced in the mirror.

My lips formed a silent *Damn*.

See, I told you it would work, Alex said.

I huffed and toweled off the dampness still clinging to my skin. *I shouldn't have looked like that for at least another day,* I thought as I pulled on the same clothes I had on last night. My hand dropped to my stomach as a wave of terror gripped me.

What if the child growing inside me was a siren?

Alex remained silent in my head, but his restless shifting didn't ease my fear. I packed up my things and headed out again. While the hotel offered a continental breakfast, I didn't feel like stale bagels and donuts. What I wanted was something quick and full of protein. On my way to the highway entrance, I pulled into a fast-food restaurant and ordered an egg sandwich in the takeout window. A few minutes later, I was on the road with food in my stomach and no actual plan for where I was going to end my journey.

Go through Sedona.

I glanced at the exit signs for State Route 179 heading towards Sedona.

Please. You deserve to see some of the beauty of the land since you're making this suicidal trek across the country.

It's not suicide. It's survival, I thought.

Alex didn't answer. The exit was fast approaching. I rolled my eyes before swerving onto the ramp, giving in to his silent protest. The flatter landscape gave way to more hills and valleys, and then the painted rocks came into view. Alex was right—this wasn't something to miss.

My stomach growled, and my attention snapped to The Red Rock Cafe on the left side of the road. The wheel turned before I had even made the decision. It had only been a little over two hours since I last ate, and I was ravenous.

There wasn't much of a crowd in the restaurant. I was seated at the front window by a young waitress named Sandy. Her glowing smile made my morning, and her bright cheery attitude was a far cry from some of the waitresses in San Diego who had that entitled point of view.

I scanned the menu, and the minute I put it down, Sandy was there with her pad and pen. I pointed towards a picture on the menu.

"You want the Eggs Benedict Florentine?"

I nodded and then flipped it to where the drinks were and tapped orange juice from the list.

"Orange juice?"

I nodded again with a smile.

"Large or small?" she asked.

I spelled out *large* with my hand, and when she raised her eyebrows, I held my hands out in a wide span.

"Large it is." She gave me a nod.

Thank you, I signed and waited for my meal.

Sandy brought my orange juice and scampered off to take another order. I glanced out the window, watching the slow-moving traffic.

The pace of the cars lulled me into a bit of a trance.

"THE NUMBER OF IMBECILES you need to collect for me has tripled because of Death's son," Fate had said, spitting the words out with venom. "He opened a breach in York that let loose some serious monstrosities."

Her red dress flared around her as she flipped through the pages of her book, sneering at each entry like she smelled something sour.

When her gaze lifted to mine, she snarled, "What the hell are you waiting for?"

I turned with my instructions and headed back to the house to collect my things for the next hunt.

I SAT UP STRAIGHTER in the booth and reached into my pocket for my phone. My hand came up empty and I berated myself for not grabbing any form of electronics for this trip.

I glanced at my pocketbook and pulled it over, rifling through it to see if perhaps Alex's phone had been tucked away while we were in Las Vegas, but I came up empty. I leaned back in the seat just as Sandy stepped to the side of the table with my meal.

I looked at the plate and sighed.

"Is there something wrong with your meal?" she asked with genuine concern.

I shook my head and made the hand gesture for a pen. She handed me her pen and a clean sheet from her pad.

I left my phone at home and needed to do a quick search on the internet. I handed her the paper and shrugged.

She pulled her smart phone out of her pocket, unlocked it, and handed it to me with a smile. "You can use my phone," she said. "I'll come get it after I go give those folks their food, okay?"

I gave her a thumbs-up and typed in York in the internet search box. Too many entries came back for unrelated things, like colleges and even New York City, which wasn't a place I wanted to hide out in. There were just too many people, and while the Hudson led to the ocean, it was not the most ideal place to recuperate.

I refined my search to the town of York and the results came back with five options in the United States. Wisconsin was out. I searched on the map for each of the others and there were only two options close enough to the shore to be viable. Between the two, the one in Maine was actually right on the shore.

I exited out of the search engine and put the phone on the corner of the table before I dug into my breakfast. The egg was perfect, and I closed my eyes, letting the creamy texture of the hollandaise sauce coat my mouth before I swallowed.

"Did you find what you needed?"

I glanced up at Sandy with a smile.

The odds were that York, Maine, wasn't the same place that Fate had been talking about when she went on her mini-rant so many years ago, but at least it gave me a true destination.

I made the sign for *thank you* and continued eating the meal.

"You're welcome." She crossed back to the counter.

When I finished my meal, I waved for the check. The total bill was less than ten dollars, but I pulled out one hundred and ten dollars, leaving it on the table without waiting for Sandy to pick it up.

Just as I was getting into the driver's side, Sandy stepped out of the door.

"Ma'am?" she called, holding up the bill and the cash. "I think you made a mistake."

I glanced over the top of the car, shook my head, and gave her a thumbs-up.

The girl beamed. "Thank you!"

I slid into my car and pulled away as Sandy gave me a hearty wave. With a smile on my face, I headed north towards Denver. As soon as I stopped for the night, I'd search out one of those big electronic stores and get myself a global positioning system and a computer. I wasn't sure a phone was such a good idea unless I bought one of those prepaid things just until I found a permanent residence. I wanted nothing linked to San Diego.

My wandering mind snapped back to my current surroundings as I pulled out of the populated town into the desert. The colors and textures of the hills to my right kept pulling my attention away from the road. The reds, greens, oranges, and grays all blended in a symphony of colors like I had never witnessed.

Alex was right—this landscape was as breathtaking as the open ocean. I was in awe of my surroundings, and thankful that the traffic had thinned out so I could gawk. By the time I merged onto 89A in Sedona, I was in sensory overload and my gas tank was on empty.

I pulled into the next gas station and went inside to use the facilities before grabbing some munchies and drinks. I also paid for the gas to fill up. While I filled up the tank, my gaze kept going towards those painted hills. I sighed. I hadn't ever ventured far from the coastline, and now a sour taste of regret filled my mouth.

I drove away from the station without a second glance. The chips and juices I had on the front seat were gone by the time I hit Flagstaff.

While there, I pulled off to fill up my tank and my juice reserves. I glanced in the mirror at the state of my skin and hair and sighed. The desert dryness was sucking the moisture right out of me, but I couldn't use another gallon of seawater until I had my morning bath.

As I paid for my juice and water, I reached over and added a map of the United States onto the pile. I also grabbed a package of cookies and some Snickers bars on a whim. With a smile, I paid the total and once outside by my car; I dumped everything in the front seat.

I unfolded the map after I pumped gas and plotted my course. The question remained. Do I continue on Interstate 40 through more desert than I cared to see or head north to Interstate 70 and the Rocky Mountains?

Alex remained quiet, waiting for me to pick the route. I traced my finger along the highways and smiled when Interstate 70 ran through Kansas, home to the world's largest ball of twine.

If I was taking a road trip with my dead husband, I might as well hit one of his bucket list items along the way. I tracked an eight-hour drive from Flagstaff, which would put me in the Grand Junction, Colorado area. I thought about pushing ahead more, but I knew by the time eight hours passed, I would be ready to eat a restaurant and pass out from the food coma.

I folded the map to Alex's soft chuckle in my mind. *Twine it is*, I thought and pulled onto the road, following the signs to US 89 North.

It took me a little over an hour to get to US 160, and the country I traveled was the most desolate of deserts. In some areas, there wasn't even a bush in sight. Just the thought of being stuck on this sand-filled land gave me a shiver so severe, I almost had to stop.

I stopped at the junction of 264 to refuel and relieve myself. A quick glance in the rearview mirror almost made me break open the cooler in the back. I matched what I looked like just a mere eight hours ago. I bought a bag of plastic cups and poured a little saltwater into the plastic. Not even a quarter cup, and set it in my cup holder next to a newly opened juice.

I pulled back onto the road and stuck my fingers into the warm liquid. Within seconds, my hand absorbed the seawater, leaving nothing in the cup. The effects were barely visible. My heart thundered in my chest, drowning out the drone of the wheels on the asphalt.

I passed the Elephant Feet landmark with only a cursory look and pressed the pedal to the floor, flying down the open highway without caring how fast I was going. I just wanted out of the desert and away from this wasteland that was draining every drop of water from my body.

Signs for Kayenta, Arizona and Navajo Nation blurred by. It wasn't until I saw the signs for US 191 North did I hear the siren behind me. I glanced at the speedometer and gasped. My needle was buried beyond the 110mph mark. I slowed and finally pulled over to the side of the road.

Why did you stop? He's going to call your license in, and you know what that means, don't you?

I ignored Alex. I knew well enough. If the officer called this in, Fate would know where I was. I didn't know how fast she could get someone out here, but just the thought of going up against her made my stomach clench.

I rolled the window down. The desert heat hit, and my throat tightened. All the juice in my stomach rolled. I covered my mouth just as the officer leaned in the window.

"Where are you going in such a hurry?"

I swallowed the bile that rose in the back of my throat. *I'm visiting family in Colorado,* I signed.

Then I covered my mouth again as my stomach did a slow roll. I threw open the door, and all the juice from the morning ride came barreling out, all over the officer's shoes. He jumped back as I spit and shivered, closing the door again.

He glanced at the steaming mess at his feet and then at the contents of the passenger seat before returning his gaze to me.

I guess I'm not handling pregnancy very well, I signed.

His forehead creased.

I touched my throat and shook my head.

"You can't talk?"

I shook my head again.

"But you understand what I'm saying."

I nodded as the stagnant scent of orange juice and bile rose from the steaming dirt. I closed my eyes and swallowed a second burn of bile.

He pressed his lips together. "Move up a couple of feet, please." He pointed ahead. His other hand remained on his firearm.

I put the car in drive. Temptation dragged nails over my skin, and I almost pushed the gas pedal to the ground. I curbed the impulse because I knew if I jumped the gun, my license plate would be called in and a chase would follow. I wasn't in any condition to deal with a night in jail.

He stepped to the window again just as my emotions ran away from me. My chin quivered and my eyes filled with tears. I made the motion of a pregnant woman over my stomach just as the tears spilled over.

"Pregnant?" he asked.

I nodded and made a writing motion.

He pulled out a pen from his shirt and handed it to me along with the back of a ticket stub.

I wrote, *I'm sorry. I was trying to get to my parents' place in Colorado before that happened. I'm not handling this pregnancy very well.* I handed him the pen and paper back.

He gave me a knowing smile. "Ginger ale and Social Teas are the only thing my wife can keep down these days. You have a whole boatload of acidic stuff on that seat. That doesn't help."

I glanced at my stash of empty wrappers and juice containers.

"Sugar and preservatives." He chuckled. "No wonder you hurled. Stick with fruits for your sugar fix. It seems to help my wife... and it will

319

help get rid of that death's door look." He stood taller and cleared his throat. "I'm going to need your license, ma'am."

My heart plummeted as I reached for my pocketbook. My hope of not getting reported died at his request. My license still had my last name as Paradox, not Cervas. My chest tightened. If I let him call my license number in, Fate would have a digital mark as to where I was.

I had no choice in the matter. It was either hand over the license, run, or use my siren. The last two options had consequences I couldn't live with, so I handed him my license while trying to control my chin tremble.

He took my license and made his way back to his car, circumventing the vomit. I sat staring in the rearview mirror as he typed in my information. My heart pumped in my chest, making my fingers and toes tingle and my head feel light. I wiped my tears away in disgust. Crying was never my thing, and annoyance filtered through at my inability to stop the tear parade.

The officer came back and handed me my license, his expression more serious than it was when he first pulled me over. "Your license is clear of any tickets, but you need to promise me you won't speed like you were. That usually comes with a hefty fine for reckless driving, but I'm giving you a break."

I nodded and signed, *I promise,* then dumped the license in my pocketbook. I added, *thank you.*

"Go on." He tilted his head towards the road.

I pulled out and kept to the speed limit until I crossed into Utah via US 191. The three-hour ride on US 191 took me from the desert flats of Arizona to the rocky terrain of Utah on one side and Colorado mountains on the other. While I had seen the Sierra Nevada range in California, this was even more majestic.

I stopped to fill up once I turned onto US 70 East. While the gas pumped, I strolled inside the shop and grabbed ginger ale like the officer had suggested. They had nothing else that tickled my fancy, so I went back out to the car.

Scanning the map, my gaze landed on a town south of where I was headed. I laughed silently at the name.

Paradox, Colorado.

If I had been in Fate's shoes, I probably would've scoured that town first. I wished I hadn't revealed all that I had when she gave me the Las Vegas job. If I had known I would be on the hunted list, I never would have divulged my weakness.

The cop had my license plate and the make and model of the vehicle. I sighed and glanced around at the cameras in the area before glancing at my wrist. The sigil I drew had faded.

An icy breeze bit at my skin. I was well aware of the ease in tracking someone with the minimal information Fate had. I shivered, wondering just how prudent it was to remain on my current track.

I figured once I hit Grand Junction, I'd have to reassess my journey and find a tattoo parlor to make this sigil permanent.

With a full tank and another hour or so on the road before I hit my destination, I pushed myself onward, even though every muscle in my body wanted to curl up and sleep. I didn't bother glancing in the rearview mirror. I already knew the state of my deteriorating body.

Hunting the Siren
Chapter 3

GRAND JUNCTION, COLORADO WAS the biggest town I had been through since I left Phoenix and it was a welcomed sight. I pulled off of US 70 onto North Avenue. I passed a couple of motels, but none of them had any places to eat that struck a chord. I didn't want to drive for food either. I needed to stretch my legs as much as I needed a seawater bath. As I passed the medical center, I spied an inn with a diner next door and pulled in with no nagging urge to keep going like all the other ones.

With food and sleep at the top of my list, I parked next to the office of the Palomino Inn. The desk clerk didn't look up from the television when I walked in. I stood at the counter while his gaze was glued to the squawk box and when he still didn't divert his eyes from whatever action was playing across the screen; I tapped the counter to get his attention.

When he finally looked up, his eyebrows rose and he scrambled to his feet, his cheeks reddening. "I'm sorry, ma'am. What can I do for you?"

I put up my index finger.

"One minute?" he asked while he chewed a wad of gum. His gaze drifted back to the television set.

I pulled a room pamphlet from the carousel next to me and pointed to it. The movement caught his attention, and I held up the picture of a room.

"Oh, you want a room?"

I nodded and said *yes* in sign language as well.

"You a deaf mute or something?" he asked.

I shook my head and tapped my throat.

"So you can hear me?"

I nodded.

"That will be fifty dollars for the night," he said, his gaze drifting again.

I really wanted to look over at the screen to see what had him so enthralled, but I thought twice when the redness in his cheeks didn't fade. He took the money I handed him and then hastily turned to grab one of the room keys off the wall.

"If you need anything, just holler," he said as he handed me the key. He blinked, and then his eyes widened. "Sorry." He laughed a high-pitched laugh. "You know what I mean."

I gave him a thumbs-up and took my leave. Once inside the room, I carted in another gallon of water. One look in the mirror told me I needed to do this now and not in the morning. My eyes were sunken and my skin pale and shallow in the cheeks. My hair looked like dried wheat. I didn't know if food would revitalize me at all at this point.

The tub had an old rubber stopper that didn't fit well, so instead of pouring the water into the tub and then stepping in, I sat down in the cold porcelain and drizzled the water over my head. What pooled in the tub absorbed into my skin moments later. Even my hands transformed, hydrating before my eyes.

I sat until every drop was taken into my skin and then stood, toweling off what remnants remained before dressing. My jeans hung on my hips, and I cursed that I never grabbed a belt. I slipped a camisole over my bra and pulled on one of Alex's old chambray work shirts. The shirt felt soft against my skin and I welcomed it as much as I had the seawater.

On the short walk to the diner, I noticed the shopping plaza next door contained not one, but two tattoo parlors. I nearly laughed at my luck.

Alex remained silent in my head. I wasn't sure if he just didn't want to spoil the upbeat mood I was in or if he just had nothing to say.

My heart squeezed. I missed him, and the weight of the loss crushed down on me to the point I didn't want to go inside the eatery, because if the waitress asked how I was doing, I might burst into tears like I had when the cop pulled me over.

I stood on the sidewalk, just staring at the little diner. It was open twenty-four hours, so I could stand in this paralysis all night if necessary. My gaze moved to the adjoining plaza. The sign for Native Ink mocked me.

My feet turned and moved towards the tattoo shop instead. Crying while a needle full of ink pierced my skin was much more palatable than bawling alone at a diner. I stepped inside the reception area.

A girl with jet-black hair and a nose piercing looked up and smiled. "What can we do for you today, ma'am?"

I hated being called ma'am, but I guessed with the wedding ring still on my finger, she couldn't really refer to me as a miss anymore.

Tattoo. I signed and walked to the counter, making the motion for pen and paper. She didn't seem the least bit fazed by my sign language and handed me both a pen and paper with a smile. I took a few minutes to draw the sigil in detail for her. Once I was sure it was exactly right, I handed my drawing to her and pointed to the back of my shoulder.

She glanced at the detailed drawing and nodded. "You want it this size?" She held up the paper.

I nodded.

"Turn around," she said, and I did. "You want this on your shoulder?" She touched the muscular part of my shoulder. "Or here on your shoulder blade?" She tapped lower on my back, right over my shoulder blade.

I put up two fingers to indicate her second choice.

"Shoulder blade, it is," she said.

I smiled, turning back with a nod.

"That will be two hundred dollars, please."

I pulled the cash out from my wallet and handed it over.

The receptionist smiled and waved to the couch. "Tim will be out in a moment. He is just finishing up with a client. Please have a seat."

I signed, *thank you.*

She signed back, *you're welcome*, before she disappeared into the back with my drawing.

I turned my attention to the various tattoo choices mounted on the walls.

The man that appeared with my paper in his hand was built solid and loomed tall from my perch in the chair. His expression was serious as he studied the piece of paper in his hand, but the moment he looked up, his face broke out in a friendly smile that put me at ease.

"Jules tells me you want this on your shoulder blade?" He turned the picture around.

I nodded.

"I'm Tim, but everyone here calls me Lil' Mex." He extended his hand.

I stood, shaking it. As soon as our hands parted, I signed my name.

Lil' Mex turned to his receptionist who took her seat at the counter.

"She said her name is Kylee."

"You read lips, Kylee?" he asked when he turned back to me.

I shook my head and pointed to my ears
before I gave a thumbs-up. Then I touched my
throat with a shake of my head.

A crease appeared between his eyes. "You can
hear, but you can't talk?"

I gave him another thumbs-up with a smile.

"Have you ever had a tattoo?"

I signed *no* and shook my head.

"Okay." He nodded for me to follow him.

I stepped into a small hallway that led to an
immaculate room with three chairs and a table.
The table reminded me of the physical therapy
tables that Alex had to use when he hurt his
back. A sterile scent hung on the air and Lil'
Mex pointed me to one of the low back chairs
while he took a seat on the other side of the
room with my picture.

He traced it out on paper and then showed
his drawing to me. He had captured the sigil
perfectly, so I gave him a thumbs-up. I peeled off
my work shirt as he crossed and sat down,
spinning the chair so my back faced him.

Lil' Mex cleaned the spot on my shoulder
blade and then pressed the paper he used to
draw the sigil onto the same spot. He waited a
minute and then peeled the paper away.

"Let's make sure this is on where you'd like
it." He waved for me to follow him to the
mirrored wall and handed me a mirror.

I looked at the reflection of the outline on my
shoulder blade, then handed him the mirror and
smiled. *Perfect,* I signed.

He gave me a nod and led me back to the
chair. As soon as I settled in, he pressed the ink
gun to my back. The low hum of the tool filled

my senses, as did the sensation of being scratched. Seconds later, the hum stopped.

"How does that feel?" Lil' Mex asked.

I gave him a thumbs-up. Even if it had been like someone tearing my skin off with a blowtorch, I would have given the thumbs-up. I needed the sigil permanent. It would keep my location a secret, and the one I drew on my arm was just about gone.

Lil' Mex hummed along with the song piped into the studio as he crafted my tattoo. Occasionally, he wiped my back and went back to finishing my ink.

My stomach growled loud enough for Lil' Mex to pause.

I'm okay, I signed with my left hand.

He nodded and went back to work. The hum of the needle stopped again, and he wiped my back with a satisfied nod. "Take a look." He handed me the mirror again.

I stepped in front of the wall mirror, turning my back to it, and lifted the handheld one. I studied the design with a critical eye, making sure every dot and symbol was placed just so. If even one squiggle or dot was misplaced, the tattoo wouldn't protect me at all.

That looks really good, Alex whispered in my head. *Damn sexy.*

Heat filled my cheeks, and I moved my gaze from my back to my own eyes, where Alex hid. *Shush.* I couldn't have him talking to me about things that were sexy. It just slammed home my loss all the more.

Satisfied with Lil' Mex's craftsmanship, I lowered the mirror and gave him a smile and a nod. He waved me back to the seat, where he cleaned off the tattoo and covered it with plastic.

He pulled off his gloves and turned the chair towards me. "Since it's already dinner time, I'd suggest you keep that film on until morning. Then wash with soap and water and apply moisturizing cream to the area at least twice a day." He stepped to the desk and pulled a sheet of paper. "You can get specific washes and creams here if you'd like, or go to the local drugstore. Just don't get anything with fragrances, and I'd suggest an antibiotic cream for tomorrow and the day after if you don't buy the brands we offer here."

He handed me the sheet which held the specific after-care instructions along with the brands of creams and body washes they recommended using. I read through the instructions while I pulled the work shirt back over my shoulders.

My stomach growled again, enough to bring heat to my cheeks and a smile to Lil' Mex's face.

"If you have any questions, feel free to stop back in, or you can text us any time."

Thank you, I signed and wandered to the front desk where they had after-care products for sale. I purchased the ultimate tattoo care box and headed out the door with my instructions and after-care kit in a bag.

The diner beckoned me, and I crossed the parking lot directly to the little food shop before my stomach rumbling turned sour. Once seated, my gaze kept drifting from the menu in my hand to the rotating dessert display. Specifically, the chocolate cake. Every time that sucker came around, it was like a magnet for my eyes.

I sighed and forced myself to pick something. I didn't want steak or chicken or fish. I didn't want salad. All I seemed to want was the entire chocolate cake in the display case.

The waitress came to the table with her pad in hand. Her dark hair was piled on her head in a messy up-do, and it bobbed as she stood waiting for me to make a decision.

"Do you need more time?" she asked.

I scanned the menu again, and when my gaze fell on the all-day breakfast menu, my stomach made a growling noise that would have put a rabid dog to shame. I tuned the menu towards her and tapped the Eggs Benedict Hearty Breakfast, which included hash browns along with the main course.

"Eggs Benedict. Will that be all?"

I put up two fingers.

"Two servings?" she asked with her eyebrows arched.

I nodded and then tapped the orange juice.

"Two?"

I shook my head and put up a single finger. *And water*, I signed.

She stared at my hands and then looked at me. "I'm sorry, sweetie, I don't read sign language."

I made the motion for the pen and paper, and she handed me the order slip and her pen. I wrote ice water on her sheet and handed both the pad and pen back to her.

She smiled. "Coming right up."

My gaze kept traveling to the chocolate cake, and every time, my mouth watered. I tried focusing elsewhere, but it was no use. By the time the waitress came with my food, I was ready to break through the glass and shove the cake into my mouth. Manners be damned.

The moment she put the eggs in front of me, my rumbling stomach set me into action. I must have made a spectacle of myself, because when I looked up from my nearly empty plates, a few of the patrons near my table were staring at me.

Heat filled my entire face, and I shrugged and made the motion of a pregnant belly. A few of them smiled and turned their attention away, but one teenager kept staring at me in a way that made me shift in my seat.

The waitress stepped into my line of sight with a smile. "How was it?" she asked as she picked up my plate.

I gave her a smile. My stomach was sated for the time being, but I still craved that damn chocolate cake.

"Is there anything else I can get you?"

"I pointed to the cake as it passed on the rotating shelf."

"Chocolate cake?" she asked.

I gave her a thumbs-up.

"With a scoop of vanilla ice cream?"

I licked my lips and nodded.

She cleared the plates and the kid that had been staring at me was gone. The waitress cut a piece of cake and scooped a generous amount of ice cream on top. The drizzle of chocolate sauce over the ice cream secured her a hefty tip. My mouth watered as she crossed the diner with the cake in one hand and a water pitcher in the other.

The first bite transcended me to heaven, and a hum started in the back of my throat. I swallowed hard, shutting the purr down. As much as my siren wanted to sing the praises of this dessert, the last thing I wanted to do was infect these people, even though the cake was as close to orgasmic as I was ever going to get again.

You'll find someone else.

Alex's voice invaded my bliss, turning my meal sour. I stared at the half-eaten cake and my throat tightened. My appetite vanished along with my dry eyes. Mist blurred my vision. I took a deep inhalation before slowly letting it out.

His words were not welcomed.

I wasn't ever going to let anyone as close to my heart as I had let Alex get.

My hand dropped to my belly, and a chill gripped me. I knew my thoughts were a lie. I already had a life that I cared about beyond my own, and I would do whatever was necessary to keep our child safe.

Hunting the Siren
Chapter 4

AN ITCH ON MY shoulder pulled me from a sound sleep. I reached back, and my fingers skimmed over plastic. My eyes popped open, and I glanced around, momentarily disoriented and reaching for Alex.

The empty bed met my hand. The dream of being with him seemed so real. Aching loss gripped my chest, and I closed my eyes, wishing for the dream instead of this vast emptiness in my soul.

Getting my bearings, I sat up and looked at the dresser across the room. My backpack sat unopened since I packed the wedding album and my cash into it outside of the hotel last night. That seemed more pragmatic than leaving it in the car, like I had done down in Phoenix.

The tattoo kit sat on top of the backpack, just waiting for me to open it. My overnight bag was less compact. It sat open with my clothing in a chaotic jumble. I had done nothing to neaten it since I showered last night. My gaze landed on the last gallon jug of seawater. I bit my lip. The skin cracked, and I licked blood from the split, wondering just what the hell I was going to do when I ran out of seawater.

My deterioration without the elixir seemed on overdrive, and I only had the big cooler of saltwater left in the back seat of my car.

A shiver skipped up my spine, and I trembled with the force of it. Kicking off the sheets, I avoided the mirrors and focused on a hot shower and taking care of my tattoo before I embarked on absorbing the gallon of seawater in the room.

Once I finished doing as the instructions stated, I toweled off and jammed the plug into the drain. Instead of pouring the gallon over my head like I had done the previous night, I drizzled it down the front of my body, careful to avoid my tattooed shoulder. I wasn't sure how the tattoo would react to the salt, and I didn't want to ruin my illusion of safety.

The salt water never even hit the floor of the tub. It absorbed on contact, and the effects were immediate. I swore I could feel my cells expand, hydrated and happy. My stomach growled, and I sighed. I needed to get on the road, but all I craved were those damned eggs Benedict, which was not a quick drive-through meal.

I rubbed my belly. *Today, you'll just have to settle for an egg on a muffin or something because we need to get to the ocean.* An ungodly rumble was my jilted stomach's answer, but I had to get moving if I had a prayer of reaching Missouri by nightfall.

I grabbed a quick breakfast and topped my car off at a roadside gas and donut shop. The roads wound higher into the hills, and mountains surrounded the road, daunting at times and offering wide vistas at other times. It was grand and beautiful in the same way the Painted Desert had been.

I was so consumed with the scenery and focusing on staying on the winding roads that I hadn't touched either the snacks or drinks piled around my backpack on the front seat. Entering Vale was like entering something out of a fairy tale with the amounts of green surrounding me. The river that paralleled the highway drew my attention, and I sighed. I wish fresh water had the same effect on me that the ocean did. I could gladly get lost in this lush land.

As soon as I passed through Denver, my ears popped as the elevation changed as dramatically as the landscape. The flat lands lay before me. I ended up stopping in Watkins to fill up and grab a bite to eat. My lips were already dry, and one glance at my reflection was enough for me to scoop a cupful of water from the cooler in the back seat and stick my finger in it.

The water disappeared almost as fast as it had this morning. I glanced in the mirror, and the creases around my eyes filled in with plump and hydrated skin.

With my appearance more normal, I stepped out of the car and headed into the little diner for my lunch. As I sat down, I scanned the restaurant out of habit. My gaze landed on a familiar face, and I shivered. The teen who had been staring at me in Grand Junction sat at the counter. His eyes were on my reflection in the mirror behind the counter.

I went to stand, and the world tilted. I sat back down, hard. My stomach cramped, and I nearly doubled over from the muscle spasm. The child inside me demanded food, so whether or not the kid was following me, I couldn't leave without following the demands of my body.

"Are you okay?"

I glanced up at the young waitress staring down at me, and I forced myself to straighten. I nodded and pointed to the menu item.

"Eggs Benedict?" she asked.

I confirmed with a nod and the sign for *yes,* then tapped orange juice on the menu.

"Orange juice," she said. "Can I get you any coffee?"

I shook my head. I didn't need caffeine. Not at this point, anyway. I still had five hours or so before I got to see the big ball of twine and then another three or four hours after that to cross over the state line into Missouri.

The waitress smiled and turned, her blonde ponytail whipping around with her.

The teenager was no longer at the counter. My gaze darted around and then out at the parking lot. There was no sign of the stranger. However, the feeling of being watched still clung to me. Unease filtered into my bones right beside the gnawing hunger in my belly.

Watching the parking lot, I let my mind wander, trying to pinpoint the moment I got pregnant. It couldn't have been in Las Vegas. That would have been way too soon.

I think it was the night on the beach.

Alex's voice filled my head. I smiled at the memory. It had been late, and we had been out watching the sunset, drinking wine. Lots of wine. The night was a blur of discarded clothing and laughter as we dared to make love out in the open, wondering if someone was going to stumble upon us. We had moved from the beach to the shower and then to the bed until we exhausted ourselves.

My smile faded, and the pang of loss squeezed my heart.

I will miss that, too, Alex whispered.

He didn't know the half of it. He was the only man who I gave everything to. Sure, I had been married and thought I had been in love before, but all the other relationships I attempted paled compared to the connection I had with Alex. I tried to ignore it for years, but every time he came and sat down next to me on the beach, it was as if the other piece of my soul had arrived. I'm not sure he understood how frightening that was for me and how much of a loss his death was.

I know. I am part of you now, so I exist inside your pain.

"Here you go," the waitress said, startling me out of my thoughts. She placed both my meal and my orange juice on the table. "If you need anything else, just give me a shout."

I gave her a tight smile, and she bounced away to take the next table's order. I forced the food down my throat despite the complete lack of appetite that missing Alex brought on. If I skipped the meal, I would pay dearly for it later, and I couldn't stop every five minutes to throw up, although I wasn't sure food was the answer to that dilemma.

I waved for the check as I downed the last of the orange juice. I covered my meal and a decent tip and headed to the car, hyperaware of my surroundings. Despite the lingering feeling of being watched, I focused on my tattoo maintenance, rubbing the lotion into the back of my shoulder before I continued my cross-country trek.

I pulled out on I-70 eastbound and scanned the radio stations, settling on one that boasted current country hits. God bless him, Alex sang along in my head. His endearing off-tune timbre tickled me enough so I wanted to join him. But I knew better, even on this nearly empty straightaway. My siren voice could create a toxic poison, so I settled for just tapping my foot in rhythm.

When I pulled off I-70 and headed towards Cawker City, Alex chuckled.

What?

Really? You are going to see the biggest ball of twine?

I smiled and glanced in the rearview mirror, meeting my gaze. The one Alex shared with me. It had been his joke, and I thought it would please him to follow through on it now that I'd subjected myself to a long, landlocked trip.

His laughter filled my ears. It was filled with the same type of joy found in a child, and it sent a thrill through me. While I could never cuddle in his arms again, still being able to hear his laughter helped ease my pain.

He was the only damned soul that communicated directly with me. All the others faded to nothing when they died. Sure, I felt their energy, but it joined with mine, making me stronger and more resilient. Alex was different. I had lured him with my siren to save him from the bicorn. It was the only way, and it killed a part of me. If the bicorn hadn't killed him, I would have had to do it. Maybe not initially, but eventually, as the madness overtook him.

I followed the signs and finally pulled up in front of the building, announcing the biggest ball of twine. Alex giggled again, and I couldn't help but join him as I walked into the little store to buy my ticket and use the restroom.

Minutes later, I stood in the covered gazebo and stared at the ten-foot ball of twine. I pressed my lips together against a smile and turned to leave.

A shiver gripped me as I thought I glimpsed the same face I had seen earlier. Alex quieted down in my mind, too. My intuition prickled, and I scanned the horizon as I picked up my pace to a slow jog.

My heart pounded in my chest. I caught the camera on the side of the welcome center out of the corner of my eye and a frigid chill layered on my skin. There was only one person trying to track me down. As I turned the corner, I bumped smack into the teenager I had seen at the coffee shop.

He stumbled backwards, both eyebrows rising in surprise as he stared at me. His shock quickly turned, and his eyes narrowed as he fumbled with his pockets.

My hands clenched. As did my jaw. This close up, I could see under the facade. He wasn't human, but I had no idea what kind of beast he was. I just knew he was tracking me. Before he could free his hands from his pockets, I struck out, punching him in the throat hard enough to do significant damage.

I wasn't sure how much intelligence Fate had on me, but I was just as deadly with my hands as I was with any manner of weapons.

He dropped to his knees and clasped his throat. I skirted around him, jumped in my car, and peeled out before Fate and her minions arrived.

I didn't look back. Instead, I floored the gas until my needle was buried beyond a hundred miles per hour. The car shook with the speed. I had an open road in front of me, and a quick glance in the mirror showed me there was no tail following me.

Idiot, I scolded myself. I should have been more cautious and diligent after lunch. Seeing the same face in two different locations was a problem. It meant Fate knew the path I was taking across the country. I glanced at the map on my passenger seat, wondering if her lackey looked at where I was headed. It was there in black and white had he bothered to look in the window.

My heart raced. I tried to get hold of the jitters accosting me. I glanced back at the road and my eyes nearly jumped out of my skull. I swerved to avoid hitting Leviathan, a monster the size of a Tyrannosaurus Rex, who was blocking the road.

I hadn't seen Leviathan since I snuck out of the gates of hell with my brother. The shock of seeing him in his natural form and not a glamor sucked all the moisture from my mouth. If he was here, then Fate and Death weren't far behind.

I slammed on my brakes to make the narrow space between his legs. Everything in my car shifted, including the cooler in the back seat. Water rushed across my feet. I silently cursed. If I made it out of here alive, my means of rejuvenating while away from the ocean had just been drastically drained. Damn it all to hell.

By some miracle, I cleared Leviathan's legs and continued careening down the highway, unsure of whether to head north or continue to I-70. The faster I got to a shoreline, any shoreline, the better. I turned off the main road, jostling the remaining seawater in the cooler and on the floor.

Find a more populated road.

I couldn't have agreed more with Alex's suggestion because Leviathan wouldn't be caught dead in his native form with other people around. I gunned it, praying that the direction I was heading would be worth it, but with nothing

but flat plains surrounding me, my faith
floundered.

Hunting the Siren
Chapter 5

INTERSTATE 70 HAD MORE traffic than I expected. I kept checking the rearview mirror for signs of anyone following me. The encounter with Leviathan left me quivering in the driver's seat. I slipped off my left sneaker and let the standing water absorb into my skin. I had a feeling I'd need every drop I could squeeze out of the flooring.

My heart slammed in my chest, creating shockwaves through me every time I thought I recognized a car behind me. With my mind playing tricks, exhaustion took its ugly toll on me. My eyelids became heavy, as heavy as my foot, and I knew if I didn't stop soon, I was going to end up in one of the wheat fields bordering the road.

I needed food. I glanced at the array of empty wrappers on the passenger seat next to me. Nothing was left. I had pillaged the food stash on the way to the largest ball of twine.

The gas gauge was near empty as well. I scanned the horizon, hoping to see something that would save my tired ass. In the distance, past the lines of cars driving on the highway, I saw a glimmer of light. I just hoped I would reach it before the gas ran out.

My engine puttered within sight of the gas station, and I was able to coax it the few hundred feet farther. It rolled to a stop within reach of the gas tank and I sighed. I didn't know whether to gas up first or address my rumbling stomach.

My belly made the choice for me, cramping at the first scent of food. I put the fuel dispenser in my tank and headed inside. When my arms were full of snacks and drinks, I crossed to the counter and dumped it all with an uneasy smile.

I gave the cashier enough for the food and my fill-up and headed out to the car with a grocery bag. I took a moment to clean out the front seat before I started the gas pump. Next, I opened the back door and sighed as I pushed the cooler back to an upright position on the seat. One look inside at the thin layer of water barely covering the bottom of the cooler squeezed my throat closed.

If I hadn't stopped at that damn ball of twine…

I shut the lid. It was enough to perhaps get me through Kansas City, but after that, I wasn't sure what my form would look like once I got to my destination.

If I got to my destination.

I shivered, closed the back door, and focused on the gas pump. My mind kept turning over my options. All of them bleak, especially with just how tired I was after being on the road for close to twelve hours. I still had another twenty-four hours of driving before I arrived in Maine.

That didn't include any stops.

Being in a hotel room, vulnerable, for two nights left me cold, and I entertained trying to drive straight through.

That's a recipe for disaster, and you know it. Alex said.

He was right. If I attempted it, I would end up in an accident, and then who knows what would happen to me and the baby? My hand glided down my front over my still flat stomach.

The gas pump clicked, so I hung the fuel dispenser back on the pump.

With all my ideas exhausted, I slid back in the car and took off without collecting my change. I didn't have a choice. I had to stop, and a hotel was more secure than the side of the road, especially with Leviathan on the prowl.

Soon, I crossed into Missouri and uttered a silent sigh of gratitude. I started looking for hotels and considered going upscale instead of roadside, but I didn't want to be trapped in a building with a bounty on my head. I wanted multiple ways out. I decided Kansas City wasn't the place to pull over and plant for the night, so

I went farther east until I saw a sign for America's Best Value Inn right off the highway.

There were only three cars in the parking lot, so getting lost in the crowd wasn't an option, but the motel had doors at street level, which would do, considering my eyelids were drooping. I didn't really have much of a choice.

I signed in and got my room key. As I stood in the parking lot, I parked opposite my room. If Fate and her cronies could follow me to the ball of twine, it might be smart to give the illusion of being at the farthest point from where I actually was. I hauled the backpack over my shoulder and paused, glancing in the back at the cooler.

There was so little water, I wondered if saving it was prudent, but I could already feel the dryness in my lips. The desk attendant had given me a questionable eye when I walked into get the room. With a sigh, I decided perhaps I should power up before I went in search of food.

I opened the back door and sat on the edge of the seat, opening the cooler. I dipped my hand in the water, and it barely covered the first set of knuckles on my fingers. A sucking sound filled the car, and within a matter of seconds, the water was gone. My cells expanded with hydration. Relief swept through my form.

My next stop was my trunk. I took a quick glance around and then opened it. I plundered through my weapons cache and pulled out a couple of ancient daggers that would stop almost anything that came for me. If I ran into that blue-eyed kid again, I'd be ready.

I stashed the weapons, along with a change of clothes, into my backpack and locked up my car. With a quick glance around, I hurried across the parking lot and fit the key into the hotel room door. Once inside, I swept my hair up into a ponytail and splashed cool water on my face.

My stomach reminded me I needed to eat. I glanced up at my reflection and sighed. With dark shadows under my eyes, I looked just as exhausted as I felt.

You're still beautiful to me.

I rolled my eyes at Alex's commentary and gave my reflection my "yeah, right" expression.

You are.

I signed *thank you* to myself and turned away from the mirror. No sense in talking to the ghost in my head at the moment. He already knew I was in a bad place just through being in there with me.

Pregnant. On the run. No clue of why I took this brainless adventure. I should have done the Gulf Coast route. Then at least I could have just rented a boat, gone out to sea, and disappeared, but something was calling me to Maine.

If that was where Death's son was, then maybe he held the key to my salvation.

Hunting the Siren
Chapter 6

THE ONLY DECENT RESTAURANT in the area was a ten-minute drive from the hotel. The food did nothing for my stomach or my mood. Luckily, I didn't see that kid from Cawker City while I ate. I wasn't in the mood to deal with either him or Leviathan.

I drove back to the hotel and paused in my seat as a shiver traversed up my spine. I pulled the dagger out of the backpack and then slung the strap over my shoulder before I got out of the car. The evening shadows made the parking lot seem menacing.

"Kylee?"

The familiar, feminine voice pierced the traffic noise in the background. My heart jumped into my throat, but I kept going, veering towards the office instead of my room. The itch on my shoulder reminded me I had protection against Fate's detection, so the questioning lilt in her voice helped make my decision.

Fate shouldn't have sought me out.

I spun, releasing the knife. Thunder rolled through my blood. I sprinted towards the highway, hoping to catch a ride in one of the eighteen-wheelers passing by before Fate could catch up to me. Her cry of pain didn't stop my legs from moving as adrenaline ravaged through me, giving me more than enough energy to make the eastbound lane.

I stuck out my thumb as I jogged backwards, and much to my surprise, the first tractor trailer pulled to a stop.

Be careful!

I didn't need Alex's cautions. I already knew this could be a trap and had my hand on the other dagger stowed in the side of the bag.

I hauled myself into the passenger seat with a smile. I didn't get that underlying unease that usually alerted me to another monster.

"Where you headed?" The trucker looked as harmless as some of the elderly homeless people I saw occasionally on the streets of San Diego. His bald head reflected the lights, and the rest of his body seemed to be draped in clothing that at one time might have fit, but now looked as if it was at least two sizes too big on his slight frame.

I smiled and set my backpack between my feet before I spelled out *Maine* with my hands.

He blinked and cocked his head. "Maryland?"

Surprised that he got a couple letters, I shook my head and signed each letter slowly.

"M. A. I. N. E," he repeated.

I gave him a thumbs-up.

"I can take you as far as Buffalo if you don't mind me rambling on."

I don't mind you rambling if you don't mind me falling asleep on you; I signed.

"Name's Burt." He put his hand out.

I shook it, and then slowly signed my name.

"K. Y. L. E. E. Kylee?"

I nodded.

"Well, Kylee, welcome to my rig." He shifted the truck into gear and pulled out from the side of the road.

I glanced at the side-view mirror, and the adrenaline fueling my awareness bled away as we put more and more distance between us and the hotel. I bit my lip at the loss of all my priceless weapons in the trunk. At least I had the forethought to stash my cash in my backpack, although it had been difficult to stuff it all in, along with my wedding album. The knife was still in reach and hidden from Burt's view, but I was sure I wouldn't need it.

Not with how much he actually was rambling. I wondered if he talked to himself when there wasn't anyone else in the cab. He hadn't been kidding. His musings were much more personal than I expected.

His voice lulled me into a semi-stupor, and I found it hard to keep my eyes open and my mind alert. It reminded me of the lure of a siren.

My eyes flew open. I shifted in the seat and glanced at him out of the corner of my eye.

He didn't even look over at me, just kept on describing his latest argument with his wife and how upset it had made him to have to leave to haul this load across the country. He wished he didn't need the money. He wished he could make her understand. Instead, he had left her sulking in the kitchen.

He sighed heavily.

"I don't even know why I'm telling you all this. It's not like you can hear me," he said softly.

I glanced out the window, debating on whether or not I should correct him, but it seemed too much like eaves dropping. I waved my hand in the dark cab, and he glanced my way. I tapped my ear closest to him and gave him a thumbs-up and then my throat with a thumbs down.

The man turned red. "You heard all that?"

I nodded. I knew what disappointing someone I loved was like. I had hurt Alex every time I turned down his proposal, but I had been right. The moment I gave in, the moment I said yes, it all went to shit.

Marrying you didn't kill me, Alex piped in at my train of thought.

I ignored him. My focus was on the driver next to me, who was hurting so much that he had to unload his pent-up frustrations and sorrows on a total stranger.

Call her, I signed.

"She was pretty upset," he said.

You love her, right?

He stared at my hands. "More than she knows. I can't leave her with insurmountable debt. We need this run, even though I may lose time with her."

What's insurmountable?

"My treatment cost us seventy thousand dollars and it didn't work." He nearly growled the statement out.

And this truck run will get you that? Surprise arched my eyebrows.

He let out a laugh. "Not even close. Neither will the one coming back, but I can't leave my wife with that kind of debt attached to our lives. She'll lose everything when I go."

I leaned over and unzipped my backpack. I pulled out two stacks of bills from my stash. Each stack was as thick as a ream of paper. I put them on the console before I zipped up my bag.

The truck swerved, so I knew he had seen the money.

Will this do? I signed and then picked up the two stacks, offering them to him.

Surprise manifested in his wide eyes and a slack jaw. He pulled the vehicle over to the side of the road before he actually looked at me.

"Did you rob a bank or something?" he asked, his voice squeaking.

I shook my head and handed him the stacks. *It's my rainy day fund,* I signed.

Do not tell him there's an entire backpack of money, or you won't be getting out of this cab without a hell of a fight.

I almost rolled my eyes at Alex's narrative in my head, but I heeded his advice.

Burt giggled as he fanned through the money. "This is a lot of money for a rainy day fund."

I shrugged and crossed my arms.

"And what does your husband think of you running around with this kind of cash on you?"

He's not here anymore. Tears blurred my eyes, and I blinked them away. It was still raw, like an open wound. We had been together, in bed, less than a week ago. I shook the oppressive grief away and tried to smile.

"He left you?" he asked, his voice rising.

He died. Life is precious, so you shouldn't be wasting your time out here on the road. You should be with your wife.

He bit his lip, and his brow creased. I slowed down my hands and repeated what I had said. Burt slowly repeated the words my hands formed, and when my hands stopped moving, he looked down at the money and then back at me. He pressed his lips together and nodded.

"You're probably right, but I can't take this from you." He handed the cash back to me. He put the truck in gear and pulled back onto the road.

I sat staring at the money, wondering why he wouldn't just take the gift.

"I'd never be able to explain it to my wife. She would think I robbed a bank," he said, as if he knew where my thoughts had wandered.

I put the money in the cup holders on the console in front of him. I would figure out how to leave it with him as a thank-you for helping me cross the country.

Do you mind if I take a nap?

He glanced at my question and shook his head. "Not at all. You look like you could use a little sleep."

Exhaustion pummeled my muscles. I did little more than offer him a smile of gratitude before I leaned against the door and closed my eyes. Trusting the truck driver could get me killed, but my intuition remained calm, and he had given me no reason to think he would try to harm me.

As I drifted to sleep, I prayed I was right, but I was too tired to remain vigilant.

Hunting the Siren
Chapter 7

THE DOWNSHIFTING OF THE engine stirred me from my sleep. I stretched, my joints crackling and popping with the movement, and blinked at the lightening sky. I'd slept the entire night, which made sense the more I tried to shift in the seat. I had stiffened considerably while I slept.

Burt gave me a tired smile and tilted his head towards the roadside grill and the gas station beyond. A trucker's paradise.

"It's time to refuel." He pointed towards the restaurant. "I'm not talking about just my gas tank either."

My stomach answered for me by roaring loud enough to be heard over the truck's engine.

Burt chuckled. "You sound like you could use a chow break, too."

I nodded.

"While you were sleeping, I did some thinking," he said as he pulled off the highway. "If I can find someone to take you as close to your destination as possible at this truck stop, I'm going to accept your offer and follow your advice. I'll figure out what to tell my wife, but you are right. Life is too short for me to waste my last days on the road." His smile seemed strained as he downshifted. "Who knows? Maybe we will get lucky and find you a ride right to New England."

I tried to moisten my lips, but my tongue was as dry as my lips felt. I flipped the visor down, hoping for a mirror to see the damage the night had produced. Unfortunately, there was no mirror, but with the sideways glances from Burt, I was feeling very self-conscious.

He slowed the rig, turning into the parking lot, and headed straight for the diesel pumps. The minute he stopped, he tucked the money into the overhead bin above him, giving me that same tense smile.

Is everything okay? I signed before he opened the driver's door.

"I'm just tired," he said. This time his expression was more natural. "And you look worse than I feel, so..."

My hand dropped to my belly, and I glanced down at it before looking back up at him. Burt

stared at my hand, the crease between his
eyebrows deepening. His eyes widened.

"Pregnant?" he asked in a hushed whisper.

I gave him a slow nod.

"No wonder you look like death just smiled
upon you. You go on ahead and get some food in
you. I'm sure that will help."

I slid out of the truck and grabbed my
backpack. My stomach growled again as I
crossed the pavement. With my mind still foggy
and my bladder singing, I headed for the
restrooms first.

After I did my business, I crossed to the sink
and slid my hands under the faucet, waiting for
the automated stream of water. My gaze stared
at the tap for a minute before my mind
registered the knob. I turned it and the water
flowed. With my hands under the cool liquid, I
chanced a look in the mirror.

My hair looked as if I had been in the worst
desert sand storm. Stripped of moisture, it just
lay in dried layers. My curls looked more like a
frizzy mass. I dared to look at my face. My lips
held jagged cracks and my skin had that
leathery quality about it. It had been less than
twelve hours since I had my saltwater fix. I had
no clue how bad the next twenty-four hours
would be. Even my eyeballs were dry.

I lifted a handful of water to my mouth and
took a sip, hoping it would satiate my dry
tongue. Even swishing the water around my
mouth, but the minute I spit it out, my mouth
became the Sahara again.

Good lord, no wonder Burt had given me that questionable look. I resembled one of Death's emissaries.

I splashed water on my face and dried off with a paper towel before heading into the belly of the restaurant with my backpack slung over my shoulder. I scanned the patrons, looking for Burt. On the second pass, I saw him leaning over a table in conversation.

He straightened as I approached, smiling. "I found you a ride east."

I stared at the boy I had knocked out in Kansas and took a step backwards. Fear knocked my heart against my chest. I turned, sprinting out of the diner. I ran toward the parked trucks without turning back. Once in the middle of the big rigs, I scanned plates for anything near the direction I needed to go. It was a gamble, but when my gaze fell on New Hampshire plates, I ran towards the rig and took a breath as I tried the door handle. It was unlocked. I launched into the passenger seat.

I looked up to see a startled man in the driver's seat and gave him a sheepish smile. He had a map in his hand, and I pointed to the coastline of New Hampshire before pressing my hands together in a silent plea.

"You need to get to New Hampshire," he said, still sporting that incredulous expression.

I nodded and glanced toward the restaurant. Burt was standing outside with the kid scanning the parking lot. My breath locked in my throat. I scrunched down on the floor.

The truck driver glanced in the same direction I had. "Crazy ex or something?"

I just nodded.

"Been there. Lived to tell the tale." He rubbed his shoulder and scanned the lot. "Why don't you hop in back and I'll take care of this."

I glanced at the shadowed bed in the back of the truck.

Don't. Alex's warning was loud enough for me to wince against the boom in my head.

I ignored him and skittered to the back. The driver undid the curtains, closing me in. The click of the truck locks sounded. I reached into the backpack for my knife. The nerve endings in my hands tingled around the handle as I sat in the darkened space.

The engine fired up, and the truck rolled forward a few feet before the high-pitched whine of brakes filled the cab. The truck vibrated as it sat idle.

The whir of a window rolling down sounded.

"What can I do for you?" the driver asked.

"Have you seen a blonde woman running through the parking lot?" Burt asked.

"I thought I saw someone running that way," the truck driver said, and the hum of the window followed. The gears shifted, and the truck picked up speed.

My skin tingled, and I couldn't tell whether it was from relief or the tension that filled me. If I had been the driver, I would have asked why, especially if the person was in my vehicle. Unease scratched at the surface. When the rig slowed and passed over the rumble strip, coming to a stop, my entire body tensed.

The engine shut off, and a moment later, the curtain pulled back. The driver's lips formed a smile, and it wasn't friendly.

"You know, I usually have to seek out my victims, but here you are, just falling right into my lap." He pulled a blade from the sheath on his hip.

I told you not to go back here! Alex shouted in my head.

I moved my knife into view and gave him the same smile, tilting my head.

His smile faltered, and a nasty gleam filled his eyes. He grinned. "I like 'em feisty."

I sucked my lower lip between my teeth, debating. I was at a disadvantage, huddled in the bed's corner with my backpack between my knees. Standing would put me in range of his knife. It would also put me in range with *my* knife.

He reached out and grabbed my ankle, yanking me towards him.

My heart leaped into my throat. I opened my mouth, forcing my siren song out of the tightness. I controlled it to a soft lullaby, and he froze, just staring at me with the knife poised for attack.

"Let go," I sang.

His hand dropped from my ankle.

I was damning this man, but I didn't care. I wasn't his first, but I would be the last hitchhiker he ever picked up.

"Drop the knife and drive," I sang.

His knife clattered to the floor, and I snatched it along with my backpack, taking the passenger seat as he pulled onto the road. He was my puppet, just like those men the bicorn had controlled. My stomach flipped at the thought, and I swallowed the burn of bile.

He put the truck in gear with an expressionless face.

I wondered if I just gave myself away, but I had a feeling this man was as far from innocent as any of the monsters I had hunted over the millennium.

"What were you planning on doing to me?" I crooned softly enough that my voice wouldn't be heard outside of this tin can.

He glanced over at me, his eyes lingering with a longing that made me sick. "I was going to fuck you, and then kill you until you pulled the knife. Then I was going to cut you and fuck you while you bled out."

I shivered as his gaze went back to the road.

"How many have you done this to?" I sang.

"I don't know. Fifteen or twenty." He shrugged. "I drop them in the nearest waterway."

How I ended up in a truck with a serial killer was beyond me, but it also took away that twinge of guilt for controlling him with my siren. I would have to ensure he was under control, because I couldn't imagine the damage he would do if he went rogue. A part of me would relish ending him. I just hoped I'd have the strength to kill the bastard when we got to Maine.

"Drive and don't stop until I tell you." The melody filled the cab.

He slowly nodded. "Where to?"

"York, Maine," I sang.

I unbuckled my seat belt and stepped in back to find something to eat before my stomach emptied the churning acid all over the floorboards. The closed curtains created a web of doubt, so I secured them before I opened the refrigerator. I didn't know what I was hoping for, but a bushel of apples and a twelve pack of water was enough to get my stomach in an uproar.

I plucked an apple from the crate and water from the door. Before continuing my food search, I sat down and all but inhaled the fruit. I tossed the core into a small can behind the driver's seat, then started opening cabinets. I found a stash of potato chips, fruit snacks, and a shoe box.

Pulling the box down gave me a chill, but I shook it off before removing the top. I stared at the snapshots in the box. They were all from those old Polaroid cameras where the film spits out a picture. The content of the photographs was enough to make me want to slice his head off. Dozens of bona fide crime photos.

Crimes he gleefully committed.

My impression that the driver was a sly son of a bitch was an understatement. I closed the box and put it back on the shelf while trying to calm my stomach down.

The apple didn't sit well with this new information. A part of me just wanted to slice his throat and be done with it, but I needed him to get me the rest of the way. I wasn't sure how I would dispose of him, but it would be in a way that would leave his pastime exposed so his victim's families could have closure.

Alex had said nothing since he told me not to climb in back. His angry quiet radiated in waves all the way to the surface of my skin, heating me to a near boil.

I've got this. Trust me.

He huffed at me but remained silent.

I grabbed the box of fruit snacks and water and tumbled into the passenger seat. I didn't ask the driver his name. I didn't want to know. A part of me wished I didn't have to ditch Burt at the truck stop. He had been so much more pleasant to travel with than the serial killer sitting next to me.

My energy was sapped, and I needed the ocean to regain my strength. If this asshat went homicidal on me, I wasn't sure I could stop him, even with my siren.

Hunting the Siren
Chapter 8

DESPITE MY VIGILANCE, MY eyes kept drooping closed and my head bobbed. I jerked in the seat yet again. My blurred vision cleared as signs for Ohio met my gaze. I blinked and shifted, my bladder too full.

With a sigh, I sang, "Pull over at the next gas station where you can fill up." I just hoped that would be at the next exit. Otherwise, I was going to soil my pants.

The truck driver nodded and pulled off the next exit. Within a few hundred feet, a gas station with diesel pumps appeared, and he pulled in and parked thc truck next to the pump. He stared aimlessly out the window.

"Turn off the truck and fill the gas tank. Then get back into the truck and wait for me." The tune was soft and just a fraction over the idling engine.

He glanced at me with a slow nod.

I thought about threatening him, but he was still in a compliant mood, so I just hopped out of the truck at the same time he did and nearly ran into the store.

My gaze darted around until I caught the restroom sign just beyond the mini donut shop. I booked to it, slid to a stop before the door, and tried the handle. It gave, and I was in with my pants around my ankles before I realized there was just a urinal. I didn't care. I squatted over that thing and just let her rip. I started chuckling because I had heard more than a time or two that the only thing worse than getting between a pregnant woman and food was getting between her and a bathroom.

Now I understood.

I finished, washed my hands, and went back into the belly of the store without so much as a glance in the mirror. I knew what I looked like. I could see the bones in my hands and feel the stretch of my drying skin. I needed food. I had already pillaged all the apples and snacks in the truck, so I went aisle by aisle until I could carry no more and dumped it all on the counter. I reached for my wallet and closed my eyes. My money was in the truck.

I put up my finger, patted my pocket, and then pointed out at the truck.

"Your wallet's in the truck?" the cashier said.

I nodded and put my finger up again as I headed towards the door. I opened the passenger door, reached into the front pocket of my backpack, and pulled out a couple of bills. The driver gave me a tilted head, so I gave him the sign for one minute.

I ran back inside with a crisp hundred-dollar bill and handed it to the cashier. My total kitty was forty-three dollars and fifty-two cents. The cashier handed me my change and pushed the already bagged items my way.

Thank you, I signed, then picked up the bags and trotted back to the truck.

When I opened the door, my heart dropped. The driver's seat was empty. I pushed the bags onto the floor mat next to my backpack and started back towards the store.

The driver waltzed out with his zipper down and a bottle of water in his hand. His eyes narrowed at me, and I returned to my passenger seat. He climbed in the driver's seat and dropped the water into the holder, sending a glare my way.

"What? I had to take a piss."

The sheer fact he disobeyed my order gave me doubts my siren was strong enough to contain the maniac. I waited until the door closed.

"Drive fast," I sang with forcefulness.

And drive he did. He cut the last leg of the trip from eleven to ten, arriving in the little coastal town of York, Maine, just before daybreak.

At the first sign of water, I made him pull into a street where a small harbor surrounded the end of the road at the bottom of a steep hill.

"Park here," I sang, and he obeyed. As much as I wanted to run down to that lifesaving water, I had to make sure this psychopath didn't hurt anyone else. "Take out your knife."

He obeyed the lullaby of my voice.

"Tip over your heart," I sang low, like a whisper.

He placed the tip of the blade over his heart and stared forward, waiting for the next set of instructions.

"Bury the blade to the hilt." A sour taste filled my mouth as the song rolled from my tongue.

The wet sound of steel piercing human skin filled the cab, releasing the bastard's soul with his last breath.

That soul was poison, and I did not want it inside me. I clamped my mouth closed as the ghost slammed me into the door, insisting on merging with me. I slipped from his foggy grip, jumping into the back area, frantically trying to recall the words to an ancient banishing spell.

His angry wail made me cover my ears. The old Latin words sang from my lips as he barreled towards me. His angry snarl cut off and the ghostly spirit dropped to the floor, unable to continue his rebellion.

With him momentarily down, I jumped into action. I turned and grabbed the shoe box, dumping the pictures into the space between the chairs. Then I wiped down everything I had touched.

With my backpack slung over my shoulders, I released the brake and threw the truck in neutral. A slow roll started. I stepped onto the running board and slammed the door shut, locking the ghost of a dead man inside with all his sins.

Before the truck picked up too much speed, I threw myself to the ground, rolling away onto the grass next to the sidewalk. The impact knocked the wind from me. I stared as the eighteen-wheeler careened down the hill, over the boat ramp, and onto the beach. Even the sand didn't slow the beast down. After the surf swallowed the truck, I laid my head against my backpack.

I needed that salt water, and I needed it now.

I rolled onto my hands and knees before getting up onto shaking legs. I didn't care about my rumbling stomach or the exhaustion making my body weak. Each step towards the water brought forth a wave of dizziness. I stepped onto the sand, and my stomach cramped, bringing me to my knees. Without the energy to stand, I crawled towards my salvation.

The water was frigid to the touch, but I didn't care. I crawled into the surf until the water reached my elbows and the ends of my hair touched the water. My dehydrated skin took on a new elasticity as each drop of water absorbed into me and rejuvenated every cell. Even my scalp tingled from the cool sensation of hydration. I climbed to my feet, and water rolled down my arms, drenching my jeans as the wet fabric clung to my skin.

The sun crested the horizon, and I stared in wonder. It had been a very long time since I had seen a proper sunrise over the ocean. Molasses painted the few clouds, penetrating the deep blue of the night sky.

My hand dropped to my belly as I witnessed the birth of another sunrise. I glanced down at the slight bump stretching my skin, slowly rubbing the cherished being growing in my belly. I caught an air bubble where the truck disappeared, and a twinge of guilt bit at my stomach.

At least he wasn't an innocent, and by killing him, I probably saved at least a dozen lives.

A cool ocean breeze chilled my skin, creating a web of bumps along my arms and legs and a shiver that ran from my tailbone to my neck. The reaction wasn't normal. The tremble morphed into a shake, and I nearly stumbled when I glanced over my shoulder. Fear gripped every muscle. My hand dropped protectively over my stomach.

The teenager in shorts and black Pink Floyd T-shirt that had been following me since Grand Junction wasn't what scared me, even though the scythe in his hand should have. The fact that Death had come for me himself should have terrified me, but it was the untethered German Sheppard standing next to him, with his teeth bared, that nearly sent me diving into the shallow surf.

"We've been looking for you," he said. His voice held the quality of maturity, like he had escaped the hell of puberty, but he would never age from the form he held. And just like Fate, this version of Death had taken his post long before his prime.

I wanted to sign *no shit*, but I was frozen in place. Fear raked every nerve ending, numbing them. A dull roar sounded in my ears.

"Get her, Levi," he said to the dog.

The dog growled, but the façade he wore wavered. Leviathan grew to his imposing size, shadowing the beach, and his clawed paw swiped in my direction. I turned, trying to protect my abdomen. The beast hit with the force of a wrecking ball.

I sailed through the air like a rag doll that had been drop kicked.

Based on their open-mouthed expressions, I didn't think Leviathan or Death expected me to be thrown so far. I had a moment to relish their shock before the pain of his open-handed punch sank in.

I thought he smashed my rib cage, and I had issues drawing a breath. Cold water splashed around me on impact. A sharp pain prickled through my scalp. I gasped, drawing the sea into my lungs before everything went black.

Hunting the Siren
Chapter 9

VOICES AROUND ME REGISTERED, as well as the fact I wasn't breathing seawater. I tried to focus on the words, but it was all just noise. Too many heated people talking at once.

"Aunt Val, please help her," a deep male voice cut through the rest.

"I am trying," a female that I could only assume was Aunt Val said. Hands inspected the wounds on my side. "I don't know what the hell could have caused these. Where did you find her?"

"One minute I was fishing in the rocks, and the next, she splashed in the water less than a yard away. I have no idea how she got there, and she was far enough out to rule out falling from the rocks," a voice argued above me. "Just fix her, and we can find out what happened."

If I could have laughed, I would have. Only the ocean could mend my body. I tried to pry my eyes open, but they stayed shut. Moving my arm or leg or even my head produced the same results. Nothing. It was as if I was trapped in my body without a way to communicate.

"I'm not sure if you can hear me or not, but this is going to hurt," the woman whispered, close enough to feel her breath on my eyelids. Then lips brushed my forehead.

Agony filled my form, burning through my skin like a wildfire. Yet I couldn't scream, but Alex could, and his cry of pain filled my head.

The same voice that whispered in my ear gasped. "What is that thing?" The voice wavered like she had lost all strength.

As soon as the pain abated, memories flashed before my eyes. They weren't mine, and they certainly weren't Alex's. The picture show in my brain continued while my skin itched, mending like when the ocean healed me. I thought the memories were my victims' memories until I saw an image of Lucifer.

I drew a great inhalation into my lungs as I sat up. My eyes flew open. Terror gripped every cell, and I scrambled to my feet, spinning around to take in the people surrounding me. My heart jumped in my chest.

Lucifer wasn't among them.

I glanced at my torn and bloody shirt and picked it up to inspect my wounds. Perfect skin met my gaze instead of Leviathan's handiwork. I ran my fingers over the area his claws had punctured as awe filled me.

I raised my gaze to the three people a few feet away. They all had variations of brunette hair that ranged from the woman's warm chestnut hair to the youngest man's almost black hair. The woman, whose memories I now shared, was on the ground, and the two men gathered around her. All three of them existed in a haze of bright light that seemed to come from within each of their beings. All three of them could have walked into a Los Angeles modeling agency and had work lined up for weeks with a snap of their fingers.

Their names remained locked in the memories pinging around in my brain.

When the man cradling the woman's head in his lap glanced up at me, my chest tightened. A familiarity spread over me, but I couldn't quite place where I had seen his bright blue eyes before. They narrowed and his lips tightened as a tingle ran across my scalp.

Leave her alone! Alex growled in my head.

The man's eyes widened like he'd heard my dead husband's voice.

The woman stirred, drawing his attention.

The other man turned, his clothes and hair darkened from the ocean water. Random drops ran down his angelic face, and his deep-set eyes were a blue that made my heart skip. A friendly smile formed on his lips, and he approached me cautiously like I was a wounded animal.

His calm mannerisms drew a smile to my lips.

"Hi, I'm Michael Andreas. And you are?" he asked when he was close enough to reach out and touch me. His voice was even more melodic than Alex's was.

I signed my name, unsure if anyone would know sign language.

"Kylee Cervas," he spoke and signed at the same time, surprising me. "Do you know where you are?"

York, Maine, I signed, hoping I was still there, but who knows how far Leviathan had thrown me.

His nod confirming my whereabouts settled some of my nerves.

"What are you?" the woman asked.

She was now sitting beside the man who I still couldn't place, but deep down, I knew I should know his name. Unfortunately, the memories I now had didn't readily pull his name from the layers of information accosting my head.

Her hair shimmered in the sunshine, making her pale features starker than I would assume was normal. I didn't know how to explain what I was to this woman. She obviously guessed I was more than human.

I could ask you the same, I signed, trying to make sense of the memories I had been fed.

Both the woman and the man laughed and glanced at each other.

"I'm Valerie Ryan," the woman said as she climbed to her feet. "Usually I don't pass out when I heal someone, but then again, I don't usually get assaulted with thousands of years of memories, either."

My eyebrows arched, and I popped my mouth closed after a moment. When she offered her hand, I shook it.

"This is my husband, CJ." She waved towards the man behind her. "And Michael, our neighbor."

My gaze jumped to the man. CJ Ryan. The memories snapped into place and mine with them. CJ Ryan, the famous crooner with the voice that lulled his audience like a siren.

My hands broke out in a sweat, and heat filled my cheeks. The man chuckled at my reaction. There weren't many people that I got all fangirlish over, but CJ Ryan up close was just as stunning as he was on television. Although the television never picked up the shine coming from his core, that made me want to squint.

His lips toyed with a grin, and he looked away. A crease appeared between his eyes as he glanced at his wife. "Did you say thousands of years of memories?"

Valerie glanced at him and nodded. "She's older than Damian was. At least I think she is from the onslaught of memories." They both glanced at me as if for confirmation.

I found her choice of words interesting. Trying to shuffle through the download she gave me was near impossible. It wasn't linear, like one person's memories were. It seemed to be more of a conglomeration of many lives, not one.

CJ stared at me, his eyes narrowing. And that tickle in my head occurred again.

How old was Damian? As soon as I signed his name, the memories surfaced. I gave a small huff. He was just a baby compared to me. *Can I meet him?* As soon as I asked, I regretted it.

Michael's sweet smile faded and sorrow filled his eyes.

"Damian was my father. He's been dead for almost fifteen years."

I dropped my gaze to the ragged remains of my shirt. My hand naturally went to the flat area over where my child grew.

"The baby is fine," Valerie said.

"Can you tell us what happened out there?" Michael asked, handing me my dripping backpack.

My breath locked in my chest at the sight of the soaked backpack. My chest squeezed as I yanked it from his grip and ripped the bag open. The only memory of my wedding sat in the middle, soaked. I grasped it and dropped the bag, giving no mind to the wet bundles of cash that dropped onto the ground. The idea that the only mementos I had of that day were ruined made me sink to my knees with the book clasped to my chest.

Valerie took a seat next to me and peeled the book from my arms. Her husband handed her a roll of paper towels as I shook helplessly next to her. My heart hurt at seeing Alex's smile on each page she turned. The pain of his loss pulsed through my body. This was not how I wanted to see my wedding album. Valerie carefully mopped up the water from each page with the kind of care that only a lifelong friend would give. Her kindness touched me.

"I'm sorry for your loss," she said softly after she cleaned the last page and closed the book, handing it to me.

What are you? I signed, opting for asking the direct question rather than trying to find it in the slush inside my head.

"Angel descendant," she said, like it made all the sense in the world. "And you?"

I'm a siren, and yes, I'm older than Damian was by a few thousand years.

"So, the memory flood... That was all you?"

I think so. But yours wasn't just you, right?

Valerie laughed and glanced at her husband. "No. It was a whole host of memories from my father-in-law's to Damian's." She climbed to her feet and offered me her hand.

I gathered the wedding album and let her help me up. *Is someone in your family deaf?*

CJ's smile faltered, and he shook his head. "My brother had to learn sign language when he was nine, but he wasn't deaf."

The circumstances bloomed in my head, and I bit my lower lip. His brother had been at the mercy of a serial killer who liked to operate on his victims. He survived the ordeal, but not without his tongue. I shivered and glanced out at the ocean.

In all my years walking the earth, this was by far the most unique situation I had ever been in. The only angel I ever encountered had been the fallen one, and he was a bastard of epic proportion. I had seen auras like theirs before, but there had never been an explanation.

Do all angel descendants shine?

Valerie smiled and shrugged. "My best friend once told me we do."

I chewed on the inside of my cheek and turned to Michael. *Thank you for saving my life.*

"You're welcome. But I still don't understand what happened."

You don't want to know. I didn't want to drag these people into my problems. I had taken enough of their time and energy, and now someone else besides Alex had my history.

Someone else knew how to kill a siren.

The sliders on the back of the house opened, and the man who stepped out froze me in place. I trembled as my own memories accosted me. The suave good looks, crystal blue eyes, and bright aura threaded with black took me back thousands of years to the darkest days of my life.

Lucifer.

I shuffled through the memories Valerie had infused and came up with his name. Tom Ryan. His gaze shot to mine and he winced, like my thoughts had reached him. He blinked before his gaze traveled in the air around me, like he could see something the rest of the group couldn't.

"Why are so many ghosts tethered to you?" he asked.

I cocked my head. *Tethered?*

He raised an eyebrow, challenging me like I knew what he was seeing.

After a few moments of scrutiny from everyone I signed, *I would imagine they are the souls that fell to my siren.*

"Damn," Tom said.

I picked up my backpack and shoved the wet money back inside. *I should go.* I signed and glanced around for an easy exit. There wasn't any, and I looked at Michael. *Can you show me out of here?*

Before I could escape the growing crowd, Valerie asked, "What attacked you?"

Leviathan. Death's pet.

They all stared at my hands, and they arched their eyebrows like I was off my rocker.

"Death's pet?" Valerie asked, as if she were unsure what my hands had spelled out.

I nodded.

As if bringing my point home, the teenager holding his dog's collar materialized on the point just beyond the swimming pool. And this time, Fate was with him.

Silence blanketed the backyard. My heart thundered in my chest. I took a step backwards, right into the hard chest of Michael.

His hands grasped my arms, and his voice whispered softly in my ear. "Don't worry, my uncle won't let anything happen to you."

"Kylee," Fate said, her voice sharp with anger.

"Julia?" Tom asked, cocking his head as he studied the teenagers standing on the bluff.

Fate turned towards him. "This is none of your..." she said, pointing at him, but her voice faltered as she stared, her eyes widening with recognition.

"Nick?" he said, even more exasperated than before.

This time, the kid glanced at Tom and offered a tilted smilc. "It's been a while."

I was truly screwed if these people knew Fate and Death.

I tried to break out of Michael's grip, but a giant tiger jumped over the wall, shocking me to stillness. It hissed and paced in front of where Michael and I were standing, its aura as bright as Michael's. Its attention was solely focused on Leviathan.

The dog bared its teeth at the tiger, issuing a growl that rivaled the tiger's hiss.

"It seems your dog isn't a dog at all, is it?" Michael said from behind me.

I glanced back at him.

"My sister can sense supernatural threats," he said, nodding towards the tiger.

I wondered why she hadn't pounced on me.

"Grace, this isn't your fight," CJ said sternly and pointed behind where we stood.

The tiger gave him a cursory glance and crouched low, focusing on Leviathan.

"Grace, I think we have this," Michael said.

The transformation from beast to beauty took a blink, stunning me more than I already was. She certainly was Michael's sister, with jet black hair and an olive complexion that reminded me of a Greek goddess. She had the same angelic beauty as Michael, but her demeanor was more predatory.

"It's been so long since I sharpened my claws." She sulked as she wandered behind us.

CJ stepped forward. "Nick, as in Nick Ramsay?"

The teen smiled. "That's who I used to be before I had to take this job." A scythe appeared in his hand, and he shrugged.

"Funny, we have never run into you," CJ said, leveling a stony stare at the boy. "And I've died at least once," he added before he crossed his arms. "I've even been to heaven and can't say I ever saw either of you." His tone challenged their station.

"Really, CJ, this isn't your fight," Fate interrupted, stepping between Death and the Ryan clan. "Kylee broke her contract, and we are obligated to return her to where she belongs."

"And where is that?" Michael said from behind me. His hands were still firmly on my arms, like he could protect me from what was coming.

"Hell," both Fate and Death said in unison.

Tom stepped next to his brother. "No one deserves to be sentenced to hell." The challenge in his voice was clear.

"It's not for us to say whether or not it is deserved. She broke the one rule that is explicit in her contract. She used her siren, and innocent people died."

Eyes shifted to me.

"I would have done the same had CJ died in my arms," Valerie said. "I have her memories. I endured the pain with her. She did not intend to kill. It was a wail of sorrow, and unfortunately, someone was driving too close to where they were held hostage and was affected by the siren. That is not a willful breach of contract."

"Innocents died," Fate said.

"Innocents die every day," Tom said, glancing at Valerie. "I trust my sister-in-law. If she thinks this woman is worth saving, I stand with her."

He glanced at the rest of his family. "We stand by her."

My stomach plummeted.

"What makes you think you can stop us?" Fate said, but Death put his hand on her arm.

CJ laughed. "I'm pretty sure I can stop anything you throw my way."

Fear peppered my tongue, turning my mouth sour. These people didn't understand Leviathan was in their midst.

Tom glanced my way and winked.

"I'm not here for a fight." Death stepped to the side. "But if that's what you want…"

Leviathan growled and grew into his imposing form. Tremors filled my skin. Michael stepped closer, his chest pressed against my back.

"You came onto my property trying to take one of our guests to a place few truly deserve, and you issue a threat?" CJ snarled and put his hand out.

A blast of air rocketed from where he stood and launched Leviathan into the stratosphere. I didn't see where the beast landed. The shell-shocked expressions on both Fate and Death's face as they looked out over the ocean were priceless.

CJ glared at Fate and Death. "You know who I am. You know what I'm capable of, and yet you still decided to fuck with me?"

"Just because you killed Lucifer doesn't give you the right to stand in the way of us doing our job," Death said.

Killed Lucifer? I stared at CJ, frantically shuffling through Valerie's memories for that information, but all I kept seeing was a blackened lawn, headless bodies, and Tom almost ripped in half.

"Next to Lucifer, you and Julia are anticlimactic," CJ said.

Death's lips pressed together.

"Besides, if you are so worried about innocent lives being sacrificed, what about the baby growing inside her?" CJ added, waving in my direction. "You're going to damn that child to hell? That seems more insidious than her losing control when her husband died. It seems to me that *you* are the villains in this scenario."

Death and Fate exchanged a glance and then turned their attention to me.

"Is this true?" Fate asked.

I nodded, and my hand fell protectively against my stomach.

"But the contract." Fate looked down at her notepad. "It's binding, and I can't undo it."

"There are always ways around a contract," Tom said. "What if we freed the souls tethered to her? Would that be enough to rework whatever fucked up contract you hold?"

My heart leaped into my throat. I didn't know what would happen to me if the souls I absorbed were freed. I certainly didn't want to live without Alex.

I'm not going anywhere, Alex said, his voice firm in my head.

Tom looked at the spot right next to me before glancing at me directly. "Your husband, I presume?"

Yes, I signed.

Fate bit her lip and studied the pad in front of her. She glanced at Death and shrugged. "I don't know if that would work. Let me see what I can do."

I'm sorry I threw the knife at you, I signed.

She rubbed her arm. "Your aim was off. It just nicked me." Fate turned to the group. "Make sure she stays here where we can find her."

"Ask the angels. They always have the answers," Grace said from behind Michael.

Fate cocked her head and then nodded. "I will. Just make sure she stays put."

"Don't come back unless you have a plan to fix this," CJ said. "Because if you come back with the idea you are going to deliver her to hell, you better damn well bring the entire population of hell along with you to have a prayer's chance of taking her off my property."

Death's face pinched in aggravation before he and Fate blinked out, leaving a heavy silence and all eyes on me.

You killed Lucifer? I signed.

CJ smiled, but it was as cold as a northern ice tundra. "Come on, let's get you fed before the death squad comes back." He turned and crossed through the sliders.

Everyone followed. I hesitated. Michael still had his hands on my arms and he coaxed me forward.

"They're good people. They won't let anything happen to you."

I glanced back at him. His blue eyes held sincerity and his soft smile put me at ease. It only took a moment, and then I followed the angel descendants, even though I didn't know if they would be my salvation, or my demise.

Hunting the Siren
Chapter 10

THE PLATE OF EGGS, toast, and home fries were better than any dinner I had visited on my way east. I signed my thank you and dug into the feast. Nearly dying and then being brought back to life by a natural healer made for a fierce hunger, which took all of my attention away from the conversations flowing around me. When the last morsel disappeared into my mouth, I washed it down with the full glass of orange juice and then leaned back in the chair.

"What happened to your voice?" Tom asked from the other side of the table.

I squinted at him. *Fate took my voice.*

"Julia?" He pointed towards the backyard.

*No. The bitch that had the job from the time I
was created until Julia took the position. The
original Fate sent me to kill my brother, and I had
to use my siren to stop pirates from killing me
before I completed the job. She took my voice to
spite me.* I signed. *Julia tried to give it back, but
she only succeeded in giving me my siren, not my
voice.* I shrugged.

Michael reached over my shoulder and
cleared my plate. After putting my dishes in the
sink behind us, he took the seat next to me. I
studied his profile. While CJ and Tom Ryan were
ruggedly handsome men, Michael Andreas
outshined them in both looks and brightness.

*Some of you are more than just angel
descendants. Michael and his sister's auras are
brighter than CJ's and CJ's is brighter than yours
and Tom's. Why?* I signed to Valerie.

"Michael, Grace, and their brother, Gabriel,
are trilogies with a more direct bloodline. Their
father was the archangel Gabriel's son. CJ is
also a trilogy, but further removed. And the rest
of us only have one or two angel bloodlines
flowing in our veins," Valerie explained. "In this
room, you have descendants of the host of
archangels. Michael, Gabriel, Raphael, Uriel,
and Lucifer."

I shivered at the mention of Lucifer.

"Michael, Gabriel, and Lucifer are all dead.
Raphael and Uriel are stuck in Heaven since
they gave their grace to CJ."

Lucifer is really dead?

CJ reached over the table and touched my
forehead. I was no longer sitting in the kitchen.
Instead, I was stalking across the bloodied back

yard towards Lucifer. It took me a second to realize I was reliving CJ's memory.

TOM LAY ON THE ground covered in blood, his gaze locked with mine as a sliver of hope filled his mind, crushing another piece of my heart. Seeing him this near death nearly ripped the righteous fury out of my bones. I resisted, knowing if I let loose too soon, we were toast. Instead, I let the image fuel the anger inside me, controlling my muscles to provide maximum strength to each of my calculated strikes.

Tom's thought whispered in my ear just as Lucifer revealed the knife Tom had just warned me about. Lucifer swiped and only met air as I parried out of the way, giving me the opening to grab hold of his wrist and crank it until the knife fell to the ground. Unarming Lucifer was as easy as taking a sticky lollipop from a child's hand.

Each fist that connected with Lucifer's body brought forth a satisfaction I should have been shamed by, but I embraced it, gaining power from it like the fury building in every cell. The bastard deserved ever broken bone and bruised muscle he got.

His fists connected with me, as well, but I didn't register pain from even one of his blows. Maybe Valerie's healing mojo was still working its magic.

I didn't have much more time. Tom was slipping into the darkness, which fueled me even more. My fist connected just below Lucifer's rib cage, lifting him off the ground with the power of it. The blow vibrated all the way to my shoulder, but it was enough to drop the devil to his knee.

Lucifer spit blood through his teeth and glared up at me. Before he could rise, I grabbed him in a headlock, crying my rage as I twisted. Bone splintered and skin split, and everything inside me burst with white hot wrath. With one final yank, Lucifer's head severed from his body. My angel fire swept over the backyard, blackening the ground along with the king of hell's body even before it hit the dirt.

THE VISION SHIFTED, AND I sat at the kitchen table blinking, my form trembling from the intensity of emotions that came with the memory. My heart hammered in my chest and my breath wheezed. I didn't know whether to drop to my knees and beg for mercy or to act casual, as if I saw the demise of an archangel every day.

Michael's hand covered mine, snapping me fully into the present.

What. The. Hell? Alex's gasping thought filled my head.

I pulled my hand away from Michael's soft grip and reached for the water glass still in front of me. The water sloshed as I brought it to my lips and forced a sip down my tight throat. CJ chuckled from the other side of the table.

I understood how this man could easily challenge Death and Fate. He had taken on the beast and won. Death, Fate, and even Leviathan were like a sparring match at the gym in comparison.

He stood, clearing the rest of the plates.

Why are you helping me? I signed once my hands stopped shaking.

"Because it seems like the right thing to do." CJ put his hand on my shoulder. "We..."—he twirled his finger to indicate everyone in the room—"know what evil is, and you aren't it."

How do you know?

He smiled. "My wife would know. She has your memories, remember?" He turned his attention to the sink. "Why don't you go relax on the couch. It's much more comfortable than the kitchen chairs."

I stood on shaking legs and crossed into the family room, then took a seat in the corner facing the doors where my backpack sat. Aggravation at my helplessness burned my skin. As much of an ally as this family posed, I couldn't, in good conscience, tangle them in my mess.

I calculated my odds of a getaway.

Valerie took a seat across from me. "Tell me about Alex."

I raised an eyebrow.

"I know. I have the memories, but I think it would do you some good to talk about him."

I can hear her, you know, Alex piped in.

I rolled my eyes at both of them and started signing. *Alex was my neighbor and became my friend. I shied away from friendship for obvious reasons, but he kind of wormed his way into my heart. The day I was told to hunt down my brother was the day he made his first move on me. I didn't dissuade him either. If I had, he'd still be alive.*

"You don't know that," Valerie said.

I stared her down until she dropped her gaze, then I continued. *He never knew quite what I did. I mean, who really understands what a paranormal investigator does, anyway?*

Tom laughed. "I own a paranormal investigation agency."

I leaned back in the seat and studied him for a minute, my aggravation at feeling helpless growing beyond my control. *What kind of paranormal situations do you investigate?* My snark was lost in translation.

"Ghosts mostly. But I've had my fair share of demons as well."

So, no bicorns, or gorgons. How about Medusa or a Minotaur?

Tom shook his head. "I've had my fill of demons, vampires, and ghosts. You're the first siren I've ever met."

I am no longer a true siren. Yes, I still hold the capability of siren song, but what you see today is what Fate turned me into after I escaped from Lucifer with my brother. The brother I was later commanded to kill. I'm enslaved by Fate, obligated to hunt down creatures that escaped from hell during a breach. But, as I learned recently, I am only obligated to hunt down those that cross the line. Therefore, my contract will truly never end. I'm bound to Fate's whims for eternity. Anger blew past my surface. *This was not my choice.* I took a breath and closed my eyes. *I'm the best at what I do, but it is not my choice to live an eternity alone. You asked about Alex. I made the mistake of letting him in, and he died because of it.* When I opened my eyes, everyone in the room was staring at me.

"I see ghosts. I never asked for that," Tom said, and bitterness threaded through his voice. "I never asked for my tongue to be cut out or my dead wife's to be sewn back in. I never asked to choose between my best friend and my daughter, either." He gave me a shrug. "Unfortunately, neither my daughter nor my best friend survived. So, you'll find zero sympathy from me." His hard gaze locked with mine.

This family, while being as strong and amazing as they were, had already lost too much. I climbed to my feet and started towards the door. Staying was a mistake, and I wasn't about to drag these people into a losing battle.

CJ stepped into my path, stopping me. His gaze held both compassion and an unyielding hardness that flamed the fury building in my soul.

Move. I signed. *You don't need to be part of my shit show.*

"Sorry, not happening."

I had two choices: give in to the anger and let my siren loose to get my way, or fight my way out. These people didn't deserve to be damned, so I executed a spin kick aimed at his chest.

But my entire body stopped in mid-air with my heel a hair away from his chest. I gulped air.

"Are you quite done with your little show?" he asked and pushed my leg away.

Whatever suspended me in the air released, and I crumpled to the ground next to the couch. The only being I'd ever encountered that had that kind of control was Lucifer.

I can't stay.

"Yes, you can. And there is a way to fix this."

I opened my mouth, but only a puff of air came out. I clenched my hands in frustration, believing him naïve for thinking he could fix something that was millenniums old.

The soft expression on CJ's face hardened, and his focus moved away from my face in an arc, like his eyes wielded a blade.

Pain ripped through my head, dropping me to my knees. A hand clamped over my mouth and shut off any hope of wailing my siren to stop whatever fresh hell they were doling out.

A soft voice whispered in my ear, but I couldn't hear the words, not with the agony overwhelming me.

Alex's thundering "No!" filled my head and then cut off, like our connection had been severed.

Silence blanketed my world. I welcomed the black wave that took me under.

Hunting the Siren
Chapter 11

ACOOL, DAMP CLOTH wiped my forehead, dulling the throbbing pain. The minute it was drawn away, the pounding returned. I winced, wondering what brought on this hellish agony. The cloth wiped again, slow and steady, reminding me of a mother doting on a sick child.

I forced my eyes open. Blonde hair hung in my field of view. I didn't remember anyone with blonde hair, but my eyes wouldn't focus. My eyelids dropped again. The soothing cloth continued to slowly mop my forehead.

A sigh followed.

"I know you're awake," a voice whispered softly.

It was familiar in an eerie way. I forced my eyes open again, focusing on the fawn eyes looking down on me. I tried to move away.

Fate whispered, "Shhh," and mopped my forehead again with enough care to bring tears to my eyes.

"Why?" I blinked when the word actually came out of my mouth. My eyes widened, and I tried to sit up. "You gave me my voice back?"

Julia pushed me back on a bed in an unfamiliar bedroom. "Just lay back and I'll explain as best I can." She ran the cloth over my face one more time before laying the cool washcloth over my forehead.

"There wasn't a way to break the contract." She stood and crossed to the window. "So I asked if there was any way to void the contract." She let out a soft laugh. "It's amazing what the angels will tell you when you ask the right question, especially when their kin are knee deep in the situation and Leviathan wants to tear every head off." She turned back to me. "I can't blame him. CJ knocked him halfway across the Atlantic."

I let out a surprised laugh, the sound of it shocking enough to stall my brain for a moment. "You know CJ?" I asked, still stunned that my voice was back.

"Believe it or not, they used to babysit me." She gave me a smile. "Nick and I are from York."

I glanced at my hands.

"But you knew that, didn't you?"

"I remember the old Fate mentioning that Death's son was from York during one of her infamous rants."

"Well, it was a smart tactical move on your part. Unfortunately, you left a map in your car, so we knew where you were headed. Your car should be here in a day or two."

"Why? Why am I not chained in hell?"

She stared at me for a moment and then licked her lips. "You're mortal."

"What?"

"That was the only way to make your contract null and void."

My hand dropped to my belly, and my heart squeezed. "And my child?" I asked, praying whatever they did hadn't terminated my pregnancy.

Fate took a deep breath. "The baby is fine."

Relief flooded every cell, and I fell back on the mattress. I expected Alex to pipe in and tell me, of course, the baby was fine, but the utter silence in my head triggered a new set of alarms. I met Fate's gaze.

"Alex didn't want to go," she said. "But we convinced him he would better serve you and your child from heaven rather than become a bitter, angry ghost that was forever earth bound."

The pain in my head was nothing compared to the hurt in my chest. He was gone. Forever. Tears formed, blurring my vision. I didn't know whether or not to be angry. At least he wouldn't be sentenced to an eternity in hell alongside me.

"You'll see him again someday," she said. "As long as you don't go on a murder spree."

I slowly sat up, staring at her. "I'm bound..."

She shook her head. "Your siren was bound for hell. Another loophole that the angels told me about. I honestly didn't know if the Ryan's could do what I asked of them or not, but we had to try. Otherwise…" She shook her head, either unable or unwilling to finish that sentence. "Anyway, you will grow old, and when your time is up, I'll be there with Nick to bring you home."

She glanced out the window again. "You know, York is a wonderful place to bring up a family." She turned, walking out the bedroom door.

I was flabbergasted.

Mortal.

I didn't know what to do with the information, so I pinched my arm hard enough to draw a wince. A knock on the door drew my attention, and I looked into Michael's kind blue eyes.

"Hi," I said, my voice soft and scratchy.

His eyebrows arched. "Nice bonus." He stepped inside the room. He waved at the accommodations. "I'm sorry it isn't a five-star hotel…"

"It's not a prison cell or a hospital bed, so…" I picked up the washcloth that had fallen into my lap and set it on the bedside table. "I assume I'm in CJ's house?"

"Safe assumption." He shoved his hands into his pockets. "Can I get you anything?"

"Do you have anything for a headache?"

He turned and disappeared from the room, coming back a few minutes later with a glass of water and two Tylenol capsules. "Val said you can take this. She also said the headache may last for a few days."

I took the pills and downed them with the water.

"I'm supposed to give you this," Michael said, pulling a folded paper out of his pocket. He handed it to me and gave me a nod. "If you need anything, just yell."

I unfolded the paper and stared at the handwriting. A lump formed in my throat, and my vision blurred under the sudden barrage of tears.

HEY BABE,

First, let me tell you how truly strange it is to be using someone else's body to write this note. But it was the only way I was going to agree to let go. I wanted to say goodbye in my own words, in my own way.

You gave me light when my world was dark, and I loved you with everything I had, despite how infuriating you could be. You were not the reason why I died. Please don't blame yourself for that monster. I was the one who erred. I didn't plunge the blade in the right spot. Hell, I should have listened to you and stayed in San Diego, but the thought of you being hurt never settled well with me. Call it macho bullshit if you'd like, but that is how I am wired.

Besides, if I hadn't gone to Las Vegas with you, we would have never married. I'm not sure how far along you are, but I'd like to think maybe the little he or she in your belly is our Vegas miracle. Take care of our little bundle.

One more thing. Don't spend the rest of your life mourning me. I don't want that for you or for

*our child. There is a light out there for you. You
will know it when it comes along. Even if the
timing seems inappropriate, know you have my
blessing.*

*Live and love in my honor and remember, you
don't have eternity to let go this time.*

Don't waste the moments away in sorrow.

Smile for me, even through the tears.

Love and light, until we see each other again...

Alejandro.

TEARS OVERFLOWED IN A torrent. I held the
paper to my breast, wishing for his voice in my
ear one more time. I curled my knees to my
chest and let the fountain go until it ran dry.

When I looked up, Tom stood in the doorway.
He handed me a box of tissues. "It may be the
wrong time, but we're looking for another
partner at our firm. I could always use someone
with your skills."

I laughed. "My skills were solidly built around
my siren."

"That's not what I understand. What I was
told is you took down all manner of beasts
without your siren."

I wiped my face. "I was, however, immortal,
so that gave me an edge I no longer have."

"I've agreed to help Fate chase her rogue
monsters down," he said.

I huffed and swung my legs over the side of
the bed. "You must be daft," I muttered under
my breath.

Tom laughed and took a seat next to me on
the bed. "I've never professed to be the smart

brother," he said. "But I can wield angel fire, and I closed all of hell's portals. Unfortunately, I'm also the one who harbors the devil's grace."

I glanced at him and then back down at the letter in my hand. "Can you do that same memory thing your brother does?"

He nodded.

I held the letter up. "Show me this."

"Kylee..." He sighed.

"You're the ghost whisperer. Show me my husband's goodbye."

His lips twitched at the tag I gave him, and he rolled his eyes. Before I could insist, he tapped my forehead.

"NO!" ALEX BELLOWED AND grabbed for me.

A host of ghosts with broken tethers rose above me as I sank to the ground, paralyzed by the pain of their release. I seized, and Alex threaded his hand through mine, holding fast while the rest of the dead were ushered out of the room. His severed tether waved in the air above us.

Valerie dropped to her knee next to me to roll me on my side as my body jerked on the ground.

"You're killing her!" Alex yelled, his ghostly essence turning red with aggravation.

"No, we're not. We're trying to save her," Fate said as she stepped through the door.

Death waited on the back lawn with a very unsettled Leviathan, pacing back and forth.

"You want to bring her back to hell!" Alex argued, trying to block her advance while clinging to me.

Tom stepped in front of Fate, blocking Alex from her. "Trust me, we are trying to save your wife and child, but we need your help."

"You're out of your fucking mind!"

"Alex, I know she never trusted me. Not fully, but I never wanted to hold her to the insane contract she signed. I had no choice. If I don't deliver her siren to hell, I will be in breach of contract. You don't want that on your head."

"I don't give a damn. I'm not letting you take her." He squared up in front of me without letting go of my hand.

"I do not want to take Kylee. The angels gave me a way to save her. It's a little unorthodox, but it will make it so none of us are breaching the contract," Fate said, articulating carefully with her hands out like she was trying to calm Leviathan instead of the ghost of my dead husband.

Alex stared at her. "You're serious."

"Yes. I need her siren. Now, will you help me save your wife?" She held a small glass bottle out to Alex.

He gazed down at my prone body with a nod and took the vial in his hand. "I don't know how to do this," he said. "Fate, the one before you, yanked it from her throat."

"That bitch didn't take her siren. She took her voice. It's different. The siren is actually a part of her. It was used to anchor all those soul tethers. You need to pull it out and shove it in that container."

Tiny worry lines formed around his eyes. "What will happen to her?"

"She will become mortal."

Alex's eyes widened, and he looked at the cluster of tethers floating above my head. "Mortal?" His mouth worked around the word. He licked his lips, glancing back at Fate and then at the only other person in the room who could see him.

Tom nodded. "It's not going to be pretty, but she will survive."

"You can guarantee that?" Alex asked.

Tom pointed at Valerie. "She will make sure of it."

Valerie glanced up at him with a tense smile.

Alex crouched down next to me and unclasped his hand from mine. He swept the lot of tethers into his hands as close to my head as possible. He looked over his shoulder at Tom. "What happens if she lets the siren loose before I can get it out?"

Tom gave a nervous laugh. "Then I think we are all doomed." He shrugged. "The key is to not stop once you start. No matter what."

Alex gave a nod and took a deep breath, wrapping the tethers around his fist until they were taut. The muscles in his arms contracted. "Here goes nothing." He yanked.

My body jerked. My eyes flew open, shimmering like a true siren, and the tethers pooled together to form a scaly gray circle on my forehead.

"Hold her!" Alex said, trying to rise to his feet with the tethers grasped tight. The muscles in his back flexed, followed by his neck.

The ghostly bellow that followed made me shiver.

Tom's hand shot out, grabbing the tethers below Alex's hand and adding his strength to my husband's.

The sound of wet flesh bursting filled the room.

"Jesus Christ," Alex cried, but the vial disappeared behind his ghostly essence.

Tom stumbled backwards, catching the edge of the couch with a bloodstained hand. Alex turned, giving Tom a full view of my body and the hole in my forehead. Valerie's lips landed on a clean spot next to the tear in my skull, and light danced across my form, pooling around the gaping wound.

Alex shoved the vial at Fate and then fell to his knees next to me. "I'm so sorry, baby." His hands cradled my face and his lips brushed against mine. "I'm so sorry."

The light surrounding me faded, and my ragged breathing evened out. Valerie checked my pulse and glanced up at Tom.

"She seems to be stabilizing," she said.

"Good. I will be right back. I have a siren to deliver." Fate gave Tom a nod before she disappeared.

Tom squatted next to Alex. "It's your turn now," he said softly.

Alex drew his eyebrows together. "I'm not leaving her."

"You need to move on," Tom said.

"Look, I get it. I'm a ghost, but she's my wife, and she is carrying my child. I am not leaving."

"Do you have any experiences with ghosts?" Tom asked.

Alex's mouth popped open and then closed. He looked at me and let out a high-pitched laugh. His nervous laugh. "A little. But…"

"But what? You'll never turn out like those bitter and violent ghosts you encountered?"

Alex met Tom's gaze. "I wouldn't."

"You will. It is inevitable. Do you want to end up hurting Kylee or your child?"

"God, no!" He recoiled from Tom's question, his hand still clasped mine.

"Then come with us," Fate said from the doorway.

"I can't leave her." He caressed my cheek. "She would never forgive me for leaving."

"She'll forgive you," Fate said, crossing the distance. She held out her hand.

Alex glanced at her and then at Tom. "I need to talk to her before I make a decision," he said.

"It doesn't work that way," Fate said. "The window closes."

"How long before that happens?"

"It will close long before she wakes," Fate said.

"Do I have time to write a letter?"

Fate nodded. Tom stood, pulled out a pad of paper and a pen, and set them on the table. Alex attempted multiple times to physically maneuver the pen, but to no avail.

Tom picked up the pen for him.

"She needs to see my handwriting," he said through clenched teeth. "Otherwise, she won't believe it was from me."

"Is she okay to be moved?" Michael asked, squatting next to Valerie and my still unconscious form.

"Yes. Take her up to the guest room while we hash this out," Valerie said.

Michael scooped me up in his arms and carried me to the stairway. He didn't make it more than the first step when Alex's ghost slammed into him.

Tom blinked. One minute Alex had been at the table next to him and the next, he'd merged right into Michael.

"Shit." Tom swiped the paper and pen off the table and lumbered after Michael.

When Michael turned into the bedroom at the top of the stairs, Tom muttered under his breath, following him in and waiting until the ghost laid me on the bed. Then he slammed the pen and paper on the desk.

"Write fast, otherwise I'm bouncing you the hell out of my godson." His growl filled the room.

Michael turned and his blue eyes were muddied with ghostly brown ones. Alex nodded and sat down, scribing his letter. When he finished, he folded it and put it in Michael's shirt pocket.

"Make sure she gets this when she wakes." Alex patted the pocket.

His ghostly essence peeled away from Michael. Tom's clenched fists relaxed.

Michael took a great inhalation and coughed. "Holy crap," he said. "What the hell was that?"

"That is what it's like to be possessed," Tom said. "Are you okay?"

"Yeah."

"Good. Keep an eye on her." Tom grabbed Alex's arm and dragged the ghost downstairs. "I don't take kindly to ghost possessions," he said, giving Alex a sideways glare.

"He was touching my wife."

"For Christ's sake, he was just carrying her up to the bedroom."

Alex pressed his lips together and glanced at Tom's grip on his arm. "He has designs on my wife."

Tom yanked him to the right toward Fate. "He doesn't have designs. He is just intrigued by her. We all are."

Alex scoffed and turned his attention to Fate. "I'm not ready for this," he said.

"I promise you'll see her again someday." Fate took Alex's hand, leading him outside to where Death waited.

TOM'S BLUE EYES CAME back into focus as his fingers left my forehead.

"No emotions?" I asked, thinking back to CJ's mind share. His had come with all the horror and fury of the moment, but Tom's mind share was without emotional tags beyond the few physical cues I got.

Tom chuckled. "No. I can allow you to see my memories without my emotions attached. I wasn't inclined to share my thoughts with a stranger, no matter how beautiful she is."

Heat filled my cheeks as I glanced down at the letter still in my hands.

"Don't worry, I'm not hitting on you. My wife would skin me alive."

I laughed and gave him a sideways look.

"And I'm serious about a job. Having someone with your wealth of experience would do us some good. Plus, I understand you own an arsenal that is exceptional."

"Yeah, it's pretty special. I appreciate the offer, but I'm not sure if I'm going to stay."

Valerie stepped into the room with a cup of water and offered it to me. "Stop trying to get her to come work for you," she scolded Tom, and then turned to me. "Totally up to you, but if you decide to stay, we have plenty of room, as do the Andreases next door, or if you're more comfortable, there are some great hotels in the area."

Tom stood and headed out of the room, pausing in the doorway. "It's not always the best to be alone after losing someone you love." He glanced over his shoulder at me. "Take it from someone who has been in your shoes."

Valerie watched him go and then shrugged. "He means well."

"He does. But I really don't know you, and being around familiar things, things I shared with Alex, might lessen the pain after a time. Besides, if I'm truly free from being a paranormal bounty hunter, well, I don't know if I want to continue that line of work. I might just try my hand at something less threatening."

Valerie grinned. "Like what?"

"I don't know. Anything but chasing down monsters."

Hunting the Siren
Chapter 12

FATE WAS TRUE TO her word. My car was delivered to the Ryans two days later, just the way I had left it. The inside smelled of stale seawater, and when I opened the door, I nearly threw up at the stench. The Ryan's were kind enough to take it down to the auto shop for a full detailing of the interior after we emptied the weapons from the trunk.

While they had been the perfect hosts, I was restless, and I wanted home. I wanted my bed and the smell of Alex's aftershave. I had arrangements to make. Every time I thought of those details, my throat tightened. I also owed

Alex's girls a visit. They deserved to know what happened to their father.

It had only been a week since his death, but it felt like a lifetime.

I stood at the edge of the water on the small beach close to the Ryans' house. The cold water lapped at my toes. I forced myself to stand in the Atlantic and soak in the expanse before me. The bite in the fall air, along with the frigid sea numbing my feet, was enough to produce a shiver. Gooseflesh covered my arms.

"How free am I, Fate?" I whispered.

The air shimmered next to me and Fate appeared, her gaze on the ocean.

"You are mortal, Kylee. Free of all the benefits and drawbacks of being a siren. You can drive through the desert without shriveling up into a walking corpse. You can sing."

I glanced at her. "I can sing?"

"Yes. You can sing without driving humans insane."

I let out a laugh and tried out a scale. It sounded glorious to me, but Fate's forced smile told me that maybe I had more of Alex's tone deafness than I cared to admit. The sheer fact I could now sing along to the songs blaring on the radio brightened my heart.

"Thank you," I said, knowing what she did for me was a gift. One I wasn't sure I'd ever be able to repay.

"I understand you turned Tom Ryan down," she said.

My muscles tensed. I nodded, expecting the worst.

She smiled. "Good. That's no life to raise a child in."

This little sprig of a woman continued to surprise me.

"And I was serious about this town. It's a really great place to raise a child. It isn't San Diego. Life here is set at a much different pace, one you might find suits you more than the west coast."

"Are you telling me I have to stay here?"

Fate turned to me and took both my hands. "No. You are free. I'm just partial to this town. It's a magical place. One where children can play without worrying about monsters." She gave my hands a squeeze and let go. "It's where I met Nick."

"San Diego is where I met Alex," I said.

Fate nodded. "I know."

A breeze picked up, and I stepped out of the water. "I want to go home."

"Well, if you ever need me..."

"Thank you. I hope I never need to make that call."

Fate laughed, gave me a quick nod, and blinked out.

I trudged back to the house to find my newly cleaned car sitting in the driveway and Michael leaning against the driver's side door.

"Hey," I said as I approached.

"I understand you're heading home." He shoved his hands in his pockets and looked at the ground.

"Yes. I have some things to take care of back in San Diego."

He shifted his weight and looked out over the front yard. "Any chance you'd welcome company for the ride?"

My heart skipped a beat, and my eyebrows arched. "Why?"

He sighed. "I'm in need of a change of scenery. Besides, I've never been to San Diego, and I thought it would be a cool place to catch some waves while I figure out what I want to do for the rest of my life."

I bit my lower lip and studied him, debating. Eventually, my practical side won out. With two drivers, we would get home faster than with one.

"Have you ever seen the world's biggest ball of twine?" I asked.

The smile grew on his lips, making his aura brighten. "No. Have you ever seen the Cadillac Ranch in Amarillo?"

"Nope, can't say that I have."

"Sounds like an epic road trip to me," he said with an infectious grin.

I couldn't help but smile with him. "Fine. I'm leaving as soon as I collect my things. If you're not ready, I'm leaving without you."

"I'll be ready." He trotted off to the neighboring house.

I watched him go, wondering at the wisdom of my decision. A part of me expected Alex to pipe in with some sort of sarcastic remark. Instead, silence reigned, and a small part of me rejoiced at the thought of a new adventure.

"I hope you like off-key singing," I muttered under my breath and headed inside the Ryan residence to say my goodbyes.

The End

Kylee's story isn't over. You can read more of her in Homecoming, the second book in The Fire Cursed Trilogy.

Check out the sneak peek below!

About J.E. Taylor

J.E. Taylor is a USA Today bestselling author, a publisher, an editor, a manuscript formatter, a mother, a wife, a business analyst, and a Supernatural fangirl. Not necessarily in that order. She first sat down to seriously write in February of 2007 after her daughter asked:

"Mom, if you could do anything, what would you do?"

From that moment on, she hasn't looked back.

Besides being co-owner of Novel Concept Publishing, Ms. Taylor also moonlights as a Senior Editor of Allegory E-zine, an online venue for Science Fiction, Fantasy and Horror, and co-host of the popular YouTube talk show Spilling Ink.

She lives in New Hampshire with her husband and during the summer months enjoys her weekends on the shore in southern Maine.

Visit her at www.jetaylor75.com to check out her other titles and sign up for her newsletter for early previews of her upcoming books, release announcements, and special opportunities for free swag!

I traded a glance with Kylee as my heart jumped with the rev of the engine. That internal rush took over, and I kneeled on the couch to get a look out the window. I felt like a two-year-old in a toy store.

Some of Tom's memories filtered in. He knew how to fly a plane, and I grinned, glancing at the cockpit. I had his skills, his experience to tap into.

I could fly this plane.

"Why are you grinning like that?" Kylee asked. Stress layered over her sweet voice, making it sharper than she probably anticipated.

"I know how to fly a plane," I said and winked.

She cocked her head, and I tapped my temple. My smile was so wide that my cheeks hurt. I really wanted to fly the plane, too, but from the paleness in Kylee's cheeks, I wasn't sure she could deal with a teenager taking control of such a large toy.

"Please don't do that. It will give me a heart attack," she said.

I laughed, feeling giddy as we started to speed up on the runway. Blood pumped in my veins, heating my skin with a pleasant warmth. The sudden lift off dropped my stomach for a moment, and all I could do was smile. This was so out of the ordinary that I couldn't understand why Kylee was so afraid.

Levi crawled over to her to find some comfort since I was all about this rush. It was parallel to what making love to Alex had been like. Surreal.

The sudden reminder of Alex cooled whatever enthusiasm I was feeling, and I slumped in the chair.

"He really got under your skin, didn't he?" Kylee asked.

"Yeah," I said. "He was so angry with me." I looked down at my hands. "I just couldn't. Otherwise, I wouldn't leave."

"He is having a rough time of it, isn't he?"

"Yes, and I had a shot at Lucifer, and I didn't take it because he had Alex's soul stored on a chain around his neck. I hesitated and my opportunity vanished. He was angry at me for that, too."

"The things we do for love aren't always the best or the brightest."

"Tell me about your Alex." I wanted to change the subject.

"Alejandro." She sighed. "He died on a job, and if he hadn't been killed by the thing we were hunting, I would have had to put him down."

She met my gaze. "He heard my siren's song, and that is a death sentence for a human unless they can kill the siren themselves."

"A siren?" I cocked my head. "You mean a mermaid like Ariel?"

Kylee burst out laughing. "No, sweetheart. Sirens are most surely not like the little mermaid. They are more like a horrific swamp creature that drives people into murderous rage with their songs."

"Oh." I glanced out the window. There was so much I needed to learn about this world and the supernatural creatures that I might be facing. "Can you teach me about the things out there?" I hooked my thumb towards the window. "I need to know what we might face at the breaches."

"It depends how deep the breaches go. I think we may only be dealing with demons, but if there are more things getting loose..." She let out a low whistle. "I certainly hope that's all, because if the breach goes deep enough, I can't fathom what could get loose."

I waited.

She rubbed her face. "Jinn, vampires, witches, soul eaters, sirens, bicorns, shifters, wendigos, banshees." She took a big breath and shrugged.

"What, no Frankenstein or mummies?" I asked, trying to stifle a smile. I had read the romanticized versions of a lot of the creatures she'd listed, and my mother's hand-me-down books hadn't educated me beyond the monster's basic need, like blood for a vampire, or wishes for a genie. So, I had zero frame of reference outside of the soul eaters I had experienced with Alex, and they had scared the crap out of me.

She leaned forward and narrowed her eyes. "This isn't a joke. If those things get out, who knows how many will die. It's bad enough if demons and hellhounds get loose."

"I'm sorry." I bit my lip and tried to figure out a way to erase the fiery anger in her gaze. "What if I tell you what I know, and you correct me when I go down the wrong path?"

She nodded and rolled her hand for me to continue.

"Vampires survive on blood and can't go out in the light?"

"Yes. Their venom is poison to a human. And most of the ones I ever encountered were mindless. They drank until their victim was drained. And if the victim got away, the poison would kill them within a day."

I shivered at the thought.

"Jinn or genies grant wishes?"

The bark of her laugh filled the plane. "That is partially true. Humans lose their life force to the jinn. Each wish takes a piece until there is nothing left. In that way, they are like soul eaters, with one exception. They don't leave the people alive. Because people are greedy beings, they always come back for more than one wish. There have only been a handful of people who have walked away from a Jinn before the third and fatal wish occurs."

I didn't really want to hear more. I would assume the rest of the pack was as equally as horrific as the vampire and the jinn, but I pressed forward.

"Shifters turn into animals?" I asked, afraid of the answers.

She nodded. "They have a healthy taste for human flesh, as do all carnivores. However, these aren't as easy to distinguish from the other monsters. Some refuse to eat humans. They have laws against it, but there always seems to be one in the pack that rebels. Those are the ones that are in hell. And yes, they can turn into almost any animal they choose."

"You told me about sirens, and I have dealt with soul eaters. So, what does a bicorn do?"

She licked her lips. "They feed on virtue. They steal souls and keep the victims as their slaves." She glanced away. "Wendigos eat humans, and banshees are a little like sirens, except they don't drive you mad. You just go blind and then your brain hemorrhages."

"What about witches?" That was the only being she rattled off that she hadn't covered.

"Witches are a little like shifters in that they aren't always evil, but they can certainly hex you to death if they are one of Lucifer's minions."

"Well, okay, then," I muttered, now more uneasy about this endeavor than I was before. I just thought I had to worry about demons, which were bad enough, but now I had to worry about all these other creatures.

Pick up The Fire Cursed Trilogy to read
more... find it on
https://books.JETaylor75.com!